the
Lost
and
Found
Girl

Also by Maisey Yates

Confessions from the Quilting Circle
Secrets from a Happy Marriage

Gold Valley

Smooth-Talking Cowboy
Untamed Cowboy
Good Time Cowboy
A Tall, Dark Cowboy Christmas
Unbroken Cowboy
Cowboy to the Core
Lone Wolf Cowboy
Cowboy Christmas Redemption
The Bad Boy of Redemption Ranch
The Hero of Hope Springs
The Last Christmas Cowboy
The Heartbreaker of Echo Pass
Rodeo Christmas at Evergreen Ranch
The True Cowboy of Sunset Ridge

Copper Ridge

Part Time Cowboy
Brokedown Cowboy
Bad News Cowboy
The Cowboy Way
One Night Charmer
Tough Luck Hero
Last Chance Rebel
Slow Burn Cowboy
Down Home Cowboy
Wild Ride Cowboy
Christmastime Cowboy

For more books by Maisey Yates,
visit www.maiseyyates.com.

Look for Maisey Yates's next novel,
Unbridled Cowboy
available now from HQN.

MAISEY YATES

the Lost and Found Girl

HQN

HQN®

ISBN-13: 978-1-335-42750-2

The Lost and Found Girl

HQN
22 Adelaide St. West, 41st Floor
Toronto, Ontario M5H 4E3, Canada
www.Harlequin.com

Printed in U.S.A.

To Mom, wish you were here.

the
Lost
and
Found
Girl

The Miraculous Ruby McKee

BY DALE WAINWRIGHT

Pear Blossom Gazette, December 5, 2005

It was five years ago, on a cold December night, when three young girls made a miraculous discovery that changed the town of Pear Blossom forever. While walking home from choir practice on that night, Marianne, Lydia and Dahlia McKee discovered a small baby, bundled up and abandoned upon Sentinel Bridge. Sentinel Bridge is the largest covered bridge in the area, built in 1917 to join two halves of the town, restored in the early 1990s as part of an effort to reinvigorate the community of Pear Blossom. The bridge itself crosses Willow Creek, connecting the main thoroughfare of town with many of the community ranches and orchards.

On the night of December 23, 2000, however, the bridge served as something more than a simple connection of pieces of the community. It played host to a miracle. The infant that was found there could so easily have succumbed to the elements. The girls might not have noticed a tiny, quiet bundle in the darkness of the bridge. And yet, she was found.

Now a thriving, happy kindergartner, Ruby was adopted by the very family who found her that night. A McKee in name, but part of the entire town of Pear Blossom. It was Ruby's Miracle that reinvigorated interest in Pear Blossom. That revived the festivals, tourism, the historical society. The international headlines about the Miracle Christmas Child shone a spotlight on the picturesque town and landed Pear Blossom in tourism magazines and lists of the most desirable communities to visit, to buy a home in, or to start a small business in. This reinvigorated Main Street and brought new vigor to the town.

It is easy to look at this night as a miracle, for a child's life was saved. But it is said in the town of Pear Blossom that Ruby McKee herself is miraculous.

1

RUBY

Only two truly remarkable things had ever happened in the small town of Pear Blossom, Oregon. The first occurred in 1999, when Caitlin Groves disappeared one fall evening on her way home from her boyfriend's family orchard.

The second was in 2000, when newborn Ruby McKee was discovered on Sentinel Bridge, the day before Christmas Eve.

It wasn't as if Pear Blossom hadn't had excitement before then. There was the introduction of pear orchards—an event which ultimately determined the town's name—in the late 1800s. Outlaws who lay in wait to rob the mail coaches, and wolves and mountain lions who made meals of the farmers' animals. The introduction of the railroad, electricity and a particularly active society of suffragettes, when women were lobbying for the right to vote.

But all of that blended into the broader context of history, not entirely dissimilar to the goings-on of every town in every part of the world, as men fought to tame a wild land and the land rose up and fought back.

Caitlin's disappearance and Ruby's appearance felt both specific and personal, and had scarred and healed—if Ruby took the proclamations of various citizens too literally, which she really tried not to do—the community.

Mostly, as Ruby got out of the car she'd hired at the airport and stood in front of Sentinel Bridge with a suitcase in one hand, she marveled at how idyllic and the same it all seemed.

The bridge itself was battered from the years. The wood dark and marred, but sturdy as ever. A white circle with a white 1917, denoting the year of its construction, was stenciled in the top center of the bridge, just above the tunnel that led to the other side, a pinhole of light visible in the darkness across the way.

It was only open to foot traffic now, with a road curving wide around it and carrying cars to the other side a different way. For years, Sentinel Bridge was closed, and it wasn't until a community outreach and education effort in the early nineties that it was reopened for people to walk on.

Ruby could have had the driver take her a different route.

But she wanted to cross the bridge.

"Are you sure you want me to leave you here?" her driver asked.

She'd told him when she'd gotten into his car that she was from here originally, and he'd still spent the drive explaining local landmarks to her, so she wasn't all that surprised he didn't trust her directive to leave her in the middle of nowhere.

He was the kind of man who just *knew best.*

They'd just driven through the town proper. All brick—red and white and yellow—the sidewalks lined with trees whose leaves matched as early fall took hold. It was early, and the town had still been sleepy, most of the shops closed. There had been a runner or two out, an older man—Tom Swenson—walking his dog. But otherwise it had been empty. Still, it bore more marks of civilization than where they stood now.

The bridge was nearly engulfed in trees, some of which were evergreen, others beginning to show rusted hints of autumn around the edges. A golden shaft of light cut over the treetops, bathing the front of the bridge in a warm glow, illuminating the long wooden walk—where the road ended—that led to the covered portion, but shrouding the entrance in darkness.

She could see what the man in the car saw. Something abandoned and eerie and disquieting.

But Ruby only saw the road home.

"It's fine," she said.

She did not explain that her parents' farm was just up the road, and she walked this way all the time.

That it was only a quarter of a mile from where she'd been found as a baby.

She had to cross the bridge nearly every day when she was in town, so she didn't always think of it. But some days, days like this after she'd been away awhile, she had a strange, hushed feeling in her heart, like she was about to pay homage at a grave.

"If you're sure." His tone clearly said she shouldn't be, but he still took her easy wave as his invitation to go.

Ruby turned away from the retreating car and smiled, wrapping both hands around the handle of her battered brown suitcase. It wasn't weathered from her own use. She'd picked it up at a charity shop in York, England, because she'd thought it had a good aesthetic and it was just small enough to be a carry-on, but wasn't like one of those black wheeled things that everyone else had.

She'd cursed while she'd lugged it through Heathrow and Newark and Denver, then finally Medford. Those wheely bags that were not unique at all had seemed more attractive each time her shoulders and arms throbbed from carrying the very lovely suitcase.

Ruby's love of history was oftentimes not practical.

But it didn't matter now. The ache in her arms had faded and she was nearly home.

Her parents would have come to pick her up from the airport but Ruby had swapped her flight in Denver to an earlier one so she didn't have to hang around for half the day. It had just meant getting up and rushing out of the airport adjacent hotel she'd stayed in for only a couple of hours. Her Newark flight had gotten in at eleven thirty the night before and by the time she'd collected her bags, gotten to the hotel and stumbled into bed, it had been nearly one in the morning.

Then she'd been up again at three for the five o'clock flight into Medford, which had set her back on the ground around the time she'd taken off. Which had made her feel gritty and exhausted and wholly uncertain of the time. She'd passed through so many time zones nothing felt real.

She waved the driver off and took the first step forward. She paused at the entry to the bridge. She looked back over her shoulder at the bright sunshine around her and then took a step forward into the darkness. Light came up through the cracks between the wood on the ground and the walls. At the center of the bridge, there were two windows with no glass that looked out over the river below. It was by those windows that she'd been found.

She walked briskly through the bridge and then stopped. In spite of herself. She often walked on this bridge and never felt a thing. She rarely felt inclined to ponder the night that she was found. If she got ridiculous about that too often, then she would never get anything done. After all, she had to cross this bridge to get home.

But she was moving back to town, not just returning for a visit, and it felt right to mark the occasion with a stop at the place of her salvation. She paused for a moment, right at the spot between the two openings that looked out on the water.

She had been placed just there. Down on the ground. Wrapped in a blanket, but still so desperately tiny and alone.

She had always thought about the moment when her sisters had picked her up and brought her back to their parents. It was the moment that came before that she had a hard time with. The one where someone—it had to have been her birth mother—had set her down there, leaving her to fate. To die if she died, or live if she was found. And thankfully she'd been found, but there had been no way for the person who had set her there to know that would happen.

It had gotten below freezing that night.

If Marianne, Lydia and Dahlia hadn't come walking through from the Christmas play rehearsal, then...

She didn't cry. But a strange sort of hollowness spread out in her chest.

But she ignored it and decided to press on toward home. She walked through the darkness of the bridge, watching as the light, the exit, loomed larger.

And once she was outside, she could breathe. Because it didn't matter what had happened there. What mattered was every step she had taken thereafter. What mattered was this road back home.

She walked up the gravel-covered road, kicking rocks out of her way as she went. It was delightfully cold, the crisp morning a reminder of exactly why she loved Pear Blossom. It was completely silent out here except for the odd braying of a donkey and chirping birds. She looked down at the view below, at the way the mist hung over the pear trees in the orchard. The way it created a ring around the mountain, the proud peak standing out above it. A blanket of green and gold, rimmed with misty rose.

She breathed in deep and kept on walking, relishing the silence, relishing the sense of home.

She had spent the last four years studying history. Mostly abroad. She had engaged in every exchange program she could, because what was the point of studying history if you limited yourself to a country that was as young as the United States and to a coast as new as the West Coast.

She could remember the awe that she'd experienced walking on streets that were more than just a couple of hundred years old. The immense breadth of time that she had felt. And she had… Well, she had hoped that she would find answers somewhere. Because she had always believed that the answers to what ails you in the present could be found somewhere in the past.

And she'd explored the past. Thoroughly. Many different facets of it. And along the way, she'd done a bit of exploring of herself.

After all, that was half the reason she'd left. To try and figure out who she was outside of this place where everyone knew her, and her story.

Though, when she got close to people, it didn't take long for them to discover her story. It was, after all, in the news.

Of course, she always found it interesting who discovered it on their own. Because that was revealing.

Who googled their friends.

Ruby obviously googled her friends, but that was because of her own background and experience. If those same friends had an equally salacious background, then it was forgivable. But if they were boring, then she found it deeply suspicious that they engaged in such activities.

She came over a slight rise in the road and before her was the McKee family farm. It had been in the McKee family for generations. And Ruby felt a profound sense of connection to it. It might not be her legacy by blood, but that had never mattered to the McKees, and it didn't matter to her either. This town was part of who she was.

And maybe that was why no matter how she had searched elsewhere, she was drawn back here.

Dana Groves, her old mentor, had called her six months ago to tell her an archivist position was being created in the historical society with some newly allocated funds, and had offered the job to Ruby.

Ruby loved Pear Blossom, but she'd also felt like it was really important for her to go out in the world and see what else existed.

It was *easy* for her to be in Pear Blossom. People here loved her.

It had been a fascinating experience to go to a place where that wasn't automatically the case. Of course, she hadn't stayed in one place very long. After going to the University of Washington, she had gotten involved in different study abroad programs, and she had moved between them as often as she could. Studying in Italy, France, Spain, coming to the States briefly for her graduation ceremony in May, and then going back overseas to spend a few months in England, finishing up some elective study programs.

But then, she'd found that instructive too. Being in a constant state of meeting new people. And for a while, the sheer differentness of it all had fed her in a way that had quieted that restlessness. She had been learning. Learning and experiencing and...

Well, part of her had wondered if her first job needed to be away from home. To continue her education.

But then six months ago her sister's husband had died.

And Dana's offer of a job in Pear Blosson after she finished her degree had suddenly seemed like fate. Because Ruby had to come and try to make things better for Lydia.

Marianne and Dahlia were worried about Lydia, who had retreated into herself and had barely shed a single tear.

She's acting just like our parents. No fuss, no muss. No crying over spilled milk or dead husbands.

Clearly miserable, in other words.

And Ruby knew she was *needed.*

One thing about being saved, about being spared from death, was the *certainty* you were spared for a reason.

Ruby had been saved by her sisters. And if they ever needed her...

Well, she would be here.

Fixing Lydia, fixing all of this, maybe it was what she was meant to do.

And all of the melancholy that she had felt a moment before faded. Lifted like a weight taken off of her shoulders. And she started to walk a little bit faster, letting the momentum carry her down the hill toward the farm.

She branched off of the main road, moving down the narrow, bumpy drive that led up to the white farmhouse her father continually repainted to keep it in the best shape possible. One of the many things she had learned from her father.

That taking care of the things that took care of you, that held your family, that held history, was important, and a point of pride.

The McKees had never been a rich family, but her childhood had been stable. Wonderful. Her parents had helped her do the work to get scholarships to go to college. Because they wouldn't have been able to pay for the entirety of it on their own.

Ruby had gotten good grades. She'd volunteered at the historical society exhaustively, from the time she was thirteen years old all the way up until she graduated. Her relevant community service and the essays that she'd written about it were exemplary. And she could only credit the influence of her mother for that.

Andie McKee was meticulous, loving and strict all at once.

Ruby picked up the pace then, letting her suitcase sway as she ran, holding on to her dress and keeping her boots from getting tangled up in the long hem as she ran up the pitted driveway to the front porch.

She stopped at the bottom step, breathing hard. Then she walked up and knocked on the door. It was early, but she knew her parents were awake. Likely had been for a while. They might be in their sixties, but you didn't retire from farm life.

The front door opened, and her mom stopped, still wiping her hands on her apron. "Ruby," she said, throwing her arms out and pulling her in for a hug.

She pushed Ruby back, examining her, and Ruby did some examining of her own. The last time she'd been home had been six months ago, for Mac's funeral, and then she'd seen her parents, Dahlia and Marianne at her graduation five months ago. And of course, her mother looked much the same. But there was something about all the spaces between visits that made her start to picture her mom as she'd been when Ruby had been a kid.

She never pictured her with all these lines on her face, with her hair more gray than light brown. She seemed smaller somehow, as if each passing year had taken something from her.

But when she looked at her mother's eyes, she didn't get that sense. Because the joy in her eyes shone as brightly as it ever had.

"Why didn't you tell us you were coming so early?"

"I changed my flight last night," Ruby said, wandering into the small, well-worn kitchen. It was clean, meticulously so, and it was in almost unbelievably good working order. The appliances were not new, neither were the cabinets, neither was the floor or the counter. But her father kept everything in such a well-maintained state, that it was as if she had walked back in time, into the kitchen as it had been in the 1950s.

Her father had never liked modern appliances, preferring the original wood-burning stove and an old-fashioned furnace. Air-conditioning had been a foreign concept in Ruby's life until she had started going and visiting friends' houses. The one concession he'd made was getting a more modernized refrigerator.

Even he had to admit that there was a better way than an icebox.

"Well, we would've come to get you." Her mother opened the fridge and took out a bottle of orange juice, then retrieved a loaf from the bread box. Each movement decisive and economical as she put a slice of bread in the toaster.

"I know, Mom," Ruby said. "That's why I didn't tell you. Because I didn't want you getting up and driving to Medford. Anyway, it was easy to get a car."

Pear Blossom was almost an hour away from the larger town of Medford, the hub that many people used for hospitals and big box shopping. And for the airport. Ruby had never spent much time there.

Going mostly for special trips when some of her friends had convinced her mom that going shopping at the mall was an important rite of passage.

Andie preferred to get everything she could from Pear Blossom. It wasn't part of that local movement or anything like that. Her parents had a deep sense of community, and they always had. Along with a lot of practicality. Even if small, local businesses couldn't sell things for as cheap as a big box store, by the time they drove to go pick up an item, by the time they expended the time and the gas, and put money in the pockets of a stranger rather than a neighbor, it all truly didn't seem worth it. Ruby's meals had been farm-to-table far before it was cool.

"Did you just get in from England?"

"Yesterday."

"You must be dead on your feet. Put down your suitcase and go get some sleep." Then the toast popped up and her mom put it on a plate, slathered it in butter and set it on the table. In direct opposition to her words, she clearly thought Ruby needed food before sleep.

She took a juice cup down from the cabinet, and Ruby interrupted that. "I'll take some coffee. I can't go to sleep. I need to stay up. Otherwise I'm never going to get back on the right time zone."

"What's the rush?"

"I start at the historical society in a few days," Ruby said.

"In a few days."

"It doesn't make any sense to let the grass grow under my feet. To sleep when I could just as easily power through and acclimate."

"You sound like your father."

"Who sounds like me?" Jed McKee walked into the room then, putting a hat over his bald head. His face had the set look of a man who smiled sparingly, but when he saw Ruby, the change was immediate. "Well, as I live and breathe."

"Good to see you, Dad," she said.

She found herself swept nearly off her feet as she was pulled in for a big hug, a decisive kiss dropped on her cheek. "Good to see you, kiddo. And you're back with us. For keeps now."

"Yeah," she said. She waited for a sense of claustrophobia or failure or something to settle over her. But it didn't.

"So, are we moving you into your old bedroom?"

"No," she said. "I don't have a place yet, but I'm going to find one."

"I'm sure that there will be a lot of people who can find space for you," her mom said.

"I don't want the Ruby discount."

It was a joke in her family. Free coffee, free candy and free ice cream had been a hallmark of Ruby's growing up years. Another thing that she'd had to get used to when she'd gone away to the real world. People did not shower her with free items or treat her like she was a special, magical creature in any way.

And no, that wasn't the reason she'd come back home.

"Does that mean I can have it?" her dad asked.

"By all means," Ruby said.

"You know, we finished renovating the shed for Dahlia. There are two bedrooms in there now. Not sure it's hugely different than living in the house here, but you don't have your parents breathing down your neck."

The shed was misnamed, because of course nothing under her father's watch was anything half so shabby as a shed. Ruby preferred to call it a cottage, which was infinitely more charming and romantic. It had started its life as a shed and become a very cute garden cottage.

"Dee is living in the cottage?" Ruby asked.

She hadn't seen her sister in the five months since graduation, but she would have thought she'd have mentioned that.

"She's working her way up to a full-time position at the *Gazette*, plus doing freelance writing, so she quit the job at the coffee shop."

She'd have thought she'd mention *that* too.

"Oh," Ruby said. "Well, good for her."

One point for the cottage was that it was on the opposite end of the property to the farmhouse, which would have her in proximity to her parents, but distant proximity. And she and Dahlia had shared a room as kids, so a two-room cottage would be spacious compared to that. It butted up against the neighboring pear orchard, and John Brewer was an utter recluse that she would never have to worry about encountering.

"If you'd like the other bedroom in there, Rubes, it's all yours."

"I should...probably talk to Dahlia about it?"

"She doesn't pay rent on it," her dad said. "My money renovated it."

It was a pragmatic take, for certain, but Ruby would be the one who had to live with a sister filled with resentment if she didn't want her there, not her dad.

"I'll talk to Dee," she said.

"You can stay in the house, for now, though, right?" her mom asked hopefully.

"Yes, of course," Ruby said.

In fact, she really wanted to do that. Because honestly, she was too exhausted to do any sort of taking care of herself. And that was the greatest and best thing about being back home. Her mother's cooking. And hopefully soon some of her mother's coffee.

She had coffee with both of her parents before her father went out to start work, and then her mother ushered her upstairs to her bedroom. Initially, she'd shared a room with Dahlia, but once Marianne and Lydia had moved out, she and Dahlia'd had their own rooms, and they were still much the same as they'd been when she and her sister had moved out.

Ruby's room was sweet and girly with a floral, yellow bedspread and a gold daybed. She had a tatted rug that covered the newly refinished wood floor. Her father, of course, refinished the floors every time they started to look worn.

Her mother took her suitcase out of her hand and swept it over to the bed, popping it open.

Ruby blinked, giving belated thanks that she had not packed too many intimate things in that suitcase. She had been traveling with a carry-on, and she hadn't wanted airport security going through her personal items right in front of her.

The condoms she'd bought in Europe had stayed in Europe. And good thing too, since her mother was now pulling things out of the suitcase and beginning to put them away.

"Mom," Ruby said, "you don't have to do that."

"I want to." She frowned. "I don't know how you've been living with so few things for so long."

"I have perfected the art of not having much. And there wasn't a whole lot I couldn't leave behind, anyway. Moving between programs as often as I did, it's better to travel light. Though, I did send a few things home. So, don't be deceived. There is follow-up."

"Good," her mom said. "I would be a bit concerned if you came away from all of that with no souvenirs."

"The souvenir was the education," Ruby said. "Honestly. The museums. The historical sites. It wasn't like anything... I can't believe it's over."

"I'm a little surprised you didn't end up settling there. In Italy or England. They were your favorites, weren't they?"

"Yes," she said slowly. "And I thought about it. But... I don't know, there's this opportunity here, and I got to know this town doing the work I did with the historical society. Doing the living history I did with the historical society…"

"Yes, I remember it well, since I sewed your dresses."

"It just seemed like maybe it would be a waste to not try this. Plus, I miss you guys. I can't imagine being away permanently." She almost mentioned Mac. Almost mentioned Lydia's loss. But the air of determined *all rightness* in the air was too firm and she didn't want to disturb it.

"I can't imagine it either," her mom said, wrapping her arm around her and giving her a kiss on the head. "But I always knew that you were destined for big things, Ruby McKee."

She didn't say why, but Ruby knew it all the same. She'd been spared for some reason, after all. Everyone thought that. And so, she must be destined for some sort of greatness.

Ruby had never really felt all that great. Because as much as she valued the miracle that was her life, it was the other side of it that lingered. She'd been saved, it was true.

But first she'd been left to die.

She stood and went to the window, looked out over the familiar landscape, then squared her shoulders, as if to shake off the thought.

It didn't do to dwell on the dark sides of the past, not when there was so much brightness all around.

Ruby wanted to bring brightness.

It was why she was here.

2

First Presbyterian Church of Pear Blossom
CHRISTMAS PAGEANT
MARY—Lydia McKee
JOSEPH—Benjamin Smith
BABY JESUS—Hattie Mayfield
ANGEL OF THE LORD—Ruby McKee
THREE WISE MEN—Elizabeth Albright, Shannon Smith, Heath Mayfield
SHEPHERDS—Analise Johnson, Corbin Johnson, Aiden Mayfield
SHEEP—Jade Springer, Callie Springer, Sarah Marsh
OLD DONKEY—Dahlia McKee

DAHLIA

Ruby was home. Her mother had texted her a few minutes earlier, as if Dahlia had forgotten her younger sister would be here today. She shut her laptop off promptly at three, stretching at her small desk and looking around her office—which was essentially a closet.

She took the brass watering can off the windowsill and poured some water on her fiddle-leaf fig, which was beginning to look poorly, much to her chagrin.

It had been an office warming gift from her sister Marianne at Dahlia's request. She'd thought that greenery might enliven the space more than a painting. Maybe she should have just gotten some abstract art for the wall. Something that she didn't have to keep alive.

But the changes she'd made in the last five months—and the office itself—felt like an important step in her new, adult life, and she had thought that maybe a plant was a good way to commemorate that. Of course, she hadn't anticipated failing at the plan, and she really hoped that it wasn't a harbinger of doom for the rest of the endeavor.

She had been working at Spruce Coffee on Main Street for years while she wrote various pieces for websites and magazines. That was before she had gotten up the nerve to approach Dale Wainwright about being the first employee of the *Pear Blossom Gazette* in more than a decade. The newspaper was coming up on its one hundredth year and Dahlia felt a keen connection to the publication. After all, when they had first discovered her sister Ruby on the bridge, reporters had become a constant in her life. And most specifically, reporters working at the *Gazette*. Back then, the building had been filled with different staff. And that was before everything had moved on to the internet, damaging physical circulation, especially for a publication in a small town like this one. There had been an economic decline in the early 2000s, a dip in businesses on Main Street and in circulation of the newspaper.

But there was a change in town in the last ten years. Younger people had moved here looking for a simpler life, and more tourists chose to spend time in the small town, with businesses on Main Street finding their footing again now that local restaurants, banks and boutique stores were at the center of a revolution.

What Dahlia wanted to see was a return to print media as

well. And to local news. News that really focused on the community.

She and Ruby had always been history nerds. They'd volunteered together at the historical society. Dahlia loved the mysteries of history. She loved old newspapers and piecing together information about the day through the lens of reporting and interviews. Ruby, though, seemed to like the quiet, bookish aspect of it. A much more fantasy-driven idea of what it meant to make that a career. Ruby had always imagined being impoverished—in a romanticized sense, naturally. And unemployable.

But that was the kind of thing they'd laughed about in their shared room as kids, while Ruby brooded about misters Darcy and Rochester.

I would love to be a poor, starving archivist warming myself by a pitiful fire surrounded by stacks of books.

Ruby, you missed lunch yesterday and almost chewed my arm off.

I mean it in the sense that I will have a small garret, my research and all the baguettes and cheese I want. A glamorous starvation.

So...not starvation.

And anyway, I wouldn't stay poor if a duke found me.

Dukes are not likely to find starving archivists in Pear Blossom.

Then I'll have to go somewhere else.

And now she was back.

Dahlia stood up, put her laptop in her leather bag and walked to the door of the office, flicking the lights off and shutting the door behind her. Dale hadn't even come in today. He was pretty solidly half work-at-home and half at the office. But he maintained that as a man well over the age of retirement, that was fair. Dahlia didn't mind having the place to herself, but she went to the office every day, even if she didn't have to.

Much like her preference for newsprint over websites, she liked being in the office. It made her feel more like she was living her dream.

Sitting in the shed on her computer made her feel like a blog-

27

ger. She wanted to feel like a journalist. It was what she'd gone to school for, after all.

She walked down the narrow hall, lined with awards spanning the years that proclaimed the *Gazette* a town favorite—it was the only paper in town—and photos of the town's most notable events.

Right at the very end of the hall was a grainy, black-and-white newsprint shot of a baby.

Ruby.

It always made Dahlia pause. It was impossible for her to not get completely lost in her memories, and with them a profound sense of sadness, which no one seemed to share but her.

Someone had abandoned Ruby.

Left her on a bridge to die.

And Dahlia had always felt that no one wanted to dig too deeply into that.

All Dahlia ever wanted to do was dig.

She sighed and turned away from the picture, then walked out the front door, jamming her key in the lock and turning it till it clicked.

She stepped away from the door and ran almost smack into Ruby. "Dee!"

"Rubes?" She shook her head and stared, her sister's presence completely out of context.

Ruby laughed and jingled along with it. Dahlia always made it a game to try and quickly identify which piece of Ruby's jewelry was making her sound like a human wind chime, because there was always something. Earrings today.

"Or her doppelgänger," Ruby said cheerfully. "I could have a doppelgänger, you know. Or a twin. Maybe only one of us was abandoned."

Dahlia rolled her eyes. "We've been through this. You don't have half an amulet."

"I *was* found with a necklace."

"Not one with a missing half."

Ruby pretended to look crestfallen. "Right. Well. In that case, I guess that rules out a twin. In *this* dimension."

"You better hope there's no interdimensional twin. Because that would be an evil one."

"How do you know I'm not the evil twin?"

Dahlia laughed and pulled her sister in for a hug. "You are most definitely an evil twin, Rubes."

"Can I see the office?"

"I just locked up," Dahlia said.

"Please?" She treated her to a wide smile.

"Oh, all right, but there's nothing much to see."

"I still want to see." Ruby cleared her throat and her gold earrings moved too, punctuating the sound with their own. "Why didn't you tell me about the new job?"

There were too many answers to that question, and each one was complicated. Mostly, though, it came down to Dahlia's nature, which was always in opposition to itself. If she failed, she didn't want anyone to know—least of all Ruby, who never failed at anything. But she was also proud and had been desperate to tell Ruby.

"It was new," she said, which was honest. "And I kind of bulldozed Dale into creating the position, so I guess I just kept being afraid I'd blow it and he'd fire me."

"But he hasn't," Ruby pointed out.

Dahlia smiled. "No."

Dahlia unlocked the door and pushed it open. Ruby floated in past her. Ruby always seemed to float.

"How was England?" Dahlia asked. She'd been once when she was in college, and she'd suddenly understood Ruby's obsession with all things Austen and high tea related.

"Amazing." She shifted and her blond hair slipped over her shoulder, catching the light. "Everything I could have ever hoped that it would be."

"And you're sure you want to trade in your fabulous life abroad for a life back here?"

"Yeah," she said. "For now."

They walked down the hall and Dahlia waited to see if Ruby would notice the picture of herself. She didn't. It said a lot about how... Ubiquitous the Legend of Ruby was here. That a picture of herself on the wall as a baby was visual white noise.

"I haven't been in here since I was a kid selling candy bars for school," Ruby said. "It looks the same."

Dahlia looked down at the orange carpet, and the fake wood paneled walls.

"Yeah," Dahlia said, "except pretty much no one works here now." She pushed her office door open again. "Here it is. It's... tiny."

"A potted plant. You're such a hipster," Ruby said.

"As if you're not?"

"Absolutely not," Ruby said, tugging at the ruffled collar of her dress.

"How long has it been since you've been in a secondhand store?"

Her sister looked around shiftily. "I am conscious of my environmental impact, Dee. And, broke."

"Somehow," Dahlia said, "I don't think that was your primary motivation for going to this supposed thrift store."

"You don't know me."

"But I do," she said, feeling a small bubble of excitement in her chest. Ruby was going to lose her mind over this, and Dahlia had been dying to show her.

You could have told her before she came back...

She could have. She hadn't.

She wasn't floaty like Ruby. She didn't light up the room or jingle when she moved. But she knew what sparked Ruby's interest. And being able to channel Ruby's brightness made her feel like some of it belonged to her too.

She and Ruby were different. Oil and water different. Night and day different. Optimist and realist-thank-you-very-much different. But they both loved this town, and they loved the history of it, and no matter what changed in their lives, whether they were close or distant, like shifting tides in the ocean, that truth remained.

"I know you *well*," Dahlia continued. "Come here, and I'll show you something more interesting than my office."

She walked Ruby the rest of the way past the hall, down the offices that no longer housed anyone, and Dale's office, to a room at the very end of the hall.

"What is it?" Ruby asked.

"The archive." She swung the door open to reveal walls of newspaper. "Every paper the *Gazette* has ever published, in hard form."

"Noooo," Ruby said, her eyes getting wide. "Aren't they all digitized somewhere?"

"Not all of them."

"Well, I want to do that. As part of my work with the historical society."

"That would be great, Rubes. Just let me know. Anytime you want to come down and dig around."

"Always," Ruby said. "Forever."

"We better go," Dahlia said. "I have some freelance stuff to fiddle with before dinner. Though, Marianne is still at The Apothecary," Dahlia said. "Do you want to go say hi?"

They made their way back down the hall and stepped outside again.

"Yes," Ruby said. "It's why I'm here. I couldn't wait to see you. I figured I would come wander around until dinner. Also, I was falling asleep on my feet."

"You could've just...slept," Dahlia pointed out.

"You sound like Mom," Ruby groused.

"Gee, thanks," Dahlia said.

31

"No problem."

Dahlia was about to launch into a monologue on all the ways she was not their mother when Ruby stopped abruptly on the sidewalk and turned, waving. "Hi, Mr. Davis!"

Dahlia followed Ruby's gaze to the bank across the street. The little bank was housed in red brick like all the other buildings on that block. Quaint on the outside, and on the inside, bearing most of the markers of the original Rochelle Bank, which had been founded by the Rochelle family back in the 1800s. And right out front was Mr. Davis, the owner of the only supermarket in town.

"Hi, Ruby," he said. "I hope you're back for good this time!"

People asked Ruby that every time they came to visit, though Dahlia was absolutely certain the news that Ruby was indeed back for good had made its way onto the prayer chain.

A great way to share town news without technically engaging in gossip.

"I am," Ruby called, then shrugged her shoulders and turned, continuing to walk down the redbrick sidewalk. Her sister tilted her face up toward the sun, and smiled dreamily. And Dahlia could only marvel at the entire interaction. Everyone always seemed delighted to have their day interrupted by Ruby. And really, *everyone* wasn't an exaggeration. Everyone remembered her. Everyone... They all liked her.

Not that Dahlia was unliked. But she was just more serious than Ruby, who was quirky dipped in brightness and glitter. An eternally sunny woman-child, who existed in a state of constant delight. Whereas Dahlia had been concerning the church choir director since she was twelve and had shown up at rehearsal for the Christmas pageant with black fingernails.

That had been the last year she had participated in that.

She just didn't bring out joy or generosity in people the way Ruby did.

She'd been told she was intense. By more than one man she'd dated.

Obviously not a compliment.

It wasn't a problem limited to Pear Blossom. She'd found she had the same issues when she'd been at college. The thing was, Dahlia believed in the truth. Finding it, telling it.

It was what made her a good journalist.

And no, she didn't have a fantasy about traveling the world and uncovering hard-hitting stories. Her interests lay much closer to home, in the people and places around her. But she'd always been interested in the small, unusual things. In the quiet people.

She wanted to dig in, go deep, get to the bottom of the ordinary. She believed that was where the truly extraordinary lived.

Of course, casual interviews would be easier if she had Ruby's people skills. People had called Dahlia's gaze both "intimidating" and "laser like," and sometimes her eagerness to go right for the deep waters didn't benefit her.

But then again she imagined that grilling Ron Davis over the buying habits of the local populace in the internet age had come across as a tad bit… Well…

Intense.

And they went on like that, moving down the sidewalk, pausing for Ruby to greet Molly Hudson, the church secretary, and Pastor Lawrence. After greeting the latter, Dahlia's boot caught on one of the raised edges of the sidewalk bricks, and she nearly pitched forward, but Ruby grabbed hold of her arm. The two of them stumbled about three steps together, and Ruby snickered, still holding her arm. "What exactly do you do without me?"

Dahlia brushed her hands down over her skirt. "Walk down the street without stopping every two seconds to have a chat."

Ruby grinned. "How boring."

Their arms still linked, they stopped in front of their sister's boutique. The Apothecary was one of the most successful shops on Main Street. It was small, carrying a highly curated selection of bath and beauty products, plus a small selection of cotton and linen clothing, all made in small batches, with all-natural ingredients. Marianne did brisk business both in town and online.

Ruby pushed the white door open, and they were immediately swallowed up by the scent of lavender and soap. Marianne let out a short scream, and stood up quickly behind the white counter. She flew around to their side in a flurry of caramel-colored highlights and floral chiffon. "You're home!"

She flung herself at Ruby, who laughed and embraced her back.

"You knew she was coming," Dahlia said.

"But not here. Not this early. I'm so happy to see you." Marianne waved a manicured hand in the air, her bracelets jingling. "Tell me everything. Tell us about London. And now that you're home, and I don't have to worry about you, tell me about all the crazy things you did. *Please* tell me you did some crazy things."

Ruby ducked her head, her cheeks turning pink.

"Oh, yay," Marianne said. "Please tell all that I might live through you."

She went back behind the counter and grabbed a few bottles of lotion, putting them on the edge, a clear indicator that she wanted them to sample something. Dahlia was never one to turn down a free sample. And Ruby was never one to disappoint, so they both chose different bottles and squirted some onto their hands.

"I did a lot of wine tasting in Italy. And many a pub crawl occurred in England."

Marianne rolled her eyes. "Is that it? What I want to know is, did Italian men occur?"

"At least one," Ruby said.

"And how was it?" Marianne fixed Ruby with a keen look.

"You do not want to hear about that," Ruby said.

"I do. Please indulge me." Marianne clasped her hands in an

over-the-top begging posture. "I have a business and a husband and children. And I am not a world traveler."

"It's not like you couldn't travel if you wanted to," Dahlia pointed out.

"Did you not hear the euphemism under my words? I am not a *world traveler*. I have not slept with European men. I have not slept with anyone but my husband, in point of fact, so I am owed stories."

Marianne was nothing if not dramatic. Always.

And had been so since she was a teenager.

"Gosh," Dahlia said. "If you wanted to hear stories of disappointing extramarital sex, you could've always asked me."

"The Italian guy was not disappointing," Ruby said. "Cannot say the same for the French guy."

"Shame. Details on the French Disappointment," Marianne said.

"Well. I think I was supposed to feel exceptionally grateful. But honestly I was bored. He wanted to watch a black-and-white movie after? I really wanted to leave."

"And… Did you?" Dahlia asked, interested in spite of herself.

"Yes. Because, I feel that as it was my sexual exploration, I was free to do as I wished."

"Good for you," Marianne said. "I support you in theory."

"Do you wish that you…are you—" Ruby looked at Marianne keenly "—sad that you're not a world traveler?"

Another thing Dahlia was curious about, in spite of herself.

"No," Marianne said. "I love Jackson. I love him entirely and completely, with my heart and my body. That doesn't mean I don't want to hear stories of people who are more adventurous than I."

"Well, I had some adventures." Ruby shrugged. "That was the point."

"It was why you broke up with *Darling Heath*," Dahlia said.

Ruby tilted her head back as if she could not contain the force of her eye roll. "Don't call him that. We are not thirteen."

"I'm sorry," Marianne said. "I can't take a real live man named Heath seriously."

Ruby sniffed. "That's because you never read the classics. It's close enough to Heathcliff to appeal to me greatly."

"But not when there were European adventures to see to."

"I didn't think it was fair to either of us. Anyway, he went away to school too."

"And he is also back," Marianne said.

Ruby shrugged. "Good for Heath."

"Are you too busy for Heath?" Dahlia asked.

"Well, I report to Dana starting next Monday. So yes. I'm going to be pretty busy. There hasn't been an actual archivist at the Pear Blossom historical society for years. And I think most of…everything has just been kind of left in boxes."

Marianne grimaced. "I'm not sure why you're subjecting yourself to working with Dana Groves."

"I *like* Dana," Ruby said. "Anyway. She's sad. People shouldn't be so mean."

"She's mean," Marianne said.

"People are mean to her," Dahlia said.

She was not one to see the best in people, but she and Ruby had worked with Dana at the museum, where she coordinated living history programs around town.

Dahlia was notorious for her defense of Dana, and that wasn't even an exaggeration.

Every town, she supposed, had that madwoman who was accused of witchcraft by gangs of young children and ostracized by the sort of people who had neatly kept lawns and kept all their personal business carefully concealed—the better to make their neighbors envy them.

In Pear Blossom, that woman was Dana Groves.

Dahlia couldn't explain how Dana had gone from object of

pity to one of scorn and distrust. At least, she couldn't identify the stages of it. Except that the town had moved on from her tragedy, and she had not.

Coupled with the fact that if something happened to a woman or girl, and it might involve sex, then she was seen as to blame in some way.

And by extension, the mother was absolutely to blame.

Dana had been a single mother, and the fact her daughter had disappeared—and her daughter's boyfriend was most certainly responsible—had eventually been laid at her feet.

The problem was, by the time Dahlia was in high school, Caitlin's disappearance wasn't what people thought of when they thought of Dana, not specifically.

She was the hag that lived on the corner, the museum troll.

Dahlia had never seen her that way. Dahlia hadn't forgotten her sadness.

But it was like Pear Blossom had been determined to blot out Dana's sadness with the joy of finding Ruby, and Dahlia had never seen how that canceled out a tragedy.

But then, she was the one who had always seen something quite tragic in Ruby.

Dahlia's reputation was firmly linked to Dana. Since Dahlia had once screamed down the entire football team for throwing rocks at Dana's windows, and had, in fact, thrown a rock that had hit the star fullback in the shoulder and told the "pack of pricks" where they could shove their rocks.

That had done nothing to boost Dahlia's popularity, oddly.

"I don't see how everyone can be so mean about her," Ruby said. "How can you not look at her and think about everything she's lost?"

Dahlia felt kinship with Ruby just then. While Dahlia didn't feel like her compassion for Dana came from kindness, she knew Ruby's did.

"You went to school with Caitlin," Ruby said to Marianne. "Wasn't she only like a year ahead of you?"

Marianne looked ashamed. "I know. It's hard to remember from before. I don't usually… Consciously connect the two things. I know I should. Caitlin was… I mean, I didn't really know her. She was always busy with her boyfriend."

The boyfriend.

Everyone knew it had been the boyfriend.

He'd been vilified in town, in the *Gazette*. He'd even been arrested, but he'd never been convicted because there hadn't been sufficient evidence.

There had never been a body. There had never been anything.

Dana had never even seen justice done for her daughter. She'd never had closure. And once the initial impact of the tragedy had passed, the town had moved on, and eventually Dana had become nothing but a reminder of bad things.

Which had ultimately put her in the category of bad things.

The idea sat heavy in Dahlia's stomach.

"Dana is always nice to me," Ruby said.

"Well, that's just that patented Ruby magic," Marianne said, wiggling her fingers and twisting one of her rings back into place. "Which lotion is best?"

Ruby grabbed hold of Dahlia's hand and lifted it to her nose. Then she sniffed her own hand. She tapped on Dahlia's hand. "I like that one better. What is it?"

"Yours is lavender and salt, Dahlia's is cedar."

"Salt?" Dahlia asked. "Salt, Marianne. Really."

"As in like sea salt," Marianne said. "It has a scent."

"Next thing you know you're going to sell air."

"Pear Blossom Air," Marianne said, grinning. "I really could."

She could. Everything about Marianne appeared effortless. Easy. Like air. Flawless skin and just a hint of makeup. Loose-fitting clothing and hair that just seemed to fall in waves as if

THE LOST AND FOUND GIRL

by accident, when Dahlia suspected her sister did nothing by accident at all.

She wore six hundred dollars of *shrug, this old thing* most of the time, but was too filled with grace to say *this old thing* out loud. She said it with a smile and a wave of her hand when faced with compliments.

"Do it," Dahlia said.

"If you promise to give me a feature in the paper."

"Sure. Front page. Local Con Artist Sells Air to Unsuspecting Public."

"I demand a retraction," Marianne said, eyes narrowed.

"Okay, but while it's the three of us," Ruby said, her eyes going very bright and alert, "tell me what's going on with Lydia."

"Uh…" Marianne looked at Dahlia.

Dahlia frowned. "She's Lydia."

"Exactly," said Marianne.

"Meaning?" Ruby asked.

"She's working to avoid having a feeling, but she's obviously devastated," Marianne said.

Ruby's eyes were now large and glassy with unshed tears. "I feel so guilty I didn't come right back home."

"Hey," Dahlia said. "Like I told you at the time, we were all here with her."

"Jackson and I help with the kids," Marianne said. "So do Mom and Dad. Chase helps with the farm."

"But I could have…comforted her."

Dahlia sighed. "Honey, her husband died. You can't just… smile and make it better."

Ruby frowned. "I'm not saying that I can, but I want to be there for her."

"You know how she is," Marianne said. "She doesn't like to share her feelings, and she's really not sharing them now."

And Dahlia could see that Ruby was taking none of this on board. Ruby was determined to fix their sister's very real, deep grief, as if she could do it with her mere presence. To Ruby's credit, she didn't like people to be unhappy.

That was also a deeply annoying thing about Ruby.

They all loved Mac like a brother. Lydia had been with Mac since she was thirteen. He was enmeshed in who they were, and it was just… Hard.

His ALS diagnosis had been devastating. His decline gutting. His death still sudden and unexpected in a terrible way.

They'd known it was coming, but when it had, it had still felt like…it had to be a dream. A joke. It hadn't felt real.

And as to how Lydia was coping? It was impossible to say.

Dahlia had never been the closest to Lydia growing up, but the older she got she thought it was maybe because they were too much the same. Marianne and Ruby showed their emotions easily. Screaming and throwing their hands around and demanding people smell lotion. Waving at people from across the street with broad gestures and loud greetings.

Dahlia and Lydia were just much more reserved. And Dahlia knew that her fashion sense—with her blunt bangs and extreme bob, her hair dyed black and her short skirts and thigh-high socks—horrified Lydia. And that Lydia herself would never admit that they were alike at all. But they both felt things deeply. And while Dahlia was a staunch advocate of the truth…

That didn't often extend to speaking of the deeper feelings inside her.

"Her whole life is different," Marianne said. "And you know Mom and Dad try but they're…they're terrible at dealing with things like this."

Ruby frowned. "What?"

"Ruby, come on. They want everyone to just soldier on when things are hard, and that's what Lydia always tries to do, but it can't be healthy."

"I don't think Mom and Dad are like that," Ruby said.

Marianne's mouth went firm for a moment. "Well, maybe they aren't with you."

Ruby seemed to shed that comment with ease. "I'm just really worried about her, and I want to help however I can."

Mac and Lydia had been such a perfect fit. The kind of couple that had made Dahlia believe someday she could find a person that would fit her that way.

They'd both dreamed of a simple, homesteading life. Both of them committed to working their farm and raising their children. And since Mac had died, there had been a hole in the family. Ever since his diagnosis, really. They'd known that he would die. But given that he had an early onset version of the disease, his prognosis had been better than someone who showed signs of the disease in their later years.

But it hadn't happened that way, and it was the black hole of numbness that Lydia had fallen into that terrified Dahlia the most. Because her sister hadn't wailed or thrown herself on the ground and screamed at an endless, unfeeling sky. She had gotten up, smoothed her hands down the front of her apron and said: *I have to feed the livestock.*

And while Dahlia could understand the stoicism, she was also increasingly bothered by all of it.

It was that part of her that was always out for the truth that felt the dishonesty of it and feared it would eat her sister alive. She felt like a coward not charging in and saying it, but she'd learned a long time ago that her brand of honesty was often seen as abrasive and perhaps charging in and asking if Lydia had a moment to talk about her deep, unending grief would not be well received.

Ruby, on the other hand, was always well received.

"Shall we go?" Marianne asked.

"It's not time for you to close, is it?" Dahlia asked.

"Not really. But it's fine. Town is dead today anyway."

41

Of course, Marianne thought nothing about closing the shop for Ruby.

And when she looked at Ruby, who was smiling effortlessly, her blue eyes sparkling that particular way they did, she could see why people thought of her as something miraculous.

Marianne turned the sign, picked up her phone and used it to turn all the lights in the room off, along with locking the place up tight.

"Dahlia finds my modernization of this classic building appalling," Marianne said as they stepped out onto the street.

"I'm not your ally for that," Ruby said. "I'm even more analog than Dahlia."

"It makes no sense," Marianne said. "You know you can appreciate all the charm of this small historic town without living in the Dark Ages."

"I love the Dark Ages," Ruby said, practically skipping down the street. And of course not tripping.

"You do not love the Dark Ages," Marianne said, maddeningly sage, as she was wont to be. "You love the idea of a desperately handsome and brooding man wiping your fevered brow while you *nearly* perish from an illness. Only nearly."

"True," Ruby said. "And I do like my men to have all their teeth, so it's more a vague fantasy than any real yearning."

"Hmm," Marianne agreed.

They paused at the end of the sidewalk. "Where are you parked?" Marianne asked.

"Oh, I parked down at the supermarket."

"I'm parked at the newspaper office," Dahlia said.

"I'm parked behind The Apothecary. So I have gone in the wrong direction."

"See you at Mom and Dad's?"

"Yep," Ruby said.

But as Dahlia turned to go along with Marianne, Ruby grabbed her arm.

"So," Ruby said, turning those wide blue eyes on in such a manner that Dahlia knew the following sentence was certain to irritate. "Dad said I could stay in the cottage."

Dahlia laughed. She couldn't help herself.

Because hadn't it always been this way?

She'd had her own room, and then Ruby had appeared. And the town had sent cribs and bassinets and diapers and toys that had overflowed into Dahlia's space. Not a bit of it for her, and leaving very little space for her on top of it.

"I told him he had to ask you," Ruby said. "But you know how Dad is. He said you don't pay rent and blah blah his land. But I don't want to stay there if it bothers you."

Dahlia wondered for a full five seconds what would happen if she told Ruby no. If she just said: *Nope, not going to work. Find somewhere else to bunk.*

But Ruby, for all that she was asking, knew Dahlia wouldn't do that. And Dahlia, for all that she was annoyed, knew that she wouldn't either.

"There are two bedrooms in *the shed*, Rubes." She persisted in saying *shed* because Ruby wouldn't call it that. "There's no reason you can't stay there."

"Oh, thank you!" Ruby lurched forward and wrapped her arms around Dahlia's neck, and Dahlia responded with a light pat on her sister's back. "We can carpool!" she said when they separated.

"We'll see, Rubes."

"Okay, that's good enough. I can't wait to see what you've done with the cottage."

"Mostly stacked books in there. You'll need your own desk."

"I can do that."

"Okay, see you tonight."

As Dahlia watched Ruby walk away, her blond hair bouncing behind her, she reflected on the earlier strangeness of walking with her younger sister. It was the kind of thing she was used to, but it hit her harder because it had been months since Ruby had been in town.

Ruby had come back all sun and smiles, and as usual, everyone responded to that. But what kept sticking for Dahlia was the way no one ever seemed... Curious about Ruby.

Oh, they liked her. Loved her, even.

But Dahlia saw her and always remembered baby Ruby. Small, vulnerable and left to die on the coldest night of the year.

No one had ever wanted to know how she'd come to be there, not to the extent Dahlia had, even as a child.

But why, Mom? Why would someone leave her? Doesn't it mean her mom didn't want her?

She could still remember her mom's expression getting fierce.

No, Dahlia. She was sent to me. I'm her mom. And I want her very much.

But Dahlia had burned for the whole story. Like she always did.

And everyone around her seemed to just want a fairy tale while she was desperate to *know*.

But then, that was the McKee family way. Dahlia's grandmother had died of cancer when Dahlia was ten, and no one had even told the girls she was sick.

No point dwelling, Andie had said. *You can deal with crisis when it hits, but why spend time worrying while it's waving in the distance?*

Dahlia had disagreed. Then and now.

And wanted to know. What would always amaze her was that Ruby didn't seem to want to know the truth of her origins for herself, that Ruby had adopted that McKee mindset so very deeply.

She seemed as committed to her myth as everyone else.

3

WEDDINGS—Lydia G. McKee and MacKenzie J. Spencer were married at the First Presbyterian Church of Pear Blossom on Saturday, 15 August, 2012. The Reverend Lawrence Michaels acted as officiant. The Bride is the daughter of Jedidiah and Andrea McKee, of Pear Blossom, OR. The Groom is the son of John and Martha Spencer, also of Pear Blossom. The bride's officiants were her three sisters, Marianne Martin and Dahlia and Ruby McKee, all of Pear Blossom, the groom had one attendant, a best man, Chase Andrews.

LYDIA

As Lydia pulled up to her parents' farmhouse, she felt like a rusted-out old sailing vessel. Hollow and desperately tired. And on top of that, Chase Andrews was playing the part of resolute barnacle that she couldn't seem to scrape off.

Why couldn't he be like everyone else?

The hordes that had rushed in to offer support right after Mac had died had taken more coordination than her doing it herself would have. The people she hadn't spoken to since high school who *wanted to be there for her* and *do lunch*, as if she needed to add lunch to her laundry list of necessities in the wake of her husband's death.

They'd all vanished after a month.

Not Chase.

But then he'd always been there, hadn't he? Since they were thirteen. A boy with skinny legs and dirt on his face, who had taught her and Mac every swear word in existence with a cocky expression he still wore half the time, even though his legs were no longer skinny.

He was still often covered in dirt.

But he was a farmer, in fairness.

Well, she'd managed to get away from him, at least. Though he was still at the farm doing chores she hadn't asked him to do. He had his own land, after all, and she was not his responsibility. But he didn't seem to want to hear it. No matter how many times she said it to him. He'd said that Mac wanted him there.

Mac was dead. Mac couldn't want *anything*. Not anymore.

She stared ahead for a minute, gripping the steering wheel, pushing her mind into a blank, shallow space. She didn't need to think about Mac. She didn't need to think about Chase, or his tendency to overstep and make her feel homicidal. Ruby was back in town. The kids were thrilled that their favorite aunt was home. She was their favorite aunt because she was the most scarce, obviously. Which made her mysterious and fascinating, and… Well, who was Lydia kidding? Ruby had that effect on everyone. Whether she was around all the time or not.

Ruby was a lot. A kind of a lot Lydia wasn't sure she was prepared for, but…

Her kids really could use the distraction. So she was glad she was back, for that reason if for no other reason right at the moment.

Her daughter let out a shriek and burst out of the car, flinging herself toward the farmhouse, where Lydia suddenly realized Ruby was standing in the doorway.

"Aren't you going?" she asked her son.

"I was waiting for you," he said.

She could see Riley's eyes looking at her in the rearview mirror, big and far too serious for an eight-year-old.

Riley was the image of his father. Except Mac had never looked like that. Never so serious or grave. Not even when he knew he was dying.

Riley felt the death of his father particularly deep. Felt the burden of becoming the man of the house, and she could talk about gender roles and how that was outdated and all kinds of things, but it wouldn't change the weight that little boy had taken onto his shoulders. That was another thing she put at Chase's door. Because it was the kind of thing Chase acted like mattered. This man of the house stuff. And he'd stepped in like he… Like he practically owned the place.

Lydia hadn't asked for another man around the house. Frankly, she'd been ready to…

She'd been ready to try life without one.

"Let's go," she said to Riley.

They got out of the car, and she did her best to smile. She'd never been effusive, even back before. So it wasn't like she had to perform overmuch now. It was sort of a relief. Ruby waited for her, didn't go parading down the steps at a breakneck pace or anything like that. She just sort of stood there.

So *subdued* for her younger sister.

Lord.

When Mac had first died, there had been a lot to do. Life involved a lot of paperwork, death even more. During that time her parents had talked about it, had helped with the practicalities.

But those were long since managed, and now they didn't talk about it, because they didn't have to.

But Ruby… Ruby was giving her big, sad eyes that made Lydia want to yell at her.

Because Ruby hadn't been here for the last six months. She'd come for the funeral and gone back to school and then on to

England, and now she was standing there expectantly when Lydia just wanted to have dinner after a long day.

"How are you?"

"Not fragile," Lydia said, harder than she'd intended.

Ruby's eyes widened a fraction. "Okay. That's good to know."

Ruby bent down and scooped Hazel up, kissing her dark hair. Hazel looked so joyous and carefree, and for a moment, Lydia was frozen by a deep sense of jealousy. Jealousy that her daughter could feel happiness like that.

Jealousy that for a moment Hazel didn't have to feel burdened by reality.

Great. You're a wonderful mother, Lydia. You resent your daughter's happiness. Your six-year-old child's happiness.

She walked into her parents' house, and she did her best to leave some of her angst behind. She just needed to get her head on straight and to be in the moment, because all of her problems would still be waiting for her when she got back.

When she walked in, the scent of pot roast enveloped her, and her sisters were already seated at the table. And in that moment she felt alone in this room full of people because no one really knew her. Not anymore. No one understood this.

She didn't even understand.

She took a breath and fixed a small smile to her face. "Is there something I can help with, Mom?"

"We have it all ready," her mom said, waving a hand, which, as far as Lydia knew, meant that her mother wasn't allowing anyone to pitch in.

So Lydia ignored her and elbowed her way into the tiny kitchen area, going ahead and stirring the pot of gravy on the stove. Then she transferred the rolls to a basket, and set them at the center of the table, pouring the gravy into her mother's cream-colored gravy boat imprinted with geese wearing heart charms and blue ribbons.

She helped put a matching set of plates on the table, and by the time she was finished with that, dinner was served.

"Did you kill the fatted calf?" Dahlia asked from her position down at the end of the table, and Lydia's lips twitched.

Ruby might not exactly be the prodigal, but it was a close enough approximation.

"Yes," her dad said. "Afterward we will be gifting your sister a coat of many colors."

"Wrong Bible story, Dad," Dahlia said.

"Oh, so you do remember the Scriptures?" He shot a wink at Dahlia, who was giving him a mock glare.

And on that note, her father took hold of Lydia's hand, and Marianne's, which was the cue for everyone else at the table to join hands and bow their heads. He said a brief grace, and Lydia realized that she hadn't been paying attention to it at all, and when he said amen, it didn't echo inside her at all.

She wasn't exactly on speaking terms with God at the moment.

She shoved that thought aside and busied herself fixing plates for her children, cutting up the meat and potatoes into small pieces, which earned her an indignant look from Riley.

Her niece and nephew, Marianne's children, had dished out their own plates, and she could see the future right in front of her. When her kids would be a little bit more self-sufficient, and she felt guilty for wanting to speed up time.

You weren't supposed to want that. You were supposed to enjoy these years. But these had just been some of the worst years. And it wasn't her kids' fault, but she was tired and she needed help.

You have help.

Well, it wasn't the help she'd asked for. Or the help she wanted. Her husband had gotten sick and it had ruined everything.

Thankfully, with her entire family around the table, conversation flowed easily, and she didn't have to contribute much to it.

"Do you kids want to get into the board games?"

There was an enthusiastic squeal from the children, and her mom got up from the table and walked into the small living room. Lydia could hear her fussing around with the game closet, and acting on muscle memory, she and her sisters got up and began to clear the table. Mama cooked, and it was their job to clean up.

It wasn't an instinct that ever went away.

Marianne took an apron down from the peg and wrapped it around her waist, and she somehow managed to look like the pages of an ad, with her floral dress and that piece of linen tied just so, her hair swept partway up, and a twinkling light in her eyes. Dahlia didn't bother with an apron, likely because the only colors available were pastel or floral.

Ruby chose the white, pinafore-style apron that went over her head and tied around her waist, ruffles around the bottom and the top. It almost looked like it belonged with the pale blue dress she was wearing.

And it reminded her again of childhood.

Lydia went and grabbed an apron without looking at it, then paused for a second, looking down at her own worn jeans, and her hands, one of which had a blister right on the palm, cracked and bleeding. She pushed all that to the side and gathered the plates from the table, putting the stack of them by the sink.

I don't need a dishwasher. And anyway, they don't sing while they work.

Her father's cheerful words came back and echoed in her head just then. And as if she'd read her thoughts, Ruby started to sing.

None of them were overly gifted musically, except for Ruby. Her voice likely inherited from an ancestor the rest of them didn't share.

They weren't tone-deaf, by any stretch, but Ruby had a sweet, clear voice that reminded Lydia of a songbird. Marianne joined in singing, filling the sink with water and twirling the dishrag. Lydia exchanged a glance with Dahlia.

"Do you think they'll notice if we duck out on the chores?" Dahlia asked.

"Yes," Lydia said. "And they'll tattle."

Dahlia smiled.

Lydia grabbed a dishrag and started to wipe down the counter, while Marianne and Ruby filled up all the space at the sink. Many hands make light work.

One of her mother's favorite things to say, and she thought of it now as they quickly tidied up the kitchen.

When they finished, Marianne put the kettle on. And once it had boiled, she poured four mugs of hot water. Ruby began hunting around for the tea bags. "Let me just check in on Jackson," Marianne said. She returned a minute later, flashing a thumbs-up. "Jackson and Dad are talking about hunting spots, so I can guarantee you that that can go on for as long as I want it to."

They took their cups of tea and filed out the front door, sitting on the wooden chairs that were positioned there on the porch. It was dark out, only the porch light casting a golden glow directly around them, shrouding the view of the farm in darkness.

"How was England?" Lydia asked Ruby.

"Great," she said. "Really great. But I'm happy to be home."

"If I ran away to England, I might not come back," Lydia said. And then tried to force a smile so she didn't sound quite so grim.

She hadn't meant it to sound that way.

"Well, this is home," Ruby said, her smile overly cheery. "I couldn't imagine not coming back."

Ruby lowered her face over her mug of tea, the steam rising up around her. Lydia didn't often catalog the differences between the rest of them and Ruby.

Ruby was Ruby, so she didn't stop to think particularly about her differences.

But she'd been gone awhile, and there were just some things she noticed. The way her sister's nose sloped, where the rest of them had a slight bump on the bridge.

Her pale blond hair where the rest of them were darker. Her top lip was thinner than the bottom, a sharp vee cut down into the top. Where Lydia and her sisters had a rounder, fuller top lip. Ruby was part of them. As much part of them as any other member of the family.

But there were distinct little mysteries about her.

"I wanted to be near you," Ruby said, her eyes so full of sympathy that they made Lydia freeze. Made her feel pinned to the spot by all of Ruby's earnestness.

It felt like Ruby had just dropped a heap of obligation onto her chest.

"Ruby, please tell me you didn't make a decision about your whole future because you thought I needed you here."

What did she expect her to say? Or do? Lydia had been managing on her own for six months. She didn't have the energy for help. She didn't want to make a… A chore list for Ruby so that Ruby could feel helpful.

It had been a relief when people had stopped doing that. She'd been inundated in the first weeks after Mac died. Phone calls and messages and offers of food. It had been nice, but it had been…

A lot.

"I got a job also," Ruby said, looking down into her tea. "But shouldn't I want to be here for you? You were all…you were all there for me. You found me."

And onto the obligation was heaped guilt.

Lydia sighed. "Ruby, I am glad to have you back."

How the hell had she ended up managing Ruby's feelings?

"If you need help with the kids or with…with farm chores."

Lydia laughed. "I do not want your help with farm chores. That's like asking a cow for help with knitting."

Ruby wrinkled her nose. "Are cows helpful with knitting?"

"No, Ruby, they don't have thumbs. And you don't know how to do manual labor."

"I just...don't want you to be sad."

"Well. I'm sad," Lydia said. "And I'm going to be for..." Maybe forever. This terrible sadness she had no name for. "A while. So don't make it your mission, please. You will end up thwarted."

"God knows none of us needs to have a thwarted Ruby roaming around," Marianne said.

"What would that even look like?" Dahlia asked.

"Hey!" Now Ruby was looking wounded.

"Tell us more about your wild adventures," Marianne said, lifting her teacup to her lips, smiling.

"Wild adventures?" Lydia asked.

"I have it on Ruby's authority that there were Italian men," Marianne said.

That broke something in Lydia's vision. Cracked the glass she looked at her sister through. Because of course Ruby wasn't a baby, any more than Dahlia was, but she had a difficult time seeing either of them as fully grown women. And the thought of Ruby fooling around with European men was a strange one indeed.

Still she was very happy for the subject change, and if putting Ruby in the hot seat eased the gravity of the moment...

She supposed that made Ruby helpful. Just in unexpected ways.

"Just two," Ruby said, sounding defensive.

"And a Frenchman."

"Just *the one*," Ruby said dryly.

"Any Englishmen?" Lydia asked. "You were always a big one for Mr. Darcy."

"I am not a sex tourist," Ruby said crisply. "Though, yes."

"And again, you came back home why?" Marianne asked.

"Because they weren't *my* Mr. Darcy. None of them were more than a paragraph of my story."

It was a strange choice of words. They weren't more than a paragraph of her story. And it pushed Lydia off-kilter even more.

She'd thought she knew her story. Every line.

"But you know it is strange," Ruby said. "I thought that… I thought maybe that's where the answers were. Traveling. Seeing the world. Having experiences beyond my high school boyfriend. But I didn't find anything there. I mean, I found some things. But it just wasn't… It wasn't this."

Lydia had thought Mac was her whole book, and he'd been a few chapters, and then…

What was left?

What came next?

She didn't know.

But for a moment, Lydia chose to let go of the dread. She chose to release her hold on her sense of uncertainty.

Because Ruby filled her mind with images of a book, and when she thought of it like that, it seemed so easy to flip back a few pages. This moment felt like it could be placed at any point in time. Maybe she would go back inside, go upstairs and find her old bed there, go to sleep in her room.

Maybe she would go home, and Mac would be there. All those things seemed about possible right now. Thanks to that cocoon of darkness outside, the familiarity of the porch light and the tea, and the presence of her sisters.

So she chose to take a breath and just live in this moment of suspended time. Because all too soon *now* would be crushing, clear and unavoidable. But it wasn't at the moment.

Right now, she'd stay on this page and not think at all of the pages up ahead.

4

BIRTH ANNOUNCEMENTS—To Marianne and Jackson Martin, of Pear Blossom, OR, a baby girl, Ava Helene Martin, born at Rogue Valley Medical Center September 5, 2007

MARIANNE

"Do you think Dahlia is going to dye her hair pink and start going through another rebellious phase?"

Marianne walked out of the bathroom, rubbing at her face in a circular motion, making sure every last bit of her luxurious (expensive) moisturizer sank into her skin. She looked over at her husband, who was grinning at her, the lines around his mouth deeper than they'd been seventeen years ago, but she could still see the boy there who had first stolen her heart. She could see him with the years and without them and loved both. Just as she still loved him.

"Why exactly?" she asked.

He shrugged his shirt off, chucking it in the hamper by the dresser—God bless the man, it had only taken ten years to train him to do that—and walked over to their bed, sinking down onto the pale blue bedspread.

"Because she always gets weird when Ruby is in town, and now she's going to be here for... For good?"

"As I understand it," Marianne said, "Dee and Ruby are really close."

"Sure," Jackson said. "But that doesn't mean you don't have... sibling stuff there."

"Sibling stuff," she repeated, turning to the mirror above the dresser and adjusting her bun.

"I'm just going to take it down," he said.

She shot him a flat look.

"They're close in age," he continued. "It makes it a thing. That's why Asher drives me nuts," he said, talking about his brother who was only a year and a half older than him. "I was always so close to everything he did, but not quite as good. Until I outgrew him. And Ruby is...well, she's Ruby."

"We're all close," Marianne said. "I don't know what to tell you."

"All right, but I'm going to place bets. Pink hair by Christmas."

"All right, I'll take that bet."

He lay back on the bed, and she cataloged the movements of his muscles as he did. They'd been married for seventeen years. His body was a familiar enough sight, but she still enjoyed it.

It might not be with that same sort of recklessness that had overtaken her when they'd met in their early twenties, but it was definitely there.

She could both check him out and have a conversation with him at the same time.

Necessary, all things considered. They had lives. She couldn't get lost in lust every time she looked at him.

And there was so much life. Marianne felt buried in it sometimes. Helping Lydia with Riley and Hazel, trying to help shoulder her grief.

"We should have Christmas with your family again this year."

"Jackson..."

They had a deal that they were supposed to split the holidays between his family and hers, and they'd done Christmas with the McKees last year.

"It's the first year with Mac gone," he said, his voice getting heavy at the mention of his brother-in-law. "I don't think we should miss Christmas Day too."

Marianne couldn't disagree with that, but of course if her mother-in-law did, it would be Marianne who heard about it later, not Jackson.

And if her parents weren't so... So damned terrible when things were dark, then maybe they could just go on as they'd originally planned. But as much as Lydia was distant, and that was her choice, Marianne knew some of it was just the learned coping mechanisms of a McKee.

Her teenage years had been... Grim.

She didn't even like to think about them. She'd just been so dark and depressed all the time and her parents had left her to it. Ignore it, and it'll go away.

And Marianne was the oldest, so she was the one they'd made all their major mistakes on. While Ruby, of course, was the fairy princess everyone found a constant delight and who benefited from all their previous years of...

Oh. There were those sibling dynamics Jackson had mentioned.

"Let me deal with my mom," he said, as if he had read part of her mind.

"Thanks," she said, flinging her arms around him and bringing them both down onto the bed.

He grinned, moving his hand down to her lower back. "You're very welcome."

There were things, and she knew it. Things they needed to talk about. They hadn't gone on a vacation in years. Getting the store going, getting the online storefront established, kids and school and her family...

And Ava. Lord, Ava. Who was fifteen, volatile and reminded Marianne way too much of herself at that age.

They needed to talk about it. They needed to figure out how to take care of them, and not just everyone else. Mac's death had shaken the foundation of the family. Mac was one of Jackson's best friends, not just a brother-in-law. He had been family to Marianne. Ava and Hunter had adored him. And in the months since, they'd tried so hard to keep up normalcy for Riley and Hazel while also trying to *be there*. Not just pretend it hadn't happened. Not just pretend it was all fine.

There was so much stuff out there, beyond their bedroom door. So much life. So much worry. But in Jackson she'd always found... Peace. Calm.

There were years of her life that were just... A blur. But she remembered the day she first met him. The day she first saw his face. It had all come into focus.

And here, in this room, it was just the two of them, and it was like that first day.

Like everything made sense.

"I love you, you know," she said. "I think I forgot to say it today. The store gets really busy and we get really busy and..."

"I know," he said, kissing her. "I don't forget you love me."

"Thank you."

His smile turned wicked, and she really did love it when he was wicked. That he still could be, even after all this time. "You could keep thanking me verbally or..."

She gave him her own wicked smile right back. "My pleasure."

5

1917—The new bridge will connect the orchards with the town and bear more weight than the previous bridges. After a vote at the town hall meeting, Sentinel Bridge is the agreed upon name.

RUBY

Courtesy of her jet lag, Ruby was up and ready to investigate the cottage by six o'clock the next morning. But she had to wait until she was reasonably sure that Dahlia was up.

She peered out the window and looked across the field, and it didn't seem like her sister's car was parked in front of the little cottage. Dahlia had always been an early riser.

The keys were hung up on the peg by the door, and she put on a pair of hunter green rubber boots beneath her dress, ready to cross the great, murky fields that stood between her and the dwelling.

She slipped a long woolen cardigan on over the dress and wrapped it tightly around her body as she walked out of the house and down the front steps, across the driveway to the first, weed-filled field that stood between her and the dwelling. The sky was washed in pink, the edges of the clouds rimmed with bright gold from the rising sun. The trees, which were beginning to turn on autumn's red tide, looked like they were on fire now, as the morning took hold of the scenery with not a blooming gentleness, but a gong, declaring sunlight over the sleeping world, demanding wakefulness.

She picked through the weeds, grimacing as the taller shoots went up beneath her dress and scraped the sides of her thighs. The air was sharp, and if she took it in too deep, it sliced at her throat. And all the same, she found it deeply comforting to be here on a morning like this. A morning that reminded her of walking to school as a child.

A morning that reminded her of home.

Of seasons past and all things familiar. Of those foundational years that had built her into who she was. And it made the back of her neck as prickly as her eyes, that thought.

The field gave way to a forest, and the cottage was settled beneath the trees there. It was like walking back into the night. The sun couldn't penetrate the immensity of the pines. The soft, rich soil was carpeted with moss and ferns.

At the back, her father had added an A-frame. There were windows all over, and she noticed that a velvet green moss had grown thick on the roof, just as it had everywhere else around. She stuck the key into the door and turned the lock, making her way inside.

It was desperately cute and quaint, and she had always loved it, from the moment her father fixed it up, and was entranced by the idea of staying in it. And with Dahlia, just like when they were kids. And they'd stayed up late talking about their desperate romantic fantasies and their plans for the future.

Dahlia wanted to write articles. For all her sister sometimes seemed stoic and hard to reach when they talked, when she wrote she poured her soul out. When they were kids, Dahlia had written breathless romances—in the vein of Jane Austen, of course, but always with a suggestive scene of the hero and heroine disappearing behind closed doors.

Ruby had loved them.

Ruby had loved that time in their lives. The idea of living in it again made her feel… Just so very good.

There was a little bookshelf in the entry, built-in, stacked with Dahlia's books, and Ruby had a feeling there was going to be a tussle over shelf space. That was predominantly what she had shipped back to the States, in a flat rate box, because it was cheaper than paying the exorbitant airline fees for anything that heavy.

And Ruby was nothing if not a book pack rat.

There were two very small bedrooms, and one had the door firmly shut, the other opened. Ruby pushed the door open. The room was sparse and clearly not Dahlia's. There was a small twin bed pressed against a wall of windows that backed the woods.

Not just the woods.

The Brewer orchard.

She stood there at the window and stared out for a long time. There was something… Unsettling about the orchard. About the Brewers themselves.

They were placed firmly on Pear Blossom's list of pariahs.

Her mother had cautioned them to stay away from the property, though when no other incidences occurred, Ruby had always found it a little bit sad. But Nathan Brewer's parents had been ostracized along with him.

She didn't remember his mother at all. She'd died when Ruby was maybe four or five. But while Nathan had left, his father had stayed, regardless of the fact that people in town have their opinions. He still went out drinking at the bar; he still had his stalwart friends, as far as Ruby knew.

But that was how Pear Blossom was. When an opinion was set, it was set.

Nathan Brewer had been tried and found guilty of murder

by the citizens, and that was all that mattered. Whether or not a court could convict him was irrelevant.

She turned away from the window. She didn't need to be thinking about murder while contemplating moving into her new room. Much less in the context of the orchard that was just on the other side of where she would rest her head at night.

Of course, the orchard had been searched. When Caitlin Groves had gone missing, search and rescue had brought dogs out, and members of the community had formed a line, both on foot and on horseback, and combed the whole property and the surrounding woods.

At least, that was what her father had said when he had relayed the story years later. It was impossible to live in town and not know about it, even though it had happened before she was born. Because posters of Caitlin remained up in town. Pear Blossom's only missing person's case.

For a moment, a strange sensation settled over Ruby's skin. A missing person. She could be a missing person, really. Kidnapped, taken away from her mother. Brought out to Pear Blossom, left on Sentinel Bridge. Maybe she was on a poster somewhere. How would she ever know?

It was unlikely, but that was one of her more simplistic fantasies. Of course, it led to the possibility that she was a kidnapped princess. Not that she really believed that, but in her opinion, it would have been a failure of imagination to never entertain the more fantastical options.

Secret princess or an heiress of some kind.

Yes, of course she had thought of that.

And there were enough books on the subject that it seemed like it had happened sometimes. She had thought—really—that it might be true when she was maybe thirteen. She had thought that perhaps her love of soft pillows and England related to her potential status as monarchy. But in the end she had been forced to admit that a missing princess would have likely been headline news enough that she would at least be able to find out which one she was and coordinate dates.

No such luck.

Come to that, if she were anyone who had been reported missing, it was likely that the news stories from when she was found would have alerted people.

It wasn't like she needed those kinds of childish, easy fantasies. She didn't. But the alternative brought back that hollow feeling.

And so she pushed it off to the side, and imagined it flying away on the wind, because she did not need to wallow in sadness of any kind.

She wandered into the living room and looked out the windows there, wrapping her arms around herself, and then she caught sight of some movement in the trees. She took a step back and kept on staring. Wondering if it was a deer or maybe a bear. She sort of hoped so. She was in the market for a little bit of adventure.

But the movement continued, and when the figure moved into a clearing, it was not a bear.

There was a man standing here.

But it wasn't an old man. He was young, tall with dark hair and a dark beard. She couldn't make out his facial features from that distance, but she saw the moment that he saw her. Watching him through the window. He didn't move, and neither did she. And then, with a trickling sort of dread, she realized exactly who she was looking at.

She turned sharply, slamming her back against the wall, making it so she couldn't be seen from where he stood. She huffed out a breath that turned into a laugh, her heart hammering against her chest. Because of course he would have seen her. That she had scrambled and hid. And the front door was unlocked, so if he wanted to come and investigate, if he wanted to get to her... There was no barrier.

But she stayed like that, frozen for two whole minutes. And

when she turned back to look out the window, she didn't see him at all.

She texted Dahlia, who was at the local coffee shop working on an article, and Ruby met her there and relayed the story over caffeine.

"Do you think you hallucinated it?" she asked.

"No, I'm sure that he was there. Ninety percent. I'm not usually given to hallucinating the existence of men."

"Do you think it was *him*?" Dahlia asked.

"I don't know," Ruby said. "I mean, it would make most sense. Unless his dad hired someone to…"

"John Brewer died," Dahlia said. "A month ago."

"Oh," Ruby said.

"So I mean, it could be a new owner, it could be… I don't know what they ended up doing with the property. I didn't see it go up for sale, but that doesn't mean it wasn't sold." Dahlia pulled a face. "I'm not really up for living next to a murderer."

"I mean, we don't know if he's a murderer."

Dahlia scoffed. "Rubes, he was her boyfriend. He was the last person to see her alive. He's…well, it's almost always the intimate partner, that's just a fact."

Ruby looked down into her coffee. "Or he isn't."

She didn't know why she felt the need to defend him. She never had before.

"This isn't *Jane Eyre*. If a man locks his mad wife in the attic, he's a monster, not a hero."

"Speaking in metaphor, obviously," Ruby said.

"Obviously."

Ruby looked around the café. "I'm headed over to the museum today."

"I didn't think you started until Monday."

"I don't," Ruby said. "But I'm eager to get started and I don't have anything else to do."

"Aren't you recovering from jet lag?"

"Sort of. But I don't like being bored. Lydia's kids are in school so I can't do anything to help with them." Ruby felt… Lost then, and she searched Dahlia's face for answers, which she didn't find.

"What exactly did you think you were going to do to help Lydia?"

Ruby shrugged. "Just be here. It seems wrong for us all to be separated right now. And anyway, I can help if she needs something."

"Most people would take the vacation." Dahlia pointed one chipped nail on the table.

She shrugged. "I love being back here, but what happens when I spend a leisurely morning doing nothing? I start thinking that I see scary men standing outside my window."

"Well, in fairness you might have."

"It's *unnerving*," she said again.

The door to the coffeehouse opened, and Ruby fought the urge to slide under the table.

Because it was someone she knew. Very well.

"Well, look who it is," Dahlia said, following Ruby's line of sight to the door. "Darling Heath."

"Please don't call him that," Ruby said out of the side of her mouth.

And she hoped, she really did, that he would walk on to the counter and just not see them.

But alas.

"Ruby?" He smiled, which surprised Ruby because there had been no smiling when they had broken up four years ago. Of course, that was four years ago, and undoubtedly as many things had changed in his life as had changed in hers since then. "I heard you were moving back."

"You heard correctly," she said.

"Working at the museum?"

"Yeah," she said. "I'm going to be an archivist. I'm also going to help with displays in duration and things like that. You know how it is here. Many hats."

"Of course."

"Hi, Heath," Dahlia said, smiling broadly, and Ruby wanted to dump her coffee on her sister.

"Hi, Dahlia," he said, backing up slightly. He was intimidated by Dahlia. A lot of men were.

Ruby admired that about her sister. That she was indefinably terrifying to the male species. Ruby herself could not claim to unsettle anyone. Not that she wanted to intimidate Heath. She didn't know if she really wanted to talk to him either.

He was the same. A comforting sort of handsomeness that felt good to look at. Smooth around the edges and just pleasing, without creating any reckless heat in her.

"Are you still working at your dad's?" she asked.

"Yeah," he said. "It's good work. And I don't mind it."

Living the cabinetmaking dream, apparently. Not that there was anything wrong with that. It just wasn't what he had wanted to do when they'd been together. And certainly not what he'd gone away to college for. But Heath's unrealized dreams were not her responsibility.

You are also back, Ruby.

That was *different*. She was working at the museum, with Dana. It was what she'd gone to school for.

"I'd like to have coffee sometime," he said.

She shifted. "Sure. I'm… Not now. I'm headed out to…the museum."

"Are you walking?"

"Yes," she said.

"I'll walk you."

"Dahlia, are you…walking over to the newspaper office now?" Ruby asked, somewhat hopefully.

"No," Dahlia said, grinning.

And Ruby didn't really know how to politely decline his offer, and Ruby could tell that her sister wasn't about to bail her out. And fair enough, really. She was an adult. If she really didn't want to walk with him she should say. It wasn't that she didn't want to. It was just that… Well, she didn't want to.

But instead, she found herself waiting as he ordered coffee, then meandered back to her table, and then she picked up her own coffee and began to walk out the door with him.

"It is nice to see you," he said, once they were out on the street.

Ruby surveyed the main street, the neat little square that sat in the center, where the road forked and the two lanes went around a patch of grass with trees whose leaves were beginning to change. Many of the businesses had American flags waving with overpronounced patriotism in the breeze, the redbrick facades bright, the trim a sharp white. She wondered how many coats of paint had gone over that trim in the years since the buildings had gone up. Probably hundreds. That was maybe not even an exaggeration. One layer of paint going straight over the other, drying crisp and white and new.

And if you are thinking about drying paint while walking next to a man, you really are not interested.

She looked at him and his boyish features and thought maybe she really ought to feel more for the man she had thought was her first true love. She knew now that she had never loved him. She had been enraptured by the idea of being in love. She'd been such a fierce romantic.

Maybe she still was.

But distance had well and truly broken any bond she had initially felt with Heath. "I think it's good that you're back," he said, sort of abruptly.

"You do?" She hoped this wasn't leading to any kind of declaration.

"The town doesn't feel right without you, Ruby. You're like the mascot."

She laughed. She couldn't help herself. "A mascot?" She immediately imagined herself doing a jig at the center of the town square.

"Yeah, you know. You made the town famous."

The sentiment was seriously disconcerting. "I don't know that I did that."

"Well, certainly more famous than it was."

She wrinkled her nose. "Bridge baby? Is that the name of my mascot?"

"That's sort of grim, Ruby," he said.

"It is sort of grim," she said, her scalp prickling. "I mean if you think about it. And, now I am."

"Sorry. That must be weird." He looked at her, like he was seeing her for the first time. "To have people bring it up. I'm sorry."

She was unsure of what to call the emotion that was turning over in her chest. "You know, Heath, don't worry about it. I don't even really think about it. Well, I did when I left. I noticed how different it was. You know, when people didn't know. But I chose to come back, and I knew what I was coming back to."

"I won't bring it up again."

"I'm not really…" The museum was in sight. An impressive building that stood apart from the others in town, with a low stone wall all around the expansive green lawn at the front. It was red brick, two stories tall, with the same white trim as many of the other buildings in town. There was a flagpole at the edge of the lawn with the Oregon state flag flying beneath an American flag. And next to that was a statue of a cowboy riding a horse with a lasso frozen above his head. She cleared her throat.

"Right now I'm creating space around myself to explore my new role at the museum and support my sister, so…"

He stopped walking abruptly. "That's not why… I swear, Ruby, I just… I want to be friends."

Heat suffused her face and she…stumbled slightly while walking. Which she did not do. He wanted to be friends.

Friends.

He wasn't hitting on her.

Friends.

Her lips twitched. She wasn't entirely sure what she thought about that. And honestly, she wouldn't have believed it was possible when she left. When breaking up with him had felt fraught, but the right thing to do. And standing next to him now, four years later, it didn't feel fraught at all. "All right," she said cautiously. "I'm not opposed to that."

He laughed, and he smiled, and he really was very handsome when he smiled. "Well, glad you're not opposed to me."

"I didn't mean it like that."

"I know." He nudged her elbow with his. "Hey, I'll see you around."

"Yeah," she said. "See you around."

He branched off in another direction, and she watched him, feeling for a moment like she was standing sideways.

Mascot.

Friends.

And for some reason she saw the image of that man again, burned into her mind.

This was not the triumphant morning she'd envisioned. It wasn't even 9:00 a.m., and she felt frightened, challenged and embarrassed.

And slightly scraped raw.

Mascot.

That's grim.

She cleared her throat and squared her shoulders.

She was not *grim*.

She was a *miracle*.

She walked down the pathway that carried her to the broad steps that led up to the grand entryway of the museum, and with each step she tried to picture pieces of the morning falling away.

With each step, she turned her focus to what was real. Right in front of her.

This building had originally been a common area for the town. A place where the citizens could hold meetings, weddings. Parties. So much of the foundational town history had occurred within those walls. And now it stood as a testament to educating people about how the town had been created.

She stood in front of the tall black doors to the museum for a moment. She hadn't been back here for a couple of years, and she was suddenly awash in nostalgia. She could remember getting a special release from school to do presentations at the museum during Heritage Days. When fourth graders from schools in the surrounding area would come and do state education for days. Pear Blossom was one of their sites because of its strong historic programs, living history and intact historic buildings.

They guided the kids through presentations on the Oregon Trail, on the origins of the state's symbols—birds, flags, animals—and gave demonstrations on churning butter, washing clothes and baking. She had worked in nearly every station throughout the years, and for some reason, standing there, she wanted a bottled coffee and a can of Pringles. Because it was the snack she had brought with her every day when she'd been sixteen. And the memory was inexorably tied to the location.

She had always found that funny. When she went on a road trip she always wanted a bag of Ritz Chips, which were hard to find in grocery stores now. When she went back to the Rochelle house—where she had done living history during the summer at fourteen and fifteen—she wanted a chocolate muffin and a bottle of tropical juice, which was a terrible combination, but for some reason it was what she had had as her snack then.

England had been scones and cream tea. France crepes with honey and croque monsieur.

Vastly superior to muffins and juice.

But still, this memory, this moment, was so visceral she could hardly breathe past it. It was strange, the things that became part of your personal history. Perhaps Sentinel Bridge was understandable. Muffins and juice was a little bit odd. But it was all those things that made up a person, she supposed.

And what about the things that came before? The things that she didn't know about.

One thing she knew for certain, as a student of history, was that you couldn't know everything of the past. It was impossible. You could do your best to piece together clues, but you could never really know what people had been thinking. Who they were.

She had accepted that about her own life.

She was fine with it.

The museum was shockingly cool and lit darkly in the entryway. The walnut floors were scarred and shiny, the chandelier that hung overhead worked—wavy glass, likely original. Ruby loved old glass. Imperfect, full of bubbles and wobbles. She heard footsteps coming from one of the back rooms, easy because the place was hushed like a church, and a moment later a woman with short, steel gray hair and loose-fitting clothing befitting a historian, in Ruby's opinion, smiled as she approached her. "You're early."

"Hi, Dana," Ruby said. "I couldn't stay away, now that everything is set."

"Somehow that doesn't surprise me."

Dana didn't hug her. But Dana wasn't... Huggy. Of course, Ruby also didn't find her to be terrifying the way the rest of the town did.

Her eyes were pale and sharp, and her voice was clipped. She was obsessed with history, things in the past, and not at all as interested in things in the present. But, given her life, Ruby couldn't blame her. Ruby didn't pity her—Dana was far too sturdy for that. But she was... Aware.

Because along with her gauzy shawls, Dana had a grief that

wrapped itself around her like a garment. It was just there. It didn't matter if you knew her story or not. You could feel it. A part of her as much as her blue eyes or the lines around her mouth.

Ruby could remember feeling drawn to her from the first time she'd ever seen her. It had been at Pear Blossom Elementary when Ruby was in kindergarten, and a couple of kids from the high school had come in pioneer clothing to do a demonstration on what it was like in the Wild West days of the town. Ruby had been riveted. Gold panning, laundry, butter churning, tin punching. She'd wanted to learn more about all of it.

Dana had been the one overseeing the activities, and so Ruby had known she was the one she had to talk to.

She hadn't even noticed other people avoided the unsmiling woman. She hadn't even noticed she was unsmiling.

And she had come away from the meeting with a stack of brochures, which to young Ruby had meant the entire world.

Whether she had wanted one, Dana had earned a friend for life that day.

"We just finished a new display. But the whole back wing needs to be reset. I don't know if you had any ideas."

"Well," Ruby said, thrown off-balance for a second, but realizing that she shouldn't be that surprised that Dana had gotten right down to it. She wasn't really one for small talk or chitchat. She certainly wasn't going to ask Ruby anything about her time overseas. Unless it was to find out about which historical sites she had visited.

But she wasn't going to want to know about Italian men.

Which was fine.

Ruby didn't really want to share about that with her anyway.

Dana had long been like a family member to Ruby. But like a sort of distant, grumpy aunt.

"I thought that I would look and see what we have," she said. "I want to see what kind of state the archives are in."

"We haven't had an archivist in official capacity, so I imagine you will find it..."

"Anarchist archival?"

"I think that's slightly too exciting a word to use here." Dana's lips twitched with just the slightest bit of humor, and Ruby felt accomplished.

She did make people happy.

She was here for a reason.

"Well, I'm looking forward to gathering and reorganizing all of the resources. Looking at the catalog of artifacts and seeing what we can feature. Especially for the holidays. I think when tourists start to come in for Victorian Christmas we should have some kind of coinciding theme."

"You do have ideas," Dana said, and if Ruby hadn't known better, she would've thought that her tone was approving.

"Yeah, I guess I have a few. Or rather, I have a direction."

There was a staircase toward the back of the building, dark walnut steps and more of that bright white on the banister. The museum was large and cavernous. And very empty. But on a weekday that wasn't unusual. Especially in the fall. Over summer, people came to stay, and again over Christmas, but otherwise there was a lot of weekend traffic. Very much the usual tourism cycle.

She followed Dana up the stairs and down the hall. And toward a part of the museum she had never been in before. The ceilings were high, the moldings ornate, and Ruby felt like she could easily compose poetry about them. Dana pushed the door open, and a rush of satisfaction washed over Ruby. It was a library. A proper library. With big, weighty bookshelves built into the walls. Each one of them absolutely filled to the bursting point. With folios filled with documents, books and artifacts that were on display.

"This is your office," Dana said.

"Really?" Ruby asked, turning a circle, aware that she looked a little bit like an overeager golden retriever.

"Yes," Dana said. "There's a microfiche, for records that haven't been fully digitized. There are some that are digitized."

"Do you have the *Pear Blossom Gazette*?"

"Some," she said. "Notable events. Announcements about World Wars I and II, the paper from 9/11. But the majority of the archive is housed in their offices."

"Mmm. Dahlia showed me yesterday. I might want to use some. I love old newspapers," Ruby said. "I like to find the smallest local paper wherever I go and go back through different articles. It gives you such a picture of the place."

"Well, better you than me," said Dana. "I don't have the patience to read newsprint."

"I have infinite patience for it," Ruby said.

"There are clothes," Dana said. "They're in a wardrobe over there in the corner."

"Clothes?" Ruby asked. "Well, we have to do a clothing display."

"I thought you might like that. I remember you were very into the costuming when you did living history."

"The costumes, in my opinion, are sort of the point."

"The education is the point," Dana said.

Ruby smiled.

"Either way," Ruby said. "I'm… I'm glad to be back."

"It's yours," Dana said. "We still do a manual time card. Make sure you fill it out with your hours for the day before you leave."

"I don't start till Monday," Ruby said.

"You can fill out hours for today, Ruby," Dana said.

And then she turned around and walked out of the room, leaving Ruby alone in her dusty sanctuary. She was feeling… Well, like she had made a very good decision. She had just been left alone in a room filled with records. Archives. Journals. Records. Historical clothing. And it was her job. She was getting paid to spend the day going through all these things. Meticulously combing through and putting them in order. Building stories from them that would make them accessible to the public. Giving other people the insight into history that Ruby had.

She walked over to the bookshelves, and she didn't know where to begin.

December 23, 2000.

The date seemed to hit her brain and stick.

Her day.

Not her birthday. Her Found Day.

She never celebrated her birthday in December. They didn't know the exact date and they'd arbitrarily assigned her December 21, but it was too close to Christmas, and since it was an estimated birthdate anyway, she'd always preferred to take a half birthday. So she could have a whole week of celebrations and free birthday coffee and cookies at the store that did it, when she was not already stuffed full of Christmas cookies.

But the day she was found…

That always resonated. No matter what.

No. She did not need to look at her day. Anyway, she'd read that newspaper article. A hundred times. Her mother had saved all of them.

Maybe. But what about other records? Other information?

What if there was more? She might have saved the article, but she didn't have the entire newspaper. What else had happened that day?

No. She really couldn't start her job doing something self-serving. Anyway, she didn't want to.

The Legend of Ruby McKee was well-worn and overtold in the town of Pear Blossom. And Ruby knew it best of all.

She got up and made her way over to the wardrobe. And opened it. The garments were stored in bags, and she unzipped the first one, pulling out a beautiful muslin dress with pin tucks around the dropped waist. There was another in a beautiful calico. And a rich green-and-purple plaid. She found a fur and a matching muff.

She went over to the computer and sat down, tapping on it and waiting for it to wake up. And once it did, she started searching different shops. That would be an interesting display. The history of fashion in Pear Blossom. In the whole of the West. How it was shaped by where people came from. She felt that she had her first solid idea.

She found ads for different fabrics and trims. And that led her on a rabbit trail, down to digitized Sears and Roebuck catalogs from the late 1800s.

She got up and began to peruse the shelves. And found some hard copies of the catalogs. She opened the first one and began to flip through the pages. It was remarkably well preserved. From March 1901. The catalog had everything. It boasted the latest in home conveniences, ads for electric lights and indoor plumbing apparatus. Victrolas. Stereoscopes. Clothing, fabric. Even houses. It made her smile. This sort of remote shopping that was so popular now was nothing new.

Her stomach didn't growl until five o'clock. She hadn't realized that she'd been sitting here that long. Hadn't realized that she'd gotten so lost in looking at everything. But she'd always been like that.

She went over to the files. There were police records. Stretching back to the 1860s. And newer...

She found the bundle that was labeled December 2000.

She grabbed hold of that file, and then the one for January 2001.

She'd never had a look at actual police reports from either Caitlin's disappearance or her appearance. And it made her feel... Like she was being slightly nosy when it came to digging into Caitlin, because of Dana, but...

She was curious.

Emerging from the room and out into the hallway startled

her. Because she hadn't realized how dim it was in there. But there was only one window for the whole large room, and as a result the large windows that lined the hall made her feel like a bemused bat emerging from a cave before its time. She nearly ran into Dana, who was halfway up the stairs when she was going down. "I was just coming to get you. I'm ready to leave and lock up. I won't have a copy of keys for you until Monday."

"That's okay," she said, feeling slightly edgy and a bit like she'd been caught, even though she was allowed to look at whatever she wanted. "I'll walk you to your car."

"You don't have to do that."

Dana always pushed off overly friendly gestures, but Ruby had always wondered if she secretly liked them.

"I know. You're always telling me what I don't *have* to do, Dana. I don't listen—you know that."

"Your sister listens," Dana said.

"Dahlia is a fake rebel."

"I like her."

That was exceedingly high praise coming from Dana.

Ruby and Dana walked out the front door, and Ruby paused for a moment to take in the golden evening. The sun was beginning to lower, but the air still had that rich cast to it. There was something about October. It was particularly beautiful here. She'd always thought so.

A crisp breeze blew up, and she held the strap of her bag more tightly, lowering her head, her hair blowing in the wind.

As they made their way down the street, no one stopped to chat. A few people waved at Ruby, but several people looked away quickly and acted like they didn't see them. Ruby had never been quite so conscious of how different it was than when she walked alone—or with one of her sisters or a friend.

"I saw Heath earlier," Ruby said, determined to push past the odd sensation inside her. "You remember Heath? He was my... I dated him in high school."

"Yes," Dana said. "Floppy-haired boy. He used to hang around waiting for you to be finished with your shift."

"Yes. That is him. Floppy hair and all." She cleared her throat. "He called me the town mascot."

Dana did something totally unexpected then. She laughed. Rusty and in the back of her throat, like it wasn't a sound she was accustomed to making. "Well, he isn't wrong."

"He isn't?" Ruby asked, feeling betrayed by this.

Dana should have said it was ridiculous and validated her earlier feelings, identified it as stupidity. Silliness.

"It says nothing about you, Ruby McKee, and everything about them. You were...a miracle." But she didn't say the word the way most people did. "And now you're...well, the mascot of how great we all are. Not all of us, of course." That was accompanied by a wry smile, stretched thin on Dana's narrow face.

Ruby paused and stared at Dana, at the grooves in her forehead and between her brows, by her mouth, etched into her skin. And she saw the ghosts of laugh lines by her blue eyes. Evidence of joy that had passed away before those lines had become deep and decisive. The grooves worn the deepest were anger, sorrow.

"You don't think I'm a miracle, Dana?" She tried to ask it in a light tone. Self-deprecating, even, but it came out...*seeking*, and Ruby was left embarrassed by it.

"You're a smart, capable young woman with a good head on your shoulders, when it isn't in the clouds. That's a kind of miraculous, I suppose." They carried on walking. "But... You know when they found you it was...it was like you were supposed to replace what we lost. And I suppose for them you did."

Ruby's stomach turned sour.

Caitlin.

Dana had never, ever talked to her about this before. And Ruby didn't know why she was doing it now. Ruby wanted her to stop, in fact. Which she realized with a certain amount of horror and shame. Because she considered Dana a friend, and she should want to hear her hard truths, and here she was, wanting to cover her ears while the older woman spoke.

"Miraculous," Dana said. "That's what they thought and I... Ruby, it was a tragedy. I... I couldn't believe some woman would leave her child, her baby, like that. Not after my own baby was taken from me. I..." Dana stopped walking and Ruby looked at her, expecting to see tears.

But she didn't.

All she saw was anger.

"I couldn't fathom who would do that. Who would...she left you to die."

The words punctured Ruby's stomach, made her feel deflated and hurt and *tragic*. And she wished she had covered her ears.

But she didn't.

And Dana didn't stop talking.

"Of course, my first thought was to blame her. But that's what we do. It's what we do."

"What is?"

Dana looked her square in the face. "We blame the mother."

Ruby hadn't. Ruby hadn't blamed anyone. She was...she had been rescued, and that was what counted, not the rest of it.

"I... I'm not angry about it," Ruby said. "I'm just happy. I'm happy that I'm here. You know, not everyone gets to be so confident their life has a purpose. My life was saved and I... I'm meant to do something with it, I suppose."

"My daughter's life meant something too. And she's still gone."

Dana started to walk faster and Ruby had to trot to keep up, her each step making pain radiate in her chest. "I... I didn't mean..."

"Settle down, I know you didn't." Dana sighed. "Everyone wants easy answers, easy fixes. You can't fix tragedy."

Then they were standing by Dana's car, and Ruby didn't

know if she was relieved or sorry. "I guess I'll see you Monday," Ruby said.

"That is one thing I like about you," Dana said. "I don't scare you."

Then she got into her car and left Ruby standing there feeling… Like Dana did in fact scare her.

But not half as much as the things she had said.

6

The March of Progress

BY JAN EBERSOL

MARCH 5, 1883—With the new railway comes new opportunities in Southern Oregon. The new Eden Valley Orchard in Medford has capitalized on this new era of export, and it seems the expansion is happening here too. The land owned by Thaddeus Brewer boasts 400 acres of pears, expected to be ready to harvest next season.

DAHLIA

When Dahlia arrived back at the shed that night, Ruby wasn't there. She could tell she had been. The door to her room was flung open and there were boxes everywhere.

Dahlia locked the front door behind her, then went to check the back and make sure it was locked too.

What if the man Ruby had seen really was Nathan Brewer? Though it seemed like if it were Nathan Brewer, rumors about him would have been flying already.

Dahlia heard a key in the lock a moment later, and then Ruby. "Hi," she said.

"I was worried about you," Dahlia said.

"Why?" Ruby frowned.

"Because you saw a man skulking around earlier."

"Ah, right," Ruby said, as if she'd forgotten about the skulking man. "Can you help me carry stuff in from the car?"

"What did you get?"

"Everything," Ruby said. "Retail therapy, Dee. It's a thing."

She vanished out the front door again, into the twilight.

"Are you using Mom and Dad's car?"

"Mom said I could," Ruby said, bending over and digging into the back of the small SUV. "She said Dad never goes to town anyway."

Dahlia supposed that she shouldn't find that annoying. Particularly considering she was living on her parents' property for free.

Ruby appeared, not with bags as Dahlia expected, but a very large box. "I drove into Medford. I went to Target. You said that I needed my own desk."

"Why are you retail therapizing?" Dahlia asked, watching as Ruby hefted the long box and carried it inside. Then she went to the back of the car and grabbed hold of the bags that were sitting in there. There were many.

"I had a whole day," Ruby said, waving her hand. "And I felt bad, so I thought I should throw some money at it and make it go away."

"You realize this is a very small space, right?"

"Yes. I do. I needed a desk, though, and I needed storage. But my desk can go next to yours."

Cozily, Dahlia thought with much annoyance.

"Yeah," Dahlia said.

"Also, I got some succulents," Ruby said. "Because of your plant."

Dahlia shook her head. "You're a whole thing—do you know that?"

"What?"

"You came in here and basically took over, and just when I start to get irritated at you... I can't."

"I don't want you to be irritated with me."

"I know," Dahlia said. "I know you don't. And I can't stay irritated at you anyway."

"I didn't mean to take over either. I'm just trying to... Help."

Dahlia grimaced. "You always are."

She watched as her sister made manic about the room, unloading her bags and putting knickknacks on every available surface.

"What bad emotion exactly are you banishing?"

"Heath called me a mascot," Ruby said. "And then Dana... well, she was Dana."

"I'm sorry. Heath called you a what?" Dahlia frowned.

"A mascot. The town mascot."

"While I would love it if the high school were in fact The Fighting Rubies, I don't think your head could stand to get any bigger."

Ruby's eyes went large, and her frown deepened. "My head is big?"

"Oh, for heaven's sake, Rubes. I was teasing you."

"Dana said I'm not a miracle."

And while Dahlia *really* wanted to tease Ruby about being devastated that someone didn't find her miraculous, she could feel there was something more serious there, and she didn't want to be mean. Poking at Ruby was fine. Knocking some of her glitter off on occasion was Dahlia's sisterly duty to the whole of the world.

But she didn't want to hurt her.

"Can you expand on that?" Dahlia asked.

"I mean...she said she always found me really tragic and... Anyway, it was fine—it was just a really uncomfortable conversation."

Dahlia felt the strangest echo inside of her. A radiant pain that also felt oddly satisfied. Because she'd felt that. Always. Even at four. That there was a deep sadness to Ruby's abandonment, and a story. One that no one seemed interested in discovering.

"I agree with her," Dahlia said.

"You...you agree?"

Dahlia's breath caught on an indignant sound. "I'm not...trying to be mean, so please stop with the big eyes. But have you honestly never...wondered about why you were left? Or thought it had to be some insane tragedy? I mean, you were abandoned. You could have died."

"I didn't, though," Ruby insisted. "Because you found me."

"Yes, we did. And it was chance. The odds of a sad ending were much higher."

"I just don't like to think of it that way."

"I understand that," Dahlia said. "But you know, you don't see things the way I do and you never have."

"Glass half-full," Ruby said, then gestured to Dahlia. "Glass half-empty."

"That's not true," Dahlia said. "Not necessarily. I want to know how the glass came to be the way it is. If someone filled it halfway, I guess it's half-full. But if someone drank from it, it's half-empty. What happened matters. Why it happened matters."

Dahlia didn't know why it bothered her so much. Why she wanted Ruby to care about the answers all of a sudden. Except she'd always been this way. She'd always wanted the answers while it had seemed like the people around her preferred *stories*.

"I care about the truth," Ruby said. "It's not like I'm...living a lie. It's just...perspective. And I didn't like Heath saying I was a mascot any more than I like Dana saying I'm a...a tragedy. I'm a *person*."

Dahlia sighed. "I know that, Rubes. I just... Aren't you curious?"

"I...not usually. Once I realized I definitely wasn't a secret princess, it all became less interesting. I just... I don't know, I was going to say I just want to be a normal person, but that's a lie, isn't it?"

Yes.

"I can't answer that for you."

"I want to be special."

Dahlia stared at her sister, who from her point of view had been treated as special from the moment she'd been found. "You are the girl who lived," she said. "You couldn't be any more special."

Ruby huffed a breath and looked to the side, scrubbing at the bridge of her nose before looking back over at Dahlia. "I just… Look, I did… I grabbed some police records from the museum today. I don't even know why. No, I do. It was what Heath said. It got me in a funky headspace and then Dana…"

"What police records?"

"I got a file that should have the police report from the night I was found."

Interest prickled the back of Dahlia's neck. "Can I see it?"

"Sure. I haven't looked at it yet. I…dumped it off and went back out to shop."

Ruby walked out of the room and into her bedroom, returning with a file, which she shoved in Dahlia's hand before heading back to the car. She came back in with a giant bag filled with blankets and another with pillows spilling out the top. She grinned sheepishly. "I needed blankets too."

"Uh-huh," Dahlia said.

Ruby shoved those into the bedroom and shut the door, then came to stand by Dahlia.

Dahlia looked it over critically. Pear Blossom Police Department. December 23, 2000.

There was an exhaustive description of Ruby and her condition. And witness statements.

She paused when she got to her own. She had been four years

old. It said simply: "There was a baby. She was crying. Distress likely caused by a combination of hunger and the cold."

Dahlia felt an unexpected swell of emotion in her chest, and the memory felt so fresh. The sadness she'd felt then, the confusion. She'd been so young she'd always felt like she was missing pieces of what had happened, especially because her own feelings about it had been so different from the whole town's.

Except Dana's, apparently.

"Wow. I… I've never seen this," Dahlia said.

She handed it to Ruby, who looked at it while squinting, as if she didn't want to see it too clearly. Ruby didn't frown. Instead she looked… Calm. Her expression glassy and smooth.

"I know this story," Ruby said. "It's just strange to read what you all said to the police."

And for the first time Dahlia really considered that Ruby's myth sold her sister short a bit. As if her survival had been so unquestionably meant to be, that she'd never truly been in peril. That she'd been magical, and therefore not… A fighter.

"You're a story, Ruby. You always have been. Just making you into a miracle is kind of selling you short. You're not a tragedy, because you survived."

The corner of Ruby's mouth twitched. "That makes me sound kind of tough."

"I've been looking for stories," Dahlia said slowly. "Stories about the town. It's something I've been thinking about, mulling over. The people who live here love it here. They really do. And there are a lot of new people. People who don't know what made this place. But this is… This is what I need to do. A series of articles rediscovering the town. The history, the arrival of pears into the economy, the building of these different businesses. The disappearance of Caitlin Groves. And you. I'd like to do a real profile on you. Gather new interviews and perspectives. I want to reinvigorate interest in the paper, and I think this could do it."

"I...look, Dahlia, if you want to do history, I'm here for that. I can even make museum displays to coincide with the story. A history of businesses in town? There used to be a feature... They don't do it anymore. It was in the paper. It was called No Longer on the Map. And it went over what used to be on Main Street, what isn't there anymore. You could write about them and I could make mock storefronts and everything."

Ruby was brightening and trying to move away from the serious stuff already. "Okay, that does sound great." Dahlia gripped the edge of the police report. "But this...this is the substance of the town. I want to write about this. I want to write about you."

"What is there to write about?" Ruby asked. "It's been written."

"We were never interviewed. We were kids. Me, Lydia and Marianne, I mean. And you haven't been."

"Dahlia..."

Dahlia stared back down at the police report and remembered. "I was four. And for some reason I remember very clearly that I'd just cut my hair to chin length, and it felt really grown-up. I'm having a hard time describing the feeling. I see things but I don't... I'm not sure if I'm remembering or if I'm making things up, you know?" She squinted as if that would help her cast her mind back. "I've heard everyone else talk about it so much."

Except... She hadn't really. They talked about the event, but not the moment they'd *found* Ruby. And those two things seemed very different.

It was like still pictures. There wasn't sound. But she had a vision of the bridge. It was dark out, and Lydia was holding a flashlight. She was *pretty* sure Lydia was. And her sisters were both tall, which was funny because she was taller than both of them now.

She was walking in front of them trying to stay in the beam of light. And she could remember seeing it. A little bundle. Like a baby doll. And in her mind there was one clear image, of the light falling across that red, wrinkled face.

The first time she'd seen Ruby.

"I just remember it was really cold," she said to Ruby. "And we were… We were rehearsing for the Christmas play. And I was in the choir. So we were dressed as angels. I think I had a white sheet on. And I don't have a clue why I remember that. But I remember trying to squeeze the baggy white sleeves into my coat before we left. And I felt like I couldn't move my arms right. But Mom wasn't there. It was Lydia and Marianne bundling me up. So they didn't do a good job. Then we walked outside and it was cold. I could see my breath. And I remember the bridge. The boards were squeaky. And I thought it was scary. Because it was like walking into a mouth. And I didn't like it. I guess it's not really a memory from that night. It's just how I felt about the bridge. And you were there. In a little blanket."

Ruby was staring at her now, not so immune now. Wanting the story now.

"Who picked me up?" Ruby asked.

Dahlia frowned. "I don't remember. I remember that when you did get picked up, something fell out of the blanket. It was your necklace. The silver bells."

Ruby nodded.

"I picked them up," Dahlia said.

And right then she could feel it between her fingertips. Cold from the air outside. So cold. It was a miracle that Ruby had survived. Dahlia had been out there with a coat, and she could remember. She could remember how cold it was, and Ruby had been just a tiny thing, wrapped in a blanket.

"I put them in my coat pocket," Dahlia said. "And… I remember being home. And I remember police." She shook her head. "That's really all. I was just…in preschool. I can remember making a turkey with my hand, but I can't totally remember all that. You're my sister. That's what it was. From that day forward. I mean… There were discussions. I remember being upset, because Mom said she didn't know if we could keep you. Because someone might be looking for you. I remember praying that whoever it was didn't find you, because they didn't deserve you. They left you. I didn't want you to go away. I felt like we found you and you were ours. So we should get to keep you."

Ruby was uncharacteristically silent, and she noticed that there were tears in her eyes. "I didn't know that."

"I guess I never told you."

She had wanted Ruby so desperately, so very badly. A baby, because then she wasn't the baby anymore, and it made her feel older and more important.

And after the honeymoon phase she had started to resent her sometimes. Because she was loud and red-faced and noisy. Because Dahlia didn't get all the attention that she used to. And she could also remember telling her mother that she wished that they would send her back. She could remember saying that she was tired of Ruby and she hoped whoever was looking for her found her. At that point she'd been a terrible two-year-old to Dahlia's emotional six. And her mother had told her they'd adopted Ruby, and she was part of her family. Just the same as they were. And they could no more send Ruby back than they could send Marianne or Lydia away.

She didn't tell Ruby that part. Because always, always at the end of one of those fits she felt terrible guilt. And then fear. Fear that that vague hope had made its way out to the universe and someone would come for Ruby. Come and take her away. It was like that always. A seesaw of guilt and resentment. The adjustment period wasn't smooth.

"I never asked," Ruby said.

Dahlia looked at Ruby, hard. "Why not?"

"I don't know. Maybe because I… Dahlia, I know I'm not a secret princess. I know that… I do know that there's something half-empty there. I just…don't see how it would help me to know that. I've always preferred to just focus on the fact that I'm here for a reason, saved for a reason and…it makes me brave. It gives me a purpose and I don't know what this is going to do for me."

Ruby was sincere. Always. "Well, maybe it's not about what it would do for you. I mean, Ruby, history is your thing. What does history do for the people that have passed on? Nothing. It's about what we can all learn from it, right? It's about…the way it touches us in the present. You and I both believe, so deeply, in that."

"Caitlin too, though? I worry about Dana…"

"I would never do anything to hurt Dana," Dahlia said. "You know that. But it would feel wrong to leave either of you out of these kinds of…retrospectives."

"Hmm."

"Do you object to being the subject of a retrospective?"

Ruby scrunched her nose. "I guess not. I trust you, Dee. I know you aren't going to write anything that bothers me."

Dahlia wasn't sure about that, though, since it was clear a great many of the truths Dahlia saw in her sister's past did hurt her.

Maybe Ruby floated so none of it touched her.

So her feet never hit the ground and she never had to feel it.

And Dahlia wasn't looking to write a puff piece. She wanted to write something new, something that hadn't been written yet about Ruby McKee.

About Pear Blossom.

"I'll tell you what, I'll bring back all the Ruby papers tomorrow from the office."

"I have a scrapbook. Of me. I think I've seen everything there is to see."

Dahlia shrugged. "Don't you think sometimes you can look at something at a different time and see…something completely new?"

A strange expression crossed Ruby's face. "Yeah, I... I guess that's true."

"What?"

"I've been feeling that way all day. I'm on these streets, and I know them so well. But I keep noticing things I never did before. Like the way people avoid Dana. I feel like I *knew* it, but I never really...felt it like I did today."

"So maybe it's the perfect time to revisit things."

"Maybe," Ruby said. "Yeah, okay. I think...yeah."

"Not exactly an enthusiastic buy-in, but I'll take it."

Dahlia had often felt out of place in this bright, shiny town, but she'd always felt connected to it too. It was hard to explain. How much she cared about the history, and how compelled she felt to dig into the secrets that were here.

After all, she was part of one of them. And she had the best resource right in front of her.

Now she had a mission. And when Dahlia McKee had a mission, she was never deterred.

7

Highwaymen Afoot in Pear Blossom

BY JOHN HARDY

1918—A traveler from out of town was ambushed by highwaymen on Sentinel Bridge. It is believed to be connected to a string of such robberies happening up and down the coast. It is not believed the citizens of Pear Blossom are in any current danger, as the general method of these marauders has been to rob once, then move on to new territory where the law is not actively seeking them.

RUBY

Ruby was bone-tired by the end of the day. She'd spent the whole day with Hazel and Riley, and she had exhausted her bag of Cool Aunt Tricks. She had myriad fun clothes for dress-up and was pretty good at various dance challenges from the internet.

She loved Riley and Hazel. But when it came to being there for Lydia…she had sort of expected her sister to actually spend some time with her. But Lydia had been out on the farm all day, butting heads with Chase, most likely, and Ruby had been on kid duty, until they'd all gone to dinner at their parents.

It was hideously embarrassing to realize how much of her Save

Lydia Mission was about her own feelings, and even worse to realize… That realizing it didn't change the way she felt.

Now she was finally back at the cottage with the newspapers Dahlia had promised.

And she was… Ugh.

She was trepidatious. And she was never that. It irritated her.

Ruby settled back into the cottage and stacked the newspapers beside her bed by the window, shivering slightly as she looked out into the darkness. *He* could be out there and she wouldn't know it.

"Good lord," she muttered, getting up and drawing the curtains.

She'd lived in cities full of strangers where there was almost certainly a criminal somewhere on the same street. A predator of some sort. And yet there was something intimate about knowing who the person was. About knowing what he might've done. About being here and feeling in danger. In this place that had always been a haven for her. For her specifically. Because hadn't Sentinel Bridge shielded her? And hadn't the people here taken her in and loved her?

Or maybe she just had an overactive imagination, and she was applying all sorts of special meaning to the situation that simply didn't exist.

She pulled out the newspaper article that had appeared the day after she'd been found.

Baby Found on Sentinel Bridge

A newborn baby girl was found on Sentinel Bridge on the evening of December 23. Marianne, Lydia and Dahlia McKee were walking home from choir practice when they happened upon the bundle…

It was an article that Ruby had read before. One that her mother had cut out and tucked away in her baby book. Her blanket from that day and the necklace that had been placed with her were wrapped up in the same keepsake box.

She looked at the rest of the paper. There were ads for various sales. A story about puppies for Christmas and a bit of national news.

But it was the other story that occupied the front page of the *Pear Blossom Gazette* that stopped her cold.

Brewer's Trial Postponed

The trial of Nathan Brewer has been postponed indefinitely. The defense is challenging the charges on the basis that there is not enough evidence, and that Brewer has been held unlawfully. The defense posits that because no body has been found, nor any evidence suggesting violence occurred, Brewer cannot be implicated in the disappearance or possible death of Caitlin Groves.

This is a devastating blow to a community in mourning. It has been more than a year since our town's greatest tragedy, and we are no closer to justice, or answers. This event has left a deep and lasting scar. If we cannot now trust our own neighbors, as we always have, throughout the history of our town, what will we become? If we cannot root out the bad apples among us with veracity, if we can have no recourse or justice, what will this community become?

It was the strangest thing, to see this story right next to her own.

Hadn't Dana just made the link between herself and Caitlin yesterday?

The town acted like her appearance canceled out the loss of Caitlin.

She grabbed another newspaper at random, one from the middle of January.

There was nothing about her, or Nathan. There was a piece about smudge pots and their history. But when she grabbed the paper for the week of January 20, there was mention of Nathan again.

Charges Dropped, Brewer to be Released.

She skimmed the article, her eyes landing on the final few paragraphs.

Dana Groves is distraught, her eyes hollow. The single mother has no one else to help to shoulder this burden. She is a woman alone. A wayward teen daughter, who spent nights out with a boyfriend, likely engaging in risky behaviors, likely already causing undue stress, the loss of that child has broken her. Perhaps it is only residents of this town who can truly grasp the gravity of the situation. Certainly not officials sitting in their ivory towers in Salem. They are unaffected by the tragedy of one teenage girl, potentially murdered by one of the people she trusted the most. For now, for Dana, for the community of Pear Blossom, it feels as if Caitlin has been taken all over again.

"He knows something," Groves' mother asserted. "He was the last person to see her. And he's the only one who knows what happened to her. I just want the truth."

But the truth is proving to be elusive, subject to the whims of a justice system that is more concerned with keeping the letter of the law than seeing actual justice done. The state of Oregon may forget, the nation most certainly will. But the town of Pear Blossom will not.

Well, they hadn't. Ruby knew that for sure. Because there were no villains hated half so much in the town as the Brewer family. And Nathan Brewer was here. Why?

She knew why she was back. To find herself. To be with her family. To connect with this town who loved her so much, almost as much as she loved it in return.

Why would you come back to a town that hated you?

Well, probably because he needed money, and he needed to fix up the house and the land to sell it. That would make the most sense.

Her eyes were prickly, and she was sleepy.

I don't know what this is going to do for me.

Well, maybe it's not about what it would do for you.

That was all fine for Dahlia to say, but it was Ruby's life that was being excavated.

She sighed heavily and got up from the bed, stretching. She surveyed the tidy, small space. The light wood floor was clean and uncluttered, the few open shelves on her wall were filled with books. Her bed was made and ready for her. As ready for her as she was for it.

She pulled the blankets back, crawling beneath the covers. But she kept seeing newsprint behind her eyelids. And in spite of herself, she was trying to read it until she finally lapsed into unconsciousness.

And when she did, there was no rest.

Because she felt like she was awake again, standing there on the backside of Sentinel Bridge. The path behind her looked impossibly long and unfamiliar. The trees overgrown. There were fall leaves on the ground, and the wind was cold. She had a sense of foreboding that stretched all around her, and she didn't want to go into the bridge. She was afraid of it.

But she had no choice other than to keep walking forward. As if each footstep was compelled by a force more powerful than herself. But the passage through the bridge was dark. And still, she kept walking forward. She wanted to tell herself to stop. But she couldn't. It was like the body wasn't hers.

She took her first step into the bridge. Then another.

And the darkness swallowed her whole.

8

Chase dared Mac to climb up the rocks at the park and he could have fallen and smashed his head. I told Mrs. Spencer and she grounded him. Mac said that was mean of me, but I don't care.

LYDIA MCKEE'S DIARY, AGE 13

LYDIA

When Lydia got back to the property from dropping her kids off at school, he was already there.

She wasn't in the mood for Chase. She wasn't in the mood for... Much of anything. And she had agreed to go over to Marianne's house tonight for a girls' dinner. Which was very low on her list of things she wanted to do.

She loved her sisters. She did. Marianne was a rock, but Marianne also made it clear Lydia didn't have to be. She was so understanding and wonderful, to a degree that made Lydia feel guilty because she never felt like she could quite give Marianne what she expected.

Then there was Dahlia, who was bracing, and honest, and somewhat too close to the truth for Lydia's taste right now.

And Ruby...

Oh, Ruby. She loved her baby sister so much.

But...

Ruby had a way of unintentionally making other people's feelings about her. Ruby didn't want anyone to be unhappy, and she made it her mission to cheer people and Lydia just didn't want cheering.

The way she looked at Lydia... Like she wanted to see into her head, her heart, and examine her grief. It made Lydia want to hide from her.

But Ruby had helped with the kids all day Saturday, so there was that.

Oh, she was so tired of herself. She was so tangled up in everything. Her own feelings, her own resentments. And Chase wasn't helping.

Mac's best friend and foster brother had never really been her favorite person. She found him crass. And his laconic manner and extreme confidence hit her in all the wrong places. Not only that, his grief was just a bit much for her to bear. It was clear in the way that Chase mourned Mac. It was pure. In a way her own grief wasn't.

She could deal with someone who was annoying. That was the least of her worries. It was dealing with someone who made her feel guilty. Who made her feel like a fraud... Yeah, that was what she resented.

She got out of the car just as Chase was circling back to his work truck. He had on a faded denim jacket and a pair of tan, Carhartt pants that clung to his workman's physique with more loving care than she felt was strictly necessary.

"Good morning," he said as she got out of the car.

"Yeah. I guess. What have you been up to?"

"Just went and fed the pigs. Haven't been out to collect the eggs, but I know you like to do that."

He looked almost boyish when he said that, and it made her want to snap at him. "And we care what I like now?"

"I thought I'd haul the tractor out later, help out with the field." He said that like she hadn't just been spiteful about the eggs.

"I didn't ask for your help," she said.

"No," Chase said. "But Mac did. And this was his plan too. Same as the kids are his kids, as well as yours. And I figure if that's what he wanted, it's my duty to make sure that some of this is done the way he saw fit."

"He's dead," Lydia said, making a wide berth around his person as she headed toward the house.

She was a *bitch*. She really was such a bitch.

And she was angry with herself. For saying that to Chase, and for the fact that saying it didn't make her want to cry.

"I'm aware of that. Would you like some coffee?"

She stopped, her shoulders sagging. "Were you in my house?"

"No. I brought some coffee with me."

She looked at Chase, and she suddenly felt tired. And he looked strong. Tall and broad shouldered, with pale blue eyes and blond hair. When she'd first gotten to know him, at thirteen, he'd been cute, and then he'd transitioned into a boyish handsomeness, his looks appealing to large swaths of Pear Blossom's female population.

It had been truly irritating to be around. But in Mac's eyes Chase could do no wrong. His foster brother *knew about the world*. And had all the women he could possibly want—not that Mac wanted that. He was perfectly happy with her! He always hurried to say—in an endless source of streetwise confidence.

He was that bad boy most girls couldn't get enough of and all Lydia had wanted was safe. When Lydia was twelve, Caitlin Groves had disappeared. Presumably killed by her boyfriend. And then she'd found a baby on a bridge when she was thirteen, and that had only confirmed to her that the world had seemed vast and scary.

Bad boys were the last thing she could imagine wanting.

And yet, she seemed to be stuck with one.

And now there were lines around those eyes and grooves around his mouth, representative of the years that had passed and all they had cost him. His face holding ghosts of emotions that had come before, and now a permanent sort of grimness that had come about with Mac's death.

She directed her focus past his shoulder, at the mountains beyond that had the audacity to look the same.

"Yeah, I'll take some coffee."

He took out his thermos, unscrewed the lid and poured a bit of coffee into it. He took a step toward her when she didn't move toward him, handing it to her.

She sighed and leaned back against the passenger side of her car, and he mirrored her stance, leaning against the side of his truck.

"It's been six months," he said. "Do you think you're ever going to accept that I'm helping you here?"

"It's been six months," she countered. "Do you think you're ever going to accept that I'm not comfortable with it?"

"Why?"

She didn't have words for that. Rather, it was a whole cascade of feeling. Bound up in her own secrets, her feelings about Mac and her feelings about Chase.

The resentment that she had felt early on at Mac's closeness with him and the strange sort of resentment that she had decided was because it seemed like Mac could be more open with Chase than he ever was with her. And in the years that she was married, she had come to realize that Chase wasn't the issue at all. But she had never really shaken the resentment of him.

Maybe because the promise of Mac seemed to be what Chase had gotten, and she hadn't felt like that was the case for her. And that lie, the lie of who she and Mac had been, the lie of what had been between them and how she grieved... It stood as a pillar between her and her entire family. And it was even worse with Chase, because she didn't care about him. But he cared about Mac, and she…

Well, it didn't bear thinking about. But that was the problem—when he was around, she thought about it. She thought about it obsessively and endlessly.

"Because I'm not." She cleared her throat. "I was unaware that as a grieving widow I needed to give a dissertation on my feelings."

"I loved him too," Chase said.

She tightened her arms around herself. "I know you did."

"He was like a brother to me. I might have been back and forth between my house and theirs, but his mother is more a mother to me than my own has ever been…"

"You don't know what bothers me, Chase," she said.

Because how could she ever say. How could she ever say that she had been on the verge of asking for a divorce when he was diagnosed with ALS. How could she ever untangle the impossibility of all that grief? Of the role she was stuck playing. And that she did *genuinely* grieve him as the father of her children. A man who had died too young.

As the man she had *wanted* to love.

But she just hadn't. Not anymore. Not like that.

But you couldn't be the woman who left a dying man.

At least, *she* couldn't have done it.

Because she *had* loved him, loved his family, and hers loved him. Because she had *married* him. Because she had vowed she would be there in sickness, and they'd had years of health before, so didn't she have to do that part?

So all of her plans had been put on hold. The life she'd painstakingly decided to build for herself as a divorced woman.

It hadn't been an easy conclusion to come to even when he hadn't been sick. She'd known it would mean untangling lives that were so enmeshed in each other that the process would be painful. Would leave damage and scars.

And she'd decided it was time, because they both deserved more than a life of quiet resentments that were aging into bitter roots, down deep in the lowest parts of their souls.

She'd decided to take that step.

And then the path had turned again, and while she might have been able to figure out how to live as a divorced woman, she hadn't yet discovered how to live as a widow.

She hadn't anticipated how much it would tangle her up in the grieving. And how much it would make her feel boxed in.

How much it would leave her unable to deal with her feelings.

"You can tell me," he said.

She imagined a wall going up between them. Smooth, pristine and impossible to scale. "Yeah, I'm gonna pass on that. You and I were never friends. It's not going to happen now."

"I don't need to be your friend," Chase said. "I know that might shock you."

She started to walk away from him, her own words echoing in her head. *We were never friends.*

They hadn't been. It had been him and Mac, thick as thieves, and she'd been along for the ride, mooning over Mac's blue eyes and brown hair and dimples. He'd been sweet, she'd thought. She hadn't liked Chase's overabundance of energy, his quick temper or his blunt observations.

Later, though, she'd realized Mac's sweetness was a deep passiveness. He went along with things. And when life got hard, he took a step back. He went out drinking even when she didn't want him to. If he didn't want to deal with a problem, he didn't.

And there was nothing she could do to make him.

They might not have *fought*, but she realized now it wasn't because he was nicer or kinder than the average man.

"I heard your sister's back," Chase said.

She stopped, her shoulders stiffening.

"Yes," she said. "She is."

"I'd like to see her sometime."

She gritted her teeth. "If you're trying to angle yourself into a position to hit on Ruby—"

"I don't have any interest in Ruby that way. But it's nice to know that you have such a low opinion of me."

She ground her back teeth together, feeling so awful in her own skin because this was just meanness for the sake of it and she couldn't seem to stop. "Your reputation precedes you."

"I'm a single man, Lydia. What I do with my spare time is my business. But I guarantee you it's not going to cross over into your family. I was just making conversation. Being polite. Not sure if you're familiar with the concept. They taught us trashy foster kids manners because they assumed we wouldn't pick them up naturally, not sure how it worked for your kind."

"And yet, I keep thinking that you'll take a hint. But you never do."

"I hear you," he said, moving away from the truck, and something about that swift, smooth motion sent her heart straight up into the center of her throat. "But you may have noticed that I'm not interested in doing your bidding. My best friend died. He doesn't get to see his kids grow up. And the last thing he said to me was that he wanted me to make sure that this farm didn't suffer. That *you* didn't suffer. If I'm your medicine, then so be it. But I will make sure you swallow the pill."

Her heart was hammering so hard she felt dizzy with it, and she couldn't quite say why.

There was an intensity to his gaze that she couldn't contain. He was firing it straight into her, and there was nowhere for it to go. She had done her level best to live in some kind of softened state that denied reality for the last six months. And he was pushing something so real, so authentic, right into her that she just...

She turned and walked away from him. Started to move toward the farmhouse.

"I'll be back with the tractor," he said.

"Great," she returned.

"You don't really mean that."

"You don't know what I mean."

"At this point, I know you well enough to be able to make some guesses. I also know better than to tell you what they are because I don't want you to bite my hand off."

There was so much she wanted to say to him. But she also just didn't want to deal, so she made the decision not to. So she just walked away from him. Went into the house and let the screen door slam behind her. An angry, therapeutic sound.

But only the slammed door felt like therapy. The rest was just the same.

Her bottling it up.

Her not dealing.

She stood in the quiet of the farmhouse and let out a long, slow breath. She looked at all the pictures on the wall, extending down the hall. Her wedding picture. Pictures of them when she had been pregnant with Riley. Baby pictures of them with Hazel.

Her and Mac. Together for what was supposed to be forever. Except she'd been intent on shattering that...

Mac never knew.

She felt furious about that, sometimes late at night. Her head and heart and throat crowded with all the things she'd never gotten to say. Angry things about years spent in unhappiness. About all that he'd done wrong.

She'd said the nice things. Every one. That was what you did when someone was dying.

She'd said he was a good father. He was, when he was around.

She'd said she was glad for their time together.

In truth, she was just glad they had the kids.

But she'd swallowed it all down. Her truth, her pain.

But these pictures stayed up on the wall, not because of the

husband he'd been, but because of the husband she wanted everyone to believe he was.

"You were kind of a terrible husband," she said, right to the
picture. "And I loved you. And I still do, really. Just not like
that. Not for a long time. So. Just so you know."

The little speech hadn't done anything to make her feel better, because nothing had changed. Nothing at all.

And she was going to have to get herself together so that she
could have dinner tonight.

One thing was certain, she was not going to hide in the house.
She was not going to let Chase know that he got to her.

So she took a deep breath. She had eggs to collect.

9

*I hate this town. I want to go away and write for a big newspaper.
I want to go to London, or New York. I just want something bigger.*

MARIANNE MCKEE'S DIARY, AGE 14

MARIANNE

"How about we go to the toy section, you guys?"

Ruby looked down at Riley and Hazel and extended her hands, smiling brightly. Marianne glanced over at Lydia, who was looking around the brightly lit, large store appearing slightly dazed. She hadn't thought about it, but she wondered if this was the first time Lydia had ventured away from Pear Blossom since Mac's death. They had talked about a lot of things, but whether or not she had gone into Medford to go to one of the big box stores was not one of the things.

"Lydia?" Ruby addressed her sister.

"Yeah," Lydia said, blinking. "Sure. Don't ask your aunt Ruby for anything."

"You can ask for things," Ruby said, leading her niece and nephew off.

"She's going to spoil them," Lydia said.

"So what?" Marianne asked. "That's not your problem. It's Ruby's problem. Let her handle it."

Lydia laughed. "I don't do letting other people handle it very well."

She couldn't help it. She looked over at Dahlia, who shot her a quick glance. So, clearly she couldn't help it either. Luckily, Lydia didn't really notice the exchange. The one that had clearly said, we are aware that you are emotionally stunted.

Ava was standing a very teenage ten paces away from them, pacing in a circle and ignoring them extremely purposefully.

"Come on," Marianne said, beckoning her daughter. "Let's go look at clothes."

"I can look by myself," Ava said, walking quickly in front of them toward the junior section.

"I want to see them," Marianne said. "I'm paying, after all."

And she wanted to spend some time with Ava. Of course, the trip to Medford had turned into a whole family circus, with her sisters and her niece and nephew coming along as well. Though, in some ways she imagined it was better than if she had just tried to come with Ava by herself. At least she was excited to spend time with Ruby, and often with Dahlia. The cool young aunts who didn't have mom energy like herself and Lydia.

Ava grumbled something, and at this point, Marianne knew better than to ask exactly what her daughter had said, unless she wanted to get into grounding her in the middle of the store. And she did not. They were supposed to be having a nice day.

It was nice that Ava still had a great relationship with her father. It really was. Marianne shouldn't be jealous of Jackson at all. It was just that she was Ava's mother. She was the one who cared so much about making sure that she did a better job for her daughter during her tumultuous teenage years than her parents had done for her. And she was repaid with grousing.

Fine.

It was all fine.

"Do you like this, Aunt Dahlia?" Ava held up a short, velvet dress with small flowers all over it.

"Very cool," Dahlia responded.

And that seemed to please Ava. Marianne turned and grabbed a furry jacket off of a rack. "I like this," she said.

"I don't like that," Ava said, turning back to the dresses. Marianne shot Dahlia a dirty look, but Dahlia didn't notice. Her sister—who was a full-grown adult—was busy picking through the juniors clothes and holding them up to herself.

"Of course she doesn't like that," Marianne muttered, stalking through and pretending to look at some scrunchies on a circular rack.

"My stance," Lydia said, "is that if I wore it the first time around, I don't have to wear it this time."

"I like scrunchies," Marianne said, grabbing a couple off the rack and sticking them in the shopping cart.

"I remember you used to have a giant Tupperware full of them."

"And you used to steal them."

"I did," Lydia said. "Until a certain point, when you legitimately terrified me, and I thought you might actually murder me."

"Right. About Ava's age, I believe."

Ava and Dahlia were now conferring over clothing.

"Yes."

"I don't know what to do. To stop her from turning into a monster." She grimaced. "Sorry. I shouldn't unload my crap onto you."

"Please," Lydia said. "Unload your parenting crap on me."

"You have enough to deal with."

She huffed a laugh. "I don't really have anything to deal with. Mac is gone. There's nothing I can do about it."

"You don't have to do that, Lydia. You don't have to be… Mom and Dad."

"I'm not Mom and Dad," Lydia said.

"Not at all? You're not... Holding things together because you think you have to be tough?"

Lydia rolled her eyes and grabbed a pair of heart-shaped sunglasses off of the round rack, putting them on. "I'm holding it together because what's the other option? Lying on the ground? Falling apart?"

"I like a good tantrum," Marianne said.

"And if I need to have one, I will let you know. I promise. But in the meantime, having you not treat me like an alien would be good. Have you seen the way Ruby looks at me?"

"Like she wants to hug you and cry and put you in a pouch and carry you around?"

"Yes. That's the look."

"I did notice."

"I don't want that. I do enjoy her taking the kids to look at the toys, though."

"Yeah."

"I'm grateful that right now their problems can be solved so easily." She stared at Marianne until Marianne was forced to stare back. "But something is up with Ava?"

Marianne tried to breathe past the tightness in her stomach. Lydia had said it. The thing that Marianne had been avoiding outright admitting to herself. That it was possible she was losing touch with her daughter as profoundly as her own parents had lost touch with her. And she'd never wanted that. It had been her motherhood nightmare, and she'd been scared for a few months that she was dancing on the edges of that.

"I just... I don't know." She pressed against her sternum, trying to ease the tension there. "I know how emotional and depressing being a teenage girl can be. And Mom and Dad just... They never handled it very well."

"I know," Lydia said. "Though, I don't know that I did either."

"You were my sister. You weren't supposed to handle my... Depression or whatever."

"Were you on drugs?"

Marianne laughed. "No, I wasn't on drugs. Have you been waiting twenty years to ask me that?"

"No. But I have wondered. Off and on."

"No. Nothing quite so edgy. It was just...hormones, you know? And that's scary enough on its own. I have some issues with Mom and Dad, sure. But they were good parents. I just don't want to lose touch with Ava." She frowned. "Where would one even get drugs in Pear Blossom?" Suddenly, she felt terrified. "What if you *can* get drugs in Pear Blossom?"

"Marianne," Lydia said. "Settle down."

"I'm trying on," Ava said, wandering toward the dressing rooms. Lydia, Dahlia and Marianne walked over with her, forming a line and watching the dressing room door.

"What are you talking about?" Dahlia asked.

"The inherent drama of being a teenage girl," Lydia responded.

"Ah. I remember it well." Dahlia looked down at her hands and Marianne's gaze followed. Her sister's dark red nails were chipped, which forced her to look at her own hazy blue gel nails, which were still perfect.

Lydia's, of course, were bare.

Manicures required upkeep and care so Lydia didn't try.

Marianne did everything with delicacy to keep her nails nice. It felt like control, usually. Though right now it wasn't helping at all.

Dahlia wanted it both ways.

Which seemed so very Dahlia.

"Who doesn't?" Marianne asked. Except, she didn't particularly like to remember. Even now, she couldn't really sort through it. She had just been so emotional. And she remembered desperately wanting to connect with her parents and feeling like they couldn't handle her. And that was the last thing she wanted with Ava. But Ava was getting withdrawn, and Marianne could see shades of herself there, and she had been certain that, if ever faced with this issue, she would know what to do.

"Maybe I should take her to a psychologist," Marianne said.

"Why?" Lydia asked.

"I don't know. Look, she's a good kid—she gets good grades, she does art and she writes for the school paper, but… Kids order drugs on social media apps now. It's scary."

Ava came out, wearing a crop top that showed a stripe of her midsection and a pair of high waisted jeans.

"No," Marianne said, before she could think.

"Why not?" Ava asked.

"It's against school dress code."

"I don't spend a hundred percent of my time at school, Mom," Ava said.

"But you do spend a hundred percent of the time being my daughter, and no."

"Aunt Dahlia," Ava said, turning to Dahlia. "This looks good, right?"

Dahlia looked between Marianne and Ava. "It looks good…"

"Hey," Marianne said.

"The issue isn't that it doesn't look good," Dahlia said.

"No," Marianne said. "The issue is that… The issue is that you're a kid. You don't need to try and… You don't need to try and show skin and things like that. You are a kid."

"I'm fifteen," Ava said.

"My point stands."

Ava growled and turned away, heading back into the dressing room.

"It's not that bad," Dahlia said.

Marianne looked to Lydia. "I like it," Lydia said.

"When Hazel is fifteen, I'm buying her low rise jeans and a coordinating thong."

"A crop top is not those things," Lydia said.

"Let's just go," Ava said, reappearing and breezing past Marianne.

"We don't need to go. We have to choose things for school. I don't want to order them online, because you're just going to complain. And you don't want anything that I carry in The Apothecary because it's old lady clothes."

"Which is why I don't want your opinion on my clothes," Ava said. "Because you like old lady clothes."

Marianne felt her temper begin to boil over. "Oh, Ava. I am the crypt keeper. Of your nightmares. We can finish this trip and I will be your ATM machine, only because you need clothes but you are soooo grounded. This old lady will take everything you love. You can shop with Dahlia. Lydia and I are going to go get candy bars. And you can't have any."

And for the first time maybe ever, Marianne had sympathy for her own mother. Maybe the distance had been her fault. Maybe she had been so mean that she had pushed her mother away. Maybe she hadn't recognized good intentions. Because she had good intentions.

"Are you really not going to give her any candy?" Lydia asked.

"Yeah," Marianne said. "It's my candy."

"Fair enough," Lydia said.

Then Lydia grabbed her arm and bumped into her with her shoulder. "Thanks."

"What?"

"Thanks for letting me borrow your problems for the afternoon. It feels kind of normal."

"Well, I'm glad I could help with something."

She might not be able to do anything right for Ava, but at least she had done something helpful for her sister.

They finished at the store, and Marianne ended up not even looking at Ava's clothes. But she did toss her a candy bar when they got in the car. They drove to a small burger place that was just down the road. It was a tiny little shack of a building, always overflowing with people. The kind of place where people who didn't come together ended up sharing tables. They all ordered hamburgers and went and sat on a picnic bench outside. The kids, including Ava, sat in the grass away from them. Riley and Hazel were throwing French fries at each other and picking weeds, Ava was looking at her phone.

"Thanks," Lydia said. "For distracting the kids." She smiled. "This is the first… This is the first thing that I've done that wasn't work or just going to Mom and Dad's."

"Well, I'm glad to help," Ruby said, beaming.

"Thank you for providing counsel to my teenager," Marianne said to Dahlia, and she supposed she should just be grateful that Ava did have Dahlia to look up to. She hadn't had a female relative she had considered cool that she could confide in. Or get fashion advice from.

"No problem. It's kind of validating to know that a fifteen-year-old thinks that I'm… Very retro?"

"Wow," Marianne said. "Isn't your stuff kind of vintage 1996?"

"Yes. The nineties are retro."

"That hurts," Lydia said, frowning.

"I remember telling Mom the seventies were retro," Marianne said. "History repeats and repeats and repeats, and I'm in the most annoying part of it, I swear."

"Speaking of history," Dahlia asked. "Marianne, what do you know about the building that The Apothecary's in?"

"It's been about a hundred things," Marianne answered, turning her focus to her business, which was a much less complicated situation. "But it was a jewelry shop first. When the town was built in the eighteen hundreds."

"I'm doing some research on the history of the town, for a series of articles. And I'm trying to get Ruby to play along and do the museum displays."

"I'm playing along," Ruby said. "I'm just deeply uncomfortable about the aspect that includes me."

"What are you doing about Ruby?" Lydia asked.

"It's a compendium of town history. I would be remiss to leave Ruby out of it."

"Wow. First the nineties are retro, now Ruby is history. You're not doing a lot for my self-esteem, Dahlia."

"Well," Dahlia said, "I think it's interesting."

"I think everything that can be said about Ruby and Caitlin has been said," Marianne pointed out. "Didn't the *Gazette* run exhaustive coverage of both things? They were the biggest stories Pear Blossom has ever had."

"Well, yes," Dahlia said. "I guess it's just that... I don't know. I'm curious about other angles or something. The full context of the history of the town. I'm trying to reinvigorate interest in the paper."

"I hate to break it to you," Marianne said. "But I think print circulation is on the downhill slide."

"You used to love the school paper," Dahlia said. "Used to want to write," she pointed out.

"Yes," Marianne answered. "But then I realized I was terrible at it. In any way. I like being around people too much."

"Well, I don't. I hate people," Dahlia said, grinning. "So a life spent distancing them by filtering them through the lens of their stories, and sitting by myself writing, is perfect. Anyway. I want to include some stuff about the store."

"Well, I like that," Marianne said.

"Great."

"Can't you just write a story that says I'm miraculous?" Ruby asked.

"Sorry," Dahlia said, grabbing a French fry and dipping it into Ruby's ranch. "Nothing is that simple."

Marianne looked over at Ava. Sadly. She had a feeling that Dahlia was right.

10

Ruby McKee is not perfect. She is annoying. I hate her I hate her I hate her.

DAHLIA MCKEE'S DIARY, AGE 15

DAHLIA

Dahlia was ready to pitch her idea to Dale. After talking to her sisters a few days earlier, things had just started to gel. She'd had to get everything compiled into a formal pitch, because he was nothing if not traditional in that sense, and then she officially emailed it to him, rather than walking into his office and just asking. He would also make her give him a verbal pitch. She knew that by now.

Unless of course he rejected the initial idea.

Then he would just send her an email, and they would pass in the hallway and never speak of it.

She was tapping away at her keyboard, sitting at her desk, when Dale called her on the intercom on her desk phone, which he insisted that she keep for just such an occasion.

"Can I see you in my office?"

"Sure thing," she said, standing and brushing off her skirt.

Then she walked down the hall and stood in front of his door for a moment before knocking. No points for seeming too eager.

"Come in. I want to hear your idea," he said, as if he didn't have the entirety of the idea sitting in front of him in text form.

"As you know," Dahlia began, staring at a point on the back of the wall. It still made her nervous to do things like this, even though Dale had never seemed to mind that she wasn't Ruby. That she didn't have that kind of light ease about her. In fact, he had an intensity that often matched her own, and it seemed to be compatible.

"Ruby is back for good—she took a job at the historical society, which I used to be heavily involved with also. Through our discussions, I started thinking. Our community is filled with local history, the kind of thing that you can't just gain from a Google search. And AP articles and stories that inform us of what's going on in the broader world might be important, but Pear Blossom is our home. I want to run a series of articles about the history of the town. I want to start with the founding of Pear Blossom, then do a feature on the introduction of the pear industry and the railroad into the community, followed by the effects of the world wars on the community, and then a piece about Caitlin Groves and another about Ruby McKee. Interspersed between those will be some pieces that reflect an old-style journalism that used to happen at the *Gazette*, including features on who's out and about in town, and also a No Longer on the Map feature, where I talk about businesses that are no longer here, and the way that Main Street has changed over the past hundred and fifty years. It will be in honor of the 150th year of the *Gazette*, and what I hope is that special features like this will increase interest in people subscribing to this newspaper, and not just Medford's paper or the national news. Real, human-interest pieces about our town. Where we live."

"It's a good idea," Dale said. "It's a damn good idea, Dahlia.

THE LOST AND FOUND GIRL

And you're right. Exactly the kind of thing that will bring a point of interest and difference to the paper."

Dahlia's stomach burned with satisfaction. She had known there was something here. The validation from her boss was just...it was so good. What she'd always prided herself on was seeing those in Pear Blossom who were otherwise unseen, or seen as different, or bad in some way. Like Dana. Her friend group at school had been made up of misfits—people she still kept in touch with.

Dahlia might not be accepted in the way Ruby was—with open arms and total enthusiasm. But Dahlia had her place here. And the fact her perspective could be shown to people in this way really mattered to her.

"In my opinion, it's why people moved here," Dahlia said. "For that sense of community. I want to bring them in. To the good and bad parts of our history. Make everyone who's here feel like a local. And remind the locals of what makes us unique."

"I'm interested. When can you get started?"

"Right away. The pieces on the pear industry... And the other historical pieces, those will be easier. And my sister is going to work on doing some corresponding displays at the museum. Which I can include information on in the paper. But it'll probably take me some time to get into Ruby's and Caitlin's stories. And the war stories. I want to talk to people who remember. It's not just about relaying the events, but the way that it changed things. The way that people felt."

Dale nodded. "Get started as soon as possible. God knows we have the room."

"I mean, I guess it's not a bad thing that we tend to traffic in slow news days. Dogs playing in sprinklers means nothing bad has happened, I guess."

Dale smiled. "I've always thought so."

"Can I start with you?"

"Sure," he said. He sighed. "I've covered... I covered Ruby

being found and… And Caitlin Groves' disappearance. I remember both. Vividly." His gaze took on a faraway look.

It was interesting to Dahlia, because of course she'd found Ruby. But she'd been a child. And everyone assumed Dahlia, Lydia, Marianne and Ruby would know all about Ruby and her origins, so they never spoke to them about it.

It was the same with Caitlin Groves. Dahlia couldn't even remember her disappearance, but it was something everyone in town just *knew*. Which meant they didn't speak of it, not really.

"What can you tell me about Caitlin Groves' disappearance? About the ripple that went through the community?"

"It was like a deep fracture," he said. "It's the best way I can describe it. As if a crack ran down the middle of the town. For a while, everyone banded together. They searched for her. They exhaustively combed the woods, the orchards. But once that faded, that was when the real despair set in."

"What about Dana Groves?" Dahlia asked. "When did the town turn on her?"

Dale frowned. "I don't feel the town turned on her. But she wanted answers no one could give, and… I expect people couldn't handle being reminded of tragedy constantly. I think there was hope when Nathan Brewer was arrested. But then he was released from prison after only a few years and never convicted… There was a hopelessness, a distrust that seemed to color everything. I never thought we would find our way back from that."

"But that's where Ruby comes in," Dahlia said, feeling slightly uncomfortable. And yet, she could see. She could see the way that these lines were drawn between these events.

It had entered Dahlia's mind that it was possible Ruby belonged to Caitlin. She'd considered it more than once. The only thing was the timing. She'd disappeared a tiny bit more than a year before Ruby appeared, which would mean she'd gone off, gotten pregnant and returned, and that didn't really make any sense.

"Yes," he said. "I remember that night vividly. The actual night. I got called down to the police station. And there she was. This tiny little bundle. Healthy. In spite of how freezing cold it was. I work a lot with the police and the mood down at the station had been... It had been poor. To be no closer to solving the disappearance of Caitlin Groves, to bring her mother closure... It had taken its toll on them. Tom Swenson is a dear friend of mine, and he was never the same. But that night, the night that Ruby was found... He was sitting at his desk holding her, and it was like some of the good in the world was visible again. Like some of the hope had returned. You never forget that. I never will."

"Thank you. Can I quote you?"

"Sure. Make sure you talk to Tom, though, too. I know what I saw, but he'll be able to tell you."

"I will."

She left her boss's office feeling renewed. Feeling... Enthusiastic. She went back into the archive room, and she hunted around for the papers that would've come out in the days following Caitlin's disappearance. And then she went back to the 1940s, gathering pieces from World War II. And when she had it all, she walked next door to the museum and into the building.

"Hi, Dana," she said upon entry.

Dana looked up at her, her expression unreadable. "Dahlia."

And Dahlia could remember clearly that day she'd walked by Dana's house to see that pack of football players throwing rocks at the windows. And Dahlia had been all righteous fury at fifteen.

Stop that, you pack of pricks!

They'd ignored her.

I said stop! What the hell is wrong with you? She's not a witch, and you're not tough.

Are you going to make me stop?

She'd picked up her own rock and hurled it at one of the bikes, knocking it over.

Yeah, I'll make you stop.

And Holden Striley had advanced on her like he might actually hurt her. Which was when Carter Swenson rode up on his bike, clearly also just finished with football practice, but a little bit behind the rest of the crew.

That's enough.

What, are you gonna tell Dad? Holden had advanced on him.

I don't need to do that, but I'll kick your ass if you touch her.

Then she'd looked up and had seen the curtains twitch, seen Dana's face disappearing from the window.

She shook that memory off.

"I'm not sure if Ruby said anything to you," Dahlia said. "But... I want to do some newspaper pieces, on the town history."

Dana's eyes sharpened, as if she knew exactly what Dahlia was going to say. "Is that so?"

"Yes. It's about the way different events have shaped Pear Blossom. And you know that the history of our town is not complete without mentioning Caitlin." Her throat tightened and she picked another sliver of color off her nails. She should just remove the whole manicure at this point. She also knew she wouldn't. "I also don't want you to be surprised by anything, and I don't want to cause any more harm."

"Are you worried that you'll remind me my daughter is gone? Because I remember that every day."

Pain lanced through Dahlia's chest. "I was. But I realize that's silly. Of course you do. Of course you think about it all the time. I'm sorry."

"Every day. I think about it every day. And how there's no justice for her. How her life was taken from her."

It was amazing how... At ease Dahlia felt with Dana. Not in

the middle. Not trying to be liked and trying to be truthful. She could just… Say it.

"You think she was murdered then," Dahlia said.

"I *know* she was," Dana responded. "She hasn't just been off living her life. She's gone. She's been gone since before I knew she was missing, I'm sure of it."

"Nathan…"

"He's back, you know," Dana said, her eyes getting faraway.

"Nathan is?" So it probably was Nathan that Ruby had seen.

"Yes."

"I can't believe he'd come back. It was painful for the town when he—"

"The town," Dana said, her tone scathing. "You can write all you want about how her disappearance affected the town. But you know what? The town never did have a right to act like they grieved her more than I did. They all whisper about me. And they think I'm crazy. They think maybe the problem is I was a single mother who let her fifteen-year-old run around with a boy who was just a bad apple. And you know… I was a single mother. So my behavior was suspect, and as a result so was Caitlin's. Sneaking around with a boy doing God knows what. Immoral acts, most likely."

"You think the town blamed Caitlin for…her own disappearance?"

"I think it was between every line. And if not her, then me." She shook her head. "And when they were sure they had their villain, they wanted it all to go back to normal, and I couldn't. But why did they have the right to claim it changed their lives while acting like I should…get back to how I was before? What gives them that right? They think they're her champions just because they searched when she was missing. But how did they all treat her when she was here? *She* wasn't special to anyone. Not until it was too late. And in all that, I was never special either.

And now I'm just an inconvenience. Walking around with too many bad feelings."

Her words scraped against Dahlia's soul. She knew it was true—she'd seen it. Pear Blossom absolutely defined itself by Caitlin's disappearance. One of the scars of the community, and yet they wanted it neat, didn't they? Contained. They wanted to feel sadness and regret and a bit of judgment over the whole thing.

The sort of feelings that let you keep a distance and lay just enough blame to believe it couldn't happen to you, or to your children.

"If you don't mind me asking," Dahlia said, "why did you stay?"

And for the first time Dana's face softened.

"In case she came back. I don't expect that to make any sense. Because I do think she's gone. But there's a part of me that... That could never stand to leave. This place. The house. In case she came back." She looked away. "Your sister is upstairs."

And just like that the conversation was over.

"Thank you," Dahlia said. "I really do want to write the article in a way that...that you're happy with. Would you like to see it before I hand it in?"

Dana sniffed. "If you like."

Dana didn't look at her when she said that, and it was as if she'd closed an invisible door between them. And Dahlia respected Dana enough to let it be closed.

She went up the stairs, opening two doors before she finally found the one that Ruby was behind.

She was sitting on the floor surrounded by mannequins and stacks of catalogs.

"Hey," she said.

"Hey, yourself."

"I brought you some newspapers."

Ruby's entire countenance brightened, and Dahlia had to

concede that while she and her sister might be very different people, it was a rare person who would get that excited about old newspapers, and that she had someone in her life who cared as much about that sort of obscure history was definitely a gift.

"Which newspapers?"

"More about Caitlin. And her disappearance. I also got some from the forties, which I think you'll love because the ads in them are gold."

"Thank you," Ruby said, absolutely enthusiastically.

"I talked to Dale today and he mentioned… He mentioned the toll that Caitlin's case took on Tom Swenson. On the town. And how… When they found you, Tom held you for a long time. That it seemed like it brought hope back."

Ruby looked uncomfortable. "I've heard versions of that. I mean… I'm not complaining. It's better than having people dislike me and having it nothing to do with who I am, but it's just…uncomfortable to be a symbol."

This was the first time Ruby had seemed remotely open to the conversation, though. And Dahlia had to wonder if she felt the shift the same as she did. Dana talking about Caitlin. Nathan being back. It felt like the past was pressing in, whether Dahlia was the one digging it up or not.

It felt inevitable.

"I bet," Dahlia said. "I just talked to Dana downstairs and I'm suddenly very aware that real people are impacted by these stories. And maybe I won't find anything new. It might all just be more of the same story. What if I just stir up pain and don't bring anything new to the table at all? It feels irresponsible."

"You believe in what journalism brings to the world," Ruby said. "You believe in stories. And how they can change people and shape people. I thought a lot about what I said to you, about how I'm not sure what this does for me. There's so much I don't know, and yes, it's…easier to just believe the good things. But that isn't…history."

"No." She looked at her sister and her heart squeezed. "It's not."

"It's just scary. I held myself back from wanting information and now I'm moving toward something else and I'm not sure if I want to find something, or if... I'd rather not."

"You're allowed to have complicated feelings, Rubes."

Ruby's expression turned enigmatic. "Am I?" She picked her purse up from the table and made a clear move toward the door.

"Before we go, I wanted to see if the police report for Caitlin's disappearance was here. I don't know that I'm going to be able to get a lot of useful information out of the police reports, but they're interesting. It was... Instructive to read yours."

"Let me check." She got up and went to the archives, going easily to the spot where it would be. She opened up the folders and scanned them. "I don't see it. I can see if it's digitized."

"I'll stop by the station tomorrow," Dahlia said. "It's public record. I can ask for it down there—it's faster than requesting electronic records."

"Well, I'll leave you to that then, investigative reporter."

"I'm not an investigative reporter."

"What if you find something that matters?" Ruby asked. "You're worried about being irresponsible but...but maybe it's time, Dahlia. To stir things up and see what comes out?"

That landed hard, square in the center of Dahlia's chest. "Dana said justice was never served. And she said... She said Nathan is back in town."

"For sure?"

"She seemed sure," Dahlia said. "Which makes me feel great that you saw him in the woods behind our house."

"He was never convicted of anything," Ruby said, suddenly looking thoughtful.

"Which is a miscarriage of justice."

"Is it? We don't know."

"Dana seems pretty confident. And he was dating her daughter, so I'm sure that she would know if it seemed like something she didn't believe that he could do."

"Or maybe he's just a mascot."

11

Today at school we were told to write about something we were thankful for. My teacher said I should write about being thankful I was found on the bridge, and that my mom and dad adopted me. Dahlia told me when she had that assignment she wrote about being thankful for chocolate.

RUBY MCKEE'S DIARY, AGE 12

RUBY

Ruby walked out of the museum and slung her scarf around her neck. It was legitimately chilly this afternoon, and she had spent the day curled up by the oil heater in her office, going through fabric samples and ads, looking at old sewing patterns and going through the vast array of antique sewing machines in the back room at the museum.

She'd also run across some books that indicated that some old dresses were being stored in the basement of the First Presbyterian Church, and she was going to have to go sift through those at some point. She'd given Molly Hudson a call about stopping by in a week or so and seeing if she could have a look down in the basement.

She had been thinking a lot about the articles that she'd read the other night and wanted to get home so that she could go through more of them. She had called in an order at one of her favorite restaurants, and she was just going to swing by and grab it on her way to her car. It only took a couple of minutes for her to grab fajitas for herself and Dahlia and start driving out of town.

It was twilight by the time she pulled her car up to the cottage and parked. She took out her food and turned, taking in the silence all around her.

The late afternoon rays of intense gold spilled themselves over the tops of the trees, gilded the edges of the grass. She paused for a moment, letting the breeze tangle in her hair, her dress. It was cold, but it smelled amazing. Damp leaves and pine.

Dahlia wasn't home yet. She'd said something about needing to stop to get something for the plants, and Ruby hadn't even tried to understand.

She pressed forward, unlocking the cottage and walking inside, setting her takeout on her desk. And she stopped and looked out those windows. Peering into the forest, to see if she could see anything. Or anyone.

There was nothing, of course. She was beginning to think she had hallucinated the whole thing with the man who—in her imagination—was Nathan Brewer.

She had never seen a person out there again. Not even any movement.

But you didn't hallucinate a whole person. And Dana had told Dahlia he was back.

Still, everything that she had built onto it was a little bit ridiculous. Restless, she walked back out of the house. There was just a sliver of daylight left now. She moved from the edge of the field into the trees, where it was dark. Except for some brave shafts of light that spilled through the thick trees. She hadn't explored this part of the forest at all. Not recently. When she was a kid... When she was a kid, she had come back here all the time.

Even the four years between herself and Dahlia had felt like a big separation at different points in their lives. And as a result, Ruby had spent quite a bit of time playing by herself. Knights and dragons and maidens here in this enchanted-feeling place. It had always felt like it might be touched with magic. Like the possibilities of what could be, enhanced beneath the cover of trees. The world beyond might not just be Pear Blossom, but somewhere else. Anywhere else.

A whole different kingdom. A different world.

She laughed at herself, bending over and picking a soft, white flower that grew abundantly around here. She had always called them Kitty Ears, but she wasn't sure if that was their real name. It was what her mother had always called them because of the soft velvet that covered the petals.

She closed her eyes, rubbing the blossom against her face.

And it brought her right back to the years spent growing up here. She had imagined being a princess in this forest. And she had thought maybe she really could be. Because again, why not? Why shouldn't an abandoned girl imagine that her mother had been a queen, who had a baby with a lover she could never acknowledge. A commoner, perhaps. Or maybe her father was a king, and her mother was a servant girl...

She almost laughed out loud at the memory.

She heard a loud sound in the brush behind her, and she turned and just about ran into a male figure coming up out of the trees.

She nearly swore, but the word wouldn't quite come out, and she ended up taking two stumbling steps backward, before finding herself being caught by a strong, masculine hand. At the same time, he pulled her forward, and she couldn't see anything but his eyes. Green, like the trees all around them, dark and intense.

It was him. It was most definitely him.

She wiggled, trying to get away from him, and he let go of her. "What are you doing here?"

"I might ask you the same question," he said, his words as hard as his grip had been. "This is my land."

"No," she said. "This is my dad's land."

"Line's back there," he said, pointing behind her.

"Oh," she said. "I didn't realize that I… I didn't realize that I had gone that far. But I used to play here when I was a kid…"

"Yeah," he said. "Me too."

But of course, they weren't kids at the same time. Not if he was Nathan Brewer. Still, the idea that she had played where he had once, before he'd been accused of murder…

Before he'd *become* a murderer.

She took another step back.

"I promise I don't kill women walking alone in the forest," he said.

A sliver of ice ran down her spine, because what kind of thing was that to say.

"An interesting denial," she said. "Since I didn't say you did."

"You're a McKee," he said.

"And you're Nathan Brewer."

"See. I know who you are. You know who I am. Which means we both know what you think."

She regarded his face. It was strong, like it had been carved from stone. His jaw a hard, square angle, his nose straight and sharp. But his eyes… They were the hardest, coldest thing of all.

"You *don't* know what I think," she said.

"I have a decent idea."

"I know what people say about you."

"Congratulations. That makes you real special."

"I…"

"Stay off my property," he said.

"Well, just a second…"

"I said stay off my property."

"That isn't fair. I live right over there. And I might dispute the property line with you. It's not like you *need* to come all the way over here, when we are both well aware the house is no-where in the proximity."

"But I can. Because you know what I'm not? A prisoner. And you don't get to tell me where I can walk."

"But you get to tell me?" she asked.

"When it's my land. Yes, I do."

"I'm *Ruby* McKee," she said.

He looked at her, his gaze dismissive. "So? Is that supposed to matter to me?"

Then he turned and walked away. And Ruby could honestly say that was the first time in her entire life someone in Pear Blossom didn't care who she was.

She was shaking. She didn't realize how badly until she was back in the cottage, with the door closed and firmly locked be-hind her. And she closed every curtain in every window. He was terrifying. Big and… More than capable of doing whatever he wanted with her if he had half a mind to. And if the rumors around town were to be believed, then he was a monster. Fully capable of any terrible thing that she could conjure up.

And he didn't care that she was Ruby McKee.

She thought back to the article about her, about how the other articles written were about him.

His trial.

He hadn't been in Pear Blossom when she'd been found. He'd been in Salem. Detained and awaiting trial. Held on a host of charges.

It took her a while to remember her dinner, she was so shaken.

Dahlia arrived home and Ruby debated talking to her about Nathan, but something stopped her.

They ate their dinner and talked about the article Dahlia had started today. Ruby rattled off what she knew about the history of the town's pear industry. Then Dahlia went over to her desk and got out her laptop, popping her earbuds in and typing intensely.

Ruby went to her desk right next to her sister and pulled out that same newspaper she'd already gone over, poring over what had been written about his charges being dropped.

"He knows something."

Dana had said that. Dana, who she knew and loved. She might be able to dismiss most of the town as being gossips or hysterical when it came to this, but Dana was… Yeah, so some people found her to be difficult. But Ruby cared about her very deeply. And if Dana thought that Nathan Brewer had done something to her daughter… Well, wouldn't she know? He had been dating her. So, he would've been around.

The idea of him being right there made her shiver.

But why would he come back here to murder someone? She doubted he was a serial killer. Whatever had happened, it had probably been specifically related to their relationship. A lover's quarrel. The newspaper articles had implied that maybe she had broken up with him. That would make sense.

Even now, he radiated… Rage.

The impression of it left her feeling scorched. Made her shiver. Hot and cold all at once.

One thing her mother could not find out was that Nathan Brewer was looming around the woods. She and Dahlia would be bundled straight back into their old bedrooms.

No, she wasn't going to tell her parents. Not about this. She would tell Dahlia eventually. But Dahlia didn't really go off and wander about the woods.

"I'm going to bed," Ruby said, her eyes starting to sting around ten.

Dahlia grunted in response but didn't look up from her computer.

Ruby scrubbed herself quickly in the small shower, then put her pajamas on, flicking the lights off, climbing beneath the covers and letting sleep wash over her.

She was back out in front of the bridge. That same sense of

terror washing over her. Because there was something inside that she didn't want to see. But she was compelled to walk forward all the same. This time, the dream let her get all the way inside. And this time, she felt a strong hand wrapped around her arm, holding her there in the darkness.

And when she tried to look at who it was, she couldn't see his face.

12

1945—The troops marched over Sentinel Bridge today, down into town, a symbol of the return of normality to a town badly scarred by the loss of its missing sons. A symbol of the unity and strength in Pear Blossom. And how good triumphs over evil in the end.

LYDIA

Lydia had felt happier in some ways since the shopping trip with her sisters. And in some ways worse because she was still hiding so much from her family. But it was just so nice to be reminded that Marianne was human with issues of her own, and kids who didn't always listen. It was easy for Lydia to think that Marianne's life had turned out... Perfect.

Marianne and Jackson had this wonderful, perfect marriage. And she and Mac had been lying. To their families. To each other. To themselves.

She wasn't sure if he had known it. He'd thought they were happy, she was sure. And if she'd ever gotten to ask him for a divorce she knew it was what he would say.

But we're happy.

Because he got to do what he wanted. Because he got sex two times a week and had dinner on the table at night.

He didn't listen. He didn't share things with her. When push came to shove, he didn't really want to share his life. He wanted to be able to go out and do whatever he wanted without having to ask her, talk to her. He didn't want to be inconvenienced by her or the kids. He never said that, but it had become clear, especially after they'd had kids.

At first she'd excused it as… New parent stuff. She'd had to do the babies because she breastfed, so he couldn't feed them, and she was needed around all the time, and then she'd just told herself it was taking him a while to realize he could take on more than he was.

They'd talked about it. Or rather, she had. But it didn't change.

Until she'd just quit talking about it.

The truth was, he'd wanted to have more traditional roles than they'd agreed on when they'd married, more traditional roles than he *pretended* he wanted them to have. Even to himself.

Because she was fairly certain that he believed that he wanted to have this farm life and share responsibilities. But when it came down to it, he hadn't wanted to take care of his children in a hands-on way. Hadn't known what to do.

When it came down to it, both of them could come in from working in the fields, and he wanted there to be a fresh meal prepared for him, he wanted to go out and go drinking, and leave her there by herself. He wanted to go hang out with Chase.

She ground her back teeth together.

Chase.

The funny thing was, it was Chase that she needed to talk to. Because Chase was the person who had the practical and physical ability to help make her next steps happen. She might not be in a place where she wanted to have a deep heart-to-heart about her personal life, but… But it was time to have a discussion about this.

Dahlia's thing about writing those articles had pushed this to the forefront of her mind for some reason. Maybe it was just recognizing that… She wasn't doing anything.

Ruby was here, she had a new job. Dahlia was trying to invigorate the paper and the town and advance her dreams. Marianne was a dream. With her husband and kids and successful business.

Lydia was still living the life she'd felt stuck in for years, and there was…

There was no reason to.

She'd known what she wanted for a long time.

Three years ago she'd decided to ask Mac for a divorce. It had come after a lot of thought and more prayer than she'd done since she'd been a kid. And from that decision had come a dream. For the farm. For this land that she knew she loved more than he did.

But before she'd been able to tell him, he'd gotten diagnosed, and everything had come to a halt.

She grabbed hold of her binder, the one that had been shoved to the very back of the home office that she and Mac had rarely used, the home office that had then begun to be taken over by medical bills in the years after he got sick. That was quite frankly still taken over by medical bills that she couldn't bear to get rid of. Everything had been handled, she didn't have any debt.

Probably because he had died so quickly.

The thought stopped her in her tracks.

It was desperately unfair. Desperately unfair that he'd gotten pneumonia like he had, and that his lungs were so compromised it had…

She took resolute steps out of the office, then out of the house, down the front porch. Chase's truck was here, so she knew that he was here too. She peeked into the barn and didn't see him, then passed through to the backside, standing in the doorway, where she spotted him out in the field, driving the tractor with the plow behind it. Tilling the field.

She just stood there for a minute, watching a man who wasn't her husband working this land. Chase was a fixture around here and always had been, but still, it should've been Mac out there. Except... Would it have been? What would've happened if she had told Mac she wanted a divorce. Would Chase have still made it his mission to be there for her after his friend died if she hadn't been his grieving widow?

And what if he knew the truth now?

That question haunted her. And in that sense... She was almost glad about the way it happened. Because their kids had never been let down by their father. Yes, he had been slack. No, he hadn't been as involved as he could have been, but they weren't overly aware of it. They were little, and he wasn't that different than most of their friends' dads. They didn't know that he had been perfectly capable of spending more time with them than he did. That, unlike a lot of their friends' parents, it wasn't like he traveled for work, or even worked outside of the home.

She swallowed hard, then took a step forward. She didn't have time to stand there and ruminate. She was glad that she wore her boots, because the mud was thick and sticky, and she sank into it as she took her steps toward the tractor. He looked over his shoulder, saw her and turned the wheel, taking another half pass before stopping the vehicle and turning off the engine.

"Is the house on fire?"

"No," she said, frowning.

"It's just," he said, climbing out of the seat and jumping down onto the ground, "I would've thought the house would have to be on fire for you to come out and seek my company."

"I'm not seeking your company. I'm seeking your consultation."

"Was there an explosion?"

"Yes, there was an explosion. About six months ago my life blew up. And I didn't ask for your help then. But I'm asking for it now."

He rocked back on his heels, pressing his hand against his chest. "Ouch. But yeah, I guess that's true. What exactly is on your mind, Lydia?"

"I want to talk about the next steps for the farm."

"Okay. That's good."

"It's not making enough money as it is. Just doing the farmers market the way that we do… We can do more. I want to expand. I've been looking into beekeeping."

"That's a good idea."

"What?"

"It's a good idea, the beekeeping."

"I know that. I'm just surprised that you said so."

"We're only enemies in your head, Lydia. Not in reality."

The word stopped her cold. "I've never thought of us as enemies."

"Then why do you yap at me like a terrier every time I'm around?"

"I do not…" She blinked rapidly. "I do not yap."

He was such a pain in the butt.

He started to walk toward the barn, leaving her standing in the middle of the mud. She tromped after him, her foot nearly coming up out of her boot when it got stuck in a particularly deep patch of mud. She yanked it free, managing to retain the boot as she scrambled after him. "I don't yap. It's just that you don't listen to me. So I figure if you're intent on being around, you can help me with the expansion. I want to convert this barn."

He stopped at the doorway of the barn and looked up over his head. "To?"

"A farm store. I read about them in other places, there's one in Medford. Basically you carry the goods from the farmers market in the store. That's what I want. Our own products, plus products from the other neighboring farms. Something is localized in there all the time. There will still be the farmers market, which will have a broader range of things, but…"

"That's pretty intense."

"Yes," she agreed. "It is intense. It's going to be expensive and it's going to be a lot of work. But I cleared all the medical bills, and we had insurance… We had life insurance. There's money to do this. As long as I don't break the bank hiring people to do the work, and that is…well, that's where you come in."

How ironic that the money left behind by Mac's death would be used to do something he hadn't wanted done. But she couldn't waste time feeling guilty about that. Even though she wasn't going to… Make a book of Lydia or anything silly like that, she could appreciate what Ruby had said. There was a certain amount of getting back to who you were that just had to happen. If you were ever going to move on. If you were ever going to figure out what your life was.

Mac wasn't here. He wasn't here to deal with this life, to work on this life. Only she was. The farm was hers, and she had to make it something that she could deal with, otherwise she would be beholden to Chase for the rest of her life. She needed to make more money so that she could hire help.

Chase leveled his gaze with hers, his blue eyes as clear and sure as the sky. And everything in her stilled.

That thing in him that she'd always seen as cocky, confident, obnoxious… It was just certainty now. The kind she'd needed for a long time.

"I'm here for you," he said. "Whatever you need."

Whatever you need.

That whispered over skin, a promise that shook her.

And then he just kept on walking, heading back toward his truck.

"Are you… Are you going?"

"Yes," he said.

"You can't just go," she said.

"You're always telling me to leave. Now I can't just go?"

"You left your... Your tractor's out there."

"And I'm going to be here tomorrow. So I'm leaving it. But I have somewhere to be soon."

"You do?"

"Yes," he said. "I don't live here. I do other things."

"Oh," she said.

They just stood and looked at each other for a long moment. She couldn't quite say why. Something in her brain was trying to grasp what he might be doing, and she felt ridiculous and possibly extremely selfish that it hadn't occurred to her that Chase didn't spontaneously appear when he came to the ranch to help her out. All those times when she resented him. When she was obnoxious to him. She still had never thought about what he did when he wasn't here. She didn't think about him as a whole person. She thought about him in context with Mac.

"Are you... Going out with friends?"

"I might be." He continued toward the truck.

"Do you have a date?"

He stopped, then turned toward her. "Yeah," he said, his lips curving upward. "I have a date."

"Oh."

And she didn't know why her first thought was that it was a little bit too soon after Mac's death. But that was silly. *Chase* wasn't his widow.

She watched him get into the truck and drive away, and even though it left her feeling like she was standing on shaky ground in one regard, on another she felt resolved. She was going to do it. She was finally going to take the first step forward. And maybe she would never figure out how she was supposed to grieve the man that she had promised to love for her entire life. The man she had fallen out of love with far too soon. The man who had given her this house, who was part of why she had this dream, and who had given her her children. Who had given her this unspeakable sadness.

Maybe she would never sort out what she was supposed to feel about that. But she could do something about the ranch. And for now, that would be enough.

13

The baby never stops crying, and now I have to share a room with Lydia.

MARIANNE MCKEE'S DIARY, AGE 15

MARIANNE

Marianne could hardly hear over the enthusiastic screaming of her niece and nephew, combined with her son, Hunter, who was twelve, but was not immune to regressing to earlier childhood when his cousins were around.

Unlike Ava, who had withstood the noise for five minutes before disappearing into her room.

They were currently playing some kind of dancing game in the living room, where the gaming device picked up their movements. And it was causing massive amounts of flailing. All of the furniture was pushed into the corners of the room, and the kids were bouncing all over the place.

"Be careful," Marianne said, rushing forward and stopping Hazel from hitting her head on the corner of the coffee table, because of course Hazel had managed to migrate to the spot where the furniture was.

Even Riley was joining in with the fun, which made her feel

better, because her nephew was so affected by the loss of his father that it was uncommon to see the little boy even smile.

"Are they here for dinner?" Jackson asked, the question casual.

"Yeah," she said. "Is that okay?"

"Yeah," he said. "I'll just throw an extra couple of burgers on the grill."

"Thanks, Jackson," she said.

"No problem."

And she wondered…

She swallowed hard. "You would tell me, right? I mean, if everything that we're doing for Lydia was too much."

"Yes," Jackson said. "Have you ever known me to suffer in silence?"

"No," she said. "I guess not."

"What's bothering you?"

Marianne frowned. "I don't know. I had a very unsuccessful shopping trip with Ava."

"Ava's fine, Marianne."

"She's fine with you. She thinks everything I do and say is dumb."

"That's teenager stuff. It'll pass."

"I hope so." She sighed. "I just…"

"You need to talk to your parents is what you need to do."

She shot her husband a glare. "Why?"

"Because you're mad at them. And everything with Lydia is stirring it up, and Ruby being back and Ava being fifteen."

This was what annoyed her about Jackson. He *knew* her. Which sounded like a silly, obvious thing. But she'd always felt like Jackson knew her. From the moment she'd met him. Coming out of a time in her life when she'd just felt like a misfit. In her family, in town. There was something about him that had made her feel so much more at ease with herself. That had helped her open up.

When she had bad feelings, she didn't feel like she had to

bottle it up and hide in her room, knowing her parents would just tell her to keep her chin up, or not to be emotional. He was there and he listened.

But he also pushed.

"What is there to say? You suck at feelings and you have since I was a teenager? And now I'm afraid Lydia is bottling up her grief because if she cried in front of you, you might expire from embarrassment at such a display?" She sighed. "I can't do that. They love us. They're just from that generation. All I can do is do better for Ava."

"I think you should ask for what you need too, Mar."

"Ugh. Stop."

"And I love you."

"I love you too."

It just so happened that Lydia showed up in the middle of dinner, and not after. "You want a hamburger?" she asked.

Her sister looked tired, and... Embarrassed. "Yeah, I kind of do. Is that okay?"

"Absolutely. What's wrong, Lydia?" It was a lot easier to ask Lydia what was wrong than to sit around and ruminate on her own completely ridiculous feelings. "You look really tired."

"Thank you," Lydia said. "No, I'm fine. It's just... It's good. I talked to Chase today about... I want to start a farm store."

"That's a great idea. I know how to do a start-up. And Jackson is amazing with accounting."

"Are you hiring me out?" Jackson called from the kitchen.

"Yes," she responded.

"It just hit me when I got here that maybe this is stupid," Lydia said. "I'm exhausted as it is. I'm going to expand my business? You had my kids ever since school got out. I feel... I feel bad. I feel like I'm not actually managing everything."

Marianne had never seen her sister look so... Openly vulnerable. Lydia was that girl who never cried, even when she fell out of a tree. She'd been the perfect counterpoint to Marianne's extreme moods.

"You know, you don't have to have it all together. You don't have to know what you're doing."

"But I want to," Lydia said.

"Yeah, but what's the worst that will happen if you fail?"

She laughed. "I'll fail, Marianne."

"So?" She looked at her and said what Jackson would say to her. What she'd wished her parents would have said to her. What she wished Ava would understand about her love. "You'll still be you. And I'll still love you with everything I am."

Lydia blinked, her eyes suddenly bright. "Yeah, okay. But I'll be...wrong. I'll have made a mistake."

"So what?"

She laughed, but it sounded broken. "I don't know. Maybe I'll lose my status as the easy one?"

"I think that happened when your husband died."

She bit her lip and looked up, that same broken laugh shaking her shoulders. "Ah, dammit, Mac."

Marianne pulled Lydia in for a hug. "You're not a child, Lydia. You don't have to perform your behavior for Mom and Dad. You don't have to be calm just because I wasn't." She swallowed hard. "I'm sorry if that's why..."

Marianne had made the household feel heavy and emotional, she'd rebelled against her parents and their stoicism and it had been harder for Lydia to deal with her then. She knew that. But maybe she'd actively pushed her away.

"It's not," Lydia said, pulling away. "I just... Have you ever been afraid if you started crying, you'd never stop? My feelings have always been like that. So I just never start. Like if I...keep it in it's like holding armor over myself and...keeping myself safe." She took a shuddering breath. "I remember thinking everything here was safe. And then Caitlin disappeared, and it felt like there could be villains behind every tree. And then we found Ruby. We found a baby on a bridge, and that made everything seem… I don't know… I wanted something that felt safe and normal always. And I don't have that now."

Marianne's chest ached. She understood. Deeply. It was Jackson who gave her that feeling of safety. Satisfaction. Stability. And she'd met him later. Lydia had loved Mac since she was thirteen.

"You have us," she whispered. "We'll hang on to you, I promise. And if you cry, and you can't stop…you'll still have me."

Maybe she couldn't magically fix things with her daughter, or her parents. But she could be here for Lydia.

That at least felt like something.

14

Local Girl Missing
for More Than 48 Hours

BY DALE WAINWRIGHT

Pear Blossom Gazette, November 5, 1999

It has been forty-eight hours since Caitlin Groves, 15, went missing, after last being seen at the 300 block of East Fork Rd, and police are no closer to answering the question of what happened to the teenager. The girl's mother, Dana Groves, says that there were no problems at home, and no indication she might have been unhappy. Police have declined to offer any insight into what they believe may have occurred, and say at the moment there is no cause to believe a crime has been committed.

RUBY

When Ruby went into the museum that morning, she felt a strange, somber sort of air settling all around her. She couldn't place why. "Good morning," Dana said.

"Good morning," Ruby agreed, taking her coat off and unwinding her scarf. "I'm collecting all of the information that I can find on the fashion of the day and the local industry around here. I hope that people are interested in it. I'm finding it fascinating."

"That's good," Dana said, sounding distracted.

"I'm going to... Head upstairs."

"That's fine, Ruby," Dana said. "You don't need to keep me apprised of your every movement. There's a reason I hired you. So I wouldn't have to do the work myself."

Ruby turned to go and then... Stopped.

"Dana," she said. "I'm sorry. About how the town treated you. About how they acted...about me. That they acted like I could replace Caitlin."

"Ruby, there are a great many sins this town has to answer for. But you don't have any fault in them. It's not for you to apologize."

"No, it is. Because I've...happily accepted the adoration that has been placed on me and I... I've been happy to be their miracle."

"Because it's better than being the crazy old lady down the street."

Ruby couldn't go on then. Because she herself was complicit in her own mythology.

This myth that hurt Dana.

And in many ways, hurt Ruby too.

She thought of Nathan Brewer. The way he'd been in the woods...

"I'm just sorry," Ruby said.

"Keep your sorry, Ruby McKee," Dana said. "It won't bring her back."

On that note, Dana turned on her heel and walked out of the antechamber of the museum, leaving Ruby feeling raw.

She didn't know what could be said to that. And the weight of Dana's sadness was palpable right now.

Ruby went about her work, those words echoing inside her. It wasn't until she realized that it was November that she understood what might be going on. On a hunch, she looked up the date.

It was the twenty-third anniversary of Caitlin Groves' disappearance.

Ruby spent the entire day thinking about that. Dana had never had closure. Ever. She'd said she knew Caitlin was dead and wasn't coming back. But she'd also said… That glimmer of hope was why she couldn't leave.

Ruby had always felt connected to Dana. But it was only since Dahlia had started pushing things around that Ruby truly felt connected to Caitlin. There were things about it that echoed with her own life. The unknowns that Dana had to deal with. That she had to face. Ruby had so many of her own. Being uncertain of how she had come to be. Of where she came from.

Not knowing could drive you crazy.

Knowing is probably a burden sometimes too.

Yes. She supposed it was. Because when you didn't know, you could imagine that you were a princess. Or you could imagine that the person you loved was safe and well, just away from you.

But underneath it all, you knew.

That was the thing.

Ruby hadn't wanted to know. What not being a princess meant. It was why she'd never wanted to look too deeply into it.

Ruby had been happy to live in her fairy tale. Dana had confronted her dragon head-on.

It made Ruby feel…

Small. Cowardly.

Tears filled Ruby's eyes, and she pressed the heels of her hands against them, trying to hold them back.

Instead of crying, she went to work on her projects. The clothing project and a few of the archives that needed updating. She opened up the files she'd gotten from Dahlia.

And found November 5, 1999.

That would be two days after Caitlin went missing. There was a small article dedicated to the fact that she was missing, but it wasn't very expansive. She took out the next one, and then the next. It was when Caitlin had been missing for five days that a large portion of the newspaper's real estate was devoted to the story. About the police investigation and that Nathan Brewer was the last person she had been with.

They had gone on a date, and then gone back to the orchard. Where they went for a walk.

It chilled her. Because she had run into him at that very spot. The orchard.

She hadn't realized that she had strayed onto his property, but she had. And it was the place that Caitlin had last been seen. The door to the office opened, and Ruby shoved the newspapers down into her bag quickly.

"Ruby," Dana said. "There are some tourists here, and they're requesting more information on the display."

Dana didn't elaborate, but Ruby knew that the older woman wasn't up to giving a tour right now.

"I'll be right down," Ruby said.

She spent the last couple hours of the day visiting with an older couple from the Bay Area. Giving recommendations for what to see around town, where to eat. And of course giving them exhaustive information on anything they could've possibly wanted to know—and probably several things they didn't— about Pear Blossom. And by the time she was finished, it was time for the museum to close. She went looking for Dana, but Dana's door was closed tight. And Ruby was hesitant to disturb her.

Instead, she went back upstairs, gathered her things and headed home.

It wasn't until she was driving on the road that ran parallel to Sentinel Bridge that she realized she had brought all the newspapers with her. And when she came around a bend that met the backside of the bridge, she screamed when she saw a figure in the middle of the road. She slammed on her brakes, barely avoiding hitting the person, who was walking up out of a trench.

It took her a minute to realize it, but when she did...

It was Nathan Brewer. Clearly intoxicated. And she didn't know what the hell she was supposed to do.

She killed the engine and scrambled out of the car, powered by adrenaline and not one single organized thought. "Are you trying to get yourself killed?"

He only looked at her, a bottle of liquor in one hand. "Maybe."

"Get in the car."

He lifted a dark brow. "Really?"

"Are you going to kill me?" she asked, anger making her voice shake.

He shrugged.

If he was a murderer, he was a ridiculous one.

She went to the passenger side and opened the door for him, waiting. And finally, he got into the vehicle.

"I'll drive you back to the orchard. What are you doing?"

"It's a bad day," he said. "I don't know. I... I haven't been back here."

His speech was slurred, his voice rough.

It was the day Caitlin had disappeared. That's what it was. And all she could think was that Caitlin's mother was down at the museum having a worse day than he was.

Unless...

She looked at his profile. His head was leaning back against the seat of the car. What if he hadn't done anything? Then this was the day that his life had spiraled out of control. He was arrested for this. And his girlfriend had disappeared. And no, there was no other narrative about him in town. No other narrative but that he was guilty. She almost felt guilty entertaining the idea that he wasn't.

But she kept coming back to her own myth. Her own narrative.

And the one about Dana.

And it was just…

There were stories. Stories about everything. Fairy tales, and that's all they were.

Dahlia was trying to get to the truth. And right then, Ruby felt hungry for it.

Because a human being couldn't be a myth or a mascot.

Or a scapegoat.

It only made them unravel.

"Why are you doing this?" he asked.

There was something in his voice. Something… Sad and confused. Broken.

"Because someone's going to hit you. Possibly on purpose. I don't know how I feel about you, but there are limits to what I'm willing to do. And leaving someone to die is one of them."

Tension crept up her shoulders as she drove past her parents' driveway and down toward the road that would take her to the Brewer orchard.

"She went home," he said. "She said goodbye. And she went home. I told them that. I told them over and over again. But I told him she walked out toward the road. And then I guess one time I said something else. So my story changed. It was just that I couldn't… I couldn't remember if she went east or west. I couldn't remember. She was gone. I was worried something happened to her." He laughed, and the sound was bitter. Hard. "Something *did* happen to her, I guess. And everyone thinks it was me."

"It wasn't?" She asked directly, she figured *why not*. He didn't answer.

Not directly.

"Everyone was sure. Everyone was so sure. It was in the news. I got arrested. It was easy to blame me. It was easy. It was so damn hard when it was over. And it's never really over. It's never really over."

What he was saying was rambling. And she probably shouldn't read too deeply into it. But there was something about… The helplessness in those words—there was something about it that made her feel something… She recognized it.

There was a big hole in the story of who he was. And he didn't understand how to cross it. How to make sense of it.

Hers was all the way at the beginning of her story, and his was somewhere in the middle.

He really didn't know. How he'd gotten here. How he'd become the villain.

She knew it, because she recognized the feeling.

Of being made into something based on…

Nothing you'd done at all.

She pulled her car up to the farmhouse. "Is this where you're staying?"

The place was so run-down it hardly looked habitable at all.

"Yeah," he said. "I'm fixing it up."

She waited for him to get out of the car. But then he did, and his gait was so unsteady, that she wasn't sure he was going to be able to make it to the front door. Feeling exasperated, she got out. And she really didn't know why she couldn't leave him alone. Except… She felt wound up in this. She had been with Dana earlier, and now she was with him. And if Dana had any idea…

She wrapped her arm around his waist, surprised by how solid he was, and he smelled heavily of whiskey.

"Come on," she muttered, helping him up the rickety steps and to the farmhouse. His flannel shirt was damp, and she wondered if he had been walking through the bushes. She looked up at him, and… It was the bleakness in his eyes that captivated her. The absolute devastation. The raw hopelessness there. How could she deny that? How could she act like she was immune to it? She wasn't. And whatever he'd done... Whatever he'd done... In this moment he was a man in pain.

"You didn't lock the house," she said, as she pushed the door open and walked into the dimly lit room. It was surprisingly well-ordered. Clean for all that the exterior was ramshackle. He'd said he'd been working on the place.

"You have to be careful," she said.

"Of what? I'm the only danger in this town, aren't I?"

"I don't know," she said, gasping when he stumbled forward.

She slapped her hand on his chest as if that would do anything. As if it would steady him. It was firm and solid like the rest of him. He was... Strong. Unquestionably. And really the only reason it was notable was that right now he was so very... Not strong. And his whole body gave the indication that it should be otherwise. That he was indestructible. Unaffected by what had occurred twenty-three years ago. The picture of health, really. Except that he was stumbling around too drunk to stand. She led him over to the couch and essentially deposited him there. He went down easily, sinking onto the blue flowered material.

"Are you... Are you all right? Is there anyone I can call?"

He looked up at her, his expression blank. "No," he said.

The hardness she'd seen in his eyes was gone now, but it was replaced by a hollow, empty thing that would haunt her for the rest of her life.

She swallowed hard. "Your..." She tried to think of a relationship he might have.

"No one."

She didn't doubt it. He looked like a man with no one.

"Okay," she said.

"You can leave," he said, lying back on the couch, throwing his arm over his eyes.

"You're not going to hurt yourself, are you?"

"No," he said. "Believe me. If I was going to do that, I

153

would've done it a long time ago. Would've gotten a hold of a razor blade in prison."

"How long were you…how long were you in there?"

"Not story time."

She huffed. "Well, I just rescued you."

"Why?"

"I don't know," she said, suddenly feeling out of place in the quiet, dark room. "I really don't." He groaned. "Can I get you a water?"

"Sure," he said.

She went into the kitchen and opened two cabinets, and she came up with the water glass pretty quickly. The kitchen was spare. Not fancy, but also very clean. Again, not something she would expect. All things considered.

"Here," she said, extending the glass.

He sat up, but didn't make a move away from the couch. She held the water glass out, unmoving.

"Are you going to bring it to me?"

"Why don't you get it yourself? It'll be a good test to see if you can take a drink without hurting yourself."

"Clearly I don't have a problem taking a drink," he said. He groaned, leaning forward and managing to reach the glass, before straightening back up on the couch.

"Do you do this… Every year?"

He glared at her while he took a sip of the water. "No."

"Why this year?"

"Because I'm here," he said. "I guess I underestimated the power of that."

"I see."

"Do you?"

He finished the glass of water, then set it down on the coffee table, flopping back on the couch pretty aggressively. He had one work boot resting on the arm of the couch, the other firmly on the floor. "I used to love this place. Never thought I'd leave.

And then it became hell on earth." His eyes fluttered closed, and she realized he was about to pass out. She looked around, feeling uncertain about what she should do. He really wasn't her responsibility. He was a grown man. And not one she particularly wanted to be alone with for an extended period of time. Right now, she could pretty handily outrun him if she had do.

But... Yeah, she didn't really want to be around once he sobered up.

His breathing went even, deep, and she felt a strange sense of relief. She leaned forward and took the water glass off of the coffee table, went back into the kitchen and refilled the glass. He would need it again. A creeping sense of unease stole over her, and she turned a circle in the kitchen, taking in the details of the space.

The cabinets were painted a cheerful yellow, old-fashioned-looking hardware screwed to the doors. Nothing was updated, but it was all freshly cleaned and painted. But the appliances were definitely from the eighties, the linoleum floor a bit scarred in places.

Without making too much noise, she walked out of the kitchen and back into the living room. The couch set was also old. Overstuffed with a ruffle around the bottom. There was a staircase that led upstairs. There were no pictures hanging on the wall. There was nothing... Personal, or that seemed to carry any kind of familial significance. There were no knick-knacks. That was what was so strange. These old farmhouses... They were rarely sparse. There were usually garlands hanging above the doors and statues of geese. Decorative potpourri bowls. *Something.*

She tiptoed down the hall, toward the bathroom, and found it to be in much the same condition.

And you're snooping why?

Well, because she was here. It felt like she was standing on the site of a legend. A bad legend, but nonetheless... She was here.

And she had never imagined that she would be. Never imagined that she would be in Nathan Brewer's house. Why would she? The frustrating thing was, there wasn't anything to learn. None of the hallmarks of history that she would expect.

Well, that tells you everything, doesn't it?

Of course it did. He had come to *sanitize* his father's house. There were no marks of family here. No marks of the person who had lived here before.

She moved toward a sideboard that was pushed against the wall and stopped in front of it, staring at the drawer pulls. And before she could think it through had jerked it open. The drawer wasn't empty.

There was a framed photo resting in there, facedown.

She slowly lifted it from the drawer and turned it over.

It was a typical family portrait, taken in front of a brushed gray photo set. A mother and father standing beside each other, their hands on the shoulders of the child in front of them.

But the child's face was cut roughly from the photo, a blank hole where it should have been.

A gruff, masculine sound coming from the couch made her jump, and she dropped the picture back into the drawer and slammed it shut. She looked over at the couch, her heart hammering. He had shifted slightly, but that was all.

And she'd stayed too long.

She darted past the couch, right out the front door, back to her car, breathing hard.

She shouldn't have stayed. She shouldn't have come here at all. It was one thing to make sure that he was safe, but she didn't need to...

She didn't need to go thinking that she had things in common with Nathan Brewer.

She was Ruby McKee, the town miracle. And he was...

But no matter how much she tried, she couldn't muster up

condemnation for him. She couldn't muster up... Well, any of the things that she knew she was supposed to think about him.

All she could see was that photo. And the boy who'd been cut from his own family.

15

I do not like Carter Swenson. Every girl likes Carter Swenson. It is dull and embarrassing at the same time.

DAHLIA MCKEE'S DIARY, AGE 16

DAHLIA

The police station was tucked back behind the main street of town, right next to a park that was always packed full of local kids, rain or shine. It was a small, quaint building made of red brick, with vines climbing up the side. It looked too sleepy, as a police department in a town like this one should.

Dahlia pushed the door open and wasn't overly surprised to find the entry empty.

She wasn't sure if the officers hung out here during the day. But she had some questions, and she hoped that she could get them answered. And mostly, she hoped that she could get quick copies of the police reports.

She was still thinking about her conversation with Dale. She needed to have a talk with Tom Swenson, but he was retired now. Even so, it was common to catch him in town, or even at the department. Especially considering his son, Carter, was now the police chief of Pear Blossom.

Which was something she couldn't get over, because every time she thought of him, she thought of him as he'd been that day at Dana's, all young and rangy and angry, and too handsome for everyone's own good.

He had been two years ahead of her, and the star of the football team. Everything you'd expect from a guy like that. All-American and deeply perfect. Pretty much everything Dahlia had never been.

And of course... He'd had the audacity to be good too.

Not part of the group of boys who'd thrown rocks at Dana's, but he'd...

Well, he'd defended Dahlia.

If she was honest, and she hated to be honest about this particular thing, she'd had an embarrassing, intense crush on him that had never been returned because he had been with the predictably blonde head cheerleader.

And if she'd felt like Elizabeth Bennet, hating and wanting a man all at once, and if she had maybe written them into her stories, hoping Ruby wouldn't identify them...

Well.

But he had married the cheerleader.

Who had also divorced him a year or so ago, but that was neither here nor there.

She was *over it*.

And if she still found him to be the most attractive man she'd ever seen, and if finding his classically handsome face attractive still sent her into a shame spiral, then fine.

She remembered the first time he had pulled her over after getting a job for the department. It hadn't gone well. Not for either of them, really, because she had ended up with a ticket that itemized everything she had done wrong, and she had verbally skinned him. Which had felt satisfying at the time, but in the end, she hadn't really... Gotten anything out of that. She'd been the one who was fined, after all, and he'd seemed... Not bothered.

She had been all the way bothered. Angry, red-faced and unsettled for days.

The door opened behind her and she turned sharply. And there was Carter, tall and broad as he'd ever been, imposing in his dark blue uniform. "Can I help you?"

"Yes," she said. "I... Dahlia McKee," she said. "I don't know if you know who I am."

He looked her up and down, his expression unreadable. "I know who you are," he said. "Can I help you?"

"Yes, I'm doing a story for the newspaper."

"Okay."

She could see that engaging him was going to be like squeezing water from a stone. "I'm doing a story for the newspaper, and I was wondering if I could get some police records."

"You can order those online."

"I know. But I thought it would be much easier if I came down here."

"You could get them any number of ways."

"I *know*. But I can also get them from you."

The corner of his mouth tipped up. "You haven't changed, have you?"

"What does... Does that mean?"

"You were like this in high school, if I recall. And also when I wrote you that ticket..."

She laughed. Probably about two beats longer than she should have. But he remembered her from high school? Other than that day at Dana's, they had never interacted. And she'd been pretty sure he'd been a knight in shining armor all the time and would never remember that one particular moment. And she had been sure that by now—five years later—he would have forgotten the ticket incident.

They had, in fact, waved blandly at each other a number of

times since, and she'd been certain he waved back just because he knew her face in that way you knew the faces of people when you'd both lived in the same small town all your life.

"Oh—" she waved a hand "—I completely forgot that you wrote me a ticket. Completely forgot about it. Just, doesn't even cross my mind anymore. Not an issue. But I also just wanted to… Your dad worked on Caitlin Groves' case."

He crossed his arms over his chest and rocked back slightly on his heels. "Yeah. But if you want to hear about that, you're probably going to have to talk to him."

"I want to talk to him. But I did want to find out if you thought he would be open to that."

"I'm sure he would be. He… He talks about it sometimes. Look, I've been police chief here for the last three years. More because there was no competition than any other reason. Nepotism combined with that. But also… Pear Blossom averages a scant handful of violent crimes a year. And of those… There hasn't been a death as a result of violence in my time on the force. And as for disappearances… Beyond people getting lost in the woods for a couple of days, nothing. I know if you work in a big city, if you work most other places, that's not going to be the case. But it's different here. And it always was. My dad never worked a case like that until Caitlin. And I know that the lack of closure bothers him."

"I want the police report that was taken when Nathan Brewer was arrested. And the missing person's report that was filed when Caitlin first disappeared."

"Yeah, I can get you that." He moved away from the door, crossing the station and making his way to a computer. It was old. It looked like the kind of computer they'd done work on in elementary school. But it didn't take long, a few decisive keystrokes, and she could hear the printer firing up. "So, you work for the *Gazette* now."

"Yeah," Dahlia said. "It took a little bit to convince Dale to take on an employee. Circulation has been down the last few years…"

"I heard newspapers were dead."

"The death of print has been greatly exaggerated."

"Apparently," he said. "Here you go." He handed the files to her, and she shoved them down in her beat-up leather bag.

"Thanks," she said. "Did your dad ever… Did he ever talk about Ruby?"

"Your sister?"

"Yeah. *I am* going to talk to your dad. But… I'm just curious. About everybody's perspective. It's part of the series I'm doing. So I'd like to know how you saw it too."

"I remember that night. My dad was… His mind was blown. He couldn't stop talking about it. He kept telling my mom… He kept telling her it was a miracle."

"Did he ever have any idea how she might have ended up there?"

He shook his head. "No. I mean, the case was turned over to child services and I assume there was an investigation that stemmed from there. But as far as the police went, there was no evidence."

"Wow. Okay." She chewed the inside of her lip.

"You want to ask another question." Not phrased as a question.

"Is it that obvious?"

He smiled, and she wasn't immune to the effect of that smile. The alt girl in her had always hated the way that mainstream beauty lit her up inside. She was supposed to like *interesting* boys who wore black and wrote poetry.

She wasn't supposed to like football players.

And he'd never liked *her*. It had been Carter and Lena all the way. The royal couple of their small high school.

And then when golden boy Carter Swenson had gotten divorced from his equally golden girl, the gossip mill had gone into overdrive. But Lena had gotten the hell out of town, which meant most of the gossip went in Carter's favor.

It was said Lena had moved to *Portland*.

A more unforgivable sin did not exist in Pear Blossom.

"Yes. Go ahead."

"Did he think that Nathan Brewer did it?"

"I don't really want to speak on the record about my dad's feelings."

"Off the record," she said. "This is not... These are supposed to be pieces about the history of the town. I'm not doing an exposé. But I heard that Nathan Brewer was back in town. And, I think my sister...well, she had a *sighting*."

Carter's expression went hard. "Be careful. My dad absolutely thought that Nathan Brewer was guilty. And there was nothing he could ever do about it. He was arrested, but the charges didn't stick. Because they could never... They could never prove what crime had been committed. Now they've arrested people and charged them with murder without bodies, convicted them, but there's always more... There's always more."

"And with Nathan there was never more."

He shook his head. "She just vanished. There was never a trace of her. No blood, no...sorry. I know it's not the most pleasant topic."

"I'm fine."

"You'll see all that in the police report. The only lead we ever had was that he was the last person to see her. And they were seen going off of the main road onto the Brewer orchard. That was the last time anyone ever saw her."

"Who saw them?"

"Walter Berryman. He's... Well, he's gotta be ninety-five now if he's not gone."

She shook her head. "We'd have heard if he was."

"True. I mean, you could talk to him about it but..."

"I might. Thanks for this," she said, pointing to her bag.

"No problem. If you end up needing any more information…"

"Why would you help me? Print is dead."

"Because. This case was the biggest blight on my dad's… Not his legacy. That wasn't it. It changed him."

The words sat heavy between them.

"I think it changed all of us. We used to walk down to the store and my mom didn't think anything of it. But after that… After that, she got a lot more protective."

"My mom too."

She laughed. "I can't imagine that your mom would think she had to protect you from anything. Even in high school you were…well, you are *that*." She waved her hand up and down, and immediately felt ridiculous.

"What does that mean?"

"A human tank."

"Sure. But do moms ever see you that way?"

Dahlia shrugged. "I guess not. Anyway. Thanks. I'll definitely be in touch if I need anything else. And…"

"Do you want my dad's phone number?"

"Yes. Please."

He scribbled on a piece of paper for her, and when she left, she couldn't help but smile in amusement that she had gotten a phone number from Carter Swenson. Not that it was *his* number.

She shook her head.

Yeah, he was handsome. As handsome as ever. But infuriating, and just as out of reach. Anyway, that had nothing to do with her task at hand.

She was going to bring these reports home to Ruby. And when she did, she imagined they would have a lot to discuss.

Tonight, they were having dinner at the farmhouse, and her mother was determined to nail down a plan for Thanksgiving. She knew that Andie McKee liked to have the holiday in the farmhouse, but Marianne preferred to have it at her place, where there was modern cooking equipment and ample space. So tonight, Dahlia anticipated watching the two of them tussle over venue.

She wasn't terribly surprised that it dominated dinner conversation, and Marianne ended up winning by virtue of the fact that she did have more space, and the kids were getting bigger. Plus, with Ruby back, there was another person to consider.

Marianne ate dinner with their parents once a month, just like Dahlia did. They all got along. But it was impossible to not get along with their mom and dad. They never fought. No fuss, no muss. In spite of that, Dahlia knew Marianne was resentful of the way they'd handled her teenage depression, and the way she exploded with emotion, especially in her parenting, was a stark rebellion against the way their parents did things.

Lydia was the most like their mother, with her practical nature and naturally low-key emotions, and the two of them often seemed to communicate without words.

Ruby was nothing like their mother. And seemed to delight and surprise her constantly for that reason alone.

Dahlia loved her mom. That didn't mean she had a clue how to talk to her. She'd always aspired to be more like her, more like Lydia. But she wasn't. She was outspoken and... She felt things deeply, and didn't know how to put them into words.

So she just shoved them down deep.

She knew how to write things. She knew how to write a feeling out on paper and explain it. She just didn't always know how to... Have it.

"You need to show us the shed," Marianne said, once dinner was all finished.

"You've seen it," Dahlia said.

"Not since Ruby moved in."

And she didn't know why, but that sort of irritated her.

"It is a cottage," Ruby said, serenely.

"It's a shed," Dahlia said.

"It hasn't changed that much," Ruby said. "If you want to see how we're sharing a room like it's 2005, you're definitely welcome."

Marianne dropped a kiss on Jackson's face. "We'll be back," she said, patting her husband on the shoulder.

"Mom, is it okay if I leave Riley and Hazel?" Lydia asked.

"Of course," her mom said.

Lydia seemed… Well, slightly energized. Like there was something charged beneath her skin. An electric current of some kind. It was unusual. To say the least.

They all piled into Dahlia's car and drove around on the service road to the shed. Dahlia felt a shiver of unease as she got out of the car. Like maybe they were being watched. She shook that off and walked to the front door, unlocking it and letting them all in. "Here you go."

Ruby went ahead and flicked all the lights on. "Look, we have desks," she said.

"Wow," Lydia said. "You've done so much to this place, Dee. You never mentioned."

Dahlia had to admit that a lot of the details were Ruby's doing, and that even the encouragement for her to add succulents and other plants had made the place all the more livable. "Last time I was in here there was just a bed in your room."

"Oh," Dahlia said. "Well, I've definitely made things nicer since then."

"Well, that's good," Lydia said, looking around. "Good."

"What's up with you?" Marianne asked.

"What?"

"You," Dahlia said, "seem twitchy."

"I'm not twitchy." Lydia frowned.

"What's on your mind, then?" Marianne asked.

"Oh, nothing. It's just… I spent some time working on the plan for the farm store today. And figuring out how much it's going to cost. And trying to figure out the logistics of beekeeping."

"Bees?" Ruby asked.

"Yes," Lydia said. "Bees. For honey."

"You did not tell me that you were going to buy bees."

"Well, I'm buying bees."

Ruby wiggled her shoulders and practically jumped across the room. "That is disgusting. Bees are horrific. And a mass of bees? That is a horror movie."

"I don't think so," Lydia said. "I'm excited about my bees."

"That's what it is," Marianne said. "You're actually excited. You're actually happy."

"I don't know if I would go that far," Lydia said. "For the first time I feel like I might know what I'm doing. What I want."

"I'm happy for you," Marianne said, wrapping her arm around Lydia.

Dahlia's eyes met Lydia's. Her sister looked away. Dahlia was maybe the only one who really understood how much it cost Lydia to admit something like that. To share what was happening inside of herself. And speaking of...

"I got the police reports today, Rubes," she said.

"Police reports?" Lydia asked.

"Yeah. For the project. I wanted to get all of the information on Caitlin Groves' disappearance. It's one of the pieces that I'm working on. The effect of Caitlin going missing on the town. I also talked to Carter Swenson."

"Carter Swenson," Marianne said, her tone taking on a slightly dreamy quality. "He's looked good in every uniform he's ever worn. Football or law enforcement."

"He is a *lot* younger than you," Dahlia pointed out, archly, and refusing to internalize any of those thoughts, or admit that she had been thinking something similar earlier.

"Rude," Marianne said. "Very rude. Anyway, my daughter thinks I'm lame—maybe I need to shake things up."

"You would not cheat on Jackson," Ruby said.

"No," Marianne agreed. "I wouldn't. This is a modern age. I would simply tell Jackson I needed to go off and sow my wild oats for a while and then return home when all was well."

"And that would go over...not well at all," Dahlia said.

"No," Marianne agreed. "But, your ageism aside, I'm not dead, and I am not too old to notice that he's hot."

"Which has nothing to do with me getting those reports from him."

"Have you looked at them?" Ruby asked.

"No," she said. "I haven't had time."

"She was too busy looking at him," Marianne said sweetly. Dahlia glared.

"I'm curious," Ruby said. "I'd like to see them."

"I'll read the article when it's finished," Marianne said, frowning.

"You don't want to see the reports?"

"It turns my stomach. She was... She was a nice girl."

"I barely remember her," Lydia said. "I used to see her walking on the road sometimes. Between Nathan's orchard and the bridge."

Ruby frowned, her eyebrows pleating. "Right. She would've walked that way."

"Yeah," Lydia said. "It's the only way to get back to town. Why?"

"Nothing. Just...the bridge."

"Everyone uses that bridge," Lydia pointed out.

"No, I know," Ruby said.

They chatted for a few more minutes, and then they all rode back to the farmhouse, where they bade their goodbyes and Dahlia and Ruby returned to the shed.

"*I* want to see the police report," Ruby said.

"And I want to know what you weren't saying," Dahlia said.

"I saw *him* there."

"What?"

"Nathan Brewer. He was on the bridge. He was drunk."

"When?"

"About a week ago. It was the anniversary of Caitlin's disappearance. I saw him walking to the bridge, and he crossed over into the road and I almost hit him with my car. But I ended up giving him a ride back to the farmhouse and…"

"Ruby McKee," Dahlia said, "he's…he's dangerous."

"What if he isn't?" Ruby asked. "I just know that I can't get over the fact that everybody in town loves me. And it has nothing to do with anything I've done. Nothing to do with something I've earned. It's just because I was born. It's because I was there. Because they needed a symbol. And there I was. It could have been any baby. It didn't need to be me. Any… Any baby whose mom didn't want her. And there's just…all of this is making me think about all the horrible parts of this. I am a hand-me-down person."

"Ruby," Dahlia said. "I…"

And she could find no real satisfaction in this. In Ruby being forced to acknowledge the tragic piece of her story. Of Ruby finally seeing what Dahlia had all along. She didn't want Ruby's sparkle diminished.

As she stood there looking at her, she realized she drew as much comfort from Ruby's glitter as she did irritation.

No, more comfort. She loved Ruby's confidence. Her sparkle. She hadn't realized how much until she saw it grow dimmer.

"I'm sorry," Dahlia said. "I'm sorry that sometimes I forget."

"Forget what?"

"That you're a human being. And not just a forest sprite. But I'm still worried that you went somewhere alone with Nathan Brewer."

"If you could have seen him… He was completely wasted. In the way that he talked about her… It doesn't sound like he knows anything. He sounds confused by all of it."

"I don't know. Heavily drinking on the anniversary of his girlfriend's disappearance just sounds like guilt to me."

"No," Ruby said. "It wasn't that. And there's something wrong with that house. I saw his family picture…"

"You *went inside*."

"Yes. But listen. The family picture… His face is cut out of it."

Dahlia shivered. "It sounds like even his parents think he's a murderer."

"I'm not sure I do."

And something, a whisper of something, slid over Dahlia's skin. Because one thing she was forgetting. That as a journalist, she wasn't writing the story the way people in town had told it before. She might include their viewpoints, but she had to remember that she couldn't take what they said and connect the dots in the way that matched up to the narrative she had always believed. There had never been any evidence to convict Nathan. And she couldn't write the story as if there were.

Even though she knew that implying otherwise would hurt Dana terribly.

"What about Dana? You…you finding sympathy for him would…"

Ruby shook her head. "I don't know. Wouldn't you want to know? Wouldn't you cling to any story that made sense? And of course it makes sense. He was her boyfriend. He was the last person to see her. But that doesn't make him guilty. Just because it's what often happens doesn't mean it's what happened here."

"I know," she said. "I do. It's just… I don't know. For the purposes of my piece, you're right. I can't go making assumptions about him. But for the purposes of your safety… Ruby, you need to make some assumptions."

"I couldn't just leave him."

"Well, I'm glad you didn't. But I'm also glad that he… That he clearly couldn't do anything to you."

"Thank you for the concern," Ruby said. "It's noted. But I'm fine."

"All right. As long as you… As long as you… Just be smart."

"I promise. Anyway, I don't have time to go dealing with disastrous men right now. I have museum displays to finish. And we have police reports to look at."

"Oh, right." Dahlia dug her reports out of her bag. She opened the folder, and Ruby took one piece of paper, while Dahlia stared at the other.

"There's not really anything here we didn't know."

"I didn't know this," Ruby said, pointing to the witness statement from Walter Berryman.

"Well, I just found out about it today while I was talking to Carter."

"But that's it," Ruby said. "That's just… Nothing."

"Yeah. A whole lot of nothing."

"Sort of like my police report. Nothing we didn't know."

"Well, we can keep talking to people. Paperwork… Paperwork doesn't give you the half of it."

"No," Ruby agreed. "It doesn't."

16

Out on the Town

BY RITA SKINNER

OCTOBER 1907—The town of Pear Blossom was bustling Friday evening. Mr. and Mrs. Daniel Hawkins dined out at The Porterhouse with Mr. Evan Shaw. Mr. and Mrs. Ronald McKee dined at 501 Cherry Street with Mr. and Mrs. Carl Swenson.

LYDIA

Lydia still felt uncomfortable that her sisters had observed some sort of change in her behavior last night. She had spent the whole day working on all of her plans, and she was both stressed out to the absolute max and excited. And she didn't really know what bucket to put all of her feelings in, so she just sort of felt like they were leaking out of her. Which was... Very unusual.

And her thoughts were cut short by the arrival of Chase.

They were going over renovation logistics, and she really couldn't afford to fight him on this. Because that was what he did. She needed him. And she most especially needed him to give her that special rate that he would give because he was Mac's friend. Which meant she really couldn't afford to be his enemy.

"Hi," she said.

"You're not spitting tacks at me," he said. "That makes me nervous."

"I can't win," she said. "You're not happy when I'm mean to you, you're not happy when I'm nice to you."

"Don't get too crazy, Lydia. A greeting without acid is hardly being nice."

"Right. Let's just go to the barn."

"You have ideas?"

"I have a lot of them," she said.

They walked into the old barn together. Right now, it was a simple cement floor. And she wasn't intent on doing too much to it. It was essentially going to be a farm stand. But she needed to get the structure shored up, needed to find a way to keep the heating and cooling consistent, even if it wasn't completely finished.

"Tell me what you're thinking."

"Well, I was thinking I could put a register here." She indicated a spot in between two doors. "And back there we can have lettuce and leafy vegetables. Eggs, meat and cheese. Then with center displays that rotate out specialty ingredients. I thought that I would have fresh bread from the bakery. Things like that. All things local, fresh and yummy in one spot."

"I don't think it's going to be too difficult to fix it up."

"And the expense?"

"Don't worry about it."

"I have to worry about it. I have... This might be crazy."

"Yeah. But... It's what you want. Shouldn't you have what you want?" It was such a strange question, and it was one that no one had asked her. Life certainly hadn't asked her. She had been given things that she wanted, it was true. She loved the farm, and the farmhouse. They'd saved for it, bought it from Dale Wainwright when he and his wife had been ready to let their hobby farm go.

And she loved Riley and Hazel more than anything. Her marriage hadn't been what she'd imagined, but she hadn't wanted Mac to die.

"I don't know. I was beginning to think maybe I shouldn't."

"You gotta find some happiness," he said. He took a step toward her, then stopped. There was nothing hesitant in Chase's manner. And it wasn't hesitance she saw now. It was as if a wall had gone up and stopped him from moving forward. A powerful, otherworldly force, and she couldn't for the life of her figure out why. "Lydia, you deserve to live."

Discomfort moved like a wave beneath her skin. As to why he would say this to her... Like she... Guilt ate at her. It always did. But suddenly it was like a ravenous beast. "I'm not... It's not Mac that's making this hard. It's just garden-variety fear."

"Well, it must be tough imagining a new life when you thought you were going to be living a different one."

She huffed a long breath. "Yeah. I..."

And as she stared at Chase, she realized that she... Okay, if she told him now... If she told him now, then he might rescind his offer to do all of this for her, and that would be terrible. But he was treating her like broken glass, and she couldn't take that. Maybe she would never be able to tell her family everything about Mac. Because they'd loved him. And they loved her equally. But Chase didn't have any particular loyalty to her. It wouldn't... It wouldn't matter to him. But she just couldn't take that. Couldn't take him looking at her with pity. Pity that was misplaced. She couldn't survive being underneath the weight of that while they worked on this project. It was half of why being around him was so difficult.

And her sisters were so careful with her and so sad about Mac, and last night...

Last night she had even thought it had been fun to tell them about the bees she was still holding back and...

And she was tired. She was just so tired.

And Chase was *here* and he was *him*, and why should she have to carry all this alone?

If he wanted to help her...

If he wanted to help, then he could help by knowing the truth. Because the lie was slowly suffocating her.

"I was going to divorce him," she said.

Chase's eyes locked with hers. "What?"

"Before the diagnosis. Three years ago. I had decided that I was going to leave him."

Chase frowned. "You were going to leave Mac?"

"Yes. I was... I was miserable and so was he. But he wouldn't admit it. Every time I tried to talk to him about it, he just deflected. He said that I was imagining things. He said that... And then he would go out with you. He loved you, Chase, never me."

Chase held up his hands. "I don't know exactly what you're getting at but..."

"No. I don't mean like that. But you... You were the most defining relationship in his life. You were his brother. You were the person that he connected with. And you wonder why I found you so difficult all those years? I resented you. We've known each other since we were kids. And I thought... Surely at some point the woman that he wants to marry is going to be more important than his friend. His foster brother. But no. It never shifted that way. His friends were always more important than his family. Going out having a beer was always more important. And everybody thought that we were one thing. Destined to be together. And I did too. Because I didn't know any better. Because I didn't know anyone else. Because I didn't know any other relationship. But I can see Marianne and Jackson. I could see my parents. They're completely different from each other. My parents are traditional. My mom does the housework, my dad works and pays the bills. But they have always been in agreement about that. Marianne and Jackson are partners. He helps with her business. He supports her. And it works for them. I can't... I've never known how to articulate this, Chase. It's why no one knows. It's why... I've never said anything to anybody. Because how do you say no, he wasn't evil. Yes, I'm sad that he's gone. He was the father of my children. And he was my friend for more than half of my life. But I didn't love him like a husband anymore. And everybody thinks that I'm grieving him like a wife, and I'm not. I can't stand you thinking it too. So there you go. You have permission to hate me or..."

And suddenly, Chase took a step forward and wrapped his hand around the back of her head. And she found herself being hauled toward him, up off of her feet, and his lips were crashing down on hers.

Chase was kissing her.

Chase.

Who she had known since he was a thirteen-year-old boy, and it felt like she'd been resented by him for just as long. Who she'd resented all that time. Chase, who was here to honor her husband's memory, and who she was sure loved him more than she did. He was kissing her like she...

She'd never been kissed like this.

And for a minute, she let everything fall away. She let her world reduce to the warmth and firmness of his mouth, the scratch of his whiskers, the rough strength of his hands as they held her face, while he thoroughly explored her mouth.

She was dizzy. Drowning. And she couldn't process what on earth was happening to her. Because it was too insane. Too out of the ordinary, too... Wrong. She pushed against his chest and launched herself backward, her heart thundering hard. "I..."

"Forget about it," he said, turning and starting to walk away from her.

"I... I can't forget about it."

"Just forget it," he said. "I'll be back tomorrow to start on getting that rotten wood replaced."

"You'll be back tomorrow," she said, the words hollow. Nonsensical.

"Yes," he said.

"Chase… We need to talk about this."

"We talked," he said, his voice rough. "You weren't in love with him. He was my best friend. I lost my head for a minute. That's it."

"You still want to help me?"

"I'm to make sure you're taken care of. I promise to do that. I promised."

And then he left her standing there, her head spinning, her entire body buzzing. She had finally admitted that her marriage was a lie. And on the heels of that had received her first kiss from a man who wasn't Mac.

And it had been Chase.

And the worst part was, there were some things that suddenly slotted into place. Her discomfort with his presence, her occasional desire to rest herself on his strength even though she found him frustrating, suddenly seemed all too clear. Suddenly seemed all too obvious.

Why hadn't she recognized it before? For exactly what it was. She was attracted to him.

He was infuriating, and he was… There was just no way. It was too high stakes. All of this was. She hadn't even wanted to be in the marriage she was in, much less be in a different relationship. A new relationship.

She couldn't handle her life. She could not handle this. Not even remotely.

And if her sisters could read the strange waves of her emotions when she was dealing with just setting up the store, she was going to get caught out on this. And she couldn't risk that.

Well, Chase didn't need her to do the renovations. He knew what she wanted. She didn't have to be around him.

But somehow even the distance between them now didn't do anything to make her feel better. Because everything inside of her burned.

17

1975—After an accident involving a weak point in the wood and a drunken youth, who is recovering at Rogue Valley Medical Center, Sentinel Bridge has been deemed unsafe, and is closed to foot traffic.

RUBY

Ruby had been caught up in a flash of inspiration for her displays. In the basement she'd found all the supplies to piece together an old general store exhibit that she knew kids would love, and she'd spent days assembling it with loving care. And maybe she'd played with the register and scales a tiny bit.

Dahlia had written a wonderful piece on the pear industry, which had gone into the paper just in time for Thanksgiving break. It had been quite a boon for the small display on orchards, and the little general store she'd set up for kids to play around in. And today was a day to think, not about that, but about pie and togetherness. Thanksgiving was one of Ruby's favorite holidays. It was rivaled by Christmas, obviously, because she was basic and had never claimed to be otherwise. She'd felt melancholy and wistful the last few weeks. And she blamed her encounter with Nathan, and that she felt deeply unsettled by the entire thing, particularly while working with Dana.

But she wasn't going to think about that today. She wasn't going to think about Nathan Brewer, or the particularly disturbing side note that her investigation into herself seemed to continually take.

Instead, she got involved in dance contests with her nieces and nephews, and she felt absolutely ridiculous, but they thought it was hilarious, and making preteens laugh seemed like a pretty great achievement so she went ahead and considered that her win for the day.

For her part, Ruby had made a trifle for the get-together, a dessert that they really didn't need because there were already at least five different varieties. Bread pudding, pumpkin pie, sticky toffee cake, cranberry cake and an apple galette. But Ruby had developed a slight obsession with the layered dessert while she was in England, and she wanted to share her obsession with the family.

So, red and sweaty from dancing, she made her way into the kitchen to begin making the cream so that she could assemble her layers. She hadn't wanted to do it too early, because she didn't want her cream to go all runny. She knew people who could make one that seemed to stand up for ages, but hers just never did.

Luckily, her sister's kitchen was organized very well—she had to concede that it was better to have Thanksgiving here for that alone—and it was simple for her to find everything she needed to begin to whip it all up.

She had just gotten the bowl locked in the mixer when Lydia came into the kitchen.

"Hey," she said.

"Riley is still hungry," Lydia said. "I have to get some olives for him. He's hungry, but of course not so hungry that he can't put the food on his fingers before he eats it."

"No. Of course not," Ruby said. "It's nice to see him smile. He's too serious."

"He's... He's been pretty happy today. I'm glad."

"What about you?" Her sister looked pale and glassy-eyed today, and Ruby hadn't been able to ignore how... Haunted she seemed. But of course. It was her first Thanksgiving since Mac died. It must be awful. "Lydia, if you want to talk about..."

"About what, Ruby?" she asked, her words tart. "About how you keep looking at me like you want me to cry on command?"

"I don't... I don't want that."

"Don't you?" she pressed. "I think you can't stand that I won't show you my feelings in a way you can understand them."

"No, I want to make sure you...are having feelings," Ruby said, fighting against the anger that sprang up inside her. "I don't want you to be like..." She lowered her voice so that her words wouldn't carry. "Mom and Dad just don't deal with things. With anything. And everyone is worried about you, Lydia. It's not just me. We don't want you to just hold it in because Mom and Dad..."

"Like I'm choosing it? Like I'm performing for them? I'm not performing for anyone. I have to live with it, Ruby. I can't just sit and cry about it for two days and then get up and go on. That's what you want. For me to have a catharsis and that just isn't... I have to wake up every morning. And every morning when I do, I think... He's dead. Mac is dead. The kids' dad is dead. They don't have their dad. I want to send him a picture of Riley in his baseball uniform. Or tell him that Hazel lost a tooth, and I can't, Ruby. And I forget. It's not ever going to be sitting down and crying it out one day. It's going to be years of milestones he won't see. Forever of them wanting their dad and not having him. I can't cry it out because it doesn't end."

"Lydia..."

"You have to accept it. That's all you can do, and then you have to go on, knowing sometimes there isn't a reason or a fix or...or anything on the horizon but life without them."

"I'm sorry, Lydia," Ruby said, her voice thick. "I really didn't mean... I promise I just wanted to help. I wanted to give you something, like you gave to me. I wanted to feel like I mattered and... I just realized how many times I said *I* in that sentence about helping you."

Lydia's anger seemed to leach out of her then. "Well, that isn't unique to you. People want to help. They want to be there. And they don't realize how much of that is trying to make themselves comfortable with your pain. With death. They want to do something when there isn't anything to be done."

"I hate that. I want to do. I want to fix."

"I'm glad you're here, Ruby. You can just...be here. I better bring Riley his olives." She turned and left Ruby standing there.

And Ruby realized she hadn't given to her sister in the way she had imagined. Instead, Lydia had given her something.

You can just be here.

MARIANNE

Marianne didn't even mind how big of a mess was left after Thanksgiving was over. It had been wonderful to have the whole family together. Of course, she would like it if her husband and kids were pulling together and helping her clean a little bit more, but the kids were sprawled out on the living room floor watching Disney movies.

Having them get along, and having Ava not be sullen and withdrawn for a day, made her not want to push them.

And when last she had left him, Jackson was comatose on the couch.

He always claimed that turkey made it impossible for him to keep his eyes open, and he could not be held responsible for the fact that he couldn't withstand the aftereffects of it. She for one called baloney and felt that it was all just a whole tactical maneuver to not have to help with cleanup.

Ruby had been subdued today, and so had Lydia. But she had not had a chance to talk to them because she was so busy running around and making sure that all the food was perfect. She really did like hosting, but there was a strange sort of frenetic energy that came over her when she did. Even though it was her family. Even though they'd been to her house a hundred times when it wasn't Thanksgiving, and she didn't feel like she had to run around or serve everything on time or have everything be perfect. There was something about the holiday that brought that out in her.

She moved into the living room, to see if she could rouse Jackson, but he wasn't asleep. He was sitting up on the couch, texting.

Julie.

She could see the name pretty clearly in the top of the conversation, but she didn't know a Julie. She didn't know that Jackson knew a Julie.

"Hon?" she asked, making sure to recede behind the door slightly so that he didn't know she'd been standing behind him.

"Yep?"

She came around the corner and saw him stow his phone hastily.

"What's up?" she asked.

"Nothing," he said. "Just sleepy."

"Right. Because turkey."

"Because turkey," he agreed.

"Were you asleep?"

"Yeah," he said. "Did you need help?"

"Yeah. I would like some help."

Her world felt tilted slightly. And it wasn't because he was texting a woman, not necessarily. Except usually, if there was a woman in his phone to text, it would've been someone that she'd heard him talk about before. Someone that he dealt with for the business. Or an old friend that she would be familiar with. One of his best friends from college was a woman who was very happily married with a wife of her own, and obviously Marianne had no concerns about her. But she was familiar with the people he was in touch with. Regardless of gender, really. A completely unfamiliar name on his phone, and then a strange…

She had never caught her husband in a lie before. And it was such a small lie.

Is it?

She had been feeling so much disquiet lately. Things had felt unsettled and strange, and her life had felt *off*. And maybe she wasn't crazy or having a midlife crisis. Maybe it was because there was something going on.

Maybe Ava was sliding into a depression or a rebellion.

Maybe it was because Jackson wasn't being truthful with her.

She should just say something. She should. She had been with the man since they were in their early twenties. She usually thought nothing of saying things to him. Shocking things, dirty things. Anything.

And yet, she couldn't quite bring herself to get these words out. To ask him a question. To call out the lie. Because even though her life had started to feel small, it was still hers. At the moment it felt tenuous. Like if she said the wrong thing, it might break open. It might crack and dissolve at the foundation, and if that happened… She didn't know who she would be.

She didn't know what she would do.

She had been thinking about travel, she had been thinking about changing things. And hell, she had been joking about Carter Swenson a couple of weeks ago to her sisters, but she…

None of that was real.

Was he…

She couldn't even think it. She could not even think it. He was texting, and it wasn't that big of a deal. And she wasn't going to ask him about it. And she wasn't going to make it something that it wasn't.

She could get dramatic about it. She liked a little drama. But not now. Not over this.

It hovered at the base of her throat, making it tight and achy.

So she pushed it down. Down and down until it was so deep she couldn't feel it anymore.

Until it didn't matter.

She walked down the hall and looked at the hardwood floors she and Jackson had chosen together, then into the kitchen. Champagne bronze faucets on the bar sink and kitchen sink, white cabinets, the marble backsplash.

She really loved that backsplash. Her contractor had tried to talk her out of it because it was so expensive to buy a slab and mount it like that, but she'd known she had to have it and now she did and it was... It was perfect.

This place, this life that they'd built together was just so beautiful. And it was here and real and it was what mattered.

Her mind wandered to The Apothecary, her business, which she was so proud of. The business that had helped build this house.

This life.

It was easy to let her mind wander as she filled the sink. To the exposed red brick in her shop and the bouquets of flowers—she needed to replace them. Maybe she would get peonies?

Or maybe there was something that connected to Ruby's history thing.

Without pausing to think, she took her hands out of the sink, wiped them on her pants and picked up her phone.

"Hey, Rubes," she said. "I hope you weren't napping off a turkey."

"No," Ruby said. "I was still figuring out what to do with all of these leftovers. Besides eat them immediately. Dahlia and I have a tiny fridge in the cottage."

"You can give them to Mom and Dad."

"No way," Ruby said. "They don't get our pie."

"Well. I just wanted to talk to you about… Did you find anything out about the shop?"

"Oh," Ruby said. "I did. I'm sorry. It was owned by Silas Sullivan. He was a silversmith. He came from Boston, where he had a successful shop, and he set up a storefront here, making and selling jewelry. It closed in 1956. If you go online, there's some really great pictures. I'm going to include it in my No Longer on the Map feature. Dahlia is going to write about it in the paper. And I'm starting a big board at the museum. I'd love to take a picture of The Apothecary and put it next to the original store."

"That would be awesome," Marianne said. "Being featured in the museum is… It's great." It was a connection. It was the kind of thing she had been searching for. It was. And Jackson… It was nothing. She was going to put it out of her head. She'd already forgotten it. She was just restless. And she was being paranoid because of it. That was all.

"Yeah. Of course. You know, now that I have you, I wanted to talk to you about something else."

"Oh," Marianne said, looking into the living room and seeing Jackson and the kids. "I should go. Sorry. Can we talk later? I mean, I feel bad, because I called you to ask you about that…"

But she felt an obsessive need to go and sit next to her husband. Even though she was sure there was nothing going on. There couldn't be anything going on.

"Yeah. We'll talk later. It's nothing that needs to be solved on Thanksgiving. I'll see you."

"See you."

And then Marianne went out to join her family.

And she was grateful. To be here with them in this house. To be laughing with Jackson. Lydia's husband was gone. That was such a tragedy. She had everything.

There was no point looking for predators in the grass where there weren't any.

18

News in Brief—

FEBRUARY 3, 1865—It has come over the wire that Crispin Colfax, having left town March, 1864, in the company of a notorious woman, Belle Greaves, was killed when he was shot to death in a robbery in Portland.

DAHLIA

It hadn't been easy to get Walter Berryman to agree to see her. In fact, it had required the promise of a police escort. And that was how Dahlia found herself riding in Carter's cop car all the way up the mountain. "This is silly," she said.

"Well, you decided you wanted to interview him."

She had. Because it was twofold. It turned out that Walter was one of the few remaining living World War II veterans in Pear Blossom. And the only one who had lived here at the time of his service. That meant talking to him was going to help her accomplish elements of two different stories that she was writing, maybe even three. Walter lived up on the mountain above Sentinel Bridge. The view overlooked the McKee family farm, the Brewer orchard and other parts of the valley. And the man had lived there his entire life. He had inherited it when his parents had moved away. He had been born on that hill, and he was determined to die on that hill. At least, that was what he told Dahlia on the phone.

"I guess he's a little paranoid," Carter said.

"Fair enough, I guess," Dahlia said. "But I'm a reporter. It can't be completely unusual to him that a reporter might want to talk to him about his time in the service."

"That's not all you want to talk to him about, though, is it?"

"Well, no," she said.

The house itself was small. It made the farmhouse that Dahlia had grown up in look like a grand mansion. But it was tidy. And she wondered if somebody helped him with the upkeep.

That question was answered when she and Carter encountered Walter, who was straight-backed and full of fire from the moment he opened the front door. "I just had to make sure you weren't a scammer," he said.

"I'm not a scammer," she said. "I'm a journalist."

"Hardly a difference, is there?" he asked.

"Well. Officially," she said, "there is a difference."

"And why is it that you want to talk to me?"

"I'll wait outside," Carter said.

"No you don't. You look like your old man," Walter said, appraising Carter.

Carter shifted. "Thanks."

"He was a good cop."

"Yeah," Carter agreed.

"I figured you might be a good cop. That's why I thought I'd ask for an escort if she was going to come up here." He shook his head. "Can't be too careful."

"You don't strike me as someone who's ever lax," Dahlia said.

The older man squinted at her. "Don't flatter me."

"Oh, I wasn't. I was being completely honest."

"What is it you want to talk to me about?"

"I'm working on a series of articles about the history of Pear Blossom. And one of the things that I want to write about is the way war affected the shape of the town. How many people here went. How many young men were gone."

"The real story is in the ones that didn't come back," he said. He shook his head. "It was a terrible thing. All the young men had gone to the other war. And that was supposed to be the war that ended it all. And then... It didn't. It didn't. All the men had to send their sons off to war. My father had already fought. You know there was a family in town sent both their sons off to war. Neither of them came back. D-Day."

She didn't know what to say to that, so she said nothing and just let him continue. It was so easy to think of Pear Blossom as a magical place. But of course it hadn't been spared this sort of tragedy. This global experience.

When they got Walter talking, the stories flowed out of him. The businesses that closed, how it was to leave Pear Blossom for the first time and then come back. Seeing the world here unchanged, and yet profoundly altered in so many ways. Being profoundly altered himself.

"Thank you," she said. "I'd love to tell your story in the paper."

"Wouldn't be the first time I was written about in the paper." But she could tell that it meant something to him. This was the kind of documented record that she could help create. That she could ensure was saved for future generations. The way they were looking back on newspaper articles now.

"Before I go," she said. "I wanted to ask you about one more thing. A couple more things. You've lived up on top of this hill..."

"For my entire life."

"Right. There are two other specific events in the town's history that I'm writing about. One is the disappearance of Caitlin Groves. And the other is when Ruby McKee was found on

Sentinel Bridge. You can see the bridge and the Brewer orchard from here. I was just going over the police report for the night Caitlin disappeared. You said that you saw her."

"I did," Walter said. "I saw her go into the orchard with her boyfriend. And I might have seen her again later, at sunset."

"What?" She looked at her notes. Furiously trying to see if she'd written that down after looking at the police report, but she hadn't. She knew she hadn't.

"Yeah. She went off into the orchard with the boy. And then I saw her walking on the road later."

"The police report says the orchard was the last time you saw her."

"Well, I saw them, and then I went out back to do some work. I came back inside to make some supper. I saw someone. Walking along the road and into Sentinel Bridge."

"You didn't tell the police?"

"I was never sure it was her. Although… In the years since, I've made it her in my mind. Not sure that's the case."

"And you didn't update your statement."

"There was no new information to be gotten from that."

"If she wasn't with Nathan Brewer," Carter said, speaking for the first time, "then that means she could have encountered someone else."

Walter shook his head. "No. It was Nathan Brewer. I'm sure of that."

"What makes you so sure?"

"That whole family… They're a bunch of bad seeds. John Brewer was as mean as a snake. It was a miracle that his wife stayed with him as long as she did."

Dahlia frowned. "You knew he abused her?"

Walter nodded. "I saw things, like I said. She was a sad woman. I suspect, like a lot of those women, she was afraid she'd get killed if she left. And would she have been wrong? That poor Caitlin Groves was trying to leave the Brewer boy.

And he did to her just what his daddy would have done to his mother had she ever tried to make a break for it." He sighed. "I have some sympathy. You may not think so. I know what it does to you. To see violence. Well, I see things sometimes. I have. Ever since I got back from the war. Like ghosts. Maybe you shouldn't take what I say too seriously. That I think I saw her again. It might not have been her. It might've been a trick of the light. Like I said, I see things." He got a hollow look in his eye and looked past Dahlia, and she swallowed hard.

"If it was her..." she pressed. "If it was her walking into the bridge, she was alone."

"She seemed to be," he said. "But I didn't think anything of it. There was no missing person at the time, and everyone is free to walk on the road as they see fit. And at the time, I didn't think who it was. Just someone walking. It was only later... Way after I talked to the police that I wondered. That I even wondered if I wasn't just hungry and tired. It's not unusual to see people on the road." He rubbed his hand over his thinning hair, and Dahlia noticed a tremor. "I think it's time for you to go."

Dahlia exchanged a glance with Carter.

"Thank you for your time," Carter said, shaking the older man's hand, and Dahlia did the same.

When they were back outside and safely in the patrol car, Dahlia nearly exploded. "If he saw Caitlin Groves after he said he did in the police report..."

"She still isn't found," Carter said. "There were no clues anywhere in the vicinity. This entire area was searched. The assumption was made that if she went back to town she went via Sentinel Bridge. It was searched."

"But still. She could have encountered someone else."

"It doesn't change anything. We can't confirm it."

"The case isn't closed," Dahlia said.

"No," he said. "But I didn't think you were doing investigative journalism."

"I'm not. I mean... I don't feel qualified to. But that... It gave me chills all over."

"And you know, alternately, he's a ninety-five-year-old man who may not have a great grasp on something that happened twenty-three years ago."

"I know. But it's the possibility. That there's information out there that your father didn't have."

"The case isn't closed. If there were ever any real leads, any new pieces of evidence, you can guarantee that I would investigate it immediately."

"I know," she said.

"You say that with a lot of confidence. You know, for a woman who just reintroduced herself to me the other day when she came into the police station."

"Yeah, well. I guess... I trust you. On that level. You... Um... I don't know if you..."

"The day you yelled at the JV football team for being a bunch of dicks and throwing rocks at Dana Groves' house? Yeah, I remember."

"Oh," she said.

There was no sound in the car for a moment. Nothing but the engine, the tires meeting the road, the air coming through the vents. And it felt oppressively quiet.

She took a breath. "Yeah, thank—"

"I always thought you had guts, Dahlia McKee," he said. "And I admired that. A hell of a lot."

She felt *overheated*.

He was a cop. He wasn't a duke.

He wasn't Mr. Darcy.

And yet somehow it felt like a Darcy moment. Heated longing and yearning she couldn't quite explain.

"Well, thank you, I... I mean I was glad you weren't...them. I was thankful you stood up for her."

"It was you," he said. "I stood up for you."

Dahlia looked out the window, her palms suddenly sweaty.

Carter cleared his throat. "I could go down to Sentinel Bridge right now and do a search. For evidence. For something that would indicate... But it's been twenty-three years. We know she was around here. But other than Nathan Brewer, no one else was seen that night."

"Did you know that John Brewer was abusive?"

He looked past her. "There were rumors. But you know how it is. People talked, and that's what it was. Talk."

"Your dad never arrested him?"

"I've never talked to my dad about him. If he could have, he would have. Trust me, Dahlia. My dad hates men who hurt women, who hurt anyone. But rumors aren't evidence."

No. Of course not. But rumors had been enough to convict Nathan Brewer in the eyes of the town, and it was possible his dad's reputation had played into that.

The sins of the father...

"Thanks for driving me up here."

"No problem. It's the closest thing I've had to a date in..."

"Are you... Are you hitting on me?" She could not believe that, and moreover she could not believe she had asked.

"Well, I wasn't intentionally. But if I were..."

"Are you allowed to hit on someone while in a cop car?"

"No one's ever told me I can't."

"Is your divorce finalized?"

He drew back. "Yes. And... I'd rather not talk about it."

"Sure."

"Let me ask you something, Dahlia."

"I just tried to ask you something, and you said you didn't want to talk about it."

"And if you don't want to talk about it, then you can say so."

"Okay. Fair. Ask away."

He paused before he spoke, and she didn't have the sense he was hesitant. Just that he was waiting.

"Why do you still live in Pear Blossom?"

She hadn't expected that. "Um...my parents?"

"No. I don't think so. Why the *Pear Blossom Gazette*? You just always seemed...you seemed like the kind of girl who was bigger than here. I was shocked when I pulled you over that day, because I was shocked you were here. Even more shocked to see you had a local address."

"I thought about going other places," she said, looking out the window and trying to ignore how scratchy her eyes felt. No one had ever asked her this before. "But nothing felt...like this. And I couldn't shake that there was something here I wanted to do."

"Is this it?"

"I think so," she said. But for some reason it was a whisper.

"Why?"

"I want to..." The words got jumbled up in her throat.

I want to be special.

How sad was that? She wanted to be special, like Ruby. Ruby, who was special by the virtue of her existence.

Something Dahlia hadn't been given. And something she... Wanted. More than she'd realized.

"I just want to contribute something. I'm not a news story, Carter. But I can tell these stories. It's my...it's my gift."

They let conversation stop after that, but it wasn't uncomfortable.

He smelled amazing, and she wished she hadn't noticed that.

She had other things to think about. She was going to focus on writing up Walter Berryman's story.

And she was going to do her best not to obsess about the additional detail regarding Caitlin.

Or just how handsome Carter Swenson looked in a uniform.

Or why it made her heart feel too full that he'd asked why she stayed.

19

Grand Opening

The Grand Opening of Pear Blossom Market will be held Saturday, October 15, 1985 2 PM to 5 PM. Community BBQ! Hot dogs .50, Soda .25, Tri Tip sandwich, $1.50.

RUBY

A week after Thanksgiving and the fridge was still full of pie. Not for lack of trying on her and Dahlia's part. They were dedicated to their dessert eating, but often ate out during the week, or got takeout. And the pie was starting to eat at her, rather than her eating the pie.

That's not the problem.

No, she knew it wasn't.

She was restless. She had been restless ever since her encounter with Nathan on the anniversary of Caitlin's disappearance. Whether it made sense or not. She should be focused on getting the displays together at the museum. She still needed to stop by the church and go through the costumes. Dahlia's first article—about the pear industry in town, and the displays at the museum—had done a lot to increase the foot traffic in the museum, and she was grateful for that. Dahlia had also told her about her trip to interview Walter Berryman, and what the older man had said about the night Caitlin had disappeared. And it had got her thinking about Nathan again.

As if you stopped.

She ignored that thought. And before she could fully contemplate what she was doing, she was in the fridge getting out a piece of pie. And then she took that pie, stuck it on the passenger seat of her car and began to drive toward Nathan's house. It was really not a very smart idea, but then, Ruby wasn't known for smart ideas. Impulsive ones, certainly. And sometimes they panned out. She might just leave the pie on the doorstep. That seemed like not the worst idea.

There was a truck there, parked in front of the residence, and she had a feeling that meant he was there. And she couldn't resist the temptation. She walked up the front steps and knocked on the door.

And when he jerked it open, taller and broader than she remembered, his dark hair looking like he'd been running his fingers through it, her stomach did something strange. "Hi," she said.

"You actually came here this time? Running into each other out and about wasn't enough?" His tone was dry, his smile sardonic.

"I wanted to see how you were. And I brought you pie."

"You brought me pie?"

"Well, I was worried about you. It's just that you told me you didn't have anyone else. No one for me to call when I…"

"That wasn't my finest moment," he said. "Maybe let's not revisit it."

"That's fine," she said. "We don't have to revisit it. But I… Well, I assume that you were alone for Thanksgiving."

"You assume right."

"And I… I thought that someone ought to be in charge of making sure you get a little bit of pumpkin pie."

"You don't even know if I like pie."

"What kind of monster doesn't like pie?"

"A whole lot of people think I'm a monster, Ruby. Maybe you should take a hint."

Maybe she should.

Maybe.

But it made her really wonder... Why. Was there a monster in her too?

There might be.

People thought she was a miracle, but you didn't leave a miracle on a bridge in the middle of winter. A monster, maybe.

Maybe there was darkness in her. And it liked his.

She had never considered that before.

It made her feel breathless. Excited.

If she wasn't all glitter and sunshine... If she didn't have to be...

He walked away from the door, but he didn't close it. He left it wide-open, and she took that as an invitation to come right on inside. She held the pie out, and he just looked at her.

"What's your deal?" he asked.

She shook her head. "I don't have a deal."

"You clearly have a deal."

"All right, if you want to know. I was found on Sentinel Bridge when I was a baby. And every time I start digging into my past, *you* come up."

"Wait, back up."

"To what part?" She went ahead and took two steps forward, all but shoving the pie into his hand. "Go eat the pie."

Surprisingly, he complied, making his way to the couch and sitting down, picking up the pie in his hand and taking a bite. "It's good."

"Which part did you need me to back up to?"

"The part where you were found on a bridge."

She looked at him. Just stared. Because... It hadn't occurred to her that he wouldn't know about her. He knew she was a

McKee. But that was based on where the house was. Maybe he really didn't know. From what she'd pieced together in news reports, he'd been arrested three months after Caitlin disappeared and had spent two years in jail being held before trial. And then... She wasn't sure that he'd ever lived back in town.

"One year after Caitlin disappeared, I was found on Sentinel Bridge. And I get a lot of credit for being... Some kind of magical healing glue for the town. In the same way that you're painted as kind of a villain, I'm painted as a hero."

And they lingered in her throat, those words. And burned. She had been happy to accept that mantle. Had been thrilled by her coronation and hadn't ever looked at... At the ways others had been treated.

"How nice for you," he said.

"No, that's not why I'm saying it."

"You got found on a bridge?"

"Yes."

"Sentinel Bridge."

She nodded in affirmation. "I did. I don't know anyone from here who doesn't just... Know that."

"Well, no one here talks to me, and if you were found a year after..."

"I know. I know you were in prison."

"Why aren't you afraid of me?"

"Maybe for the same reason you aren't impressed by me. Maybe it's because I don't really know what it was like. That time. I get the feeling that everybody was... Emotionally scarred by it. Like they all felt as if their safe world was upended. My world has always felt safe. For all that I was found on a bridge, I was found. And my mom always told me I was saved for a reason. So maybe I've always felt... A little bulletproof."

He looked at her for a long moment, and there was an intensity to his gaze that made her shiver. "You just look like a girl to me."

"Well, the town will tell you I'm a very special girl, Nathan." She laughed at her own words. "Think about that. They think I'm a miracle, but I think you're right. I'm just a woman. And that means maybe you're just a man."

He shoved the last bite of pie into his mouth. "Thanks for the pie."

"You're welcome."

She waited. Waited for him to... Something.

"What?"

"Am I also going to be thanked for not running you over the other day?"

"I told you. Not my finest moment."

"Can you... Can you tell me. Can you tell me what happened when she disappeared?"

"I've told people," he said. "Exhaustively. Under oath. I don't have any interest in talking about it. Ever again."

"But it..." She shifted. "It haunts you."

He laughed, a bitter sound, and set the plate down on the coffee table. "Yes. It haunts me. And the ghosts in this fucking house are a whole lot more intense than I anticipated. No, that's not an admission of anything. My father was an asshole."

"Oh."

"And he... Oh, he loved to shove in my face that I was a *murderer*. He believed it. At least, he said he did. I don't think he did. I just think he liked the idea that maybe I was worse than he was. So I couldn't be so holier-than-thou about the fact that he used my mother for a punching bag."

"Nathan... I'm sorry."

"No. You don't need to be sorry." He looked around the room, and her gaze followed his. It made sense now, the way it had been stripped of personality. The way all memorabilia was gone. He wasn't trying to remember what life had been like here. Not even a little.

"Maybe I don't. But I am still."

"Caitlin was my girlfriend. I loved her. The way that a fifteen-year-old idiot can love another fifteen-year-old. This idea that I was some kind of crazy, jealous lover... We were *fifteen*."

"Well, things are intense when you're fifteen," Ruby said.

"Yeah, that's what I was told. By every cop who interviewed me. It's okay, kid, everybody gets upset when their girlfriend breaks up with them. When they find out they're more in love than their girlfriend. I bet that made you angry. Did it make you angry enough to hurt her?" He shook his head. "What bullshit."

"You weren't breaking up," Ruby said.

"No. And even if we were... It wasn't like that. Look, I can never know what my life would've been. Ever. It was changed completely that day. But one thing I'm pretty sure of is that Caitlin Groves would not have been a part of my life forever, even if she hadn't of disappeared. It was a regular fifteen-year-old romance. First love kind of stuff. There was nothing jealous or crazy or anything like that about it."

"You weren't sleeping with her?"

His expression went hard. "We were fifteen."

"Fifteen-year-olds have sex," Ruby said. "Or so I'm told."

"Well, we didn't. We weren't."

The full implication of that settled like acid in her stomach. What he was describing was something completely different than what she'd imagined based on the story everyone had built around it. Because of course passion had to be at the center of the decision to murder someone who wanted to leave you. But all of that was made up. And if what he was saying was true, it was just an entirely different thing.

"You were just a kid," she said.

He had been painted as somebody violent. More man than boy. But now she wondered.

Just a boy.

Like he'd said she was just a girl.

Neither one the myth they'd been made into.

He suddenly looked tired. Exhausted. And every year between then and now was apparent on his face. The cost of each
and every one of them. "I was. But it changed. Quickly. I had
never been in any trouble. And then... I lost my girlfriend. I
got arrested. I was taken away from home. And then there was
no home to go back to. And my home was never a walk in the
park, Ruby. What I'll say for Caitlin Groves is she was about the
only nice thing I ever had in my life. And of all the things that
were taken from me... My memory of her is one of the things
I resent the most. Because now I can't think of her without remembering what happened after. I forget that I cared about her,
because it makes me think that maybe I just hate her. For having the nerve to disappear when I was the last person anyone
knew she was with. I wondered for a long time if she ran away.
She ran away and she just didn't care that I was being blamed."

"Do you still think that?"

"If she didn't run away, then somebody else did something
to her. A stranger or... Someone in town."

"That's why they need to believe it was you, you know. They
need a symbol. Otherwise... The danger is still out there."

"I'm well aware." He sighed heavily. "You know, that's the
strangest thing of all. I think if she'd...stayed, our relationship
would have run its course. Nothing dramatic. I wouldn't think
of her much, but when I did I'd smile. I certainly wouldn't be
drinking myself half to death over her. Her disappearance...it
changed everything."

"Nathan..."

"Thanks for the pie."

That was as loud as any dismissal could ever be.

"All right." She picked up her plate and edged toward the door.
And for some reason she didn't want to go. She didn't understand
why she felt connected to this man. Why she felt for him at all.
But she did. It wasn't just because he was handsome and mysterious. Yes, she was prone to that sort of thing, or she always had

been in her fantasies. But he was a lot more real, a lot more dangerous feeling than some mad duke in her fantasies, or a man with a house out on the wild moors and a crazy wife in his attic.

She might be imaginative about things like that, but she also knew the difference between that and reality. This was real. And it was sticky. And dangerous.

"Take care," she said, because it seemed maybe more definitive than goodbye, which could mean for now. She was telling herself she needed to say goodbye. Because it would be better. It would be easier.

She backed out the door and went back to her car. It was dark.

When she got back to the cottage, Dahlia was already there, and she did not tell Dahlia where she had been.

"The pie is gone," Dahlia muttered, backing out of the fridge.

"Sorry," Ruby said, offering no explanation or excuse.

"You're lucky I love you," Dahlia said.

"For a variety of reasons. But, yeah, that you might not kill me for eating the pie is definitely among them."

"I think Carter Swenson hit on me," Dahlia said.

Ruby let the events of this afternoon fade away. "Really?"

"Yes."

"This is the chance to live out your secret shame-filled high school fantasies. You should get in there," Ruby said.

"I did not have shame-fueled fantasies, Rubes."

"You did. You fully did."

"Regardless, I've never been a *get in there* kind of girl."

"Well, you should try it," Ruby said, pragmatically. "I tried it."

"And what was your conclusion?"

Ruby scrunched her face. "I don't know."

"See? You don't even know."

"It was different. Different than Heath. Who was—until I left—the only person I'd ever been with."

"Right," Dahlia said.

"It was different to be in a relationship. And different to not be in one. It was an interesting journey of self-discovery. And I felt... I don't know. There was something about not feeling accountable to anybody that made it feel exciting. And like I was free. So that was fun. I'm not going to say it was satisfying every time..."

"But I can't have a fling with Carter and not be accountable. He could write me a ticket at any moment."

"Not if you don't... Speed."

"Or worse, we could spot each other in public. Like...when I'm with Dad or something. I can't avoid him, this town is too small."

"You didn't do anything like that in college?"

Dahlia shook her head. "I mean, not that I didn't have relationships. I just didn't do casual sex. I always have terrible relationships. Because I tend to gravitate toward the hipster intellectual guys who like to prove how smart they are, and usually that takes the shape of being insecure, which often ends up with them being derogatory about my intellect."

"They sound swell. Maybe you should date the jock."

"He's *divorced*," Dahlia said.

"So?"

Dahlia shifted, looking away uncomfortably. "I don't know. Would that not bother you?"

Ruby frowned. "I don't know. But then, I haven't ever thought in terms of what I want long term. You know, other than a duke with a crumbling manor house."

"Obviously."

"Anyway, that's not what we were talking about. We were talking about flings. What does it matter if he's divorced if it's just a fling?"

"I don't know," Dahlia said. "Except he was married to Lena, and she was this mesmerizing, beautiful cheerleader when I was in school, and you don't remember, because they were older."

"So you won't make a move on him because he was married to a pretty girl."

"He married *the* pretty girl. And I don't want to be his foray into trying something new. It feels reductive."

"But he's really hot," Ruby pointed out.

"Okay, I regret bringing this up. Let's go back to talking about history."

Ruby laughed. But she was relieved that Dahlia had led the conversation. Because it was all making her think of… Whatever this thing was that was happening with Nathan.

He would probably say nothing. He had been eager to get rid of her. In fairness, she was becoming a little bit of a bad penny that he couldn't lose. But she wasn't the one who had run in front of his car drunk.

"I just don't like the idea of being second," Dahlia said. "Is it so much to wish that somewhere out there is a guy who would choose me first. And best."

"No. There's nothing wrong with that."

They did move on to discussing their various projects after that, and when Ruby went to bed, her mind was still full of Nathan.

But when she went to sleep, it was the dream again.

Just the same as it had been for weeks.

She was standing in front of the bridge. Terror was tightening her throat. But she had to go inside. She was compelled to. She stopped at the mouth of the bridge and looked up, saw lights on in a house up on the hill. And then she took a step into the bridge, the darkness consuming her. And there was some force, some force compelling her through the bridge. Out to the other side. But once she was out the other side, she didn't go toward town.

Instead, she turned and stumbled toward the river.

20

Chase had the nerve to ask me how I'll know if Mac is the one if I never have another boyfriend. He says he'll have a hundred girl-friends, and then when he's in love he'll be sure. He's the most an-noying boy on the face of the earth, and he probably will have a hundred girlfriends because he's handsome, and girls are that stupid.

LYDIA MCKEE'S DIARY, AGE 15

LYDIA

Lydia didn't particularly feel like taking Ruby up on her invi-tation to bring the kids to the museum. Mostly because at this point in time facing her sisters wasn't something she wanted to do. She had been putting her head down, and being as attentive a mother as she could be. Not because she was so amazing, but more because it was easier to focus on Riley and Hazel than it was to focus on what had happened between Chase and herself.

She had told him everything.

He had kissed her.

And that was just something that she couldn't... She honestly could not wrap her head around. Or begin to deal with. She felt like a walking knot of resentment. Resentment at Mac. Resent-ment at the past. At the present. Resentment at Chase, because she had been so irritated with him being around, and then for all that, she realized that she had come to depend on him. And his kiss had rocked the foundation that she was standing on, no matter how she had pretended that it was reluctant. No matter how she had convinced herself that it was reluctant. She didn't know what to do now. She didn't know… Anything. But she had promised the kids that they would go down to the museum. She had promised Ruby that she would come check out the exhibit.

She met Marianne at Spruce Coffee, along with Hunter, who was just as excited about the museum as Riley and Hazel, though, as a preteen, was dedicated to pretending that he wasn't. Because a general store display was not supposed to be exciting when one was twelve years old.

"I need a triple shot," Marianne said. "I am dragging."

"Me too," Lydia said. "Where is Ava?"

Marianne sighed. "She is at home in bed and she didn't want to come out with us and sullen door slam."

Lydia gave her sister a sympathetic look—at least, she hoped it was sympathetic.

She hadn't been sleeping. She had been avoiding Chase like the plague, even when he came over to do work. It was just a mess.

"You okay?"

"You always ask me that. What about you?"

"I don't know. I… I thought I was fine," Marianne said.

They got their coffee and walked out of the coffee shop, a brisk breeze picking up and blowing leaves across the brick sidewalk in front of them. The kids started ahead, hopping up on cement curbs and the tops of tree planters. In general making a ruckus, as they should do. It gave them time to talk.

"You thought you were okay?"

"Yeah." She did not look okay.

As a teenager, Marianne had been completely closed off. But she'd changed since then. Meeting Jackson had changed her.

She'd talked of escaping and acted like living in a small town was prison, but she'd never said anything like that since meeting him. But this... Her hesitance. It reminded Lydia more of how Marianne used to be.

Marianne closed her eyes. "Jackson lied to me the other day," Marianne said. "And since then I've been paying extra close attention to everything he does. He's on his phone a lot."

"Marianne," Lydia said, feeling shocked down to her soul. "Jackson wouldn't... You don't think Jackson would cheat on you."

"No," Marianne said. "That's what's so scary about it. I don't. I trust him completely. But then I asked him... A simple thing. And I could see that he was texting a woman. And he told me that he'd been asleep. He didn't know I was standing behind him... *Julie.* He never talks about a Julie. And I know everyone in his life. I thought that I did. That's what's so scary. When you think you have complete transparency, and now I wonder if we do."

Lydia had no idea what a marriage with total transparency was like. Hers was full of brick walls and no-go areas. Places where neither of them dared to tread.

Mac could've had a whole secret life and she wouldn't have known. She wouldn't have asked.

"Marianne, it's not like you to not say something. Directly to him."

"I know. That's the other thing. This isn't like me, or like us. But things with Ava have been stressing me out, and I'm mad at him because I don't need to deal with this on top of it, and I don't want to. I'm just... I don't know what to do."

"Don't hold it in," Lydia said. She took a sip of her coffee. Spicy and polished like the weather outside. But it didn't do its job making her feel warm.

"I shouldn't talk to you about this. I mean..."

"Why? Because my husband is dead so you're not allowed

to complain about yours? That's not reasonable. Anyway, I was married for a long time. You've been married for a long time. Something we have in common. If we can't talk about it, Marianne, then we're not going to be able to have a relationship. At least not like the one we had."

And Lydia hadn't realized that she was holding that in. She hadn't even realized that she thought that. But it turned out she did. It was just frustrating. Infuriating. And half of it was her own fault. It wasn't all because Marianne was being careful with her. It was because she herself had closed off. Because she didn't know how to talk about this.

She felt like people had expectations of how she should feel and what she should do and it made her want to show them nothing.

And so much of this crushing feeling inside of her chest had to do with just being lonely. All these walls that were up, keeping her sisters out. Keeping everyone out.

"I'm sorry," Marianne said. "I wasn't trying to do that. I just don't want to make you sad."

"Well, I'm sad. And it's complicated. And some of… Some of me being kind of mean and keeping things to myself and not dealing with the kids…not dealing with anything…is just me. And no one can take the blame for that. It's just me."

"What's wrong?"

"We are talking about you," Lydia said.

"Yes, but that doesn't mean we can't talk about you."

"Yeah, but… Talk to Jackson. I didn't talk to Mac." Lydia felt something in her chest shift. A burden she hadn't known was there, weighing her down. "When I was feeling lonely, when I was feeling upset, when I was feeling afraid. I didn't know how to talk to him."

It felt so good to say that out loud.

To admit that to her sister.

"You were with him from the time you were thirteen. You always seemed like you talked."

"We did. About little things. And we acted like we were in the same relationship that we had begun when we were thirteen years old, and not the one that we needed to have as adults. As parents to two children. As two people who started going in different directions and didn't know what to do with it. We needed to sit down and get on the same page. And we just didn't."

"Lydia, I had no idea that you and Mac had any problems."

"I know. Which is not an accident. I can't get into all of it now. I just can't." It was way too much, and right now, it was mixed in with Chase and the kiss, and she couldn't separate it, and she really couldn't deal with that just now. "But what I can tell you is keeping all this kind of stuff pushed down... It doesn't help. Secrets are the ultimate fuel for resentment. They grow it. Feed it. Foster it. And it's resentment that you can't get past. When that person that you're supposed to be in love with becomes a flashpoint for your anger. When kissing them feels like a chore instead of an expression of love. That's what you can't get past. Don't ever let it get there."

"What if I don't like the answer to the questions? What if I don't like the end result of the confrontation?"

"You might not. But if there's something going on, then you have to face it. It won't go away just because you ignore it. I guess that's my point. Take it from me. The champion of trying to ignore things until they go away."

And it occurred to her then that she was doing it again with Chase. Ignoring what had happened between them and hoping it would go away. Avoiding him and hoping it would go away. Not coping. Not facing it head-on. Just not doing anything.

"I know that," Marianne said. The museum came into sight, and they were both conscious that they needed to change the subject soon. "I do know that. That we are going to have to talk about it. That I'm going to have to confront him."

"And maybe it's nothing."

".Then he'll get mad at me."

"Is it really that bad to know that your wife thinks that you could sleep with someone else if you wanted to? I mean, jealousy is kind of a compliment, isn't it?"

"Except when it comes to, you know, the trust that we are supposed to have in each other. And we never fight. Never."

"Marriage is long and things change. And a whole lot of issues come from making assumptions. So it's just better to not make them. It's better to get them all out in the open. I assume. I have experience with the assumptions, and not so much with successfully resolving them by sharing."

"We need to talk sometime," Marianne said, pausing at the very bottom cement step of the museum. "Really talk."

"Yeah," Lydia said. "We do." She swallowed hard. "Do you ever feel like your life is a book? And you just wish you could skip back a few pages to make some sense of where you're at now?" She swallowed again. "I feel like I'm in the middle of the story, and I'm terrified of how it's going to end. And I can't even begin to make sense of all the things that have come before it."

"Who's writing the story?"

She laughed. "I have no idea."

The kids exploded up the steps and through the front door of the museum, and Lydia winced. Because she could see Dana Groves sitting at the front desk, and she had a feeling that the older woman did not take kindly to kids running around like the museum was a gymnasium.

She hadn't seen Ruby since their awkward Thanksgiving fight that hadn't ended up being much of a fight and she didn't know if it would be tense between them now.

But thankfully, Ruby appeared, smiling in greeting. Lydia was happy to let it go on that way. "I'm so glad you're here," she said. "Let me show you the new display."

She shepherded her niece and nephews into the next room,

where there was a brilliant display set up. A counter with a cash register, all manner of old-fashioned labels printed out and wrapped around tin cans, big flour sacks full of... Well, maybe it was really flour.

"Ruby," Marianne said. "This is amazing."

"It has been very popular," Ruby said. "I'm thrilled that we were able to get it put together. There were some set pieces that I was able to borrow from the community theater. And the kids are just loving it."

The kids had already gotten aprons, and Riley had grabbed a broom and was sweeping the floor.

"He doesn't do that at home," Lydia said.

"It's good to see them play."

"He's been better lately." And Lydia would be lying if she didn't admit that deep down somewhere she was missing her partner in seriousness. As much as she wanted him to be liberated from the grief of losing his father, and as much as she knew that would be a lifelong issue, part of her just wished that...

You can't confide in your kids. You have to be an adult and have real conversations with the grown-ups around you.

That was sobering. And there were adults in her life, it was just that they were going to require details about her marriage— that much was apparent by the conversation she just had with Marianne. And probably eventually she was going to have to deal with Chase. Reckon with him.

She was so desperate to skip ahead a few pages and see where this was all going.

But somehow, she knew that it was uncharted territory, and she just didn't know if she had the wherewithal to take more new on.

"How are your other displays coming?" Marianne asked.

"Come see. It's still under construction, but I'm getting there with this section on war in Pear Blossom."

"How...holiday appropriate," Marianne said.

"Okay, it's not overly cheery. But Dahlia went and talked to Walter Berryman the other day. And he had some really interesting insights into how that affected the town. Can you imagine... Just... All those young men leaving? It must've been so obvious here. The hole it left must have been so profound. And the losses must've felt so personal."

Perhaps Lydia would find it more interesting if she didn't feel like she was neck-deep in the particular issues that came with living in a small town. The endless connections that she had to her late husband. And the way that she cared about the people who cared about him. And all right, maybe she never needed to tell his mother that she had been planning on divorcing her son. She genuinely loved her mother-in-law. And she knew that she was lucky to be able to say that. A lot of people didn't. But she'd known Sylvia for the better part of her life, and as Ruby's caseworker, the woman had been an instrumental part of bringing Ruby into their family. All of that time was tightly wound with her marriage. With that relationship.

Why was Chase never particularly close to you?

She didn't know the answer to that. All she knew was that when she thought his name, her lips burned, and she didn't particularly care for that revelation.

"Are you actually going to do a museum display about you?" Lydia asked. She really wanted to change the subject. Just in her own brain.

Ruby looked appalled. "No. I'm going to go ahead and skip the museum display on the more recent events in town. Honestly, can you imagine? It would be like building a statue of myself." She made a gagging sound. "I could erect a replica of the bridge, and put a little baby doll on it. Kids could practice rescuing me."

"Don't say that," Lydia said, "because now I'm starting to think it's a good idea."

"Oh, it's so grim," Ruby said. Her sister lapsed off somewhere, and Lydia didn't know where.

"What?" Lydia asked Ruby.

"Nothing." Except she looked like she had something she wanted to say. And Lydia could relate to that, because it was about where she was at too.

"What's grim?" Dahlia walked in wearing a black beanie, a black hoodie and black skinny jeans, looking every inch the little dark heart she'd been in high school.

"Ruby is talking about making a display of herself abandoned as a baby," Marianne said. "It is in very poor taste."

"Extremely poor," Ruby agreed.

"I like it," Dahlia said.

"So, Marianne and I were trying this thing earlier," Lydia said. "Where we were honest with each other about things."

"That sounds terrible," Ruby replied, grinning.

"It is," Marianne agreed, looking angrily at Lydia. It was clear that Marianne didn't exactly want to get into her marital issues in front of Ruby. Which was fine. She wasn't going to drag Marianne into it.

And while she stood there at the display with all of her sisters, she realized that it was her fault they were so careful with her. They couldn't read her because she wouldn't let them.

Marianne almost hadn't shared her issues because she hadn't realized Lydia could relate.

If Lydia felt distant… It was her own fault. And she needed to do something about it.

Eyes still on the display in front of her, she finally spoke the truth. "I was going to divorce him."

They all stared at her. Shocked, as she knew they would be.

"You were going to divorce… *Mac*?" Ruby asked.

"Yes."

"Our brother, Mac?" Ruby asked, and that question just about gutted Lydia.

"Yeah, well, he was your brother. He was my husband. And I… I wasn't in love with him anymore."

"Lydia…" Marianne looked shell-shocked, even with the hints Lydia had dropped earlier.

"I had… I had a plan. The farm would've gone to me, because of the way the loan was set up. Everything was in my name because of my credit history versus his. I was going to offer to let him continue to work on it, but I wanted to have a say in how everything went. And what we did. I wanted to do a farm store. The same as I'm doing now. He had been opposed to that in the past. And that's why it's taken me so long to do it now. I… I've been trapped. Trying to grieve in a way that looked like I was grieving for my husband, who I loved. And I did love him. I *did* love him."

"I had no idea," Dahlia said. "You seemed so happy together."

Lydia laughed, because how could she do anything else. It was so absurd, all this. All of this stuff she'd hidden for so long. "What does that mean? It just meant we weren't fighting in front of anyone. We didn't fight that much at home. But it was mostly because we didn't talk. We didn't share a life. He and I started building a foundation back when we were kids, and we just didn't know how to make something better and stronger from there. We carried over all the dumb, immature things that you start out with when you're experimenting with love. With sex. And we never went further from there. And people can. But they have to talk," she said to Marianne. "When you marry somebody, it's forever. And I've had so much time to think about that since he died. So much time to have one-sided conversations about the marriage that I wish we would've been brave enough to have. But instead I was just tied up in knots and ready to quit. Not ready to make compromises. Not ready to have conversations. And you know what? Now he's gone and there are no compromises to be made. So now I can just have whatever it is I want. And I want the farm store. But I have to wonder what I would've had if it had gone differently. I don't know. And I can never know. I just feel bound up in all this guilt."

And resentment. And anger at Chase. And fear over what the kiss meant. And her response.

Because if she was learning one thing about herself, it was that she had a dedicated center inside of her that seemed determined and resolute in keeping her defenses up. Keeping the truth from others, keeping the truth even from herself.

"I was more married to a story than I was to Mac in the end. To the idea that what we had could have been good. That it could be what you all thought it was. But it didn't help anyone or anything. And it's not helping me now. It's just keeping me trapped. And I don't want to be trapped anymore."

"You don't have to be trapped," Dahlia said. "He's gone."

"I don't mean it that way. He wasn't terrible. I'm sorry that he's gone. I didn't hate him. It's just... I couldn't divorce him after he got diagnosed. I couldn't do that." She sighed. "He was my friend. Before he was my husband. And I hoped that someday we'd get back there. And you know... In a lot of ways, while he was sick it was better. It was better because..." And then she unknotted the deepest knot inside of her heart, and she just sort of let her shame flow out. "I knew that it would end. That I didn't have to do it. I was afraid that I would be trapped for a long time. But..."

"Oh, Lydia," Ruby said, wrapping her arms around her.

Lydia gasped, the unexpected sob expanding in her chest. "I am a terrible person. I was so sorry when he died. I was so sorry." Tears began to fall down her cheeks, and she hoped that her kids didn't come in here, because she was having the breakdown that she had never once allowed herself. In front of her sisters. In a public museum. Standing in front of a display about World War II. About people with real problems. Who had engaged in real sacrifice, for their country, for the people around them. And she was just having a breakdown becuase she might be selfish. Because she was selfish. She knew she was. There was no *maybe* about it.

No *might* about anything. She was flawed. And she had... At her darkest moments seen her husband's sickness as her way out. As her way to stay innocent in the dissolution of their marriage. And she had gotten to play the part of martyr.

Had gotten to stay and be good.

Even though nothing that was going on inside of her was right or good. And Chase had kissed her. And fundamentally she was bitter and angry at Chase because he was a better, more loyal person than she would ever be. Because he was... He was at least a real friend. A real brother. And who was she?

What was she?

"I'm just not who anyone thinks I am," Lydia said. "And my marriage wasn't what anyone thought it was. And I'm not good, and I'm not suffering."

"You are," Dahlia said, grabbing hold of her face and holding it steady. "This is grief, Lydia. And it doesn't matter if it's grief over a man that you loved like a husband, or just grief over the hole that got torn in your life and the mess that you were left to clean up. It is still grief. And it is still real. And you were not a bad person just because you fell out of love with him. People fall out of love every day. You just had the bad luck of getting caught in an end, in a tragedy that nobody asked for. It doesn't matter if you were relieved sometimes. It doesn't matter that in dark moments you tried to find something that you could... Something that you could hang meaning on. You were the one that had to deal with what was left behind."

"Oh, Dahlia," Lydia said. "I love you. I love you because you are a little bit dark, and a little bit horrible like me. And, Ruby, I love you because you're bright and sunny, and I know that nothing I say is going to make you think that I'm a bad person. Marianne, you have a husband, please tell me that I'm awful. And I will love you for that."

"You're not awful," Marianne said. "So if you have to hate me because I won't play into your self-loathing, then so be it. Everything just sucks about this, Lydia. You couldn't have stopped it. Nobody could have. Nobody knew that he was going to get ALS. Nobody knew that he was going to get pneumonia and die. Nobody knew that the boy you fell in love with was going to become a man that you didn't want to live with, least of all you. It is not your fault. I feel terrible that Mac's life was cut short. And I loved him too. He was family. But you're the one that's left to make sense of it. You have his children. You could feel whatever way you want to about it, and you don't have to put on a show for us. And you don't have to feel guilty about the ways that you figured out how to cope with it. Yeah, it's messy. But I guess life is messy and there's just... Nothing we can do about it no matter how much we wish there was."

Lydia gasped and tried to catch her breath. Tried to reclaim her balance. But it was gone. It was all gone.

"I don't know how to cope. Even when I'm not grieving him as a husband, it's... He was a piece of me. I don't know what to do with this new shape of my life. I don't know how to explain that what I wanted was to not be married to him, and I'm still unsure of what to do now that I'm not. I don't know how to reconcile the tragedy of what happened with the strange things that pop up sometimes. About how I don't have to share custody. About how we don't have to worry about dividing things up. Of course I didn't want him to die. Of course I didn't. But he did, right?"

"Lydia, it doesn't matter what you say. It can be ugly, and it can be messed up, there has to be a place for that. There has to be a place for truth with us. Messed up, messy truth." Marianne grimaced. "And after that speech, I guess I have to deal with truth in my life too."

"What?" Ruby and Dahlia asked.

"It's not important," Marianne said. "Not right now. Let's

just… Let's focus on Lydia. Who I know hates that. You haven't let us focus on you at all. You haven't shared any of this. You've just been closing it all down and trying to go on. But of course it's impossible. This is impossible to hold on to all by yourself."

"No," Ruby said. "You shouldn't have to hold on to it yourself. You're not a story, Lydia. You're a person. A whole person. And we don't need you to be a perfect story—we need you to be you. And in the meantime, we are here to hold on to you."

And so they did. Right there, in the middle of the museum.

21

The War Abroad Begets Unity at Home

BY JOHN HARDY

MAY 8, 1946—We are not left untouched by the trials of war, just as before. But what we see here is not a splintering, rather a knitting together. As the town cares for one another, comforts the grieving, feeds the hungry and aids the sick, in the darkest of times, humanity at home is shining brightest.

DAHLIA

Dahlia still felt fragile after her time in the museum with her sisters. But she had a late afternoon coffee meeting with Tom Swenson to get to. So with trembling legs, she shut the lights off in the newspaper office and made her way to Spruce Coffee.

Tom was sitting at the table closest to the window, still a strong, imposing figure, even in his retirement.

He had always had an easy air of authority, something that Carter had now. Though Tom's seemed a little bit more old-school. A little more reserved. A little less approachable. But she always had... Good feelings about him. A sense of safety when he was around.

He was that good kind of police officer that you felt you could trust. And she had a sense of reassurance even now as she made her way over to the table.

"I didn't know what you might want," he said.

"Oh, let me buy," she said. "I appreciate you giving me your time."

"Absolutely. Carter told me that you were putting together an article on Caitlin's disappearance. And one about Ruby. And I'm more than happy to answer questions about either of those things."

There was a note of steel in his voice, but she didn't doubt that he was sincere.

"What can I get you?"

"A decaf," he said, then grimaced. "I can't go drinking caffeine at this hour."

"I shouldn't," Dahlia said.

She ended up getting herself an Earl Grey, and that black coffee for Tom.

"What started all this?" he asked.

"Well, it's a natural extension of my desire to write sort of…a town history retrospective for the *Gazette*. When you look into the history of Pear Blossom, both Ruby and Caitlin stand out. It's unavoidable. And for people who are new to town or even people like me, who were here, but were very young… I think it's a good thing to write the story again, talking to the people who lived it. I didn't just want to use documents."

He nodded slowly. "All right. Let's start with Ruby."

"Okay."

"When I got that phone call that there was a baby on Sentinel Bridge, and that the McKee girls had found her, brought her back to their parents, I couldn't believe it. I thought for sure someone was having me on."

"We thought someone was too," Dahlia said.

"I interviewed you that night."

Dahlia smiled, suddenly very conscious of the passage of years. Of the reversal in the situation. And she could remember when she had been in the police station on a plastic orange chair, her feet swinging because they didn't touch the floor.

She curled her toes in her shoes, very firmly planted on the cement floor now.

"Yes," she said. "You did. I looked at the police report recently. I didn't really tell you anything all that helpful."

"You were honest. That's all I ask of anyone. It's all useful. In the end. And the same as you interviewing me. It's all useful. Even if I can't tell you anything new. It just helps cement the truth."

"Yes," Dahlia agreed. "So Ruby..."

"You brought her into the station, your family, and we checked her over. She ended up going to the hospital. Do you remember that?"

"Yes."

"Child services came. But I got to hold her for a few hours. And I have to tell you, after feeling like I had failed another girl, holding that tiny child made me feel like there might be some good left in this world. I had been doubting it. I understand that law enforcement is a place where you see the worst of humanity. I was in the field for a long time. There were things that I loved about it. And I was shielded from the worst of things in Pear Blossom. But there's not much that can prepare you for the loss of a girl you know. Whose mother you know. It's the personal piece of it. And that the only suspect we ever had was a kid that I also knew... Something about that changes you. Ruby was the closest thing to closure that I can think of. Holding her made me feel... I don't know... It sounds so strange. But closer to something bigger than myself. Closer to God maybe."

"That's a lot. For a little baby."

"If you hadn't of happened by, she wouldn't have made it."

"I know," Dahlia said. "I think about that sometimes. About

that moment. How we could have easily not seen her, even walking by. I thought I saw something and I shouted... I spoke up. I learned something that day, about speaking up. And I felt... responsible. For her. Responsible to truth. And maybe that's why...maybe that's why this matters so much to me. If not for us being there, if not for me calling out... Ruby could have died. It's the potential tragedy that I can't stop thinking about. But it didn't end in tragedy."

"Yes, and it's all those things that made me feel like she was a gift to our town. We investigated, of course. We investigated all the leads that we could get. Any sightings of pregnant women in town. We looked to DNA databases to see if we had any matching DNA on file, and we didn't. No one was missing a baby. No pregnant women were missing. She didn't have family in any DNA databases, which was much different than it is now. It was dead ends every way we turned. But in the meantime, she became the community's baby. And of course, then your family's."

"So you never had any leads on where Ruby came from? Ever?"

"No. None. It was cold from the very beginning. That's what sticks in my mind, clear as day. We approached the bridge where she'd been, and it was just...eerie. Calm. Nothing out of place. Nothing to suggest a baby had ever been there. There were no reported missing persons that matched with her at all. Because of course we thought it was possible she had been kidnapped. But there was just... There was no indication that was true. We had thought maybe something had happened to her mother, but there were no missing persons from that time."

"Just dead ends."

He nodded in affirmation. "Dead ends. And in that sense, it did mirror Caitlin Groves' case. Because there were so few leads on her, and the one that we had ended. Abruptly. The state decided not to move forward with the case. They decided there wasn't enough evidence. But there *was* no more evidence. There was no more to be had. And I will never understand… I will never understand how that could be. Nathan Brewer was a fifteen-year-old kid, not a criminal mastermind. Older, more sophisticated men can't get away with murder."

"Do you think he did?" Dahlia said, her stomach getting tight. "Do you think Nathan Brewer got away with murder?"

He looked directly into Dahlia's eyes. "I sure as hell do."

"Can you tell me what you remember about the night Caitlin Groves went missing?"

"Her mama called the station, about nine thirty. Saying that Caitlin hadn't come home yet. She was worried, because she was out with the Brewer boy. And you know, you worry. You worry that kids are getting into the kind of trouble that you… That you don't want them in."

"Sure," she said.

"And so she was alarmed immediately. She said Caitlin was very responsible. That she had been consumed with the boyfriend and had been a little bit more secretive lately, but that she was overall a good kid. Really bright. Really good."

"My sister said that she was someone that was hard to get to know."

"She seemed sweet to me. I remember she would come into the station to report finding a dog tied up in the heat, or with a cat she'd rescued. She didn't have a father. She…she tried to do good. I tried to help mentor her a bit, be a…father figure, maybe. I think a lot of the men in town did. But it's not the same, it never is. And that sweet nature of hers, that drive to take care of strays, well, that… Nathan Brewer was the stray that bit her, in my opinion."

Dahlia bit back her opinions on the subtle judgment of single mothers buried poorly in his words. She did believe in voicing her opinions, she really did. But right now listening was more important.

"Did you wait twenty-four hours to begin searching?" she asked.

"I had a patrol car keep an eye out for her. Had someone drive around, but no, we didn't launch a full-scale search until it had been twenty-four hours. As much as I believed what Dana said, I also knew that kids will be kids. They'll get into what they get into. And there's not a whole heck of a lot you can do about it."

"Sure," Dahlia said.

"I figured she was off with Brewer. I didn't think that she was in any danger, though. Had I thought she was…we would've approached it very differently."

"I'm sure you would have," she said.

"I regret that. I wonder if we had… If we had gone in right away, things might've been different."

"You don't know that," she said. "You can't."

"No. But what I know is that I should have taken it more seriously that she was with him."

"Why?"

"You're too young to remember, Dahlia. But twenty-five years ago there was a fire. Burned up the mountain, damn near took out two orchards. It's a miracle that people living at the farms didn't die. Nathan Brewer started that fire."

Her breath caught in her throat. "What?"

"Yes. When he was just a boy. And we protected him. We protected him from the public finding out about it because he was just a child. But honestly, if I would've known back then what I know now. About psychology. About the kinds of things that people get up to… I would have had to do something. I tried to protect an innocent child, but he has a fury in him. And I know that his father was a mean bastard."

"Carter said he was never…he said you didn't know."

"There's never been anything I could *prove*, and never anything I could do about it. Jillian Brewer would never consent to press charges against her husband. Nor would she ever admit that anything was happening. She called the police one time. Just once for a situation she couldn't handle. It involved John and Nathan. And in the end, though there was an investigation from Child Protective Services, there was no proof that there was any abuse happening. I'd lay money on that there was. But just like I'd lay money on the fact that Nathan Brewer is a murderer and I have to let him walk around the town, I could never do anything about that either."

"It all seems horribly unfair," Dahlia said. "That you can know something wrong is happening and not do anything to stop it."

"The law is not always about right and wrong. It's about what you can prove. There are reasons for that. But sometimes... Sometimes justice isn't served. In the end, there's been no justice for Caitlin Groves. I regret a great many things in my life. People think regret is a pointless exercise, a weakness. But there are heavy things in life, and I don't mind carrying the heavy things. But the biggest regret I carry is not getting justice for Caitlin."

Dahlia wrapped up her interview with Tom and drove home slowly. By the time she got back to the shed, she felt thoroughly shaken by the things that he'd shared with her, and she couldn't even quite put a finger on why.

Maybe it was just the grimness of it. What it revealed about humanity. That there could be a boy that you tried to help, that you tried to do the right thing for, but you failed still. And that boy... That angry boy who had lit a fire...

Had he ever had a chance?

Carter Swenson had a loving family. He'd been the most popular boy in school. And he had grown into a popular citizen in town. But his father had been the sort of man that fought for law and order. While Nathan Brewer's father had only hurt those he was supposed to take care of.

And in the end, it seemed as if Nathan Brewer had hurt the person that he was supposed to care the most about.

Right now everything just felt so tentative. So strange. On the heels of Lydia's revelation about her marriage, Dahlia felt a little bit like her world had been turned on its head.

She was used to certainty. To trusting in her own voice even when her opinion wasn't popular.

She was feeling like it wasn't all so neat now. Not the clean, tidy story she preferred.

She got out of the car and walked into the shed, to find Ruby sprawled out on the small couch in the living area. She was holding a newspaper, propped up, her arms straight as she held it aloft.

"What are you doing?"

"Looking for answers."

"What answers, Rubes?"

Her sister looked distressed, her blond hair sticking out around her ear on one side, her floral dress rucked up past her knees.

"I wish I knew. But it's… I've been thinking a lot about stories. Dana's. Mine." She hesitated like she wanted to say something else, but didn't. "Lydia's, I guess. The situation with her and Mac."

It was so close to what Dahlia had just been thinking about, it set her back on her heels. "Yeah. I know what you mean."

"They don't help anyone," Ruby said. "And I feel…responsible for…what clinging to mine might have done to other people. If I'm a hero…someone else is a villain and…"

"You aren't responsible for the way the town treats people," Dahlia said.

But it butted up against something inside her. That part of her that harbored a small bit of jealousy where Ruby was concerned.

If Ruby was the most special, Dahlia wasn't.

Dahlia pushed that thought off.

"There are a lot of articles about me. About Mom and Dad's decision to adopt me. I'd read one of them, but I've never seen this one. The one about the Child Protective Services investigation and all the exhaustive tactics the police tried to get some leads."

"I was just talking to Tom Swenson. He said there were essentially no leads. You're mysterious, Ruby."

Ruby smiled, but her teeth gleamed in a rather menacing fashion. "How nice for me." The words sounded funny, like she was repeating someone else, not like she was saying something that had come from her.

"Ruby, he said some things about Nathan Brewer that concerned me. I know you're feeling very passionate about saving him like he was some sort of endangered mammal, but I just think it sounds like he might be… Like he might be broken."

Ruby sat up. "He is." She knew that look on Ruby's face. The one that said she was mostly listening to her own thoughts and not Dahlia. "He's like… He's like a wounded animal."

"That's just what I said. You're embarking on this like it's a mission to save an endangered animal."

"Well, maybe I feel that way."

"Tom Swenson said that he started a fire. When he was a little boy. That he started a fire that caused a lot of damage. People could have been killed."

"Were they?"

"No. But that's not the point. The point is that when he was a child he did something really destructive. Really violent. And people like that tend to escalate."

"Why didn't Chief Swenson do something about it then?"

"He was trying to spare him. And he feels guilty about that. I just don't want you in that kind of position, Ruby. You're trying to save this man, and he might fundamentally be dangerous."

"What makes you feel like I'm trying to save him?"

"I know you. And I remember you getting all bright-eyed over the horrendous dog that you rescued when you were like six. This is the same thing. You like a project."

"Maybe I also care about what's fair."

"Ruby," Dahlia said very seriously. "Just please tell me that he's like a wounded puppy to you. And not a man."

Ruby looked away. "I have encountered him about three times, Dahlia. And nothing untoward has occurred."

"*Untoward.* You're not really answering my question."

"There's nothing to answer. There's no conversation to have. Dahlia, I appreciate you're protective of me, but I've been off on my own having a life for a long time. And I can handle myself."

"Ruby, I love you, but fundamentally sometimes I think that you buy into the idea that you're miraculous. Not that it makes you *special*, but that it makes you *untouchable*. It never occurs to you that an interaction could go wrong. Or that someone might not like you. Or that the man you helped back to his house when he was drunk might be a murderer."

"I just don't think he is," she said, as maddeningly immovable as a goat. "I get that Tom thinks he is. I get that you seem to believe it too. But I just don't think so."

Dahlia could recognize when she'd hit a Ruby wall. "Promise me you'll be careful."

"Okay."

"You can't promise me you're not going to see him again?"

"No," Ruby said. "I can't. I brought him pie. I didn't tell you. Because of this."

That set her teeth right on edge. "You brought him pie?"

"Yes. Some of the Thanksgiving pie. Because I assumed that he didn't have anyone to spend Thanksgiving with. And it turned out that I was right. It turned out that he didn't have anyone to share a meal with. And everyone in this town thinks those things about him. And I just…"

"You just don't believe what everyone else does. You think you're exempt from reality because you want it to be a better story. Because you want it to have a better ending. So did Tom Swenson. Tom wanted to save him. He wanted him to have a better outcome than what he was going to get being raised by his father. He didn't want him to become that. But he did. He *did*."

"I'm sorry, Dee," Ruby said, shaking her head. "But I just don't agree. I really don't. And I can't... I can't."

"So you're going to get into a fight with your sister defending some man who is quite possibly a murderer."

"I'm going to get into a fight with my sister defending what I believe is right. I would've thought that you would understand. You didn't let those kids attack Dana—you stood up for what was right. Dahlia, I admired that about you. I always have. You stood up when it wasn't popular and you said what needed saying, and I can't believe you don't support me in this now."

"Dana was not dangerous, Ruby. Dana was the victim of a town who couldn't handle grief and wanted to make their own discomfort go away by mistreating the person who had been hurt the worst. Nathan..."

"What if he didn't do it, Dahlia! Then what? Then Caitlin wasn't the only person who went missing that day. She wasn't the only one who lost her future. And I... I care about that."

And then Ruby stormed to her room, leaving the newspaper behind. Dahlia sat down on the couch and picked up the paper. She could see the article Ruby had been reading. The one about her. About the investigation. She turned it over and started to skim the other articles. And there was one that caught her eye.

Tourism Boom for Pear Blossom

The effects of Ruby were everywhere.

She set the newspaper down. And then she decided to text Carter. And wondered if she would regret it.

I talked to your dad today.

There was the appearance of a few dots in the chat box, and then it went away. Her phone rang. She picked it up. "Hello?"

"I don't text."

She snorted. "Well, I don't talk on the phone."

"If you would like to have a conversation with me, you can do it on the phone."

"People text, Carter, I don't know what to tell you."

"Forgive me. I haven't been single since 2010. It wasn't as easy to text on the phone I had back then."

She felt a little sliver of unease. The mention of him being single. As if she wasn't just calling him to have a discussion about the current situation with her conversation with his dad or the project at hand that he had sort of found himself roped into. "Well, people are afraid of phones now."

"I thought people had phones welded to their hands at all times."

"Yes. For everything *except* phone calls."

"Makes no sense to me."

"Well, you got me to answer my phone. An amazing feat. So, I wanted to tell you about the conversation with your dad. Or at least… To tell you that I had it." And she wasn't going to tell him that she'd been thinking about him. And the chances he'd had, and how it was strange that one person could become so perfect, and another person could just get nothing at all.

"Yeah, he mentioned that you came by. He thought it was a good talk."

"I guess so. Kind of depressing."

"Being a police officer is invariably kind of depressing."

"You don't know Nathan Brewer, do you?"

"No. I'm a good ten years younger than he is."

"Yeah. Right. Of course. It's just… From your dad's perspective he was always headed for trouble."

"I know. I've heard my dad's version of events."

"Do you agree with him? Do you think that some people are just headed for trouble? That some people are destined for greatness and other people aren't?"

It was the question she was asking herself. If some people were just great like Carter and Ruby. Or if there was more to it.

She wanted to know his answer. Badly.

"No," he said. "I think we make choices. Every day. And some people have a harder set of choices in front of them. Look, I think it's easy to get jaded and forget that all the people that you deal with all the time—and trust me, a lot of my job is arresting the same people over and over again and wondering why the hell I do it—you don't always see the thing that led them there. You don't know what choices they had. You might not have liked any of them. But I do always think people have a choice."

"So you don't think he was just born bad?"

"Not any more than I think I was born good."

Her heart squeezed tight and she found herself smiling in the empty room. "Well, it was all good material for the article. Thank you for giving me his phone number."

"No problem." He sounded like he might want to say something, but then he didn't. "No problem. I'll see you around."

She hung up the phone and felt... Dissatisfied. She wanted to talk to him for longer. She wanted to see him. To tell him what was happening with Ruby and ask his opinion.

She didn't *like* that she wanted that.

And Ruby was mad at her.

It made her feel so awful.

Oh well, some days were bad. Even though they had good things in them, and the conversation with Tom Swenson had certainly been good.

It was just that the story he told wasn't one that made her happy.

But that was life, she supposed.

And there wasn't anything she could do about it.

22

Tourism Boom for Pear Blossom

BY DALE WAINWRIGHT

JULY 9, 2001—The tourism boom for Pear Blossom is in full effect this summer, as the raised visibility for the town since Ruby McKee's miraculous story was told to the world continues to heal the town in unexpected ways.

RUBY

Ruby was determined to visit Nathan. Pretty much because Dahlia had warned her off. She didn't have an excuse. Though, she had come with dinner. Fajitas, in fact. Because she liked fajitas and she normally shared them with Dahlia, and she was annoyed with Dahlia. She was gratified to see his truck in the driveway. As far as she could tell, he didn't really go anywhere. Of course he didn't, because if he did, then rumors would be all about the town, and they still weren't. And Dana had mentioned his return to Dahlia, but not to her, and for some reason that made her feel cross.

She got out of her car and walked up to the front door. And

you know, if he didn't want to talk to her, he could just not answer. But he did answer.

"Somehow, I knew it was you. Because literally no one else ever comes to my door."

"I brought you dinner. I hope you haven't had any yet."

He laughed. "I was heating up a can of tomato soup."

"Well, I brought fajitas."

He eyed her warily, like he was a bear expecting her to pull a gun out and dispatch him. Fully big enough and well able to handle himself, a natural predator, but one that still had to be cautious in certain situations. "Why?"

She smiled. "Because my sister says you're a murderer."

"I see." The expression on his face said he clearly did not.

"*I* don't think you are one."

"Let me ask you a question, Ruby McKee. Why is it that you think I'm not?"

She narrowed her eyes. "You're not, are you?"

"I've denied it until I was hoarse. I don't have it in me to say I'm not one more time."

"Well, I just believe it. You don't have to tell me. You don't have to deny it. Just know that I'll believe you. And let me come in and eat dinner with you. Because I'm hungry."

"Fine."

"I have a question for *you*, Nathan Brewer," she said, walking to the center of the room, then turning back to face him. "Why do you keep letting me in your house?"

His lips twitched. "Said the hen to the fox."

"You're more like a bear."

"Then that must make you a rabbit."

She shook her head. "No. I'm not particularly skittish. If I scared easily I would have run from you a while ago. But here I am." She lifted the bag. "Where can I take this? And you need to answer the question."

"Maybe I just keep letting you in because you're hot, and I'm a man. And the last thing I expected in Pear Blossom was to get laid, but if the potential is there, I won't close the door on it."

Heat bloomed in her cheeks. She knew that he was just saying that to get a reaction out of her, to shock her. Upset her. She didn't find it upsetting, though. "I don't recall offering anything."

"A man starts to make assumptions."

"I think you're just saying that to scare me away."

It didn't scare her, though. Not in the least.

"Why would I want to scare you away?"

"I don't know. But it seems to be the thing that you do with people. Doesn't it? You scare them. You let them think the worst."

"I didn't let anyone think a damn thing about me. They think what they want to. And that's it. I don't have a vested interest in anyone thinking something better. I'm not responsible for what they think. There's a reason that I don't live here."

"What are you doing here then?"

"Did you say you're on some kind of fact-finding mission?"

"Yes," she said. She started to get food out of the foam cartons. "You might as well eat instead of just standing there looking at me like I might be after your virtue."

He laughed. The sound was so sharp it almost cut her. "My virtue is long gone. If it was ever there."

"Well, then quit acting like I pose a threat to you. Sit. Have some food."

To her surprise, he obeyed her, which she imagined had more to do with the fact that the food looked good than it did with her powers of persuasion.

"My sister is writing an article about..." She didn't really want to bring up Caitlin. "Well, about me, and it's kind of...pushing me into looking more into my past."

She didn't mention her dreams.

"Maybe I'm just here to argue with ghosts. It's not that different, is it?"

"I don't know," she said, shaking her head, her earrings making noise as she did. "The people I'm talking to can talk back at least."

"I'm not interested in the conversation. To be quite honest I've never had one in this town. It was all people telling me what I was. Useless like my father."

"My sister told me that you started a fire."

"Did she?"

"Yes. She said that when you were a child you started a fire. That it nearly burned out of control. It's one of the things that makes Tom Swenson think that you grew up to be a murderer. That and the fact your father was violent."

"I did start a fire," he said. "Because I was angry. I'm still angry. I've been angry my whole damned life, and there was never anything that I could do about it. It was like a... A volcano inside of me waiting to erupt. And the worst thing is... Yeah, it makes me like my father."

A shiver went up her arms. "Did you... Did you ever hurt anyone?"

"No. I lit a fire. That was the closest I ever got to letting it go completely. I learned my lesson. And after that, I just kind of bottled up. The only person who made me feel like I didn't have to be constrained by that was...her. She was a better person than I'll ever be. She was... She was a good person. Kind to everyone, more than...more than just passively nice. She went out of her way to make the world better. I never would have hurt her. I didn't understand why she liked me. And I guess I thought that she was my punishment. I had her, I lost her. I didn't hurt her. But I paid for it. I paid for that sweet, beautiful girl liking me." His lips twisted, the expression on them hard. "That's not an easy thing to contend with."

"It doesn't sound to me like anything you've had to deal with was easy." She started to construct her fajita, paying careful attention to each and every step, because it did something to diffuse this feeling that seemed to be growing between them. She wasn't a stranger to attraction, but she didn't like the way this felt as if it expanded in her chest.

"Do you think that they even looked for evidence that anyone else was involved?"

"I don't know. I was either at home getting the hell beat out of me by my dad, or I was in prison. And either way, I was in hell because she was gone. That might be... That's the thing. I come back here and I remember her. That day that I was drunk, I was thinking of her. That grief had been pushed off. Till later. And later. Because I've been so busy dealing with the trash pile that is my life. You google me, you won't like the results. That's made work interesting. Friendships. Dating. Basically nonexistent."

"What do you... Do for work?"

The corner of his mouth turned up. "I'm in real estate."

"You're a Realtor?" She was deeply skeptical of that.

"No. I fix up houses and I sell them. I move around a lot. I do just fine. When you have a problem getting a job, you have to become your own boss. I'm not good at a hell of a lot, Ruby, but I'm good at surviving. Mostly to throw it in my old man's face that I can. To throw it in this damn town's face. I'll offload this place too, once it's ready. I can't wait."

He tucked into his dinner, seemingly uninterested in making conversation. But she was curious.

"What kind of houses have you renovated?"

He lifted a brow. "You're really determined to do this?"

"Yes, and you seem determined to let me. So you might as well indulge me."

"Fine. Yes. I have done all kinds of houses. I bought a place in England. Did a little remodel on that."

She tented her fingers and leaned in. "Historically accurate?"

He looked at her like she might be crazy.

"Yeah," he said.

This was... Very dangerous.

"I would've loved to see that. I'm a historian. I work for the historical society. I just got back from England."

"Well, I was in England ten years ago."

"I was twelve, ten years ago."

He shook his head. "Lord Almighty. You probably need to leave my house."

"Why?"

He sighed. "Tell me about your time in England, Ruby McKee."

He looked resigned, leaning back in his chair. And she did tell him. By the time they were done with dinner, she realized that she didn't want whatever was happening here to end. It had to.

"Maybe I'll see you again."

He shrugged. "Seems to be up to you."

"Right. Well. I'm at the cottage. You saw the cottage. You could come see me."

"And meet the business end of your daddy's rifle?"

"And possibly a can of mace from my sister. Yes."

The corner of his mouth lifted. "Sounds tempting."

"Have a good night, Nathan."

"You too, Ruby."

And she hoped that this man, who claimed he didn't have a friend, might feel like he had one now.

She left the house, her footsteps heavy as she went to the car. And for some reason, when she got back on the road, she drove past the driveway to her parents' house. For some reason, she kept on going until she got to where the road curved around the walkway to Sentinel Bridge.

She stopped the car in the middle of the road and got out, looking up at the imposing structure. This was where she was standing in her dream. The same sense of dread gripped her.

Like there was something in the bridge to be feared, even

though she knew there wasn't. She had driven past the bridge today and hadn't thought a thing of it.

But suddenly… Suddenly. It was like she was standing in that dream. Like she was in that fuzzy moment between asleep and awake that made her limbs feel like they were weighted down with iron.

She didn't want to go into the bridge. She looked back at her car, the headlights on. They blinded her. When she looked back at the bridge, it only enhanced the darkness.

She took two steps forward, then another. And an oppressive fear gripped her shoulders and pushed down. Left goose bumps all up and down her arms. And she kept going. In spite of herself.

Until the darkness of the bridge consumed her. Her heart was hammering, the only sound that she could hear.

Thundering right in her head.

She made her way over to the walkway, to those two windows where moonlight streamed through. Her breath echoed in the enclosed space, ragged and coming faster and faster. She tried to take another step forward, to follow the path that she had in her dream. But she couldn't.

She just couldn't. Instead, she turned and she ran. Back to her car. And when she got inside, she gripped the steering wheel so tight her hands hurt.

She had no idea what was happening to her. This place had never been scary for her. She had always been enveloped by a warm sense of home.

And now she just felt… The darkness here.

It was just so dark.

She turned the car around and drove back to the cottage. And when she came inside, Dahlia was standing there, looking angry. "And where have you been?"

"Don't ask questions you don't want the answers to."

"You were with him?"

"Yes."

"Ruby..."

"I don't want to hear it, Dahlia. I'm not a baby, and I don't need to be rescued. He's not a killer."

The conviction of that was much stronger after experiencing that level of fear by the bridge. If she could feel darkness, she would've felt it with Nathan if it was there, but it wasn't.

"You just... You think you know everything."

"No, you think you do," Ruby said. "You think that you secretly know everything, and I'm silly. And there is some truth to some of the stuff you said about me, but you never stop to look at your own issues, Dahlia. Maybe it's not me. Maybe I'm not the reason that you feel second-best. You *take* second best. Because it lets you skulk around and feel misunderstood. Because it lets you hide. And you like that. Just like Lydia being quiet about everything that happened with Mac. She would rather sit there and be a martyr. And you're no different. But at least she had an imploding marriage and a dead husband. What do you have? Nothing. You're still throwing a tantrum like you're a teenager and you have the nerve to call me immature. A hot guy that you had a thing for in high school seems to be interested in you, and you won't do anything about it because you're so stuck on him marrying the cheerleader, like that's about you and him not picking you and not just...him having his own life and mistakes. You're your own worst enemy, Dahlia. You're the only one who thinks you're second-best. And you make sure to keep yourself there." Ruby was breathing hard, so hard her chest hurt.

"Did you ever...have you ever once considered, Dahlia, that it isn't easy being told you should be grateful to be alive? That your parents are so lovely and wonderful for wanting you? That you're special to the town and you were saved for a reason and then you have to... Do you know what it's like to try and... find that reason when you just feel awful and you want to snarl at everyone? I don't want to be grateful every day. Sometimes

I want to just…tell the world to go to hell, like you do whenever you feel like it."

"Don't you dare say that to me," Dahlia said. "Don't you… how dare you? You can't spend twenty-two years swanning around like a cartoon cricket and then suddenly get mad about it because you can't have a bad day, or whatever the hell is wrong with you right now. But it's still about *you*. Everything is about you, even my news story is about you."

"You wanted to write it!"

"Yes, I did!" Dahlia shouted back. "But you act like I don't feel…like I don't feel second-best for a reason, Ruby. How would…anyone in my situation feel? I was the baby. I was. And then there was you. And you are newsworthy and beautiful and nicer than me, and no one…no one picks me over you. Nobody would!"

"Maybe grow your bangs out and be less of an asshole then. That should fix a couple of your issues." She felt bad about that as soon as the words left her mouth.

Her sister's bangs weren't bad.

"And maybe, Dahlia, you should worry less about my life, and everyone else's stories, and write a better one for yourself!"

Dahlia's glare turned deadly. "You've lived your whole life benefiting from everyone treating you like a miracle, and now you're mad about it, well fine. Change something then, but stop acting victimized over the fact that people care about you!"

Dahlia growled and spun around, stalking out of the room.

And then Ruby spun on her heel and went into the bedroom. She avoided sleep for as long as possible. And she was thankful that when she finally did fall asleep, it proved to be dreamless.

23

The Tragedy That Does Not End

BY DALE WAINWRIGHT

DECEMBER 21, 2000—It has been more than a year since our town's greatest tragedy, and we are no closer to justice, or answers. The change is a deep and lasting scar. If we cannot now trust our own neighbors, as we always have, throughout the history of our town, what will we become?

LYDIA

Lydia was going to have to deal with Chase today. She'd been avoiding it to the best of her ability, but they had actual things to discuss regarding the renovation of the barn.

The kids were at school, and it was a bitter cold day. So, tons of scope to deal with something she didn't want to. The weather being terrible felt like a decent accommodation for her mood, and the kids being gone meant that whatever she had to say... Well, it could be said.

The problem was, she didn't know what all she wanted to say. It had been cathartic to confide in her sisters, but it hadn't exactly given her a way forward. And there was just... There was a mountain of words to be said. And she didn't even know where to begin. Didn't have the faintest idea why she had told him to meet her at the house. And now she was pacing. Feeling nervous and sweaty. She didn't like this at all.

She had never been in an uncertain position with a man before. She had fallen into a relationship with Mac when she'd been too young to really think about any of it. And she had never… Really fallen back out of it. She had thought that she might. She'd been ready to end it, but that was the uncertainty of ending a relationship with someone she… Someone she was intimate with. Dealing with this step into physical intimacy with a man that she had absolutely no…

They didn't really know each other. For all that they'd known each other all their lives.

She never really tried to know him. In total fairness.

She heard the rumble of his truck pulling into the driveway, and she stood and waited. Until she could see his wavy silhouette through the glass of the front door. Her heart took a strange, sickening dive, and she resented that. Most of all, she resented how this made her feel like the silly high school girl she'd never gotten a chance to be. She'd been in a steady relationship at that point, and back when they were kids, compared to their peers, their relationship had not been dramatic.

Because when there was an issue, they just shoved it down deep, filed it in a box to deal with later, until there had been just so many that it was impossible to ever sort through it all. Until it was a disorganized mess of bitterness and unhandled emotion.

He knocked heavily, and she took a breath, moving to the door to open it.

His eyes were shaded by the hat that he wore, and his mouth was set into a grim line. "I have some specs you should see."

"I'm not very good at visualizing things," she said, letting him in. "So I don't know if I'll be able to… Give you the information you want."

"I'll tell you how much it's going to cost. You tell me if that's something you want to pay."

"All right. All right, that… That sounds good."

He took a step into the room, and she was suddenly overwhelmed by his presence. And it all felt so much sharper and more specific than her usual discomfort around him, and she had to wonder if the whole time it had been… This.

No.

Do not go there. Do not name it. Do not make it a pet.

Forget about it. Let it go.

"I haven't seen you," he said.

"I've been busy," she responded.

"How are Riley and Hazel doing?"

That sent a sharp stab of guilt through her. Because of course, he hadn't been around so he hadn't seen the kids, and the kids hadn't seen him. "Good. Riley's lightened up a lot."

"Why do you say it like that?"

"Oh, you and all your… Man of the house stuff. Teaching him how to do things in… It made him too serious. He felt like he was taking over for his dad."

"Well, there's an interesting thing to blame me for."

"It's eased up since you haven't been around." *A salve for your conscience, Lydia, and bitchy.*

"It's also just time passing."

"Who knows, Chase, maybe it's you. I can't help it if you don't want to take responsibility."

"I'll tell you what, Lydia, why don't you just go ahead and get it all out. Lay it all at my door. Everything you want to put there. However many boxes you need to stack up so that there's something keeping us apart."

She felt struck by that. And for some reason, tears stung her eyes. She didn't like how close to the surface her emotions had been lately.

"It's just true, Chase. It's…"

"I love Riley. I want him to feel like he has a man in his life who cares about him. And I'm not his dad. I'm not going to be his dad. But I loved Mac. He was like a brother to me. And if you want him to hear stories about him, if you want him to learn how to shoot and fix trucks and all the things his dad would've taught him, I can do that. Again, not volunteering to be his father, but I want to do something to help with that hole in his life. Hazel too, I can teach her to fix trucks if she wants. Because someday it's going to matter to her that she didn't really ever get to know Mac."

"Don't you think I know that?" She had so much anger in her, and she didn't know why it had to come out in hot, humiliating tears. She didn't want to do this. Didn't want to cry. Didn't want to break. "Don't you think I'm...unbearably conscious of the hole that's been left behind? For them. For them it's terrible. They lost their dad, and I am so very sorry for that."

"I know you are. And so am I."

"I know. You're like his ambassador. You're here for him and you..."

Suddenly, Chase's blue eyes took on a sharp edge. "I'm here for *him*?"

"Of course you are. You're here for him, you're here for his children. I get that."

"No, Lydia. You don't." He took a step toward her. "I'm here for *you*. It's been you. From the beginning."

His words fell with so much gravity, his eyes so fierce that she couldn't... She couldn't bring herself to issue a denial about what he was saying, even though she wanted to. Was desperate to. "Chase..."

"You idiot woman. I loved Mac like a brother, and that's why...that's why this is..." He reached out, taking a lock of her golden hair between his thumb and forefinger, rubbing it slightly. "Lydia. I have cared a whole lot about you since you were Lydia McKee. Not married to my best friend, but still...

you were always with him. I know you because of him. Because of his family. I care for you. *You.* And I wish that I could say I was half so gallant that I was here on his behalf. I'm not. I want to make things easier for *you.* I want to make you smile. I want to remove the burden. And every time you told me you didn't want me around, I told myself it was grief. Because I couldn't accept that maybe you just really didn't want me here."

"Chase…"

"You can't even finish a sentence."

She looked away. "What am I supposed to say?"

"Maybe there's nothing to say. It's impossible, right? This. Just like your feelings for Mac, and losing him. It's too complicated. There's no untangling it. The grief that he's gone, the anger about it. But also the…"

And even though he was saying it was impossible, he touched her face. His hands were rough from all the work he did on the land, and he was so large. And she had that urge again. That overwhelming urge to rest against him. To test the strength of his frame. Oh, how she wanted that.

"It's impossible," he said again.

But then he leaned forward, and he was kissing her again.

It was better than she remembered. Hotter, more certain.

But they weren't in the open now.

They were in the privacy of her house, with no one around. With no one to interrupt.

And she wasn't married.

Her husband was gone.

And she just felt… An overwhelming urge to jump right into whatever this was. Because there was a mountain of words. A mountain of reasons why it could never be anything.

Later.

But there was also right now. Right now, with the clouds so low and gray. Right now, with her heart tender and in shreds. Right now, with her kids at school and not home for hours.

And there was such a shortage of *right now.* You never knew when you were in your last *right now.*

And Chase had been making her feel more than anyone or anything else for the last six months. And sure, half the time it was frustration. Half the time it was a bright hot jumble of feelings that she didn't want to begin to sort through. And that was the problem. Because she knew where it would go. Because it had always been there.

Always.

And she had been so… So blind.

It was exactly what he'd said. She'd put up as many barriers as she possibly could. To foster her denial. To increase her ability to ignore what was happening. In her. Between them.

It was always you.

How could that be?

How could it even be?

But his kiss was firm and wonderful, and even if everything inside of her was decidedly not wonderful. Even if it was confused. Even if it was all sorts of terrible, it was blotted out by the brilliance of this kiss.

Everything was complicated. So complicated. And it made her want to lean into it all the more. Because at least it was good. At least it was wonderful. At least it felt good. And precious little felt good.

She grabbed hold of the front of his shirt, deepening the kiss. Increasing it. Getting lost in it.

Everything about this was a mess.

She just wanted to be a mess for a while. She had started unstitching all the things that held her together that day at the museum. And she wanted to keep going. Unravel it all until everything she was trying to hold inside was just out there.

Uncontained.

She didn't know why. But she was just… She was done with it. She was fed up. And this felt like the means to destroy it all.

He wrapped his strong arms around her, and she found herself being propelled up the stairs. It was clumsy, the two of them backing into steps, backing against the wall, unwilling to break the kiss. Like breaking it might stop all this. Might break the spell. She didn't want it to lapse. She didn't want to have a moment of clarity. She didn't want to have a second where she had a chance to think. She didn't want that at all. She wanted to drown in this. Immerse herself in this moment.

She felt like someone else. And she just wanted to be someone else.

Except when they finally did get to the bedroom, they parted for a moment, and she was unbearably conscious of the fact that it was Chase. Who she had known for so long, and who she had certainly never thought about seeing naked. Much less him seeing her naked.

She hadn't thought about her own attractiveness, her own sexuality, in so long…

Her marriage hadn't been great at the end, and their sex life had dwindled down to nothing. His illness had caused further complications with that. Even when her heart had softened toward him… Well, there had been some nice times. Some sweet, romantic times imbued with the bittersweet reality that it was coming to an end.

A prolonged goodbye.

But it hadn't been like this.

It was quite possible nothing had ever been like this. At least, she couldn't remember. His hands were rough on her body, and she reveled in it. The hallmark of a man who did so much hard labor. So much of it for her.

For her.

She had thought all this time that it was for Mac.

It was for her.

And as he stripped the clothes away from her body she forgot to be embarrassed. She forgot to be self-conscious. Because the appreciation that lit his face was far too keen. Far too extreme for her to feel any sort of insecurity. And he was… He was a glory. And it was no wonder that women told legends about him around town. He was everything he promised to be. All that hardened muscle from all that work, those broad shoulders that had been carrying so much of this burden—how had she not seen that he was carrying so much of this burden—well muscled and just the right width to grab right onto. To take some of the weight off.

And when she pressed herself against him, his skin was hot, and his body was perfect. And this was perfect.

She sighed as he laid her back on the bed, her mouth tingling and swollen from his attention. And it was all that she hadn't known she needed. A connection to him. To where she was. To her body.

It was Chase.

Chase kissing her.

Chase touching her.

Chase devouring her.

And she wanted it. All of it. Arched against his body, hot and perfectly hard. A fantasy she hadn't known she'd had.

Then he was in her. Chase.

Chase.

He was perfect somehow. This man who infuriated her, tested her. Knew her.

Wanted her.

And he took her to new heights. But when she crashed back down to earth, she was shattered—broken just like she'd been afraid she would be—and she didn't know what to do. What had seemed like a wave she could keep on riding was gone now. And her body was vibrating with the pleasure she'd just received, but she felt… Desperately lonely and sad too.

And on the heels of that, came panic. What had she been thinking? She hadn't been thinking. She had been lost in this feeling. And it had seemed like a great idea at the time. She felt like maybe this was adolescence. This deep, crawling sense of shame, the slap of clarity that came after the haze of arousal faded. She had been with one man for years. She'd had no real idea of… This.

Yes, she'd experienced the insanity that came with sex with Mac, even if it had been a while. It was just that… They'd always been together. They had always been inevitable. There had never been a sense of uncertainty or a question about what happened next.

There had been a lot of other things. A lot of resentment. A lot of disconnection. But this was something wholly new.

She rolled out of bed, desperately seeking her clothes, which had been so easy to take off. And she hadn't felt naked. Not in the least. Hadn't felt ashamed or hesitant. She had just felt eager. But all that shame had been deferred, and it had come to collect now. In spades.

She blinked back tears as she moved to cover herself. And Chase didn't move. He just sat there, all easy with himself, and with her. He just sat there, like everything was fine. Like the world hadn't shifted. Like they hadn't done something incredibly foolish.

"You weren't ready for that," he said.

"Do not tell me what I'm ready for," she shot back as she hastily covered her body.

"Well, you're acting like it's a problem."

"You don't get to… You don't…" She didn't know how she was supposed to talk to him. When he was lounging on her bed completely naked. And she couldn't help but look at him. But stare.

He was beautiful. But that didn't make him less of a mistake. A mistake that she was going to have to untangle, since they had to cope with each other.

Unless you don't.

Right. She could remove Chase from her children's life, the same way that Mac had been removed from them. She couldn't do that.

Frustration and fear tangled together.

"I'm sorry," he said, sitting up. "You didn't say that you didn't want…"

"I did. At the time."

"Yeah, that's the thing about sex. It always seems like a good idea at the time."

"I don't have any experience with this," she said.

"I know," he said. "I've known you since you were thirteen, remember?"

Yes. She had known him since she was thirteen. So, did it have to be so awkward? Did it have to be so terrible? No. It didn't. It didn't have to define them. A half hour of insanity couldn't erase everything else they were. And they might never have been close, but he was a foundational brick in her life. And how she was coping. And how she was surviving.

"Yes," she said. "You have. It's… I just need… I need space. I need to figure out what I was thinking. What I am thinking. What comes next."

"Nothing has to come next," he said.

Well, it *couldn't*. Not between the two of them. She wasn't ready, first of all. Second of all…

She couldn't even imagine. She had a volatile, difficult relationship already. She and Chase didn't even get along. He rubbed her the wrong way. He was stubborn. He was hardheaded. He was up in her business whether she wanted him to be or not.

He was… Very different from Mac.

She couldn't get Mac involved in her life if she tried—and she had. And when she thought about it, Chase had been more involved over the last six months than Mac had been during their whole marriage. And it wasn't just showing up and working. Mac did that. He did the physical work. Chase wanted to know what she needed. He wanted to know how she felt. And she had been projecting all of her issues with Mac right onto him. She had taken all of her resentment and annoyance and pushed it onto his shoulders, and he had carried it gamely. And then he had taken her to bed and given her the most incredible pleasure she could remember having.

And she still really needed him out of her bedroom.

"Please, Chase. I know I've been difficult. I know this hasn't been… Well, frankly I'm surprised you've stuck with me. At all. I certainly didn't deserve it. I need some time to figure some things out. To rethink."

"I told you," he said, getting up off of the bed, still naked and completely unashamed. He put his thumb against the bottom of her chin. "I'm here for you."

She blinked back tears and swallowed hard. And she kept her gaze focused elsewhere while he collected his own clothes.

"I just need some space," she said.

"Then you can have all the space you need."

"We can't go over the budget… I…"

"I'll handle it. Don't worry."

And he left her alone in her room, and she wished she could have him back, which was the most contrary, ridiculous thing she could think of. She had wanted him gone, and now the emptiness of the space felt too oppressive. She didn't know what to do. She didn't know where to turn.

So she called the one person that she knew would understand just how much trouble she had expressing her emotions. Just how much trouble she had admitting she had them.

"Dahlia," she said. "I really need you."

24

First Presbyterian Church of Pear Blossom
CHRISTMAS PROGRAM
INTRODUCTION: Pastor Lawrence
FIRST CHOIR SET:
Joy to the World
Carol of the Bells
Hark, the Herald Angels Sing

DAHLIA

Dahlia had ended up taking a long break over at Lydia's. Her sister was having a small breakdown over sleeping with her husband's best friend. It was understandable. Dahlia was... It was weird. She wasn't judging her really. But Chase was... Chase. She couldn't imagine Lydia apart from Mac—in spite of the recent revelations about their relationship—and her being with anyone else would be weird. But Chase. Yeah, that was messy.

You didn't know if something like that would work out. Certainly in Dahlia's life none of her love affairs had amounted to much of anything. What Lydia might be left with was just a sticky, tangled situation, all because she hadn't paused to think in pursuit of an orgasm.

And Dahlia knew it probably wasn't appropriate to feel... Happy that Lydia had called her.

And she did her best not to think of Carter as she mused on that. She was so focused on her computer screen that she didn't notice when her mom knocked on her office door. "I brought you some muffins."

Her mother's presence wasn't entirely unprecedented, but she did usually text first.

"Hi, Mom," Dahlia said. "You were... Just in the neighborhood?"

"No," she said. "I put myself in the neighborhood."

"Oh," Dahlia said. Maybe she should have asked why, but she was more curious about what muffins were available, and then also making sure nothing was wrong. Because anytime her mother acted out of character, Dahlia felt a degree of panic. Maybe because it reminded her of being a teenager who might be in trouble.

"With Ruby in town... I was just thinking you might need a little bit of special attention." Her mom came in and sat down, without asking.

"Is that special attention blueberry flavored or pumpkin?"

"Blueberry."

"Thank you," Dahlia said.

"I take it that means you might need some special attention."

Her mother was looking at her expectantly, and Dahlia didn't have a clue what to say. "I don't know."

"I worry about you. You never say if things are going okay."

And her mother wasn't one to ask, for fear of what the question would unearth. Or at least, Dahlia thought that was why.

It was another reason she...

Another reason she spoke out, though not with her parents

so much. Because in their house it had been hard, and Dahlia was always caught in the middle.

Of her desire to speak. Her desire to be right.

Her desire to be special.

"They are."

"Your dad offered to put Ruby in the shed and he didn't ask you."

"No," Dahlia said, "he didn't. But Ruby did."

"But he didn't. And I didn't know if you found that troublesome."

"I don't find it troublesome, Mother," Dahlia said. "I love Ruby."

"Of course you do. But a whole lot of your life has revolved around her. And that space was for you."

"If you were concerned about it, maybe you should've said something to Dad," Dahlia said. Guilt nipped immediately on the heels of that statement, because her mom was reaching out to her and trying to figure out how she was doing, so turning it around on her just because she was in firing range wasn't exactly fair.

"Yes," Dahlia said. "A whole lot of my life has revolved around her. And some of that is my choice right now. So yes, it's a lot of Ruby right now. But I'm writing that newspaper story about her." She took a muffin out of the basket. "Can I ask you about the day that we found Ruby?"

"I wanted to come and pay attention to you," Andie said.

"Appreciated. But one of the things I'm doing is working on this story." And it gave her an excuse to not think about her issues. How the muffins made her feel. Or whether or not she wanted to call Carter.

"I told Ruby the story at least a hundred times."

"Yes. But I want to hear the story the way you don't tell it to Ruby. I'm sure you protect her. Mom…you protect all of us." Was she really doing this? Pushing right now?

Her mom was here, dangerously close to admitting Dahlia might have feelings that were less than perfect, so maybe it was time.

Dahlia pressed. "What was it really like? Not this…not this easy miracle version. What was it like? To have your daughters bring home a baby and put her in your arms?"

Her mom frowned. "I remember it clearly. I didn't want any more children. I was definitive on that. But mostly it was because I didn't want to ever be pregnant again. I love my girls. But three felt like enough times to go through all of that. The three of you were walking back from church. Nathan Brewer was in prison at the time, so it felt safe again to have you walking around. I had been worried for a long time. I'd driven you to church, for choir practices, for all of that for months afterward. But things had seemed to settle. But you came running to the front door. Running. The three of you. Lydia was holding her. Clutched to her chest. I just remember my three red-cheeked girls looking terrified. And I was afraid at first that you were being chased by someone. And I was certain that Lydia was holding a doll. I couldn't make sense of what I was seeing."

"Of course. We could hardly believe what *we* were seeing when we happened upon her."

"That was when you started to cry. And suddenly, I started to hear what Lydia was saying. They'd found a baby. And I screamed to your father to call the police.

"I took her in my arms. I couldn't tell at first if she was cold or if my hands were warm from being inside. But I got a blanket wrapped around her and a second one. And I held her close. And all I could think was, who would do that to this sweet baby? Who would do that? All I could think was how tiny she was. How helpless. And I knew right in that moment that I would do anything to protect her. To care for her. And all my certainty that I didn't want another child went out the window when I held her. Because, as impossible as I knew it might be, she felt like she should be mine. Even before there was an investigation, I was in contact with child services."

"So you knew. Right away you knew that Ruby should be part of our family."

"I felt like God must've put her there. Right where you were going to be. And he put you there, just at the right time. And I felt like… She was meant to be. Meant to be mine. Meant to be in my arms at that moment. I just knew."

"Is there anything else? Anything else that you talked to child services about, or to the police about?"

"There were thousands of applications to adopt Ruby. People called from all over the world. But of course we were always up for the first consideration because of the circumstances. Because we wanted to keep her in town."

"Thousands?"

"Yes," Andie said. "She was worldwide news. Something that really captured people from everywhere."

"And for you?"

"She's my daughter," Andie said. "Just that. Which is everything, of course, but not more. Not more than you or Lydia or Marianne. Ruby is…easy. It's easy to follow her lead, her emotions, to be happy because she's happy."

"What about Marianne?" Dahlia asked. "I was four, I don't remember that much about her darker times, but wasn't it easy to be sad when she was sad?"

Andie tried to smile. "That's what I love about you, Dahlia. You say the things I can't." She breathed in deep. "I didn't do the right thing with Marianne when she was a teenager. And I've read about things since and I'm sure she was depressed, and the truth is, I didn't know what to do with her because it was how I was when I was young. And what I learned to do was smooth it over. Pretend everything was fine. I tried to do that with you, and I hoped…that I could be fine enough so you all would be too."

"Have you told Marianne?" She knew she hadn't. That this was the only time her mom had ever said this out loud.

"No."

"Maybe you should."

The tight nod told Dahlia she might, but it wouldn't be soon. "Enjoy your muffins, Dahlia. And…if you need anything, please come right over. I'm… I'm trying."

"I know."

Her mom stood slowly and left her office, closing the office door quietly, like she could minimize the impact of what they'd just talked about.

And what they'd just talked about was…

Special.

It wasn't easy or glittery, but it mattered.

She had to wonder if Ruby was right.

If she was just avoiding taking charge of her own story.

Maybe it wasn't the town that didn't think she was special. Maybe it was Dahlia herself.

RUBY

Ruby hadn't been to the First Presbyterian Church of Pear Blossom in quite some time. It was just that, come Sunday, all she wanted to do was sleep. And then lie around. And then do anything but go listen to a sermon and have people who had known her since she was a child ask for an update on her life.

It was a pale pink building with a classic steeple and lovely stained glass windows. It had always looked a little bit like candy to her.

There were sweets that Hattie Andrews made every year for the Christmas potluck at the church, colored marshmallows set in chocolate, called stained glass, and it always put her in mind of the church.

She hadn't realized that she was nostalgic for it until she

walked inside. The foyer was modest, with brown commercial carpet and a large fireplace. The sanctuary was the room with all the drama. It was all wood, with that dramatic arched ceiling that always reminded her of the underside of an arc. She couldn't walk in without thinking of Noah and his animals. Which had less to do with flannelgraphs, and much more to do with the architecture.

With some assistance from the church secretary, Ruby acquired hats, coats and gowns from the Victorian era to bring back to the museum.

She loaded all the costumes into the room where she intended to display them and began to look for their catalog numbers so that she could find the information on them. Some of them didn't have information, which meant she would be doing some research. And while she might not be able to find the exact origins of it, she was sure to find at least a time period to put to it.

When she finished, she got in her car and headed straight back toward her parents' place. She was having dinner there tonight. And she was really looking forward to it, because it was lasagna. She was very hungry.

She tried not to let Sentinel Bridge feel significant as she drove by. She'd been having strange sensations going over it every single time since that night she had driven down and experienced that same dread she had in her dream in real life. Her dreams had been quieter, but that moment of terror still lingered. Thankfully, it wasn't dark.

When she got past the bridge, she saw a figure walking down the gravel road, a dog on a leash. When she realized it was Tom Swenson, she slowed down when he waved.

"Hi, Chief Swenson," she said. It didn't matter that she was an adult or that he was retired, he was just always going to be Chief Swenson to her.

"Hi, Ruby. I'm glad I caught you."

"Oh?"

"There's something that I want to discuss with you."

For the second time that day she felt like she might be in trouble. And like she might have gone back in time at least a decade. "Okay?"

"I've seen your car at the Brewer place. A couple of times now."

Well, damn. She hadn't anticipated that he was going to get right to the heart of it. That anyone had seen her, really. But of course, the retired police chief had noticed and had opinions.

"Yes. I have been there," she confirmed.

She might not be hooked up to a polygraph, and he might no longer be in law enforcement, but she still felt like she had to tell the truth.

"He's dangerous," Tom said. "He might never have been convicted for what he did, but he did do it. I'm sure of that. You need to be careful. You're a good person, Ruby. And I suspect that you like to see the good in people. But sometimes there is no good. And I hope that you can trust me when I tell you that. I'm not saying this to be overprotective, or to try to control you or anything like that. But you just have to trust me."

There were so many words that crowded her throat. For some reason, she found herself wanting to defend Nathan. But she knew that there was no point. Not here or now. But she still wanted it to be said. That she just didn't believe all that.

But she knew that there was no point. So she let it sit there in her throat. Until she could swallow it. "I'll be careful."

"Don't go there again."

And she just couldn't say that she wouldn't. She just couldn't. Because while she might not be able to launch into a full-scale defense of Nathan Brewer, she couldn't promise to do what she knew she wouldn't. "Thank you for your concern, Tom. I'll see you around."

And she was halfway back to her parents' house before she realized she had called him by his first name.

25

MARIANNE

Marianne had not done what her sister had advised her to do. She had not talked to Jackson, in spite of the fact that she knew it was a good idea. In spite of the fact that she knew deep down that she needed to face all of this head-on. Instead, she decided to face it head down in the sand, and move forward as if nothing was happening. That, she thought, seemed the path of least resistance, and it was all she had the energy for right now.

Well, scenes from your teenage years.

Close yourself in your room and don't talk to anyone when you feel bad.

No wonder you're failing as a mother.

Oh, shut up.

She didn't need guff from herself on top of everything else.

What she had done was begin to do research on the original building that The Apothecary had been in. She was hoping that she could find some of the original jewelry designs and have them replicated. She could sell them in the store, and it would be a great talking point for tourists. She and Jackson had no issues discussing that. Because he was nothing if not a savvy businessman, and they connected easily there.

Normally, they connected easily everywhere, and she knew that he was becoming aware that all was not well. Still, she couldn't bring herself to be the one to bring it up. He knew that he had been texting a woman. He should say something.

Once she had decided on that, she knew that it was Ruby she had to go see. She popped the sign on the door that said she would be back in fifteen minutes and walked out the door of The Apothecary, heading down the street toward the large, stately building that housed the history of Pear Blossom.

Marianne had not always loved the town. She could remember feeling so stifled by it. And by the farmhouse and her family.

And then she'd met Jackson. He'd moved to town as a partner at his uncle's tax firm and they'd started a conversation outside the coffeehouse and she'd been... Blown away that a guy like him had chosen to be here.

His family wasn't far, just in Medford. And he liked the quieter pace.

Being around him had made her feel like the quiet wasn't so bad.

Once she'd had him, everything had felt better.

Unease filtered through her.

Did she have Jackson? She wasn't entirely sure. She had been so sure that they were happy. So sure that... They were one of those couples that was just solid. Always on the same page. Supportive. Loving. Filled with open communication. Maybe that was what people always told themselves.

Was it unavoidable that you just had blind spots? Like the big shiny SUV that she had. Sensors all over the place and backup cameras and mirrors, but there was still that one pesky spot.

When she changed lanes too quickly, sometimes she found herself getting honked at by angry drivers she had nearly sideswiped.

Maybe no matter how shiny, no matter how expensive...

There were always blind spots.

Her own was eating at her. Beginning to make her feel like nothing could be real. If she was wrong about Jackson, if she was wrong about them...

She could be wrong about anything. Everything. About how good of a mother she was to her kids. About her issues with her parents. About the way she handled Lydia and her grief and the advice she'd given her.

Jackson had been her rock for years. The thing that had given her confidence in herself.

Maybe that was the danger. In making your compass another person. If it wasn't really pointing north, then where was it pointing?

What else didn't she see?

She walked up the steps and into the museum. And thankfully, it was Ruby perched at the front desk.

"You're playing receptionist today?"

"Indeed," Ruby said, stretching. Her sister's blond hair was piled on her head and seemed to be held there with a pencil. Somewhat effortless and magical and intensely Ruby. Her floaty white dress with long sleeves and tiny pink rosebuds was as effortless as the hair.

"I wanted to know if you had anything that related to The Apothecary. You sent me all that great history, but I'm trying to find out if there's any pictures of designs. I'd like to have some of them replicated."

"That's a great idea, Marianne," Ruby said, hopping up. "And there are a bunch of old catalogs and advertisements for old businesses upstairs in the archives. Let me take you."

"Do you need to watch the front door?"

"Frankly, no. It is before lunch on a weekday. We had a rash of small kids this morning to play in the general store. But I have a feeling that nothing else will be happening until later. If it happens at all. Mostly, it's weekend stuff. And once I get the big Christmas display in, and we have tourists in for the Victorian Christmas... Well, then there will potentially be some people."

"How does the museum stay open?"

Ruby sighed. "Not easily. The historical society manages to get its funding from people who are as invested in all this as we are. But believe me, it mostly comes from wealthy patrons and not ticket sales into the museum. Anyway, they only cost a dollar. They were never designed to make money. That isn't the point."

"Why do you care about keeping it open, then? I mean, I'm not trying to be rude," she said, following Ruby down the narrow hallway to the curved staircase. "Just like I'm not trying to be rude when I asked Dahlia why she's so married to an *actual paper*, when she could just focus on online circulation, which has a much bigger reach."

"Why do you bother to have a storefront? You could just sell everything online."

"I know that," Marianne said. "But I think more people go to stores than still get paper newspapers."

"I just think someday it will matter," Ruby said. "This is a house of stories. Or at the very least, scattered pages here and there. If we don't have them, then what are we connected to? It's like Dahlia interviewing Walter. Sometimes I feel so unbearably conscious that a generation is passing away. Grandpa and Grandma's generation. They're gone already. And soon... Who's left that remembers? Who's left that fought? It's up to us to keep the record. If we don't keep the record, then the substance of truth is lost. It can be played with, tampered with. Online everything can be manipulated. Here... These are real. They're real artifacts of their time. They're not an algorithm. I just believe it's important that they exist. And that someday if somebody needs the answers, they're there."

"What made you feel that way?" Marianne wanted to know, because here she was asking for a catalog for old jewelry, like it might be important. And she wanted to know what had given Ruby this drive so long ago. Marianne knew what was driving her now. It was small and selfish. It was because she wanted to feel important. Like she was doing something that resonated, the same as her sisters. Like she was expanding her life by punching down the wall behind her and exposing the history that she had built her store upon. Getting rid of blind spots, maybe.

"Because you know where you came from. Most people do. My history is a mystery to me, and I guess part of me has always wanted to believe that if there are meticulous enough records in the world, then the answers are there somewhere. All the answers."

"I don't know that we can really have all the answers. And even if we could..." She thought of Jackson. "Do we even want them? Is it better to have some blind spots?"

"I don't know," Ruby said. "I've spent years trying not to think about it. And now I am. And it's...intense. There are very few things that I can imagine that couldn't be worse than the truth. I can conjure up a pretty twisted scenario. So yeah, I figure the truth can't be any worse."

"I don't know about that."

She was thinking of herself again.

Ruby pushed open the door to her office, which was apparently part of the archive. It was a towering room stuffed to the brim with papers and books.

"This is like your brain made manifest," she said.

"It is indeed."

Ruby walked over to a very specific space on the shelves. It all looked the same to Marianne. Then she took out a large file, and set it down on the ground. She sat right with it, her legs skewed, her dress draped down between her thighs. Ruby still seemed like a feral child, for all that she was a grown woman.

And it was another moment where Marianne envied her. The things that Ruby did always seemed… Not careless, but carefree.

And in Marianne's mind, those two things were very different.

Because Ruby cared. Resolutely and extremely about very many things. Things that other people would find small and insignificant. Ruby cared about them. Ruby seemed to care about a full array of things, from the past to the present. She wasn't sure if Ruby ever thought about her future. She seemed to just sort of trip along, but she seemed happier for it.

But then, Marianne had spent a long time making assumptions about her future. She had married Jackson, they had set about building a life and she hadn't had to wonder. They had made their meticulous house, their meticulous life, and they had made it well. And so she hadn't really worried. She had just sort of figured they would continue to add to those things. Grow yet more solid and secure.

She'd been certain she would never repeat her parents' mistakes, and yet she was so worried she was on that path with Ava. And now Jackson was…

She had spent years feeling like she'd been left to her own devices, ignored by her parents in her own home because they didn't know what to do with her.

And now when she needed Jackson most, when she needed him for their daughter, he wasn't… He didn't see. He wasn't there for her. And he should know. He'd always known, and now he was so disconnected from her he didn't.

She had thought maybe someday they would build another house, in ten years or so when their tastes changed and the kids were grown. Maybe they would move farther out of town, get a place up on a hill. But that was about all she had wondered. Dreams of material things, and everything else had felt fixed.

Now it all felt shaken. Over a couple of text messages.

It isn't that, though. It's that he was able to lie so easily.

"Here," Ruby said. "SS Silversmith. Here are a couple of flyers with holiday specials. And there are some jewels."

She passed the stack to Marianne, who started to look through them. There was a gorgeous necklace with a gem at the center. The print was done in black-and-white, so Ruby couldn't be certain what the jewel was. But it was Christmas, so she imagined it was something red. A garnet, perhaps. It was lovely, whatever it was.

"I love this," she said softly.

She leafed through the pages. "Can I take some pictures with my phone? I don't need to bring any of it with me."

"Oh, that's brilliant," Ruby said. "I don't know if I would've thought of that."

"Well, I'm not quite so dedicated to old-fashioned ways as you and Dahlia and Lydia, but I am dedicated to my digital file system. If I weren't, I would have kids' art overflowing my house. As it is, I take a picture of it and—"

She flipped to the next page, and everything stopped. It was the strangest, surreal out-of-body experience, and she couldn't explain it. But it was like she wasn't there. Like she wasn't anywhere. Just like darkness was the floor, the walls and the ceiling. And she wasn't here now. It was some other time. Any time, didn't matter.

But the necklace was there.

Ruby's necklace.

"Ruby," she said. "It's your silver bells."

"What?" Ruby scrabbled from her position up off the floor and came to stand next to her. "What are you talking about?"

"There," Marianne said, pointing to the ad from Christmas in 1927. "The silver bells necklace. It came from SS Silversmith."

Ruby's eyes went wide, her mouth dropping open. And she simply stood there. Staring, as Marianne did, at the ad containing the familiar necklace. It was a unique design, a long chain that fused together at the center, with two strands coming off the bottom and a string of silver bells.

"I'm from Pear Blossom," Ruby whispered.

"Ruby," Marianne said, her heart getting tight. "It could mean anything."

"Not *anything*. It had to have come from the store in 1927," Ruby said. "It's possible it came from a thrift store, I guess. And that it was randomly...no, it can't be anything, Marianne. It would be too coincidental. Whoever left me has to have been from here, or have family from here."

"This is...it's good, Ruby," Marianne said.

She wondered if it was. This quest Ruby was on. Her own issues with truth and her marriage right now left her feeing... Well, every discovery wasn't good.

Was truth so important?

Or was it better to simply stay happy?

"Mom has the necklace," Ruby said. "I've never worn it before. It's one of those things that seemed...too precious. A keepsake, not... I'll have to... I'll have to get it down."

She looked pale suddenly.

"Remember," Marianne said. "You're doing this for yourself. You're what matters. It's not... You don't have to do anything."

And that was said as much for herself as for Ruby.

26

In Defense of History

BY DANA GROVES

1988—The history of our town is too important to let it fall into disrepair. A boarded-up ruin where before we had a sentinel. The significance of this bridge, of what it meant to our town, to the economy here, should not be lost. I urge you, let us pursue restoration before destruction.

RUBY

Ruby was still shaken by Marianne's discovery by the time she left the museum that night.

She did her best not to telegraph any of her feelings to Dana. Though just being around Dana made her feel guilty right now, considering the relationship she was forming with Nathan.

She was beginning to feel like a double agent.

She didn't like it.

She wanted to follow this path. This path that led to Nathan and something darker and more complicated inside of her.

Dahlia's words had been eating away at her since their fight.

That Ruby had chosen the myth and had benefitted from it.

Well, okay, that was true. But she had to end it, then.

It didn't mean she was comfortable with it.

She certainly wasn't used to skirting the edge of controversy when she was home. Sure, her escapades abroad would have been frowned on if she'd been doing them here. If she'd been going out to the local bar and getting drunk and hooking up with local boys, her sisters would have had an intervention.

But if beer were wine, and it was a sexy Italian and not a guy named Brian who worked down at the lumber yards, then it was completely different. It was also in hindsight, and she'd clearly survived it. So.

Either way, she wasn't used to sneaking around.

Tonight, she'd intended to go to her mother's house and ask about the necklace. To have her get it down so Ruby could look at it, but for some reason she felt strange and raw, and wasn't sure she wanted to do it tonight. There would be plenty of time. The necklace had been sitting up in the hall closet, along with the blanket she'd been found in, for the last twenty-two years. It wasn't going anywhere.

She knew that Dahlia was going to their parents for dinner tonight, and it was likely that she was expected to as well, but she fired off a text saying that she wasn't feeling well, then batted away any offers of help and went back to the cottage.

She wanted to… She wanted to think. About what that might mean, if anything. She believed what she said to Marianne. It could mean nothing.

But it could also mean something. The necklace could be connected to a family who had been here for a long time. The necklace could be an heirloom of some kind. And if it was, did that mean there was some kind of care put into her being left?

She'd always imagined that a token being left with her indicated that somehow she mattered. But then, sometimes she'd excused it by saying people were buried with jewelry all the time. In many ways, in her heart, she had always felt like that bridge was intended to be her burial. Someone wrapping her in a blanket along with a token, as if she was being sent into the next life with something shiny.

Then maybe that wasn't it at all. Maybe it was a link. A connection.

Maybe the young woman couldn't admit what had happened. Maybe she was in danger.

You're back to imagining you're a princess.

She left the cottage dim, turning on only a lamp by her desk, and grabbed hold of some of the newspapers. Dahlia had been sifting through them like a mad person, finding articles to reprint—the little snippets about families dining out and moving around town—finding pieces of information that she could use to expand into new pieces.

It was all wonderful, and it seemed to Ruby that it had reinvigorated some interest in the paper, just like Dahlia had thought it might.

So she was pleased for her sister.

She blinked, her eyes suddenly filling with tears.

This was the first link that she had ever found to her past. The first concrete link. The necklace had come from SS Silversmith. The necklace had come from the building her sister's business was now in.

She was drawn back to Pear Blossom for a reason. And she had been right. The answers were here. The history was here.

She was from here.

She sat there, feeling as if roots were growing from the bottom of her feet, down through the floor and into the earth. That she belonged to this place. And maybe it was even more true than she had ever thought. Generations gone by of relatives here.

She saw a flash of movement out of the window, and her focus sharpened to the trees. And then there was a sort of rock-solid certainty that settled down in her chest.

Nathan.

She stood up and just sort of looked out the window, putting her hand on the glass. And he emerged from the trees. And this time, she was certain that he could see her. That he was staring full on into the cottage.

She bit her lip, and then she crooked her finger, gesturing for him to come closer. And she felt a little bit silly, but when he moved, the air went out of her lungs. He went around the front, and she scurried to the door, letting him in.

"What are you doing here?"

"I was walking. But it seems to lead me to you."

Her mouth went dry, her heart jumping against her breastbone. "I wanted to go see you tonight, but I thought... I shouldn't show up again without any notice."

"Well, I guess it was my turn."

"You want a drink?"

"Just water. I don't need to... I don't need to get back to that."

She felt silly for suggesting alcohol after the way she'd found him that day. "Oh, right. I have sparkling water. I'll have some too."

"Ruby, you can have a drink if you want."

"No," she said. "It's not that important."

And it wasn't. Not as important as having some kind of solidarity with him. And she found herself ready to talk to him about her day. Ready to share her story.

"I think I might be from Pear Blossom," she said.

"Yeah?"

And she found herself spilling out the story of how they'd found a picture of the necklace that had been placed with her.

"You really are a mystery, aren't you?"

"I guess so."

He was quiet for a moment. "What's it like? To have a family like you do? They chose you. Your mother chose you. She wanted you."

"Yeah," Ruby said. "She did. I have always felt so loved, Nathan. By everyone. By the whole community." She whispered the last part. "Sometimes I think…everyone thinks I'm this bright, shiny thing and I don't know if I'm allowed to be anything else. Anything but grateful for every breath I take, because isn't that the way it is? When you're a miracle? But I don't feel that way, more and more I don't feel that way. My sister thinks I do, and maybe I… I know I act like it, especially when I'm here. But I find myself slipping it on like a glittery coat and I just…trip down the street smiling, waving, trying to…to show everyone that I was worth all that care and commitment."

Horrifying, shocking tears gathered in the corners of her eyes. But she kept talking. "I think there's darkness in me. Under all that. But I don't understand it. I don't know what to do with it. I don't know why I feel sad when I should be happy and grateful, or why I feel angry…so angry that my mother abandoned me when I should focus on the mother who raised me, who didn't leave me to die."

"Is that darkness, or is it just being human?"

She thought of Lydia and how she'd been so desperate to fix her. And why? Because Ruby didn't want to feel the bad feelings.

The pain of losing Mac.

She didn't know how.

She sat with that softly spoken question for a moment. "I think sometimes I'm not sure if I'm allowed to be human."

Neither of them were. That truth sat there in the silence and was no less loud for neither of them giving it voice.

He said nothing for a moment. "My father was always mean. Always. And my mother just grew more and more brittle. Until she couldn't even stand to touch me. Like she might break. Or maybe it was because I look like him. And I started to get tall and big, and she thought I would hurt her too."

"You would never hurt anybody," she said.

"That's not true. I *would* hurt him. Yeah, I would. If I regret anything, it's never getting a real punch in. He got to die never knowing how much I hated him. But then, it might've been dissatisfying to let them know. Because even if I'd of told him, he probably wouldn't have cared. And that's a hell of a thing. To know that even if I told him, even if I would've shouted every angry thing inside my heart, it wouldn't matter to him. He didn't care if his wife hated him. He didn't care if his son hated him. I don't know what he cared about. Except having another drink. Except just keeping on living in his shady house with people who made him feel strong because they were cowed when he came into the room. I don't know what made him do anything. And that's what scares me."

"What?"

The light was stark on the planes of his face, the shadows dark in the hollows. His eyes were fierce, the color of whiskey or deep gold. And she couldn't look away from him. From his rage. There was a purity to it she wanted to touch. That she wished she could feel. Burning inside of her.

Because it was there, buried deep.

Anger.

At the person who'd abandoned her. At a town that had loved her, but made her a token. And she'd never let herself have it. Never let herself feel it.

And he burned with it.

Bright and hot.

It was beautiful, in a dark and glorious way she would never be able to articulate.

It was pain and something more, and Ruby knew he couldn't deny it.

For the first time she understood why someone might not want to.

Why you would sit in pain and glory in it.

"Sometimes I'm just angry," he said. "Some days I feel like I won. Because I succeeded, even if it was just to prove I could. But then some days it just feels like I'm standing on empty space, and I don't know what the hell I want." He looked at her. "You are the first person that I've talked to since I was fifteen years old. Interrogation made it so I never wanted to share anything again. It gets ingrained. Anything you say can and will be used against you, and dammit, it does. By my dad. By the police. By lawyers. By the press. The local news. Dale Wainwright has had a bee up his ass for me this whole time."

Ruby had recently read everything, and she couldn't deny that. "Yeah, the coverage here was not in your favor."

"I get it," he said. "Everyone loved her. They didn't love me."

"Caitlin knew you," she whispered. "She didn't think you were bad."

"No," he said. "No. But then she was gone and she couldn't help me. And I didn't know what the hell to do without her." He cleared his throat. "She was... She was special."

"Tell me about her."

"She was sweet. Just sweet. Not sarcastic or edgy or anything like that. She just seemed innocent and good. When she smiled, it felt like something lit up inside of me. It felt like maybe I was special."

"What happened that night?" She wasn't asking to trap him, or because she thought he'd done something wrong. Because she thought she already knew.

She was asking because she wanted the truth.

His story.

Not the one that had been written for him.

The one that had been the seed for the story written out for her.

An inescapable tangle, no matter what.

"We went for a walk in the vineyard. There were pears on the trees and I picked them for her. We sat there, and we ate them. I told her about my dad. I told her that everything was bad at home. I kissed her. She told me she... She didn't want to do anything more than that. I said that was okay. I told her

I'd never been with anybody like that, and all I wanted to do was give her a kiss. She seemed happy with that. And she kissed me again. We finished our pears, we walked awhile longer. We went to the top of this mountain and looked down at the river. There's a vantage point there, and you can see Sentinel Bridge, the creek that runs underneath it. We stayed there until it started to get dark. I walked her to the edge of the orchard, back toward the road. And I realized how late it was, and if I didn't get home, my dad was gonna beat my ass. So I left her there."

That word ended on a hard note and he sat for a moment. Saying nothing.

When he spoke again, his voice was hard. "Why did I leave her, Ruby? Why didn't I walk with her? There's a villain out there, and he's not me. But I left her. I see her standing there in my memory, getting smaller and smaller as I get farther away and something happened to her between the edge of that road and her home. I don't know what. And I don't know who. But my life just became a living hell after that. She was the best part of my life, and I would never hurt her. Not if she'd broken up with me. Not because she rejected my advances. Do you know the kinds of things they asked me? I was a fifteen-year-old virgin, who'd just had my first kiss and who knew more about violence than anyone my age should. About the way it felt to be hit, choked, held against the wall. About what it looked like when a man did those things to a woman. They accused me of *killing* her. Brutally. Doing something with her body. Of *raping* her. They said I must have."

His voice was like broken glass, and it cut Ruby. "All I could think was it must show through. That violence in my blood. Because it's my father's blood. And when I'd been in prison for a while, I started to wonder if I didn't deserve it. I knew I hadn't done anything to her, but I wondered if I was destined to do something to someone. I wondered if it was just something you couldn't hide, couldn't fight."

She touched him.

He went solid beneath her fingertips as she traced the grooves by his mouth, felt his whiskers, prickly beneath her skin.

"We get to choose," she whispered. "If I believe one thing, it's that we get to choose. Who you are. Not what people say about you, because they'll just make up their own stories, won't they? And we can't control that. I'm all good, and you're all bad, because that's how simple people are. But they don't know us. I'm just a girl who doesn't know what the hell she wants from life. I'm just a normal woman, who has never had a successful romantic relationship, who doesn't know what she wants from the future. Who turned down a very good job offer to come back home because she doesn't know herself. I'm not special. I can't heal the town. I can't even heal myself."

She looked up at him, and their eyes met. Held.

"The more I find out, the less I feel like I know," she said. She shifted, moving her face closer to his, her heart thundering. "The only thing that seems to be real, the only thing that seems to be beyond my control is you. I saw you that first day I was here. And I feel like... I just feel like..."

There weren't words.

So she kissed him.

Emotion, heat, need, all washed through her in a wave. Her sadness, his anger. It all flowed over her.

His large hand went up to cup her face, and she moved closer to him, angling her head so she could deepen the kiss.

Ruby'd had any number of first kisses.

In clubs with techno music pounding all around her, and the bass thundering in her chest to substitute for an elevated heartbeat. At fancy restaurants, where it felt like a sweet and romantic thing to do, as candlelight hovered all around them, casting it all in a sort of gauzy glow.

In the back of Heath's car, where it had felt new and special and exciting, just because it was something she had never experienced before.

More about her than about him.

But this wasn't the same. This touched a place inside of her, and lit her up. It felt frightening. The quiet that settled around them making her heartbeat seem loud in the space. The lighting wasn't romantic, the moment wasn't that sort of moment. The one where you kissed just because it was time. There was no alcohol fizzing through her veins. Just sparkling water and him. And he was enough to make her feel like she had lost all sense of time and space.

There was nothing about this kiss that was easy. Nothing about it that seemed inevitable, and at the same time, it couldn't be anything but fate.

He was older, and he was... A mess. But he was the center point on her personal map, and she kept going back to him, no matter how much she tried not to. And she couldn't explain it, not even if she was tasked with writing a full essay on the subject—and Ruby could write an argumentative essay on anything. She could only *feel* it. Taste it. Breathe him in.

Let herself drown in the moment of heat, in the friction of his whiskers against her cheek, of his rough hands moving down her arms and around her back, his fingertips pressed just up beneath the hem of her shirt.

And then it ended.

"Ruby," he said. "This can't happen."

"Why not?"

"Look at you. Look at me. This is not a fairy tale. In real life, beauty doesn't tame the beast. She just gets eaten alive."

He meant it. She could see it. In his dark, haunted eyes and in every line on that face she found beautiful. "I decided a long time ago that I'm nobody's long-lost princess. Don't put me on the same pedestal as the rest of them." She slid her thumb along that deep groove next to his mouth. "I'm just a baby that got thrown out like a bag of trash."

"No," he said, gripping her wrist and lowering her hand. "Trust me. You're a miracle. And I'm just a short path to hell."

And he got up and left. Walked right out the front door, and closed it decisively behind him. Ruby was shaking, arousal and emotion still buzzing through her blood.

She was… Wounded to the point of crying and desperate for him. And she just wanted to weep at the unfairness of it all.

Where was the miracle?

Where was the miracle in feeling something like this for a man whose heart was closed up tight? For a man who… It wasn't like she could ever… Wasn't like she could ever really be with him. Not ever. He was the town villain. Where would they go?

He was right.

Beauty and the beast only worked when they were locked away in a palace. You went down into town and people brought their pitchforks.

And she couldn't be responsible for that. Not because of her well-being, because of his.

They'd tortured him enough.

The whole world had.

It was only seven o'clock, but she found herself exhausted. She took a shower and closed herself in her room. And when she heard Dahlia come in, she didn't answer. Instead, she curled up tightly in her bed, her cheeks wet, and she told herself it was just because she hadn't dried her hair thoroughly enough after the shower.

And not because she was crying.

And then she was in front of the bridge again.

She moved through the darkness, slowly but surely, dread like a fist closing around her throat. Until she could barely breathe. Unlike the last time, she found herself propelled through the bridge, toward the water. There was something heavy resting around her neck, more than just fear. She couldn't see it, but she touched it with her hands, cold metal. She dragged her hands down the chain. A necklace. And silver bells.

And she kept on walking toward the creek. And that was when she woke up. She sat bolt upright in bed, gasping, putting her hand around her neck and feeling for the bells. But they weren't there. Because none of it was real.

But the terror rested in her chest long after she had accepted it was a dream. The fear screamed in her bones long after sleep faded.

It had been a dream. Of course it had.

But her hands felt cold as if they'd been grasping silver left out in the December chill for too long.

27

~~Carter Swenson gave me a piece of gum after gym class today, and~~ ~~I'm not going to write that in my diary because it's stupid.~~ Nothing happened today.

DAHLIA MCKEE'S DIARY, AGE 15

DAHLIA

Dahlia sat in her mother's driveway, her car idling, the cold from the air outside settling over her skin. She could go back to the shed. She could go back to the shed and have a conversation with Ruby and attempt to deal with the strange feelings that had been swirling around inside of her since... Since the muffins.

Why did she always do this?

Why did she always push everything off? Why did she always steer the conversation toward other people. Hell, she had oriented this entire project around Ruby. And the fact couldn't be denied.

And then there was Carter.

It wasn't like she was in love with him or anything like that, but he was the unobtainable. And why? *Why?*

That question was ringing in her ears when she opted to turn out toward the main road, cross the bridge and make her way back to town.

She knew where he lived. *Of course* she did. He lived in the same, lovely house that he had lived in with his wife. His wife that everyone had thought he'd been destined to have at least one single boy child with, who might spend his life being pampered and coddled and in general the apple of his parents' eyes. But she left him. She'd gone on to something else. A life somewhere else.

Dahlia hadn't spared much thought for her. Because she hadn't spared much thought for her in high school. At least, not what sort of person she was as a whole. Just as a symbol.

Maybe she was brave.

Maybe she was brave to leave that expected life that she'd been supposed to have.

But Dahlia couldn't celebrate her, not when she pulled her car up outside that house. That extremely normal suburban dream.

Her heart ached. It was a very strange sensation. To realize she was staring at something that she had never thought might be in her reach.

Because it was easier to be alternative. To paint her nails black and cut her bangs in a blunt fashion than it was to hope to aspire to the kind of beauty standards laid out in the halls of Pear Blossom High School.

That it was easier to tell herself she was different by choice. Not competing with anyone or anything.

She was walking her own, important path. That was what she told herself.

Integral in that. All the while thinking she… Wasn't.

Being afraid she wasn't.

Her heart skipped.

He was there. His car was in the driveway. And she saw him. He walked past the kitchen window, completely unaware that she was outside. Or maybe he wasn't unaware. He was a police officer, after all.

She laughed. And then she decided she'd better text him.

I am not calling you. But I am literally sitting outside in your driveway.

She looked up into the house, to see if she could see movement again. See if she could see anything. She didn't.

And finally, three little dots appeared at the bottom of the message thread. **You're outside my house?**

I am.

Come in.

She got out of the car, and shut the door behind her. Then she stopped, turned around, locked it. Walked halfway toward the door, stopped again.

Her heart was thundering hard. What exactly was she doing here? With this man who was the epitome of unobtainable. Who was the epitome of that kind of perfection prized so deeply in a town like this.

Are you a coward?

No, she wasn't a coward. Okay, she was a little bit of a coward. Consistently, a bit of a coward.

Because when her mother brought her muffins and asked to have a conversation, she changed the subject. When Carter hit on her, she changed the subject. Made a joke. She didn't try for much of anything.

And she could… She could say what she wanted about Ruby. About circumstances in her life making things difficult. But there just wasn't an excuse anymore. There was no point to any of it, not really. What did excuses get her? Nowhere new. Nowhere remotely productive. And she had this. Had this opportunity right here.

And why not take it? Why continue to be...

She was just so dour and Ruby was right. Committed to the narrative of her own inferiority, and where had that gotten her?

She liked her bangs, though, Ruby was wrong about that.

So she charged up to that front door, and she knocked.

He opened the door. "Hi. You really are here."

"I really am."

"Do you want to come in?"

It was no expression of ardent admiration. But it was somehow just right.

And talking seemed overrated. She figured talking could wait. She'd done plenty of talking. And this wasn't changing the subject. This was grabbing what she wanted with both hands. Not worrying about the woman who had lived in this house before, the perfection of this house, or all the ways that part of her had always longed to inhabit a place like this, in a sense of permanence with a man like him. Possibly him.

It wasn't the time to analyze that. It was the time to live in it.

So she stretched up on her toes, and she kissed him.

And he closed the door quickly behind them.

And after that, no words were needed.

28

Our Bridge, Our Town

BY DALE WAINWRIGHT

1991—I try to stay away from opinion pieces, and yet this merits one. The historical society still lacks the funds to complete the restoration project of Sentinel Bridge. The importance of the bridge is lost now, in a time when convenience isn't even a thought. We expect for travel to be easy. But there was a time when the orchards on the other side of the bridge could not easily get a wagon to the train station to have pears exported, and that changed when the bridge was built. It is an ingrained part of what made Pear Blossom. It should be restored, and we should all feel a sense of investment in that.

RUBY

Ruby had the display ready to go, which was great, because she needed the following day off, and while no one was depending on her to come in, she still felt like she needed to clear it with Dana. She worked fairly independently in her part of the museum, and it was nice. Of course, spending so much time alone meant she had an awful lot of time to think. Her mind wandered more often than not to Nathan. To the kiss that they'd shared. And the whole tangle of ugly emotions that went along with it.

The guilt that she felt having done that when she really did care about Dana so much. And the way that it conflicted with… With what she knew she was supposed to think about herself. What she'd been told about herself.

She didn't feel right. She didn't feel miraculous. She didn't really feel like Ruby. Not the Ruby that she had tried to be for all of these years.

And it had only been one kiss. But the revelation about the silver bells, and their origins at SS Silversmith was one that she couldn't stop picking over. On top of that, she was having difficulty sleeping, because her dreams were relentless.

Always the bridge. And always fear.

Lack of sleep was making her cranky.

But this was the problem with wondering. With wondering if they were wrong about Nathan. Which meant they could be wrong about her. There had been a feeling of invulnerability to being Ruby McKee, the miracle. Destined to heal the town of Pear Blossom, destined for great things.

But what if she wasn't. What if she was as frail and vulnerable as anyone. As likely to be a disappointment as not. As likely to fail as succeed.

As likely to make a very bad choice with a man who could be dangerous.

Except in her gut she felt like he wasn't.

But could she even trust her gut?

She wasn't even here for any of this. For this obsession. She was supposed to be helping Lydia, which was what she had to focus on now.

She squared her shoulders and walked downstairs, where Dana was seated behind the dark, curved desk right near the front doors. "If you don't need me tomorrow for anything special, I probably won't come in?"

"That's fine," Dana said.

"Okay." She let out a breath. It always stressed her out to do things like this. "I probably should've talked to you about it sooner, but I didn't know exactly what the time frame was on my sister's store. She's opening that farm store on her property."

"I remember. You told me about it."

"Yeah. So, she is hoping to open tomorrow so we have to finish some things up tonight, and then I just want to be there tomorrow, make sure she has all the help she needs with the kids."

"I gave you your job so you could make less work for me, Ruby. Not more."

"Right. I know. Which means you don't need to hear all about my personal life."

"Correct."

"I... Thank you," Ruby said. "For the job. I know... I know I already said that. But I do appreciate it. I wanted to make sure I was here for Lydia. You know, after everyone got tired of her being sad. People rally around you and then..."

"I know," Dana said, her voice more bitter this time.

"I know you do."

"She's lucky to have you." The unspoken part of that was that some people didn't have anyone. Dana hadn't had anyone.

"Ruby... After you were found... I talked to social services about you." She looked Ruby in the eye. "I wanted to adopt you."

Ruby felt completely shaken. "You did?"

"Yes. That was before... Well, before I knew your parents had formally started the adoption process. Ruby, I did think you might be a miracle. I thought you might be my miracle."

"I..."

"You don't have to say anything. I'm glad now that your parents had you. I've been glad ever since your sister told those boys to stop throwing rocks at my house. Because I realized that you had a good family. And that's better than just one bitter, single woman. You don't just have parents. You have sisters."

Ruby swallowed hard. "I feel very... I'm honored, I guess. That you wanted me."

"A lot of people wanted you, Ruby."

"Yeah. Well. People think they do. But... They just get caught up in the story, don't they? I know you weren't."

"They wouldn't let me," Dana said.

"Who?"

"Child services. They said because of the circumstances surrounding Caitlin's disappearance, and that I was single..."

"What about Caitlin's disappearance? You were never a suspect."

"It didn't matter." Her lips stretched into a thin smile. "They arrested Nathan, but it never brought them any closer to any answers. We never found her. And because there was never any closure, never any clarity... My parenting could still be part of the problem."

"Do you not think Nathan did it?" It seemed imperative to know that. So very, very important.

"I don't know," she said. "I don't know. And Tom Swenson thinks that he does. That was enough to stop the investigation. All I know is I have no answers. I don't have my daughter or her body. I was told that it made me unfit in some way to ever be a mother again. What did it solve, Ruby?"

Nothing. Ruby didn't even need to say that.

"They're wrong," Ruby said. "About you. About..."

"Go and help your sister," Dana said. "She needs you. I'm glad that she has you."

The unspoken. That it had gone the way that it needed to. That it had worked out for the best.

"You have mattered to me," Ruby said. "So much. From the time I was a kid, I wanted to know more about what you did.

And that's why I'm here. That's why I studied history. It's why… You've been an important part of my life."

Dana said nothing. She just nodded.

Ruby walked out to her car, losing track of the time as she drove to her sister's farm. She parked in front of the little barn, which had planters out in front with evergreen boughs stuffed into them.

And Ruby just stood there for a second, all of her thoughts out of order. Her ears buzzing. Because the conversation with Dana had shaken her. Because she had already been shaken by what had happened with Nathan.

She took a breath and tried to shake it off as she walked into the space, which had been beautifully transformed. It had a clean cement floor, wooden shelves and tables throughout. There were potted plants everywhere, and local art, cute tote bags hanging from a peg by the door.

Dahlia was standing on a crate in the corner, putting a hanging potted plant up on a hook. Whistling.

Marianne was standing off to the side by a mound of winter veggies, and Lydia was arranging soap and jars of honey.

Dahlia was whistling.

"You seem cheerful," Ruby said when she walked in.

"Yeah. *Why?*" Marianne asked.

"I did something nice for myself," Dahlia said. "A few different times." She hopped off the crate and grinned.

"And that was?" Marianne asked dryly. "If it's a sheet mask, you're going to have to give me the brand, because you're glowing."

"Carter Swenson."

"You what?" Ruby was shocked by that.

Because they'd had their fight, and Dahlia had gotten some fair shots in, and by the end of it Ruby hadn't felt like either of them were anything but entrenched.

You think you're the only person reevaluating things?

"Well," Lydia said. "And it's going well?"

"I don't know that it's a thing. But it's going very well. Whatever it is. I don't have time for it to be anything more than..."

"Sex?" Lydia asked.

"Lydia," Dahlia said, "children are present."

She meant Lydia's own children, who were running around outside the barn.

"Yes," Lydia said blandly. "They are. So you just...jumped into bed with him. And everything is fine?"

"Yes," Dahlia said. But there was enough of a pause, enough of a catch in her voice, that it made Ruby wonder.

"What's wrong?" Marianne asked.

"I just don't have any practice with things like this, you know, without... Anonymity. Awkward serious relationship stuff."

"Oh. Complicated," Marianne said.

"Well, I hope not. But I also wonder if to an extent complicated is unavoidable."

"Sex is complicated," Lydia said. "No way to get around that."

"Not necessarily," Ruby said, trying to remember those carefree European trysts with easy kisses that left her feeling high after.

Nothing like what Nathan had ignited in her with that touch of his mouth to hers.

"Different when you live in the same small town," Lydia pointed out.

"It feels uncomplicated at the moment," Dahlia said. "It's just that whole other shoe. I'm watching for when it's going to drop."

"Maybe there's no other shoe," Marianne said.

"Do you really think that?"

Marianne lowered her hand and looked blandly at Dahlia. "No."

"And what's going on with you?" Lydia asked. "Because you clearly are not in a better space."

"No," Marianne said. "I'm not. I know my husband lied to

me. I know he's been glued to his phone much more often than usual, and I have not brought myself to ask what in the world is going on."

"He lied to you?" Ruby asked. "About what?"

"He was…" Marianne looked distressed, as if she hadn't realized Ruby didn't know about the situation and was now resentful over having to explain. "He was texting another woman. I asked him what he was doing and he said he was napping. And why would you do that if you weren't hiding something?"

"You have to ask him," Ruby said.

"Unless I don't," Marianne said. "Because what if it makes things worse?"

"You need to talk to him," Lydia said.

"*Really*, Lydia?" Marianne asked.

"Hey," said Lydia, looking annoyed, and taking another honey jar out of a carton and putting it onto a display table. "You're supposed to be nice to me. I'm fragile."

"Can't have it both ways."

"Shouldn't you learn from my mistakes, then? You should talk to him."

"*I know*," Marianne said, sounding cross.

"We're not saying that to bother you," Lydia said. "Just because… Eventually, you have to talk about things. Trust me."

"You're depressing me," Dahlia said. "I don't want to talk about anything with Carter. I just want to keep making out with him. Among other things."

And Ruby said nothing, because there was simply no space to bring up that Dana had wanted to adopt her. And that she had kissed a man they all thought was a monster, and that now the monster didn't want to see her anymore, and that she bitterly regretted it, because for some reason she missed him like he was part of her.

But she was afraid that eventually it would all come out. That eventually they'd have to talk about it. Because what they had just said to each other was true not just of husbands. But people that shared your life.

Dahlia might be able to talk to Carter. But Carter was a citizen of this town. Not a ghost who hovered outside the fringes.

For some reason, Ruby had the oddest feeling that she related more to Nathan in that moment than to anyone else.

Maybe it was that thing inside her that wondered at its own darkness.

But she decided not to think about that.

She helped scrub and clean and arrange produce until her brain was blank. And then they all went inside and had pizza and ice cream. And she tried so hard to just smile and eat, and be happy for Lydia and all that she was accomplishing.

She just desperately didn't want to think about the hard things anymore.

"What's going on, Ruby?"

It was Lydia who asked that later, as they stood at the kitchen sink, Dahlia and Marianne in the dining room still.

"What?"

"You're quiet. And very not like you."

She tried to force a smile. "There are…things right now that are…making me really sad." Her eyes filled with tears, and she couldn't hold them back. "I'm sorry, I…"

"Tell me," Lydia said, reaching her hand out and wrapping her fingers around Ruby's wrist. "Tell me what's happening."

"Dana told me she wanted to adopt me. And that child services wouldn't let her because…something she did might have made Caitlin run away. And there's this guy and…oh, that sounds so stupid. But there is. And I hate this. I hate feeling like this."

"Ruby," Lydia said. "If I have learned any one thing from the last few years, it's that sometimes you can't outrun the rainstorm. You have to walk through it. And you don't always know when it will end."

"That's not comforting."

"It should be. You don't have to feel happy all the time."

"I came to make you feel better…"

"I do. Sometimes. But I'm grieving something complicated. And my children are hurting. And my life is… I don't know. But there's joy in it. Even when I'm sad. I have a hard time showing my feelings, and you seem to do it so easily. But don't forget, your feelings are yours, and you don't owe them to anyone. You don't have to smile to please other people."

"I don't want to feel pain, Lydia."

"I know."

"I just will for a while, though, huh?"

Lydia nodded. "Yeah. But you won't be alone."

"That was one thing Dana said…that she was glad in the end. That she didn't adopt me. Because I had sisters." Ruby swallowed hard, her chest sore. "I'm glad for that too. I'm so… grateful for you."

"Me too, Ruby."

When Ruby left, it was cold. And it started to rain.

She was walking through the rain.

There was nothing she could do about it.

But maybe that meant she couldn't make it worse.

Maybe that meant it was time to stop trying to be a miracle.

And just be Ruby.

29

Change in the Air

BY MARIANNE MCKEE

Pear Blossom High Chronicle

The leaves are beginning to turn a rusty red and the air is crisp like a good apple. The changing of the seasons is upon us. How fast this brilliant stage of autumn moves. It's to be savored. Because what is red and gold cannot stay forever. How quickly it succumbs to the chill of winter.

MARIANNE

Marianne wasn't exactly receptive to what her sisters kept saying to her. But she was starting to feel like she was going crazy. That sensation that she'd felt when she'd seen Ruby's necklace in the catalog hadn't fully gone away.

It was like the ground had fallen out from beneath her feet. And it was simply gone.

She felt disoriented. Everything around her foreign.

Jackson was her compass. Her North Star. The way that she oriented her life. He was the reason that she had begun to feel settled here. The reason that she had decided not to travel. The reason she had decided not to stay away.

They never fought, they never argued. Things were never tense. But they were now.

And if that foundation of her life, if that guiding light wasn't what she had believed it was… She didn't know what she was left with. She texted him to let him know that she was on her way home and asked if he wanted anything from the store. He didn't respond.

Ten minutes later she trudged into the house, feeling burdened because no one had come out to help her with her bags and really she might as well be single and alone if she had to handle such things by herself.

Jackson wasn't downstairs, so she went up the stairs and pushed open the bedroom door to find him sitting on the edge of the bed looking down at his phone.

"Oh, weird," she said. "I texted you, and you didn't respond to me."

"Sorry," he said. "I was just responding."

And suddenly, everything that she had been keeping inside of her boiled over. "Were you? Or were you responding to Julie?"

"What?"

"Do not look at me with that dumb, slapped with a mackerel look on your face, Jackson Martin. Because I was sure that there might be a reasonable explanation for me seeing that you were texting someone named Julie until that. Until that fake innocent look crossed your face. You have been lying to me."

"Have I?"

"Stop that. Stop asking questions that you know the answer to better than I do."

"Marianne…"

And it was like something inside her, some beast she'd lost control over, snapped its leash. And she just wanted to scream the house down. The walls to this room. It was like a great beast had woken up inside of her and she wanted to yell at him.

Yell at him in a way she hadn't for all these years. Yell at him like she'd never yelled at her parents, like she wasn't yelling at Ava, even though her daughter's sullen behavior was freaking her out.

But Jackson needed to be there for her.

He was supposed to be there.

He wasn't like everyone else. He understood her. He'd made her feel whole and safe and loved, and now he was lying to her. Pulling away.

And she was going to die if she didn't get this out, this pain building in her chest, this rage, this truth.

"How could I be so stupid? I saw that you were texting her on Thanksgiving. And I asked you what you were doing and you said nothing. You said you were sleeping. I've never heard you mention this woman's name. I know everyone that you know. You talk exhaustively to me about your friends, about the different text conversations that you have, but you have never mentioned her once. Tell me that there is an explanation for this other than the fact that you're cheating on me."

"Hang on," he said, holding his hand out and setting his phone down. "For the last three and a half weeks you've thought that I was cheating on you?"

"You were texting another woman and you lied to me. What else should I think?" she said.

He looked shocked. And that hurt. But something about his pain in that moment only galvanized her anger. He had made her feel... She'd doubted everything for weeks.

She wasn't going to just fade quietly into the background.

"For the last three and a half weeks you thought I was *cheating on you*, and you didn't say anything to me? You can get in bed with me every night, thinking that I was cheating on you. You let me kiss you, thinking that I was cheating on you. And served me dinner, thinking that I was cheating on you. And had conversations with me, while thinking I was cheating on you, and you never said a damn thing to me?"

"How am I the bad guy?" she asked, practically digging her heels into the carpet. "You're the one that was lying."

"Marianne," he said. "Please feel free to read my text stream with Julie." He picked the phone up again, opened it and held it out to her. She didn't know what to do with that. With this unfettered access to this device that had become a bad object in her mind. That had become a container of lies and betrayal. But she did exactly what he asked.

She clicked on Julie. He hadn't texted her for over a week. And the last text was about travel arrangements. She scrolled up. They were travel arrangements for Marianne and Jackson. Because he had been planning a vacation.

"She's a travel agent," he said. "And I didn't want to be on the phone with her because I didn't want to make you suspicious. Because I was trying to surprise you."

Maybe that was really all it was. Maybe that was really all it was.

She looked up at him, and the anger was gone. Replaced with hurt, exhaustion. She'd caused that. And for some reason...

"I cannot believe that you thought I would cheat on you," he said.

For some reason she couldn't find it in her to feel bad. She was just still so angry, that restless thing that had been clawing at her.

"Don't look so shocked," she said, her stomach and mouth sour. "A lot of men cheat. And women don't see it coming."

"Yeah, that's true, but do you really know what's going on in the marriages of those people? You don't know. I thought we were happy."

"We are," she said. "But you lied to me and... I'm *not*..."

She wasn't okay.

She just wasn't.

She felt like a fool, and even though he had been hiding this for a reason, the feeling wasn't gone. She'd felt alone and isolated, and it had reminded her of the darkest time in her life. When she'd been slipping under the surface of the water, and there had been no one reaching for her hand.

That anger in her was taking on a life of its own, and she had nowhere to aim it.

But he was here.

He was here, and she could aim it right at him.

"Marianne, I… I don't know what to say. I cannot believe that you just… Were in the house with me. Pretending that everything was normal when you thought that."

"*I* didn't *do* anything," she said.

"You didn't talk to me," he said, putting his hand on his chest. His heart. "Do you have any idea how much… It's insane to me to think that we lived in the same house while you thought that I betrayed you. I haven't touched another woman since we've been together. I haven't even thought about it. I don't know what to make of the idea that you think that I might be capable of that. Of hiding it from you. Of living with you while lying to you."

"*It's not fair,*" she said, tears pushing against her eyes. "It's not fair of you to act like you were the one that was betrayed when I thought…"

He took a step toward her, and she backed away. She might as well have slapped him. "You thought that I did it to you. But I didn't, Marianne. I was trying to plan a trip for us. I was trying to surprise you."

And she just didn't want to give. She didn't want to. That old anger was there, that rage that she'd thought long gone along with acne and crushes on boy band singers. That's what she felt like. An unreasonable, angry teenage girl.

"You still lied," she said. "You lied to me. So that's why it felt wrong. So don't go acting like there's something wrong with me. Like I made things up. You really weren't being honest with me."

"What kind of honesty did you want? Is a surprise a lie now?"

"I don't… I don't know. I just know that nothing feels *right* right now. Including us. And that you lied on top of everything else…"

And then he got angry. Right back.

"A surprise is only a lie if you're unhappy, and if you're unhappy, don't put it at my door and pretend I'm the one who betrayed us. Don't act like I'm the one who's dissatisfied when I'm not."

"Well, maybe I *am* unhappy!" And she didn't think she meant it. She really didn't. But she needed to say it all the same. "Who knows what they want from their life when they're twenty-two, Jackson? Maybe we were just young and stupid."

And something in his face shifted. A weight she'd never seen there, a sadness.

"We obviously need to have a talk."

"I don't want to," she said.

"You're not acting like yourself."

She wasn't. She knew it. She didn't care right now.

"Why, because I'm mad at you?"

"Marianne."

"Just go. I don't want to talk to you."

She turned away from him, and he… He left.

He stormed out of the bedroom, went down the stairs and slammed the door shut behind him. And all Marianne could do was just stand there. Because he had never done anything like that in the entirety of their marriage. Just walked away. Not told her where he was going. Not told her when he would be back. Just leaving her.

Just leaving her.

And in that moment, she felt a crushing, deep despair.

Because maybe… Maybe he really would leave her. She'd

begun picking at a thread that hadn't been loose until she started tugging. It wasn't him—it was her. It was…something to do with her parents and Ruby and Ava. Something to do with her. And she'd made it about him. She just had all this… Frustration and she'd thrown it all on the man who had always been there for her.

She'd made the loose thread. And she had picked it just enough to cause it to begin to unravel.

And she didn't know if she could ever stitch it back.

30

RUBY

It was dark when she pulled up to Nathan's. She knew what she was doing. She knew exactly what she was doing, and she couldn't regret it. Couldn't stop to second-guess herself, because then she might turn away.

She had come back to Pear Blossom because her heart had been calling her here. And more than anything, it was Nathan who had resonated with her since coming back home. She was linked to him, and she couldn't explain it. But did it matter? There were a great many things in her life that she couldn't explain. She couldn't explain how she had come to be on a bridge on the night before Christmas Eve. When the weather had been just like this. The air cold and thin and snapping, sharp against her skin.

In these days of early twilight, when darkness was more common than sunshine.

She couldn't explain that.

And so, in a way, it seemed right to be here. It seemed right to be experiencing this thing. This poison miracle that made the blood in her veins feel like it was electrified.

She got out of the car.

She was doing it again. Invading his space when he had made it clear that he didn't want her to.

But he wasn't used to this. The people in his life had given up on him. The people that were supposed to be his community had called him a monster. His own parents hadn't believed in him. The police chief thought he was rotten from childhood.

Maybe someone had to be relentless. Maybe someone had to keep kicking at the door until it was knocked down.

She knocked.

He opened up the door, his expression shaded, half-hidden in the shadows.

"Ruby."

"I know. You told me to stay away from you."

"You're not very good at following directions."

"Sadly no. I've been that way since I was a child. A little bit too independent. I always have to see why something is a bad idea for myself. I really don't learn until the mistake has been made."

He looked… Sad. Hollow. "I'm not a mistake you want to make, Ruby McKee. You are a golden girl. All I could ever do is tarnish your shine."

He was warning her away because he didn't want to resist.

Well, neither did she.

She took a step forward, closing the door behind them. And she put her hand on the center of his chest. "You are not what other people say you are. You're this." She pressed her hand more firmly against his chest, and she could feel his heart beating there. Strong and steady. And then she could feel it quicken. "You are everything inside of you that they couldn't take. You

301

are not your father's fists or your mother's disappointment. You are not the suspicion of a town full of people who are just afraid. You did not go missing when she did. You're here. And I see you."

He wrapped his hand around her wrist and took it away from his chest. "Why?" His eyes were wild, fierce, and they were searching for answers. And how could she give them? She didn't know who she was. She was sixteen years younger. And he was raw and scarred and bruised from all that he had suffered.

But if she was going to be a miracle, then she wanted to be a miracle right now. Except she didn't feel like there was any magic inside of her. Anything that made her particularly special, not right now.

She was just a woman who cared an awful lot, and who was faced with the sharp, hard reality of this man who had been so badly damaged by the people that were supposed to be... They were supposed to be his.

He'd been wounded by this community that had meant so much to her, that had rallied around her and seen her as something special.

And in him they had found their villain.

If they could be so wrong about him, then they could be wrong about her.

They could be so very wrong about her.

It felt a terrible thing that she needed so desperately for them to be wrong and right all in the same moment. Because she needed to believe that she had something special inside of her, the same as she needed to believe that he was good.

And maybe those couldn't exist together. Maybe the lie and the truth couldn't come from the same place. So both had to be true or both had to be false.

It doesn't work that way.

Those words filtered through her so strongly she had no idea where they'd come from.

If only life were so simple.

But it wasn't. It couldn't be.

These stories are just a lot of people trying to make life simple. And right then, in the middle of that truth, it made sense.

That the good object and the bad object of the town should be in one room together. Looking at each other.

As if they contained the mysteries of each other's universe.

Because they were both, and they were neither. Because they were simply what scared, confused people had decided they were. Except they were also so much more. And maybe they were the only people who could help each other find the truth.

"Because we get to decide," she said. "That's why. Because we are both what they made us. How can I go on as I have knowing that they made you into a monster the same as they shaped me into an angel? I'm not an angel. I'm not made of glass, and I can't be broken. I was left to die on a bridge. I am so much more than they think. I am flawed. And I am sad. I'm wrong, as often as I'm right. Why wouldn't you be the same?"

And that was how she found herself being pulled forward, gripped in his strong arms, held flush against his iron chest. And she could feel his heart.

She hoped that he could feel hers.

"You were the thing I didn't know I was waiting for," he said, his voice a gruff whisper.

Tears filled her eyes. "What?"

"I kept staying. I kept staying and I didn't know why. But it was for you."

He kissed her. But it wasn't that desperate, feral thing that had roared to life between them at the cottage. He kissed her not like she might break, but like she was something of exquisite value that required a gentle hand, because that was simply the reverence with which you handled such a thing.

And she relished that. That moment. Where his mouth laid claim to pieces of her soul with every brush of his lips on hers.

He lifted her up off the ground. With strength. Strength that formed a shield around her. Strength that didn't bruise.

A kind of controlled power that demonstrated to her exactly what manner of man he was. And if she had ever had any doubts, this would have shown her.

Just what he was capable of.

Not in the way that so many people thought, but that he was capable of bending his strength into a shield. Into extraordinary protectiveness. He carried her up the stairs and into the bedroom. The one he had been staying in, clearly. Not the master.

"It was an extra room. I couldn't stay in their room. I couldn't stand mine. This house is haunted."

She nodded. Because she knew just what he meant. And yet he'd stayed in it, waiting. Waiting for her, he said.

He kissed her again, and this time, some of the gentleness was stripped away, but it was no less powerful for it. Because she liked that. Knowing that he was capable of both. Knowing that she could withstand both. And that he thought so.

The kiss went on and on, and her earrings kept jingling with the motion, all bright and cheerful and wrong, and she finally worked them from her ears and tossed them somewhere on the floor.

Then she stripped his shirt up over his head, and her heart squeezed tight. He was so beautiful. His body showing the marks of physical labor. His muscles clearly defined.

She had tripped her way through Europe indulging herself in fantasies. With young men, close to her own age. And she had enjoyed them. Their lean bodies that didn't shift even with the carelessness of their lifestyle. Their muscles that existed— sleek and compact—simply because of their youth. Not fading because they spent their nights drinking, or their days eating whatever the hell they wanted.

He was different.

The efforts that he made in his life seemed to be carved into those chiseled marks on his body. The work that he did, the weight that he carried on his shoulders, what shaped him into the man he was.

Those other men—those *boys*, really—hadn't had lines on their faces. They'd been all smooth, carefree perfection. And he had lines. Trenches worn in his skin by grief. By loss. By betrayal. The map of who he was, written there on his face, clear and achingly glorious.

She imagined that in his youth, in the beginning, he'd had that sort of carefree beauty about him.

But it was ever so much more compelling worn through with all these cares. And it hurt, to see what his life had cost him. It was indescribably sad. But it *was*.

And there was no changing it.

No going back. No erasing it.

Honoring it, caring about it, *loving* it—that seemed to be the best way forward.

She kissed his face, right where his eyes crinkled. In his forehead, where the deepest groove always formed between his eyebrows, anger and fear and uncertainty all expressed in that one line. Then she went back to his mouth, consuming him, igniting a fire that might well consume them both.

An echo perhaps of the fire that he'd started when he was a boy, because he was a man who carried so much heat around inside of him, so much anger. So much injustice, that it could never be simple. It could never be softer, easy.

But that was fine. She'd tried soft and easy.

It didn't lead anywhere.

His large hands held her thighs steady, as he changed the power balance and kissed her neck, down her collarbone, as he started to strip her clothes from her body.

Ruby had never been self-conscious about her figure. And she wasn't exactly self-conscious in this moment, but she felt seen in a way that she hadn't before. His eyes were sharp, and he was assessing her in a manner that no man ever had.

But she realized it had never mattered before who they were. Just as to them it had never mattered who she was.

The closest that she had ever come was Heath in high school, but even then it had been about… Being young and close to the same sort of pretty and doing the things that felt right physically.

Who they were was in the gravity of this moment. The intensity of it. Their roots to this town grew down deep through the floor, all the way down through the earth. They were the two people least likely to make their way to each other. And yet they had. And they also seemed the two people most fated. Most likely. Most obvious.

And it was that fate that made her feel scorched.

He said nothing, instead he wrapped his arms around her and kissed her, while he somehow managed to work his way free of the rest of his clothes, bringing them both down onto the bed.

She shivered.

She had never been so extremely aware of all the places her body touched another person's. In a way that went beyond just arousal or physical desire. But they were connected. Chest to chest, thigh to thigh. And she could swear she felt her heart beating against his own.

And then she was lost, in the way that his hands moved, skimming over her curves. In the way he kissed her, touched her.

As if he knew her.

This man, who did not believe the prevailing truths of Pear Blossom, treated her like a miracle anyway.

And her whole body sang with it.

He put his hand between her thighs, his eyes intently on hers as he worked her to the peak and then pushed her over the edge. She threw her head back and cried out, and he captured her mouth with his, swallowing that pleasure down as if it made it his own.

And then he was right there, thrusting hard and strong inside of her.

And it was like a piece of herself had suddenly been placed just there in her soul. Right where it hadn't been before. Right where she had always needed it. But hadn't realized.

And as his strokes built up yet more pleasure inside of her, she realized why this was different. So very different.

Because every other sexual encounter she'd had before had been about her. Finding herself. Learning about herself.

But this was about *them*. Not what he could get out of it, and separately what she could get out of it. But about the two of them together, and the unique, inescapable alchemy that they created one with the other.

And when the wave hit the second time, they went over the edge together. And she clung to his shoulders, and let him take them both into his darkness.

Right then she felt closer to her own. But with him, she didn't have to hide it.

31

MARIANNE

It was two o'clock in the morning. And Jackson still hadn't come home. That had never happened before. Ever. He didn't… He didn't do that. He didn't stay away from home. He didn't stay out all night, not even if he was angry.

She pulled his phone up on the tracking app, and she could see that the last place it had pinged had been the bar in town. But it was off now. Not showing a location.

She threw her phone across the room, and broke it against the wall. "Dammit, Jackson," she said, to her empty bedroom, where nobody cared.

And she had to wonder if she had gone and designed the end of her marriage. Maybe he was out having sex with someone else right now? Because she had accused him of it, so why not. Why not become the thing that she thought he was.

She lay down on the bed and curled into a ball, misery cascading over her.

She didn't know how she got here. She didn't know how she had become this person. How everything had been fine, and then it wasn't. How she had been satisfied, until she wasn't.

She didn't understand any of this.

And she was afraid that it might be too late to fix it now.

LYDIA

It was four in the morning, the day she was supposed to open her shop. She never got up this early to do chores. It was ridiculous. But in the gray light of dawn, she didn't know what else to do. She couldn't sleep. It was a big day for her. The biggest.

She didn't know if Chase would show up.

He'd poured the cement pad for the patio behind the store a week ago. He'd delivered odds and ends and left them out front for her. But she hadn't really seen him. He hadn't called or texted.

She wished that she hadn't asked for space. Or that he hadn't given her what she'd asked for, which wasn't fair at all. She wished… She wished that she was brave enough to ask him what he meant when he'd said it was always her.

She wished that she was brave enough to withstand this moment, but she didn't think she was.

She'd told Ruby that there were storms you just had to walk through and… The grief of losing Mac she expected. This… She wasn't ready for this. This wasn't supposed to be her storm.

The feelings she had for this man.

She took a deep, shaking breath and went into the chicken coop, flinging some feed down before going to open the little henhouse.

The chickens flooded out, which allowed her to get in there and get her eggs.

Today she was realizing a dream. The store was stocked. She knew that other local farmers and artisans would come and support her. So much of the town would, in part because of the pity they felt for her over Mac.

This new page in her story was written, clear.

But the next one wasn't. And she was just tired of that. Tired of not knowing.

You know what you want.

Chase.

She wanted to talk to him. Touch him. Kiss him.

She wanted to be in bed with him again, under those blankets. Wanted him to hold her in his arms.

The only thing stopping her was fear. Fear of what everyone else would think.

Fear of feeling that deep.

The store was already scary enough. She didn't know if she was brave enough to take on anything else.

DAHLIA

It was six in the morning and she was driving back home to change before work. It was probably not the smartest thing to keep doing this. Or maybe she just needed to keep some clothes at Carter's, but that sounded like a commitment, neither of them had talked about anything like that.

He hadn't slept with anyone since his marriage ended. And before that, it wasn't like they'd been lighting the sheets on fire. He was really enjoying what was between them. He smiled like she was the sun when she showed up at his door.

But they never talked about the future. And never talked about anything serious. And the fact remained that she was Dahlia McKee, alternative princess of Pear Blossom High, while he was Carter Swenson, the big man on campus and most likely to succeed. She didn't know where she fit into his life.

If even Lena hadn't been able to withstand it.

But he got to her. She thought that maybe it was just because he was some kind of messed up fantasy. That he was sort of the unobtainable brass ring. But it was more than that. She liked him. She liked staying up late with him and drinking cider spiked with whiskey. She liked talking to him. About his job. About his life growing up in Pear Blossom. He didn't talk about his marriage in any great depth.

And someday, they were going to have to.

Unless they didn't have to.

Unless their relationship wasn't ever going to be more than this.

This thing where she went over without a change of clothes and had to drive all the way back out of town to get ready to go into the paper. Where they didn't share a drawer or a room, or anything, really, but a bed part-time.

And it was those conversations. That... Saying what she felt, what she wanted, that always seemed to get stuck in her throat.

She parked in front of the shed and stared blankly ahead. And she remembered Ruby as a baby. Crying, and you couldn't talk over her. Ruby always getting into a scrape. Until it felt like she couldn't demand anything more of her mother because she was already so taxed.

Dahlia pressed the heels of her hands against her eyes. Could she really be bitter about the way things had happened when Ruby was a baby? Was she honestly so... Shaped by something that had happened when she was four years old?

Aren't we all?

She thought of what Ruby had said about Nathan. About Carter.

About the difference in how they had started life.

Was that really what got to decide who you were?

That was when she realized that Ruby's car wasn't in the driveway.

She might've gone to get some coffee before she went to the museum, Dahlia supposed. Especially because the display had just opened, and maybe she wanted to get there early.

But then, Ruby's car pulled into the driveway, and her sister pulled up right next to her. And when she turned her head and saw Dahlia in the driver's seat, her eyes went wide.

Dahlia got out of the car. Ruby did the same, slowly. Fully dressed, just like Dahlia, without makeup, and with her hair completely askew. Much like Dahlia.

"Welcome to my walk of shame," Dahlia said. "Do I want to ask where yours is coming from?"

Ruby said nothing. And she didn't look…smug or cheerful or anything of the kind. She looked delicate. Fragile. Like the wind might shatter her.

And Dahlia's stomach sank.

She had a terrible feeling that she knew exactly what Ruby had done. "Please tell me that you were indulging in nostalgia with Darling Heath."

Ruby shook her head, then laughed. Bitterly. "No."

"Ruby," Dahlia said. "I… I can have some sympathy for him. Because if what you think about him is true, then he really hasn't had much of a chance. But are you sure you want to involve yourself in this…in this mess? What about Dana?"

"I don't know," Ruby said, walking ahead into the shed. "But Dana… Dana doesn't even know if he did it, Dahlia, I asked her."

"Did you tell her you wanted to sleep with him?"

"No. No, I…" Then she stopped, and her shoulders shuddered, and that scared Dahlia. Deep. "Because it's not just that. It's not just… I… I think I am falling for him. Really." She wasn't turned toward Dahlia, but she wiped at her face and Dahlia knew she was crying. "And it may not make sense to you. It doesn't really make all that much sense to me. But I have never felt this way about another person. There's something about him. There's something about what this town did to him that I feel... Makes me feel like we're the same."

"He is not the same as you. He's..."

"Who is he, Dahlia? Is he who Pear Blossom says? Am I? *Are you?* At some point we have to write our own stories, we have to decide."

All the air exited Dahlia's lungs in one gust.

Because Ruby was right.

They had to decide. And she'd... She'd always felt like she was her own person, but so much of it was a rebellion against feeling wrong. So she'd decided, she'd chosen, to be different. And that was fine except it excluded her from things she wanted.

Like Carter.

"Well," Dahlia said, slowly. "I think I'm falling for Carter. But I'm going to have to ask him if we have a future. I don't want to do it."

She exhaled long and noisily. "I get that. I don't want to be doing much of anything that I'm doing," Ruby said. "Is he worthy of your romantic stories, Dee?"

Dahlia closed her eyes, her mind going back to last night. His hands. His body. The way he moved. The way he kissed.

She hadn't understood all that when she'd spun romances out of nothing but emotion and a very good imagination. But now she'd lived life. She knew what desire was, and she knew what counted about a person.

She'd thought Carter was good-looking in high school. But she hadn't... Known him. Not like now.

And it was more than all that. Than the touching and kissing and pleasure he gave her. It was the way she felt when he held her.

The way she wanted to tell him every mundane detail about her day.

And how he always seemed...to want to know.

"He's Darcy," Dahlia said. "What about Nathan?"

"Rochester," she said, pulling a face. "I have this horrible feeling that I'm walking toward his darkness." She looked away. "I've been having this dream… And every step forward… My fear closes around my throat tighter and tighter. And I don't know where it's leading. And I don't know what it means."

"Sometimes a dream is just a dream."

"Yeah. I know. But this isn't."

"Whatever happens," Dahlia said. "Whatever happens. With Nathan, with Carter. With your dreams. With your display. With Dana. Ruby, I have been jealous of you. I have felt like I was living in your shadow. But at a certain point, it's just up to me to step out from behind it. It's not you or Mom or the town that kept me there. It's just my own insecurity. And I keep thinking that I realize that, and then I realize I'm still holding myself back. But that's my problem. I promise you that whatever happens from this moment forward, whether or not you just made a mistake or fulfilled some kind of…destiny like you seem to think, I am one hundred percent on your side. Because you're a McKee. You're my sister. It doesn't matter who left you on that bridge or why. It doesn't matter that I was the youngest, and then there was you. You are not something that was just pasted on to the end of the family. You were not sewn in wildly with careless stitches. You're a part of us. You're part of me. It was meant to be."

Ruby leaned forward and hugged Dahlia, and Dahlia felt a tear roll down her face.

"When we found you," she whispered. "When we found you, my first thought was that I hoped you would be my sister. And there were times when I regretted that thought. I wished you gone. I did. I was young, and I was petty. But right in that first moment I saw you and thought *sister*. I want you to know that."

A sob shook Ruby's shoulders. "Thank you."

"No matter what. It's the one thing you'll always be. My sister."

314

32

Heath is not a duke (I regret). But he is a good kisser. And I may have let him go further than I said I would. I don't want to be good. I want to be exciting. I would also like a duke, but one of those things seems easier to accomplish than the other.

RUBY MCKEE'S DIARY, AGE 16

RUBY

They were all there for the opening of Lydia's store. And none of them looked… Great. Ruby knew exactly why Dahlia was tired. She had been up half the night with Carter and had then come home early only to go straight to work. Lydia looked an absolute misery, her face pale, deep set bruises beneath her eyes indicating a lack of sleep while she tried to smile as customers trickled in.

Marianne just looked like she hadn't slept at all. There was something frozen about her face. Her eyes were not swollen, nor were there any dark circles. She just looked like she had been sitting up for twelve hours, refusing to close them.

Her parents were there, cheerfully wandering around the shop, along with the small crowd that had shown up. They were…as ever, unaware of the storm around them.

Ruby wondered if they didn't know on purpose.

They were such loving parents. But she could see now what Marianne's issue with them was. They didn't want to admit anything was wrong, not ever.

Even when she'd been a teenager and she'd been sneaking around with Heath having sex in his car, she was absolutely sure they'd pretended they didn't know she'd sneaked out, because they hadn't wanted to know what she was doing.

Things felt terribly wrong right now.

Even now, worrying about her sisters, she was thinking of Nathan.

Of the fact that she wished she could stroll through the store with him. Wished he could come and see her museum display next week.

But it was impossible. He couldn't walk into places like this.

She wanted to be with him again. She had slept all night in his bed, but she had woken up intermittently, just to listen to him breathe. She loved the feeling of resting her cheek on his chest, right over his heart. She just wanted to lie with him like that forever. And not worry about the implications of what being with him meant in the broader world.

There is no broader world here for him. He can't stay here.

She pressed her tongue to the roof of her mouth, trying to hold back tears.

She looked at Marianne, who just seemed miserable. And she…she hoped that if there was one benefit to having to feel these things it was the understanding that she didn't need to try to make someone feel better. She just needed to be there. Like Lydia had done for her.

She walked to Marianne and linked arms with her. "What's wrong?"

"Jackson didn't come home last night," Marianne whispered.

"What?" Ruby asked.

"We had a fight."

"About the text messages?"

She walked Marianne to the checkout counter, where Lydia had a break in the crowd, and Dahlia was standing too.

"They were nothing," Marianne said, keeping her voice soft. "The text messages. He was planning a vacation for us. When he found out that I thought he was cheating on him and didn't say anything... He was furious. He left. And for all I know he's been out... Making a truth teller of me." A tear slid down Marianne's pale face and she wiped it away. "I trusted him. For all these years I've trusted him with everything. And all it took was one text, one moment where he didn't tell me the full truth, and it made me suspect him of... Everything. What's wrong with me? Why is that in me?"

Ruby's stomach sank, her sympathy for her sister a physical pain. "Oh, Marianne..."

"Look," Dahlia said. "Men are notoriously faithless, and their penises can't be trusted. Why is it so insane of you to suspect your husband is cheating on you when husbands do it all the time?"

"Because he's not *a* husband, he's *my* husband and I know him. Because that lack of trust is... If he had accused me of that, I would've been so hurt. And I'm just looking back on everything from the last couple of months, and the thing is it's me. I'm the one that decided there was something wrong with us, and I'm the one who kept... Forcing cracks where there weren't any. Then I don't know why. I just... And what's wrong with me?"

"What's the matter with *you*?" Dahlia asked, directing the question at Lydia.

Lydia waved a hand. "Same old."

Ruby looked at Dahlia. And her sister smiled, even if sadly. Ruby was glad they were sharing. She'd often felt... Well, Lydia and Marianne had always seemed like such adults, they hadn't really shared their problems with her.

She'd felt closer to them in the past few weeks than ever before. She just wished things were easier.

But this is why you came back.

"You guys are a mess," Ruby said, wrapping her arms around Marianne. "But you know, we are sisters. Always."

"Always," Dahlia repeated, as she pulled Lydia in for a hug.

"Thanks," Lydia said, her voice muffled.

"What am I going to do?" Marianne asked.

"I don't have any answers," Ruby said. "I'm as big of a mess as you. But you can move into the cottage if it comes to that."

"It really is more of a shed," Dahlia said. "But you're welcome there."

Marianne laughed. "Okay, that's perfect."

They all knew it wasn't.

But they had each other. And that would do just fine since perfect wasn't available.

33

Crime in Portland a Rising Tide

BY DALE WAINWRIGHT

JANUARY 10, 1993—It is impossible to ignore that crime and an overall seedy quality has sunken into the streets in Portland, Oregon. This is no alarmist, anti-generation rant, but a fact backed up by crime statistics. A worrying trend in many cities in these United States. Analysis of Pear Blossom's crime statistics, however, show a world unchanged. Where children can still play outside in their yards, or walk to the store. However many monsters roam the streets in our urban center, you will not find them hiding here.

MARIANNE

Jackson had come home. Later the same day. But things had not been... Well with them since. And now it was Christmas Eve and they were all trying to get ready for the service and Marianne felt like she was going to rattle to pieces.

She'd had "Carol of the Bells" stuck in her head all day, of all the things. And it was just the weirdest thing. Because that reminded her of the night that they'd found Ruby. Because they had been singing it exhaustively all week.

Bells. Bells. Bells.

Ding dong.

She was not in the mood for Christmas carols on top of everything else.

"We are going to be late," she said, putting her earrings in and giving herself a critical look in the mirror.

Jackson was sleeping in the guest room. Ava seemed to sense the tension and was speaking to Marianne even less, while she was just great with Jackson.

Which was just *awesome.*

And she and Jackson had never spent nights apart. They just didn't do it. And now they were.

In October she thought they were this absolutely perfect couple. And suddenly they had been downgraded to the very portrait of brutal suburban misery. "Kids," she said. "Church."

The kids scrambled up from the couch and scurried off to get their shoes.

Jackson came down the stairs, looking... Remote and handsome and completely unobtainable. And Marianne had a headache.

Damn bells.

"Do you think you can put on a decent show in front of my parents?" she asked.

"Eventually we have to deal with each other," Jackson said.

"Oh, and you thought that dealing with each other would come easier if you were in the guest room?"

"Don't be like that, Marianne. You haven't talked to me. You haven't been interested in talking to me. And you know that. So don't get into that mode where you pretend this is all me."

"I don't know what to say to you. Because there's nothing I can do. I made a mistake."

"Let's just go to church," he said. He closed his eyes. "I don't know if it's fair for me to be upset with you. Because what you said is true. Men do that. But I never have."

"You left. For the whole night. To punish me. Don't pretend..."

"I wasn't punishing you. I was asking myself some questions.

Because… If I did something to make you… To make you think that's who I am, or if… I don't know what you thinking that means for us. Something is broken."

"I know," she whispered. "I just wish I could tell you what it is."

"We'll deal with that after Christmas."

She nodded. "Okay."

And at least, when they got in their SUV and started to head off to church, they looked perfect.

RUBY

"Mom," Ruby said, examining herself in the mirror. She was wearing a red, vintage wrap dress that she picked up at a charity shop while she'd been overseas. "Do you think I could wear the silver bells?"

"Well, sure," Andie said, looking surprised. "They're yours, after all."

"Yeah," Ruby said. "But I've never… I've never really worn them."

"They were always meant to go to you."

Her mother went to the hall closet and took the Ruby box down. And inside of it was the blanket she'd been wrapped in. Chills broke out over Ruby's arms. And then her mom took out a piece of white tissue paper, all wrapped up neatly. She handed it to Ruby. She unfolded it, and inside was the vaguely tarnished jewelry. It looked so fragile. And she could see the age on that necklace. It was still beautiful. It was funny how she'd thought it wasn't her style, when they seemed perfect.

Had that been set in stone? Her love of old things. When she'd been left with a piece of the town history tucked inside of her blanket?

She put it on and admired herself in the mirror. "Thank you."

Then she put her hand down and touched it, and her dream came back to her, sharp and vivid.

Along with the terror in her chest. Because she remembered that. Holding this necklace as she walked through the bridge.

She was shaking, and she tried to hide it. Was she... Was she pushing her dream into the realm of prophecy by putting these on?

She had the feeling that the dream was a memory, but it couldn't be. It couldn't be.

Because she'd never worn this necklace. And it had never happened.

She swallowed hard and forced a smile. Her mom was looking at her with tears in her eyes.

"What?" she asked.

"I had a feeling that when you were ready to get that down... I would know you were... You were grown-up, Ruby. And you are. You're that beautiful baby that had that necklace tucked into her blanket. And now... You're standing there wearing it."

"Oh, Mom," Ruby said, her throat getting tight and scratchy. "We don't need to get emotional about it."

"Maybe you don't," her mom said. "Ruby..." Tears glistened in her mother's eyes, and Ruby wondered then if she did know, more than she ever showed. "I love you."

"I love you too."

Dahlia came through the door then, wearing black, a rosebud headband in her short dark hair, the only nod to any sort of festivity one such as Dahlia would ever make.

"You look beautiful," their mom said.

"Let's go to church," Ruby said.

LYDIA

Lydia did not want to go to church. But it was Christmas Eve, and they always went. Her former mother-in-law would be there, and she would expect to see the kids there. Her parents would be there.

Chase would be there.

They had done such a good job of avoiding each other, and now they were about to come face-to-face in front of a whole bunch of people. Which, she imagined, would be its own sort of insulation. She sighed heavily and pulled the car into the church parking lot.

"Church is boring," Riley said.

"Don't say that," replied Hazel. "You'll go to hell. And then you won't see Daddy."

"Stop," Lydia said. "He's not going to hell. He could say he doesn't like church if he wants to. Church can be boring. That doesn't mean I'm going to hell."

"What if it *does*?" Hazel asked, her eyes wide.

"It doesn't," Lydia said, bundling her kids out of the car and walking up toward the church. "Since when did you start thinking about hell?"

"Because Riley got mad at me the other day and he told me to go to hell. I don't want to go to hell. Daddy's not in hell."

"Riley," Lydia scolded. "Where did you learn things like that?"

"I've heard you say it," he said.

She gritted her teeth. "When have I ever said that?"

"You said it to Uncle Chase."

Oh, well, that just did it.

"I didn't mean it. And, *you* shouldn't say it. Especially not to your sister."

What a *great start*. Her blasphemies lying out right in front of her at the threshold of the church.

Auspicious indeed.

She walked into the building, and of course *he* was right there. Standing next to her mother-in-law.

"Hi," she said.

She knew that it sounded brittle.

"Hi, Lydia."

Riley went straight to him, threw his arms around him. "I missed you, Uncle Chase."

And something bitter and acidic twisted in her stomach. Because this was just... Them here at church together. On Christmas Eve. It felt like a family thing. And suddenly in her mind she could just see it. Just this brief flash of a moment.

Like they were all here together. And then, it was just as easy to go on and see the two of them in bed together. His hands on her body.

Honestly, that was less disturbing than fantasizing about being a family.

"Hi, sweetheart." Her mother-in-law reached out and kissed her on the cheek. "How are you?"

"Good."

"I haven't had a chance to talk to you—you've just been dropping the kids off and picking them up when I visit."

"I know. I just... Very busy with the store."

"Oh, you'll have to tell me all about the store. I know Chase has been working on it. He's told me some things. But you know how men are with details."

Chase continued to be solicitous and lovely, acting very much like a son to Mac's mother.

Why was he so good?

Why was he making her imagine these kinds of things?

"My parents are over there," she said. And then she realized her sisters were there too. "My family."

"Well, we can sit over there."

She wanted to tell him no, but of course he was with Mac's mother, and she did want to sit with her.

"Okay. Okay. Then we'll sit together."

DAHLIA

Carter was standing there with his mother and father, and his sister and her husband and children. Making conversation with everyone who passed by. Of course, everyone wanted to talk to Carter. And she didn't feel like she could approach him. Because this was… Well, it was *town* territory. Not that private space they'd carved out for themselves in his bedroom. And it seemed silly that she was this reticent when she'd seen him naked. And tasted him everywhere.

But she was.

She probably shouldn't be thinking about tasting him while she was standing there in church.

"Are you really going to not go say hi to your boyfriend?"

She turned and saw Ruby standing next to her. "He is not my boyfriend."

"Still. You should go talk to him."

"And where's *your* boyfriend?"

"Probably hiding in his den, away from the judgmental gazes of the townsfolk looking to engage in another witch hunt." Ruby's glittering blue eyes were cool. "I'm not claiming to be the bastion of healthy relationships, Dahlia. I'm just saying he's right there. And if Nathan were right there, I'd go talk to him."

She looked around, and saw Lydia, who was sitting on the pew right next to Chase and looking chalky.

"How are we all in hell over the men we're sleeping with?"

Ruby shrugged. "Because that's what people do. We screw each other, and then screw up our lives. Usually at the same time."

"Eloquent," Dahlia said.

"You should go talk to them."

"And his parents will think what?"

"Does it matter what his *parents* think?"

"It does if they think I'm not good enough for him." She winced when the words came out of her mouth. How sad was that?

"Dahlia. You have to stop that."

"Fine." She couldn't even argue.

She separated from Ruby and walked across the room. And

much to her surprise, Carter wrapped his arm around her and drew her up against his waist. "Mom, Dad," he said. "You remember Dahlia McKee."

She was suddenly face-to-face with his parents, who had wide eyes, probably especially Tom, considering the two of them had just spoken. But that was before she had slept with his son.

"Hi," she said, in the awkward smiling hell of her worst nightmares.

"I didn't know you were seeing anyone," his mother said.

"It's new. But she's pretty great."

He had done it. He had made a public declaration. Without the two of them even talking. Right there in church.

"Will you sit with me?" he asked.

"Were you going to ask me to if I hadn't come over here?"

"Yes. I was just waiting for you not to be busy talking to your sister. Though, I would have busted in eventually."

"You could text," she said, dryly.

He leaned in. "I'm never going to. Just to bug you."

"Why do I love that?"

And then he kissed her. Right there in the sanctuary. Just light. A brush across her lips. "Maybe because you love *me*."

"Don't be stupid, Carter. We haven't been together very long."

"But we've known each other since we were kids. Back when we thought we knew what we were supposed to do. And now we both know we don't have to do anything. But here we are. Choosing to stand with each other. Don't you think that means a lot more than being together for years ever could?"

And she knew that he was speaking from his own experience. From his own marriage that hadn't lasted. The marriage that had seemed perfect with the woman he'd been with for so many years.

"Yeah, maybe."

And that was how she found herself sitting in the Swensons' pew.

MARIANNE

Marianne was feeling twitchy and uncomfortable, and the small strip of orange pew fabric visible between her thigh and Jackson's spoke volumes about just where they were as a couple.

But luckily, no one seemed to notice but the two of them. The kids were deeply involved in themselves, thank God, and Ruby leaned over the top of the kids and whispered something in her ear, but Marianne couldn't make it out, because Pastor Lawrence was onstage saying something and her attention was completely caught and seized by the necklace hanging around Ruby's neck.

The bells.

The bells.

The kids choir got up from their seats, her own kids included, and went to the stage. It opened somberly with "Silent Night," but she couldn't make her brain track with it.

She was breathing hard. There was a strange sort of... Panic at the center of her stomach. Almost a pain.

And when the song ended and flowed into the next, the kids picked up little handheld bells, and rang them out high and clear over the sanctuary. Denial burst into her brain with the first note.

Her vision got dark around the edges before her eyes and she sat down in the pew, not caring if it looked strange.

That song. That song and that necklace.

That song.

A memory pushed at the corner of her mind.

No.

There were blind spots for a reason.

Everyone had blind spots.

Everyone.

There were always doors you shouldn't open.

There were always corridors you shouldn't walk down.

There were always blind spots.

And ringing bells.

She looked over at Ruby, at the necklace dangling around her neck. And suddenly, she leaned forward, the memory of a sensation hitting her square in the stomach.

Of pain.

So much pain.

The wall that kept those memories out was made of pain. And she couldn't sort through it. Didn't want to. They were locked away there.

Behind that wall. The wall that she had built.

And there were reasons.

There were reasons.

Maybe you feel wrong because you're a liar.

The music swelled around her, and she found that she couldn't breathe.

And so she ran. She ran out of the sanctuary. She ran away from her husband. She ran away from her family. With a terrible truth in her chest that was beginning to grow and expand.

And the song came with her.

That terrible something started to grow. A threat she'd forgotten, a pain she'd forgotten.

Not like a penny you dropped and didn't remember. No. She'd lost this on purpose. Hidden it away.

It was never him.

It was always you.

He's not the liar.

You're the liar.

Christmas is here.

She had run from everyone, from everything, but she couldn't outrun that voice.

Because of that necklace.

Because when she'd seen the necklace, the floor had fallen

away, and it wasn't Jackson at all. It wasn't Jackson that had put her out there in space and left her unable to find her way back.

No.

She didn't even know where she was running to.

She just didn't want to hear the bells anymore.

She ran.

Until she reached the bridge.

Sentinel Bridge.

And she could see it. In her mind. Like she was watching a movie. Like it was happening to someone else. Because that was how she lived that whole year of her life. Pretending it was someone else.

And she saw a girl. Fifteen and afraid, bleeding and praying it would stop soon. And she watched as she got down onto the frozen boards of the bridge, down on her knees.

And she could feel the cold bite into her skin even now. Feel how it left her pants wet. And how her stomach had cramped up when she'd moved.

She saw the girl who was her take that hidden necklace out from underneath her sweatshirt, that baggy sweatshirt that concealed all of her secrets. From the necklace, that dark and pretty gift she had to keep secret, to the coming arrival of the baby herself.

And she watched her younger self put the necklace on the blanket.

Then Marianne dropped to her knees and threw up.

You always knew you are a liar. You always knew there was something dirty about you.

Marianne had been running for twenty-two years.

And so, with the world closing in on her heels, she kept on running.

34

Please join Mr. and Mrs. Robert Carlton

as they celebrate the wedding of their daughter,

Lena Marie Carlton,

to

Carter Thomas Swenson,

son of Tom and Alice Swenson,

on the 12th day of March, 2014 at 12 noon

at the First Presbyterian Church of Pear Blossom.

....

RSVP: Attending   Not attending ✔

DAHLIA

The entire McKee family, plus Chase and Carter, were outside the church while the service went on inside.

"She didn't take the car," Jackson said.

"Well, do you have any idea where she might've gone?" Andie asked.

"I have no idea," Jackson said. "I have no idea she... She didn't say anything to me about... Anything."

"You're in a fight, though," Dahlia said, anger spiking in her chest. "Don't pretend you don't know anything, *Jackson*."

She would punch him in his face right here.

"I don't know anything about this, Dahlia. I don't know where the hell she would run off to."

"She's just gone," Ruby said, looking around. "I checked the whole perimeter of the church. She's not there."

"What's her mental state like?" Carter asked.

"She's Marianne," Dahlia said, answering before Jackson could. "She's been upset, but there's nothing... There's nothing wrong with her mental state."

"It's not great," Jackson said.

And that made Dahlia feel awful, because she'd known her sister was upset but she wouldn't have said her mental state was bad. And she'd gotten in Jackson's face but... He did seem to understand this better than she did.

"Do you think she would hurt herself?"

Jackson looked stricken by that. "No. I don't. But... I didn't think that she would... Something's been going on with her, and I don't know what it is. She's not herself."

"Why didn't you say anything to us?" Andie said.

"Why would we?" Jackson asked. "Marianne made it clear that you never wanted to hear about her problems. This was about us and we kept it to ourselves."

"Jackson, we did want to know," her mom said.

"It was for us to handle," he said. "I didn't know she was struggling like this. To the point that she would just... Run away from church."

How far could she have gotten? Not very.

"Dahlia, come with me," Carter said. "We'll look at The Apothecary. She might've gone down to the business.

"Mr. and Mrs. McKee, if you can go and check your house,

maybe wait there, a childhood home is a place that somebody in her position might go."

"And me?" Lydia asked. She knew her mother-in-law would watch the kids.

"Check your place. Anywhere else you can think of that might've been special to her."

"Okay."

"I'm going with you," Chase said.

And Lydia didn't argue with him.

Ruby was standing there, looking forlorn. "Is there anything I can do?"

"Go to the shed. Make sure she didn't go there. And just like Lydia, if you could think of anywhere else she might've gone... Well, then go there."

"Okay."

Carter turned to Jackson. "You should go home."

"The hell I'm going home. My wife is out there somewhere."

"And you have your children. And she might go back to your house. And I'm a police officer, and I know how to look for someone. I swear to you, I will be thorough."

"But you want to bring my sister-in-law because you're sleeping with her."

"Yeah. Fine. If that's how you want to play that. I want her with me because she knows her. And I know Dahlia, which means that her information is going to be useful to me. Easy for me to filter. You have your kids. Deal with your kids."

Jackson was still brimming with male rage, but he didn't push it.

Carter grabbed Dahlia's hand and led her to his car, and he drove out of the parking lot quickly, headed toward town. She kept scanning the roadside. The roadside.

For her sister.

Her thirty-seven-year-old sister, who had kids and a husband

and who had run out of the church in the middle of service on Christmas Eve.

"Something is wrong," Dahlia said.

"I know," he said.

"What if she hurts herself?"

"You can't think like that."

"This is the kind of thing you deal with all the time, isn't it?"

"In a small town? Yes. Mostly…domestic violence. Prescription drug abuse. Mental health issues."

"I don't know if it's that. I don't know… She has been acting off. But I just thought it was this thing between her and Jackson. She thought… She thought he was having an affair."

"He wasn't?" Carter asked.

"No."

"You're sure?"

"Does it matter?" Dahlia asked.

"I don't suppose. But I like to know the details."

"Well, he couldn't have done anything *to* her. He was sitting right there."

"I know. I'm not saying that he did. I was just saying, I like to know the circumstances of the situation. What causes someone to behave this way."

They didn't speak on the five-minute drive down to town. He drove slowly, scanning the area for any sign of her.

The lights in The Apothecary were off. But Carter got out and knocked on the door.

"I'm going to have to break the lock," he said.

Dahlia nodded. He forced his way inside, and an alarm went off, sending a deafening siren through the room.

"I think you're being called to the scene," she said.

"Likely."

The call from the alarm company came through on his radio. "Police presence," he said. "You can disengage the alarm."

A moment later, the siren stopped.

They looked all over the store, but she wasn't anywhere to be found.

An hour later, no one had found her.

"Dammit," he said. "We'll find her."

She believed him. And right then she really believed the promise meant more because it was her sister.

And that was a whole change inside herself she didn't know what to do with right now.

MARIANNE

Marianne McKee knew how to hide. She'd been hiding for a long time.

She knew how to hide in her own house.

And she managed to do it again.

When she got into the shower, the water was already hot. She sank down to the floor, letting the steam close in around her. And she just... Sat.

And as the water pounded down on her skin, it seemed to strip away all those layers she'd spent years wrapping around the tender, fragile, frightened things inside of her.

As they melted away, it all came back. Patchy and slow at first and then far, far too vivid.

This moment ran parallel with another. Her, crouched in the shower tub combo at the farmhouse. With the water on. And the pain just wouldn't stop. It came in waves. But she couldn't make any sound. She couldn't make any sound.

Because then she would get caught.

Because then they would know.

And if they knew...

She couldn't even think about it. All she knew was that it was important. That nobody found out. And that if anyone ever suspected...

That it was already too late.

Fear gripped her along with each and every contraction.

But she would be quiet. She would be quiet. She was too afraid to let sound come out. She'd been too afraid for nearly nine months.

She had prayed. Every night she had prayed. That it would disappear. That she would wake up and her stomach would be flat again. Maybe that she would disappear.

Or die.

Struck down by the divine hand of God, because that she couldn't run away from.

But she was too afraid to let *him* strike her down.

And he would.

He would.

That's why she was hiding.

She could see it. Playing in her mind like a movie, because now that it was there, now that the door had been open, she couldn't stop it. She pressed her hand over her mouth just like she'd done then, stifling the scream. And she leaned forward.

And she could remember. Remember those horrible, tearing sensations moving through her body.

They'd started during choir practice. They'd been singing "Carol of the Bells."

Hark to the bells.

Sweet silver bells.

And it had just gotten worse and worse. And now it was evening, and thank God her parents had gone out Christmas shopping in Medford, because only her sisters were here.

She'd read books where they did this.

Where you could do it on your own. They did it on the Prairie.

And she could do it.

She could.

She could do it and no one would ever have to know.

She'd handled this much, and she might have something

wrong inside her that made him want her in the way he did. She might be broken. But she was still alive. And that made her some kind of strong, it had to.

So on her hands and knees in the bathtub, with water spraying down over her back, she managed to give birth to a baby. She didn't want to look and see what it was. She didn't want to know it.

She didn't want to look at it and see *him*.

She didn't want to look at it at all. And she was bleeding. There was so much blood. She was going to bé sick. But the pain was still coming, and now the baby was screaming, and she had to figure out something to do with her.

Or everyone would hear.

Using the rubber bands and the scissors that she'd brought in with her, she managed to cut the baby's umbilical cord.

And she knew that the next thing was afterbirth, because she'd read about that. But she'd never really understood what all it meant, or what it was.

She'd grown up on a farm, though, and she'd seen the indistinct mass that had followed the birth of calves and foals. She imagined she had that ahead of her.

So many things she hadn't understood until this past year. And now she knew too much.

She wanted to forget all of it.

When she didn't dream about dying, she dreamed about growing wings and escaping. Flying away from here. Where he couldn't reach her. Where this wasn't happening.

She could take her wings and land in a new place, where she wasn't Marianne and she could just start over. If no one knew, then it could be just… Gone like a dream.

But she couldn't fly away. She just had to go through the rest of it. She sat in the bottom of the shower with the baby, and she cried right along with it, as pain continued to drag, low and hard through her body, as her body finished with the process.

And she just wept. Miserable and sick.

She had to figure out what to do next. The closest thing to planning had been when she'd made her box that had the scissors and bands. And bags.

She was weak. And she was still bleeding. But there was no choice.

She had brought trash bags in with her. And she could remember news stories about girls doing this. About them putting the baby in the trash. And pretending it was never born. And for one second she thought about it. She really did. Because it would make it quiet. And it would make it go away.

And she never had to look and see what it was. She used towels to mop up the blood, and they went straight to the bag. Everything, all the horrible things that had come from her body.

But not the baby.

She couldn't put the baby in a trash bag.

She hated the baby. She hated it so much. But she couldn't do that.

She shut the water off, and she stood there, watching blood run down her legs. And then she looked down.

It was a girl.

It was a *girl*.

She didn't want to know that. Because she didn't want to know who she was.

She finished cleaning up the bathroom, she got a clean pair of underwear and put two pads in them. She opened up the medicine cabinet and took four painkillers. She wrapped the baby in a towel, because she didn't know what else to do.

She went to her bedroom, and opened up the closet. And she stared at it. She hoped the doors were heavy enough. She shoved the baby inside. Still wrapped in the towel. And she took the other bag down to the burn pile. Where she knew it would just get thrown in with everything else. She went back upstairs, and she couldn't hear a thing.

She opened up the door and saw it lying there.

Helpless.

Like her.

Except no one helped her. No one knew.

Marianne was alone.

But this baby wasn't alone. Marianne was here.

"I'm sorry." She sat on the floor and looked down at the baby. "I'm really sorry."

It was all she could say. Because she *was* sorry that this little thing was here now. And that she needed someone to take care of her. Who wasn't dirty and broken and afraid.

But she was here. And she could do something.

She hadn't been able to say anything to help herself. Hadn't been able to reach out and take anyone's hand.

But she could take hold of this child.

She picked her up off the floor and held her to her chest, tears sliding down her cheeks. She knew she had to decide what to do. Because she couldn't keep it. She had to get away from her. She wasn't supposed to exist.

She looked at the bed, at the angel costume she had.

It was just a blanket.

She grabbed it and laid it out on the bed. Then she went to the bathroom and got a washcloth, retrieved it and started to clean the baby off. Then she wrapped her in the blanket.

Her breasts hurt, but she didn't want to feed it that way. So she got a bit of milk from the kitchen and warmed it, and gave it to the baby out of a bottle that they used for puppies. She kept her like that for twenty-four hours.

Until she realized she had to get rid of her.

She'd intended to go to the police station, or hospital, and leave her there. She'd sneaked her out of the house before choir practice. The bridge between her house and town. The bridge that she knew she would cross with her sisters when she made her way back home.

Cars didn't drive over it, but people walked on it all the time. Anyone could find her in the time before practice ended.

But what if we found her?

And then she would be taken care of. For sure.

And so Marianne stopped in the middle of Sentinel Bridge and put the baby down right in a shaft of moonlight.

"I can't be your mother. I could be your sister. Maybe you could just be my sister."

"Marianne!"

Marianne was jarred out of her memory by the sound of her husband's voice through the door.

"Go away."

"Marianne," he said. "I'm going to break down the door if I have to."

"I said go away."

But he didn't. Instead, he forced the door open, and a moment later he was in the bathroom, opening up the shower door. "Marianne," he said. But then he was down on his knees right next to her, not seeming to care that his clothes were getting wet. He pulled her out onto his lap. "What happened, honey? What happened?"

"I can't say," she said. "I don't know how to say. I'm not supposed to. I'll get hurt. Or Lydia will. Or my parents."

"No one is going to hurt you," he said.

"I lied to you," she said.

"Honey, what happened?"

She looked up at him, at those eyes that she had trusted for so long. And she knew that she had to trust him with something huge. With something she hadn't even been able to trust herself with. With truths that she had buried so deep that they never even tried to knock on the door once she'd managed to close it.

Until now.

"Jackson," she said. "I'm the one that left Ruby on the bridge. I'm Ruby's mother."

35

I felt rebellious having sex with Heath. Then Dahlia told me she had sex for the first time when she was 16. Why is she always more interesting than I am? Someday, I will go to England and find a duke.

RUBY MCKEE'S DIARY, AGE 17

RUBY

It was Christmas morning and they were all gathered at her parents' house. Jackson had sent the text late last night to say that Marianne had been found. That she was home, and safe.

It was still a somber-feeling Christmas morning, a strange weight hanging in the air. Ruby wanted to go to Nathan, but she also needed badly to be with her family. But at eight thirty, Marianne walked through the door with Jackson holding her up, and the kids behind her.

"Ruby," Marianne said. "We need to talk."

"Okay."

"Marianne," her mom said, and her father rushed forward at the same time.

Jackson held up a hand. "She's going to talk to Ruby first. And... We'll see how that goes. I may need to be the one to talk to you. We'll see."

Protectiveness radiated off of Jackson in alarming waves. Her brother-in-law had always been that kind of guy, but it was different right now. He was like a human shield surrounding Marianne. Trying to keep her from breaking apart.

"Let's go upstairs," Marianne said.

She led them to her old room, and then stopped in the center of it. "Will you close the door please, Ruby."

"What's going on, Marianne?"

Marianne shook her hands out, then started pacing, one palm pressed to her forehead, the other one to her stomach.

"Marianne?" Ruby pressed, her voice fracturing.

She stopped walking, her hands still in the same place. "I know you're not going to believe me. I know you're not going to believe this. Because I barely do." She lowered her hands to her sides, then clasped them, wringing them together. "Jackson and I spent some time researching this online last night. Isn't that stupid? We had to look on the internet to see if this was the thing. Or if it was just something from movies. But it's real. You know… It only takes a few minutes to start believing your own lies."

"Marianne, you're scaring me now."

"I probably should be. Because it's scary. It's terrifying, actually. Everything about this is… It's bad, Ruby." Her eyes filled with tears.

"Marianne, just tell me."

"I've been lying to myself. I got so good at it that I ended up lying to everyone else."

"Marianne."

"It was me," she said, her voice a strangled whisper.

"*What* was you?"

"I left you on the bridge."

Ruby felt like the entire world had fractured. And everything was offset and skewed, not unrecognizable but… Changed. Forever. She could hardly breathe and she couldn't… She couldn't orient herself in this room. This room she'd been familiar with all her life.

And oh, she had underestimated this. How the truth of where she was from would alter everything about where she stood now.

"Marianne... That's impossible."

"No. It's not."

"You... You didn't... You were fifteen. And you said that Jackson is the only..."

"I lied," she said, the words broken. "I lied to everybody. And myself. I... I hid it. I hid it because I had to."

"No," Ruby said. "No. This is... Marianne, this is crazy. You are being crazy."

"I'm not," Marianne said. "It's... I wrote myself a new story, Ruby. Because I couldn't handle the one that... Because I couldn't handle the truth. I was so scared. I was so afraid. I had to be so quiet while I... I was hiding in the bathroom."

"I was born here?" Ruby asked, the words scraping her throat raw like glass. "Marianne, I was born in this house? This whole time I... This is where I was from? I'm a McKee?"

"Ruby..."

"No. I... I thought I was lost this whole time. I thought I was...brought here. I was home the whole time and no one... You didn't tell me."

"I couldn't!"

Ruby was shaking. "I... I've always questioned who I was and why and...and I never knew because you didn't want to remember."

"I know!" Marianne cried. She sank down to the bed and covered her mouth. "I know. I know. But I had to forget, Ruby, I had to. I don't know how I know that—I just do. I'm so scared. I'm so scared now that I remember." She looked up at her. "I know two things, Ruby. You had to survive. And I had to forget. If those things didn't happen... Something bad would, Ruby. Something really bad."

Ruby was angry, but right then... Right then she began to realize. Deeply. Horribly.

"Marianne, my father wasn't your...your boyfriend, was he?"

Marianne shook her head. "No. He...he...no, I don't know. I don't know."

Guilt crawled up Ruby's spine. Because yes, this was shattering and earthshaking, but what she was looking at was...

Trauma.

That was too clinical a word. To diagnostic for how wholly shattered Marianne looked now.

Marianne hadn't kept this from her to hurt her. Marianne was genuinely terrified. Her whole body shaking, her face white.

Everything about this quest had been about *her*.

About Ruby.

Who had cast herself as the heroine of this story, the baby who was found on the bridge, because of course she was the main character. Of course she was.

But there had been a girl. A fifteen-year-old, who Ruby loved, and she had been the one who'd...

Who'd left her there.

And all this digging, all this asking... Had led her here. To this moment she wasn't prepared for or equal to.

"Marianne," Ruby said slowly. "Who was it?"

"I can't remember," Marianne shouted. "My body won't let me. It's protecting me. That's just... I know it doesn't make any sense, but it is. I knew that I couldn't keep you. I knew that no one could know you were my baby. Because that would put you in danger."

"He must know. He must suspect. Is it someone from town?"

"I told you. I can't remember."

"Marianne... How..."

Marianne shook her head, her words thick with tears. "I never left you there thinking that you would die. I left you there

343

knowing that we would come back. I didn't leave you to die, Ruby. I left you to be found. By us."

"You…"

Ruby collapsed onto the bed. "You left me to be found."

"I was afraid, Ruby. And I thought… Oh, for a minute I thought maybe I'd get rid of you." Her face crumpled up. "But I couldn't do it. I couldn't do it. I kept you in here for twenty-four hours. Then I pretended to be sick and I didn't go to choir practice on time. And I left you on the bridge. And then I walked the rest of the way to the church. And when we left, I knew that I would find you."

"You…"

"You were a McKee the whole time. But Mom is your mom. I just… I didn't want to be. I didn't want to be anybody's mom. Not then."

"And you never remembered. Not when you had your kids, not when…"

She shook her head. "I remember feeling like I wasn't close to you at first. And I remember realizing that later I was. And I remember that I used to want to escape Pear Blossom. But I couldn't remember when or why that changed."

"You know now?"

She nodded. "Jackson. He made me feel like it was over. I think. I never had the words for it. All I had were feelings. Feelings that would kind of hit up against that wall. In my head. And… I don't know. He quieted it. He made me feel safe."

"What started it? What started it coming back?"

"Ava. Ava being…a teenager. And it was like something was trying to come up, and then you got here, and Dahlia was asking questions… I couldn't remember it. But it felt like more than couldn't remember. It felt like something else. And I didn't like it. And then… I don't know. Then the necklace."

"That was your necklace."

"Yes."

344

She didn't look... Interested or happy about it, though.

"Where did the necklace come from?"

"From him. I know that it did. He... He gave it to me. And I was supposed to wear it but hide it. Which is what I did. No one ever saw it. So I knew that no one would ever connect it to me. But I left it with you, because it was...it was part of the whole thing."

"Someone was abusing you, Marianne. It would probably be good if you could remember."

She shook her head. "I can't. Not right now. Please. I already... I'm already completely... I'm not who I thought I was, Ruby. I tried to glue those pages shut. I hoped it would mean that they weren't part of me. But they are. And now I have to figure out what to do with that. I can't take on... I can't go on a crusade on top of it. Please don't ask me to do that."

And for the first time, Ruby realized that her crusade—and she had been on a crusade—to solve a mystery had consequences for other people. Real, deep consequences.

That she hadn't been prepared for the full ugliness of the truth, because she had been certain that there was no surprise waiting.

She had known that it might've been a young woman. She had realized it might've been someone who'd been abused.

But not her sister. Not Marianne.

How could it be Marianne?

"I don't know what to say," Ruby said.

"Merry Christmas?"

Ruby laughed, because it was absurd. *Absurd.*

"We were always the most alike," Ruby said.

Marianne nodded. "Yeah. We were."

"I never imagined that I would find the answers I was looking for. And now that I have, I'm not sure that I know what to do with them."

"Well, I was always actively hoping to never find the truth. And now I have. And I don't know what to do with it either."

They both looked up then, and saw Andie standing in the door.

And then their mother ran to them both and held them, as she gave in to sobs that felt like they'd been waiting decades to escape.

36

Mac proposed, but he said we should keep it secret. We're both going to college, but I know nothing will change. We're meant to be.

LYDIA MCKEE'S DIARY, AGE 18

LYDIA

Christmas at the McKee house had been...surreal. There really wasn't another word for it. The revelation of Marianne's pregnancy had left their parents in emotional ruin. Realizing what Marianne had gone through without anyone knowing was a shock that was difficult for them to take on board. Lydia herself felt numb from it.

Because she remembered that dark period. Where Marianne had been like a stranger. Where she had hidden in her room and not talked to anyone.

And it all made a kind of terrible sense. Except... No one had known.

How could someone have been pregnant, living in their house, and no one had known? And she knew there were whole TV shows dedicated to surprise pregnancies, but she admitted that every time she saw an advertisement for something like that, she rolled her eyes skeptically.

Because how could something like that happen in plain view, with no one realizing? How could they have all been so blind to it?

The answer to that hit her as soon as she asked the question.

You were blind to what you didn't want to see.

She'd glossed over what her brain didn't want to see. She had done it in her marriage. Time and time again. Where she dismissed certain things, refused to see or acknowledge them. Like putting a coat of paint over rotten boards. As if looking new would do something about the decay underneath.

And what did secrets ever get you?

What did that ever solve?

"Chase," she said. She realized then that she had her phone to her ear and she hadn't even realized she'd called him. "Can you come over? Please?"

"It's Christmas," he said.

His voice was rusty, and it had a smoky tone to it. She wondered if he'd been drinking, and if he would be too drunk to drive over. It was Christmas night, after all. And she had no idea what he'd done with himself today.

"I don't want accounting help."

"I'll be there."

"Can you drive?"

"Yeah."

He arrived less than ten minutes later.

"You will not believe what happened today."

They ended up sitting on the couch in the living room. She poured whiskey for them both. And she told him everything that Marianne had confessed. Jackson had filled in a lot of details, as had Ruby. Because there was a point where Marianne had just been exhausted, and she had to go take a nap.

"Well. Hell. I would never... I mean, I remember when Ruby

was found. I don't remember Marianne looking pregnant at all before then."

"I know. The thing is, she also… Someone did it to her. Someone… Someone raped her."

"Holy shit," he said.

"She was so traumatized that she… She didn't remember. She didn't let herself remember."

"I thought that was just in movies."

"Yes. Me too. Bad ones. She's going to have to see someone. Someone who can help her. With all of that. Because how can you possibly handle blocking something out for so long and then remembering it all. Well, not all of it. Not who did it."

"Shit," he said again.

"I didn't just call you to tell you that. It's that… Secrets always come out. When you've held on to them for a long time, it's worse. Everything that was going wrong in mine and Mac's marriage was a secret. This terrible secret. I felt isolated because I couldn't tell anyone that we were falling apart. I couldn't even tell him that we were falling apart. I had gotten to a place where on my own I decided I wanted a divorce, and I was just going to ask for one. Instead of counseling, instead of anything. Because I let myself fall out of love with him. I let myself fall out of love with him without a real, deep conversation about it, and when you're not in love with someone… Fighting to save a marriage seems foolish. I came back around to loving him in some capacity in the end. Because he was the father of my children. Because he was my friend first. When we were kids. Because he was part of my life in a really unique and special way."

She looked at the wall because looking at him made her shake. "But… I don't want secrets and shadows. I don't want shame. I don't want to be afraid of what comes next in this… In this book. And I don't want to tear out any pages. I don't want to pretend that what happened between us didn't happen. It did happen. I'm not sorry about it. I just want to find a way to take what's next and be brave about it. And make sure it's what I want. And I want to be honest. I really care about you. And I didn't know what to do with that. And I didn't want you around because you made me uncomfortable. Because you made me feel things. You made me feel things that I just wasn't ready to feel. And I didn't know how to cope with it. I didn't know how to… I freaked out. I've never been with another man. And it's not even that. It's not even that. I'm letting it be like that because it's easier for me to say that. It's that it was you. You. And I've known you just as long. And it makes me ask too many *what if* questions, Chase."

"I get it, I do. I didn't expect you to know what to do with this, or us, right away. I loved Mac, but I wasn't blind to his faults."

"What did you like about him?" she asked, because she was curious, really. She'd always wondered what Mac saw in Chase, but she got it now.

He was loyal. He said it like he saw it. And he was *there*. There when you needed him. He wasn't a man who would hide from a fight, no, he'd charge right in. When she'd been young and afraid, she hadn't seen why that was good, but she saw it now.

"He had an easy way about him," Chase said. "And he didn't ask me to explain myself. He didn't judge me for where I came from, or for…having holes in my jeans. I don't have a brother, but I lived with him for five years and he became that for me. So even when I did see his flaws… I didn't love him less. But sometimes I didn't like him. I didn't like what he did to you."

She swallowed hard, dreading the next question a little. "What did you mean when you said it was always me?"

He slid off the couch and got down on his knees in front of her, taking her hands in his. "I love you, Lydia. I have loved you for most of my life. And I watched you marry someone else, because I cared an awful lot about him too. And once you were his, there wasn't a damn thing I felt like I could do about it. I watched you say vows to him. And have his kids. And then I swore to him that I would take care of you when he was gone. And all the while, I was frustrated as hell because I thought I would be a better husband to you. Because I wouldn't have been out drinking, Lydia. I would've been at home with you. I would've been at home with those kids. All I wanted was to be at home with you."

She covered her mouth with her hand, trying to stifle a sob. "I think I was almost afraid of that."

"I'm sorry that he's gone. You know he was the only brother I ever knew. You know how much I care about him. Still. About his kids knowing who he was. You know it matters to me. But that doesn't mean I don't love you. It doesn't mean I'm not damn grateful that I have a chance with you."

And for the first time, she could see all these pages ahead. And maybe that was just it, maybe what she saw at the church hadn't been a cruel hallucination, but a vision of what *could* be. And maybe her parents would find it odd. And maybe Mac's mother would be hurt by it. And maybe the kids would be confused. But she had stayed in a marriage to avoid hurting other people, and it didn't work. She knew that it didn't. So shouldn't she have a relationship that was just about the two of them? And they would weather the transition. The kids loved him. And eventually... Eventually it would be okay, but they were in a different sort of relationship. And maybe it would never be okay with Mac's mother. Maybe it would always be bad for her. Maybe it would damage Chase's relationship with her. But she couldn't control that. And they had to make this about... Them.

"I want to try this," she said. "Because the thing that makes me the most excited about the future isn't a farm store. Or more chickens. Or bees. It's being with you. It's making a family with you. And I don't know when all that changed for me. But when Mac got sick, I looked up and you were there. And when he died, you were there. And every time I have ever needed something, it's you that's been there. From before he was gone until now. You are the man who has loved me, exactly how I wanted to be loved, all these years. All this time. And, Chase, what we have... I've never felt anything like it. It terrified me, being with you."

"Do you feel scared now?"

"No."

"Do you want me?" he asked, his voice rough.

"Yes. I want you to spend the night with me. And also, every night after that."

"I have my own farm."

"Well. We'll have to rent one of them out."

"Mine?"

She shook her head. "It could be mine. I could run the store while living somewhere else."

"Let's talk to the kids. Find out if they'd rather stay in their house."

"Are you nervous about living where I lived with him?"

The corner of his mouth tipped up. "Don't I have a little bit of a right to be?"

"I can see how it might not...feel right to you. But then... Honestly... I thought maybe it would feel wrong to sleep with you in the room I shared with him. It didn't. Because what I want with you... It's a new life, Chase. It's a new chapter. There are no ghosts."

"Then let's go to bed."

And that's what they did.

37

No Justice, Says Salem

BY DALE WAINWRIGHT

2003—Yet again an appeal has been made to bring Nathan Brewer to trial, and yet again it has been denied. Those in Salem do not understand what it means to have found a monster among us here. They do not understand how each of us is connected. How this town is built on a unity they can never understand, and yet seek to destroy with their lack of care over a girl they didn't know. But we knew her. And we will never let go of our hope that justice will be served for her.

RUBY

Ruby was utterly despondent by the time she arrived at Nathan's door that night. She told him the whole story through gasping sobs, and she was just grateful that she had him there. That she had this man she knew could withstand all of this ugliness. Although she also felt guilty that he should have to take more inside of him. Because he'd been through enough.

"It was never safe here," she said. "It was never safe here. And they crucified you, telling themselves that it was. That there was nothing dark or bad until you. Until Caitlin Groves disappeared.

But it was a lie. My sister was raped by someone. Someone *here*. She was afraid for her life. She had to hide her pregnancy and hide the baby. They made you a monster because they needed to believe there was only one. Because they needed to believe that they found him. Look what they did. They became monsters to protect the solution that never existed. And how much more so was someone able to… How much more so were terrible things able to carry on because no one wanted to see them?"

"We all do it," he said, his voice soft as he held her in his arms. "We'll see what we want. And ignore what we don't. That's how our brains want to do things. Even when it comes to missing Caitlin… My memories of her are twisted up in my anger about what happened to me. And my brain doesn't let me separate all that easily. We want easy and simple because it makes us feel better."

"So they burned you for someone else's sins."

"Everyone's capable of being a monster, Ruby. Whether you want to believe it or not. It could've just as easily been me. I always wonder what I would've become if not for this."

"Maybe just happy. How about that?"

"I'm pretty happy now. Complications aside."

"I know we can't be together here," she said.

"We could be. But it wouldn't be easy."

"I don't want you to have hard. Not anymore."

"Ruby," he said. "My life got a lot easier when you came into it. You make me feel things I didn't think I could anymore."

"You were the only person I could come to." She touched the necklace around her neck. "Her abuser gave this to her. I don't think I can wear it. But it's what she left with me. I don't think I was prepared for that realization. That I'm part…monster."

Nathan brushed his knuckles over her cheek. "Ruby McKee, you are a hundred percent you. Created by the love of the people around you. That's the miracle. You're not a monster because of your father's DNA, any more than I am because of mine."

"Well. That was pretty much the nicest thing to say."

"It's just true."

"Can I spend the night, Nathan?"

"You never have to ask me that."

It was a comfort to be taken to bed. To be held in his arms. Touched by him, kissed by him. And all she thought when she drifted to sleep was that it made sense now. This darkness that lived in them both. Why they were drawn together.

Or maybe you just love him.

That was her last conscious thought before she went to sleep.

And then the dream began. The same as it always did. She was standing in front of the bridge. She saw the white 1917. She looked down and saw her shoes.

But they weren't her shoes.

She touched the necklace.

Marianne?

She walked forward, into the bridge, her fear intensifying. Growing. Dread like a monster.

But she went in. And just like the times before she was propelled out the other side and down toward the water. But this time, the dream didn't end. This time, she kept going. And this time, she was pushed down to her knees. She felt the bite of the gravel into her skin. And then she couldn't breathe. Her face was in the water.

And the water started to fill her lungs.

When she tried to scream, she found that she couldn't.

Screaming was what woke her up.

"Ruby." Nathan was holding her naked body against his, trying to calm her as she fought and thrashed like a wild animal.

"Ruby," he said. "You're okay. It's a dream."

She looked at the window and she saw that the first blush of rosy light was coming through. "I need to go to the bridge."

She got dressed, and he drove them both down to the bridge,

and he didn't ask. She stood there, her hand on her necklace. "It keeps bringing me here."

She looked up at the bridge, dark and silent. That bridge that had been part of her from the beginning. The trees closed in around it, a wreath of green against the dark wood.

It was like she could feel everything that had happened here. Feel it soaked into the wood. The fear of a traveler, robbed by bandits as they tried to cross. The desperation of a teenage girl leaving her child in the dark and the cold. The desperate loneliness of a small baby.

The terror of a teenage girl, who knew she had to cross the bridge to get home.

Who knew a monster was waiting for her inside.

"What does?" he asked.

"My dream. I keep... I keep seeing the bridge. And there's something terrifying in there. I just know there is, but I have to go through. Because it's the only way... It's the only way home."

"What?"

"It's the only way home, but this isn't the side of the bridge that takes me home. It takes me away from home. Away from your home. This is where she's standing. So it's not Marianne."

"It's a dream, Ruby."

"No, I know," she said. "I'm just trying to figure it out. Because it... It won't stop."

She went into the bridge, and she was grateful that she had Nathan with her. The darkness swallowed them both, light coming through the cracks of the weathered wood. Their footsteps echoed in the silence.

And she listened.

Listened past time.

Her heart thundered in her head, her legs shaking. It was just like the dream.

They reached the other side of the bridge and she paused, then turned the same way she'd done in her sleep. She walked down the embankment partway, her foot sliding on a loose rock. "I have to go down there."

"There?"

"To the creek." The wind curled itself around her shoulders, and she shivered. "Something happened… Nathan, something happened here."

She moved quickly, rocks and dirt giving way as she did. She stumbled but didn't fall, and then she stood there, at the edge of the water and looked up at the bridge, then looked down the stream, past the trees. It was completely secluded here.

No one would be able to see a thing.

She dropped down to her knees. And her stomach went tight. She was afraid she might vomit. She planted her hands down in front of her, in the water.

"What are you doing, Ruby?"

"It was…" Her hands slipped and she grabbed onto a large boulder that was submerged in the river, covered in algae, and it slipped almost violently down a crack between it and another rock. And she felt something.

"There's something down here." She moved, orienting herself so that she could see down into the crack. There was a glint of silver wedged tightly in the rock. In that still little pool just there where the current couldn't touch it.

She tried to grab hold of the slippery, hard thing back there in the rocks. She had trouble getting her fingers into the tight space. And once she did, she had to yank, until there was a snap and whatever had held it fast gave way.

She opened up her hand, and moved the object around, all covered in slick green grime and tarnished. A tangled-up chain, now broken in one place.

With silver bells hanging from it.

"Nathan," she whispered. "The silver bells. Marianne wasn't the only one. It wasn't only Marianne."

Suddenly, a sense of certainty washed over her. And she looked right into Nathan's eyes. "Nathan. It was Caitlin."

38

Bridge Dedication a Success

BY DALE WAINWRIGHT

1995—The dedication and reopening of Sentinel Bridge drew people from all over Southern Oregon. The barbecue was lively, with games for all ages, music and dancing. A snapshot of all that is good about our local community.

DAHLIA

Dahlia wasn't really in the mood to be back at the paper, but she had things to do. It seemed… Bizarre and trivial now to be going through the newspaper when it didn't contain anything of the truth of what had happened. Was she going to have to write about this? This hideous thing that had happened in her family?

She had told Carter and begged him not to do anything with it yet. Not to say anything to anyone. She was still reeling. Completely rocked by everything that had occurred. Her heart was just… It was just so heavy.

She pulled out the newspapers that she'd been sifting through. She had been—before all this—trying to find more information about SS Silversmith. Because of the relationship to Ruby's necklace. Ruby had been looking in the museum. And she'd been looking for references in the paper. She'd pulled some digital records and taken out the corresponding papers. Anywhere there was a mention. And she had a stack of them on her desk.

Now that the necklace had even more significance because it was something Marianne had been given by an abuser...

She started to sift through the pile of papers. Advertisements. But then, there was a wedding announcement.

Eliza Sullivan, daughter of Silas Sullivan and Mary Sullivan, married Abraham Wainwright on August 4, 1954. The bride's father is the previous owner of SS Silversmith on Main.

MARIANNE

Marianne felt hollow. Her brain felt empty. Her chest felt empty. Her tear ducts were definitely empty.

It was her mother that had surprised her. Her mother who had lain across the kitchen table and cried.

Marianne, I'm so sorry.

I didn't see.

How did I not see?

I don't know, Mom. I don't know.

She'd shouted. Cried. Her dad had cried.

She'd had to talk to Hunter and Ava.

Ava, I had something really terrible happen to me... You'd tell me, if something was happening to you, right? I was too afraid, but you know... that's what happens. They try to make you scared so you'll keep secrets.

Nothing like that has ever happened to me.

You'd tell me if it did?

Yes, Mom. I would.

It's why I get scared. When you don't talk to me.

And to her horror she'd started to cry, and it had been her

teenage daughter who'd put her hand on her head and stroked her like she was a child.

And she still didn't know everything. She still couldn't piece it all together. She tried to follow herself down old paths.

But those walls were there. And now that she was aware of them…

There was just a whole segment of memory that she turned away from. And she didn't know how to do anything other than that.

Jackson came into their bedroom. He had been intent on taking care of her ever since all of this had happened. And it was like the previous fight hadn't even happened.

"You don't have to keep bringing me food in bed," she said as he set down some coffee, bacon and eggs despite it being the middle of the afternoon.

"I want to."

"What I did to you was still wrong," Marianne said.

"It makes sense," he said. He sat on the edge of the bed. "Because you knew something wasn't true. And of course you thought it was me. How could you think it was your own brain lying to you."

"You believe me, don't you?"

"Yes. I believe you."

She took a breath, fighting tears. "I figured it out, you know. Why I wanted to escape. Obviously it was because of everything that happened here. But when I met you I felt safe again. You have always been… You made it so easy to wash it all away. Because even my restless feelings disappeared when you came into my life."

"I promise to be that for you. Always. Whatever you remember. Whatever you discover. I'm here for you. And I will protect you. I swear to you, Marianne."

"This changes things."

"If it changes anything, it just gives me that much more admiration for you. I've always thought you were one of the strongest, funniest… You're the most amazing woman I know. I've always thought so. And now I see how hard you fought to become that person. The degree that your body protected you. That your mind protected you. You are so much stronger than I even realized."

"A lot of people just remember the terrible things that happened to them instead of writing a fairy tale to live in."

"Your mind built a shield around you when you needed it. That's pretty amazing, I think."

"I told you I'd never been with anyone else. It turns out… I'd given birth before I met you."

He touched her face, so gentle she wanted to cry. "None of that matters. Not in the way you mean. But what happened to you is not the same as what we have between us. It's not the same. When I'm with you, when I touch you, it's because I love you. It's not about controlling you. And I always, always want you to want me. It is the most important thing. Because it's not about me having you, it's about us sharing something. It is not the same."

She started to cry then. Really. Because she hadn't known how much she needed to hear that.

"I haven't remembered it yet." She let out a shaky breath. "And someday I will. Someday I will, and it might make things hard for me. Just knowing that it's there…"

"You are my wife. And I love you. You are not a body for me to get off with while I ignore what's happening in your heart. With your emotions. I love all of you. And I will be patient. The last thing I want to do is add to any of the hurt…"

"You just didn't know you signed up for this."

"Yeah, that's life," he said. "*You* didn't sign up for it either. Some bastard did his best to destroy you. And you didn't let him. You did what you had to to survive. You did what you had to in order to make sure Ruby survived. And I bet you… That forgetting it was part of that. You were doing your best to set the both of you free, and to get rid of the power that he had. Maybe I didn't know going into this. But neither did you. I'm sorry that I was... I was downright petulant about the cheating thing. I'm sorry. I should've realized that right now... That whatever was happening wasn't about me. And I should've just been there for you. Instead, I abandoned you when you needed me."

"But you came and found me when I needed you most. When I told you to go away." She started crying again. "I gave birth on the floor of a bathtub by myself. But I didn't have to relive it alone. This time you were there. You were there when I needed you. You have always been there when I have needed you. When it mattered."

"And I swear that I will be. Always."

She set the food aside and drew the blanket down. And he got into bed beside her, fully clothed, and held her up against him.

Whatever was coming, she knew that they could withstand it. And there was more coming. She knew it. There were things to untangle. There was going to be a settling in to this new reality. This new truth. It might change the way she felt about Ruby. It might not. She might have flashbacks in memories that hurt. But right now, she had this house. Her bed. Her husband.

And there was a great and wonderful beauty in knowing that whatever was ahead, that wouldn't change.

LYDIA

There were two things that Lydia remembered suddenly in the middle of the afternoon while she was working out in the barn with Chase.

The first was that it was funny how Dahlia was the one who had gotten so into the newspaper when Marianne had been the one who had originally been on the paper in high school.

She had thought that recently. But she hadn't really let it sit.

The second was the visit that Dale Wainwright had paid to the property right after Mac and Lydia had bought it.

He had asked them what they intended to do with the orchards.

She'd said they would probably keep some. And then he'd said something about the far pasture. And how it had always proved difficult for growing things.

And for some reason those two things wouldn't leave her mind.

"What?" Chase asked.

It was an amazing thing, the way he was so tuned in to her moods.

"I just can't... I keep thinking about a couple of things that are really bothering me." She shook her head. "And I don't know if I'm being paranoid or not."

"Well, given everything that you found out recently... Is there such a thing as paranoid?"

"Good question."

Her phone suddenly buzzed, and she had a text from Dahlia.

Whoever can meet me in town...please meet me.

MARIANNE

They met in town at The Apothecary. Marianne had convinced Jackson that she was fine, but he'd driven her down anyway. Hunter had football practice, and Ava had wanted to walk around town after school anyway.

Dahlia was looking grave. Ruby looked like she hadn't slept. Lydia had that blank unknowable look on her face she often did.

"I was going through some records online. And I discovered something," Dahlia said.

"What?"

"Dale Wainwright is related to the family who owned SS Silversmith."

Marianne felt like a nail had been driven through her skull. *"What?"*

"Dale. Dale has a connection to the family and..."

"Oh," Marianne said, memories pushing against the partition.

Marianne started to say something, but she walked out of the store. She walked out of the store and started stumbling down the street, toward the paper office.

That's where she would find him. That's where she would find him.

And as the barrier in her mind started to dissolve, it wasn't fear that she felt. It wasn't fear.

It was righteous, unending fury.

And she saw him, standing just outside the paper office.

And he was talking to Ava.

Ava.

Who was her age.

Her age.

You're a very good writer, Marianne. I can teach you to be better.

You can't tell anyone, not ever. What would they think if they knew?

You wanted it.

You can never tell.

I'll make you sorry if you tell.

You have to get rid of it.

And she could see it. Bright and clear.

He knew. He knew about the baby. He was going to drive her to get an abortion.

It was almost Christmas.

They were standing out on the street, just like this one.

"It's too late," she'd whispered.

And she'd smiled.

Because it was too late for him to make it go away.

He'd known. The whole time. Always. That Ruby had to be his child.

And it must have terrified him.

His genes walking around advertising that he was a rapist. A pedophile.

And he was talking to her daughter.

And he knew.

She wasn't even conscious of making the decision to move. Instead, she flew across the street, screaming his name. "You monster," she said. "You absolute piece of shit. Stay away from her."

And she hit him. She hit him with her closed fists and she didn't stop.

Didn't stop until strong arms wrapped around her and pulled her away.

Jackson.

Jackson was here.

Jackson was always here.

She sagged against him, as memories flooded through her.

It was Ruby. It was Ruby that had protected her.

Marianne might be able to go missing.

But not the miracle baby too.

And the miracle baby had his blood in her veins. His DNA.

It had kept him far, far away from her. From her family.

She had never given him any trouble. Until now. And now, she would do more than cause trouble. She would light him on fire and watch him burn.

There were people staring. Staring at Marianne McKee, making a scene on the street. At Marianne McKee, screaming at a pillar of the community.

"You raped me," she said.

"And you waited too long," he said, his face as placid as ever. Because of course he never took responsibility.

Jackson released his hold on her and before she could say the next words, her husband hit Dale once. Just once. And knocked him out cold. He turned to Ava. "Tell me that bastard never touched you."

She shook her head. "No. I...he just stopped me to tell me he read my piece in the school paper. Mom..."

"It was him," she said.

"I called Carter already," Dahlia said.

Carter was there in less than five minutes, and he didn't ask who had laid Dale out cold. He handcuffed him while he regained partial consciousness, and put him in the car.

"I can hold him for twenty-four hours, maybe. Unless we find something."

"Look in the back field on my property," Lydia said, wrapping her arms around her midsection. "Dale lived there in 1999 when Caitlin Groves went missing. I think you're going to find something."

39

Caitlin Groves—One Year Later

BY DALE WAINWRIGHT

NOVEMBER 8, 2000—There are no answers on the horizon, no clear end to this nightmare. The one suspect sits in a jail cell, but he refuses to give answers to those who mourn. And until we know for certain, we hope. We hope she will come home. That she will walk through her front door one day as if she never left.

RUBY

It was late in the day when Carter came to the McKee house. He looked exhausted.

"We found a body," he said, his voice rough and heavy. "We will have to identify it via dental records. But… We found what I believe to be Caitlin Groves. Buried on what used to be Dale Wainwright's property."

Ruby sat back in her chair. "It was never a coincidence. We were connected."

The next hour went by in a blur, but as soon as she was able to, she went to see Nathan.

When he opened the door, she burst into tears. "Nathan," she said. "They found her. They found her."

He said nothing for a moment, his hand resting on her lower back. Then, he finally spoke. "She's gone?"

Ruby nodded through her tears. And then she wrapped her arms around his waist and held him. "Yes. She's gone. But she's home. And her murderer is in custody."

"I'm not in custody," he rasped.

"No, you're not. You're not a murderer. And I always knew. But now everyone else will too."

40

RUBY

It was a cold day in early March when they were finally able to have a funeral for Caitlin Groves. Information about her death had taken a while to piece together, given the amount of time it had been since the murder had taken place. But between that and scattered rantings and confessions from Dale, it had been determined that Caitlin was pregnant at the time of her death.

Miraculously, they were able to collect enough DNA to confirm that the father of the baby was Dale.

It was believed that he had met Caitlin on Sentinel Bridge the evening of her disappearance, after she had been out in the Brewer orchard with her boyfriend. He was angry about her pregnancy, and that she had a boyfriend who could potentially discover it, and the fact he was abusing her and had been for more than a year.

He took her down to the creek and they fought. He lost his temper and pushed her down and drowned her there. The police believed that was where her necklace broke off and become lodged between the rocks.

He had debated letting her body float downriver to be found. But decided instead to try and erase the evidence. He buried her in the farthest corner of his property.

He was never a suspect.

His land was never searched.

The police were so certain that they had found their villain.

Along with Dahlia and Carter, Tom had gone to their parents' house to apologize formally to them, to Marianne. He'd just come from Dana's. Dana hadn't accepted his remorse, and Ruby had silently cheered her on.

He could be sorry. He should be. But Dana didn't have to accept.

It was all slightly more complicated for her family, though. Especially with Dahlia in a relationship with Carter.

It was because of Dahlia that Marianne hadn't held on to anger at Tom, she was sure.

But when asked, she'd just smiled at Ruby and said, *I want to let it go. That was why I forgot in the first place. And now…now that it's out there. I'm not letting him win, Ruby. I'm not letting him have any part of me. I'm not just forgetting now. I'm healing.*

That same night, she and Dahlia had gone back to the cottage and slept on the living room floor in sleeping bags.

I'm sorry I thought Nathan was a murderer. I was so sure I was right about…everything. And I bought into that story, the same as everyone.

We're all wrong sometimes. Even you. I think what matters is that you try to find the truth. And if you are wrong…you admit it.

You make me sound almost saintly.

Well, no. Never that. But you're not the villain here. Don't borrow any guilt for yourself. Just use your gift, Dee. Tell the truth. To everyone.

So many people had failed. So many had looked away from signs and suspicions.

The hero had been a teenage girl.

If it hadn't been for Marianne giving birth to Ruby, saving Ruby, he might have continued to abuse girls in town. It might have gone on. There could have been more victims.

But Marianne McKee had stopped it.

When the truth started to come out, Dale Wainwright committed suicide in a prison cell.

And the lingering sense that justice couldn't truly be served nagged at Ruby.

But now Caitlin was being laid to rest. Not as she should have been twenty-three years ago, for she never should have been killed, but at the very least, as was right, given the interminable wrongness of the situation.

Nathan went with Ruby to the funeral. It was Dana who had issued the invitation.

They'd gone to her house last night and sat at her small kitchen table, the most unlikely trio.

He had talked to Dana about Caitlin. Not about her being gone. But about the girl she'd been. And Ruby had never been more sure she loved him than when she watched him give her that gift. Of new stories, new memories.

The town would be laying a symbol to rest.

But she wasn't a symbol for Nathan and Dana.

For them, she was a real person. A whole person.

Not a story.

And in the end, that was what they were all fighting for.

When the service was over, Nathan stared at Caitlin's picture for a long time. A picture of a girl who would be fifteen forever.

But Nathan wasn't fifteen, and his life hadn't ended then.

"She was just a really sweet girl," he said, heavy, hard.

Final.

Marianne, Dahlia and Lydia came to stand with them in front

of her picture. Chase was with Lydia, Carter holding Dahlia's hand. And Jackson stood behind Marianne, that committed shield, now that her mind had stopped protecting her.

He would always be there.

"I think on some level I knew. It was why I was so afraid. He had done it once and he had gotten away with it. And what would've stopped him from doing it to me?" Marianne said.

"Nothing," Ruby said.

"Nothing but you. Nothing but your birth. That was too big of a risk. Too big of a tangle."

"And thank God," Jackson said.

"I understand it's PTSD," Marianne said. "Survivor's guilt. But I just… Poor Caitlin. The exact same thing was happening to her and I didn't even know it. I never even thought about it. How many other girls before us…"

"No more," Ruby said. "That's the important thing. No more. Because of you, Marianne."

After the funeral, just the sisters went down to Sentinel Bridge. And the four of them stood there, staring up at the white circle with 1917 at the center. At that pathway home. At the place where Caitlin had stood last.

The place where Ruby had been left.

The place where Ruby had been found.

She took a breath, and she felt it all. Everything she was. The miraculous and the truly grim. The light and the dark. It was all there. It was all what made her the woman she was.

She wasn't the miracle, not on her own. She didn't have to be.

She was just one star in a sky scattered with diamond dust.

Of all the brilliant things that came with that, the freedom was the greatest. The freedom to live, to love, to be angry, sad and a little bit dark. To feel the miracle of life in most of her breaths, and sometimes the irritation of it.

To be more than a symbol, but a whole person.

"What happens now?" Ruby asked.

The breeze ruffled the leaves, the sound mingling with the birds, the river. Everything felt so sharp and real.

"Whatever we want," Lydia said.

Marianne walked to the edge of the path and leaned against the rail, looking down at the water below. The lines by her mouth looked deeper, and there was a sadness in her eyes that hadn't been there before.

The greatest gift was that their relationship felt strong still. Stronger in some ways, yes. But mostly… They were sisters. It was a sister Marianne needed now.

Ruby had asked her a few weeks ago how she was.

Getting there.

What does that mean?

I don't know. But I'll be okay. I didn't come this far to crumble now.

"Do you think there's justice on the other side?" Marianne asked. "Or do you think he got away with it?"

"I like to believe there is," Ruby said. "I like to believe that in the end of all things, there's justice." She took a deep breath of the cold, sharp air. "But what I know for sure is that *here* there's life. And we have that. It was never his story. It's ours. It doesn't matter why he did it. It doesn't matter what happened to him. What matters is us.

"He led the mob against Nathan," Ruby said. "With every word he wrote. He created a villain so that no one would look and see who the real monster was. He made the outside world the dark place so that no one could believe there was a predator here. And then when it was clear there was, he found a scapegoat and wrote the story the way he wanted everyone to see it."

"Yes," Marianne said. "He was manipulative. And dedicated to his fiction about his own position as…as a hero." She blinked rapidly.

"He was wrong, Marianne," Ruby said, reaching out and taking her hand.

Her sister's hand.

She would always be her sister.

"It's you," Ruby continued. "You were the hero all along."

Dahlia reached into her pocket and took out a small packet.

"What's that?" Ruby asked.

"Carter said that he was able to release the necklace. Since Dale is dead and there's not going to be a trial."

Ruby had hers around her neck, and she couldn't quite say why. Because they were not happy things. Not by any stretch of the imagination. And yet...

"I think I know what we should do with them." She took hers off, and Dahlia unwrapped Caitlin's. And they put both into Marianne's hand.

"We don't need them anymore. We did. They're part of what linked Caitlin to me. What linked you to Caitlin. And they helped. They helped bring out the truth. And the truth... The truth is what set us all free. It's what brought her back home. But they should rest somewhere. Somewhere not with us."

Marianne leaned out over the side of the bridge and released the necklaces down into the current.

They probably sank to the bottom there. Would probably cling to the rocks. Maybe they would get stuck again. Maybe they would end up floating all the way down to the sea. But it didn't matter. Not anymore. They didn't need to hold on to them now.

"Now what?" Ruby asked.

Marianne looked at her sisters. "Whatever we want. We're writing the story."

And so they walked across the bridge, on the road that led to home.

epilogue

Excerpt of: Heroes and Monsters

BY DAHLIA MCKEE

Pear Blossom Gazette

**PICKED UP WORLDWIDE BY
MULTIPLE NEWS SOURCES, TV AND RADIO.**

As far as the history of Pear Blossom, Oregon, has been written, only two truly remarkable things have ever happened there: the disappearance of Caitlin Groves and the discovery of a baby, later named Ruby McKee, on a bridge on Christmas Eve.

But the written history of Pear Blossom was hiding one of the town's most hideous villains, and at the same time silencing one of its greatest heroes.

Marianne McKee is miraculous.

For all the world she looked like a normal fifteen-year-old girl, complete with standard teenage angst. But Marianne was hiding a secret.

For two years she was abused by a man who had the unquestioning good faith of a tight-knit community. His reputation and his power isolated and silenced her. But it was when the most terrifying thing of all happened that Marianne was able to find the strength to save not only herself, but other girls in town who might have been groomed and abused as she was.

Ruby McKee is the living testament to Marianne's heroism.

While Ruby's appearance on that bridge was mysterious to the town, Marianne knew the truth. And so did her abuser.

Marianne hid her pregnancy for nine months. Starving herself to keep her weight down, wearing baggy sweatshirts when she couldn't hide it anymore.

She gave birth alone, in the upstairs bathroom of her family's farmhouse.

That child probably saved her life.

It is likely she saved many other girls from experiencing the same fate she did.

She was terrified of her abuser, who was later revealed to be the murderer of Caitlin Groves. And she defied him.

Marianne McKee was scared. She was hurt. She had no one to reach out to.

She believed her abuser when he said the world would believe his word over hers, and the sad truth is, he may have been right.

But Marianne was also brave.

She is a hero.

She is a miracle.

And her story needs to be told.

★ ★ ★ ★ ★

Acknowledgments

To Voltron, otherwise known as Nicole Helm, Jackie Ashenden and Megan Crane, who read everything I write and offer feedback and listen to me complain while I do it. I owe them immeasurable thanks.

As ever I owe so many thanks to my wonderful editor, Flo Nicoll, who read this book so many times and gave me incredible, incisive feedback with each pass. You're amazing, Flo. I'd be lost without you.

To my agent, Helen Breitwieser, who has been such a great support and advocate for all these years.

And a very special acknowledgment to my parents. Without them, I wouldn't be who I am. Without them, I certainly wouldn't be here. Thank you for believing in me, always.

Author Note

The idea of an abandoned baby, found and adopted by her town and struggling to piece together the truth of her past, has been with me for a few years. One of those ideas that just sits there waiting to become something more than just a seed.

I live in a small town, and I have lived in the same small town for my entire life. It is often more quirky than could ever be believably depicted in fiction. A restaurant in town was once baffled by the fact their lettuce kept going missing, and they ended up discovering the restaurant down the street was stealing their lettuce. I really need to put a lettuce heist in a book.

The other thing about small towns, though, is that people form very strong narratives about places, and about the people who live around them. Often we are reluctant to challenge these narratives, or simply have no reason to.

The Lost and Found Girl is all about those kinds of narratives. Legends that we accept as truths because they make us comfortable.

We might see someone as a Good Man simply because that's how people around us continually describe him, even though we have never seen him do anything good.

That was what I started thinking about when I wrote Ruby's story. These stories we tell ourselves are comforting. They help us understand the world. They help us feel safe. But what happens when those stories, those narratives, become shields for monsters to hide behind? We tell ourselves stories about where we live and about the people who share our homes with us.

And we don't only tell stories about other people, but about ourselves. And what happens when those stories become the cages that keep us trapped?

I'm a storyteller, it's what I do. But in many ways, we all are. We want to tell ourselves stories about the world around us because it helps us make sense of it—it makes it neater. And in writing Ruby's story, I wanted to remind myself that it's okay to be complicated, and it's important to have the bravery to disrupt the stories around us when we must, even if it stirs up uncomfortable truths.

Ruby McKee's story is about having the strength to uncover the darkness, so the light can get in. About unpacking the lies, so the truth can begin to heal. Sometimes what's right isn't what's easy.

And while the truth doesn't always offer protection, it is always what will set us free.